CREATC

Christopher Mitchell is the author of :d
in Edinburgh before living for several years in the Middle East and Greece, w
taught English. He returned to study classics and Greek tragedy and lives in Fife, Scotland with his wife and their four children.

By Christopher Mitchell

The Magelands Origins

Retreat of the Kell
The Trials of Daphne Holdfast
From the Ashes

The Magelands Epic

The Queen's Executioner
The Severed City
Needs of the Empire
Sacrifice
Fragile Empire
Storm Mage
Soulwitch Rises
Renegade Gods

The Magelands Eternal Siege

The Mortal Blade
The Dragon's Blade
The Prince's Blade
Falls of Iron
Paths of Fire
Gates of Ruin
City of Salve
Red City

City Ascendant
Dragon Eyre Badblood
Dragon Eyre Ashfall
Dragon Eyre Blackrose
Dreams of Kell
God Restrainer
Holdfast Imperium
World's End

The Magelands Dominion

Serpent Dominion
Demon Witch
Death Seer
Blood Burden
Kin Strife
Tempest's Edge
Creator of Worlds
Palace of the Almighty

Masters and Makers

Fall Seldom Kings
The Making of Abigone

Cover Design by Sasha Almazan and Gene Mollica, G&S Cover Design Studio. LLC.
Maps by Irina French

Brigdomin Books Ltd
First Edition, August 2024
Ebook Edition © August 2024
ISBN 978-1-915978-35-6

ACKNOWLEDGEMENTS

I would like to thank the following for all their support during the writing of the Magelands Dominion - my wife, Lisa Mitchell, who read every chapter as soon as it was drafted and kept me going in the right direction; my parents for their unstinting support; Marilyn Hopwood for reading the books in their early stages; James Aitken for his encouragement; and Grant and Gordon of the Film Club for their support.

Thanks also to my Advance Reader team, for all your help during the last few weeks before publication.

DRAMATIS PERSONAE

Plateau City

Kyra Holdfast, Karalyn's Daughter (17)

Thorn Holdfast, Empress

Kelsey Holdfast, Herald of the Empire

Naxor, Imperial Chamberlain

Brogan ae Bridget, Imperial Treasurer

Bedig ae Brannig, Lord Marshal

Caelius Logos, Imperial Quartermaster

Van Logos, Banner Major General

Calpurnia Holdfast, Kelsey and Van's daughter (7)

Caelius Holdfast, Kelsey and Van's son (4)

Elbannon, University Professor

Gallea, University Professor

Nadia, University Professor

Ravi, University Professor

Achan, University Professor

Rosie Jackdaw, Visiting Professor

Dazi, Student

Hold Fast Estate, Holdings

Cael Holdfast, Karalyn's Son (17)

Celine Holdfast, Estate Manager

Cole Holdfast, Trainee Estate Manager (18)

Arrosa, Estate Worker (16)

Marium, Estate Worker

Soula, Estate Worker

Tarrun, Estate Worker

Colsbury

Karalyn Holdfast, Immortal Dream Mage

Carden Holdfast, Karalyn's Son (2)

Caitlyn Holdfast, Karalyn's Daughter (almost 1)

Shella, Imperial Chancellor

Lucius Cardova, Imperial Constable

Olo'osso, Retired Pirate

Frostback, Silver Dragon

Halfclaw, Blue/Green Dragon

Great Tunnel, Rahain

Lahnos Laimos, Commander, Imperial Army

Sigum Mon Sigel, Friend of Lahnos

Efizel, Bullan Sergeant Major

Dolwyn, Lieutenant, Imperial Army

Zamata, Athumia

Bailey, Theodora's Brother

Bauchlie, President

Ulna, Dragon Eyre

Blackrose, Queen of the Eastern Rim

Maddie Jackdaw, Blackrose's Rider

Sable Holdfast, Retired Agent

Alara'osso (Lara), Sable's Partner

Anaj'osso (Joss), Sable and Lara's Son (5)

Alindi'osso (Lindi), Sable and Lara's Daughter (Almost 1)

City of Salve

Emily Aurelian, Queen of the City

Daniel Aurelian, King of the City

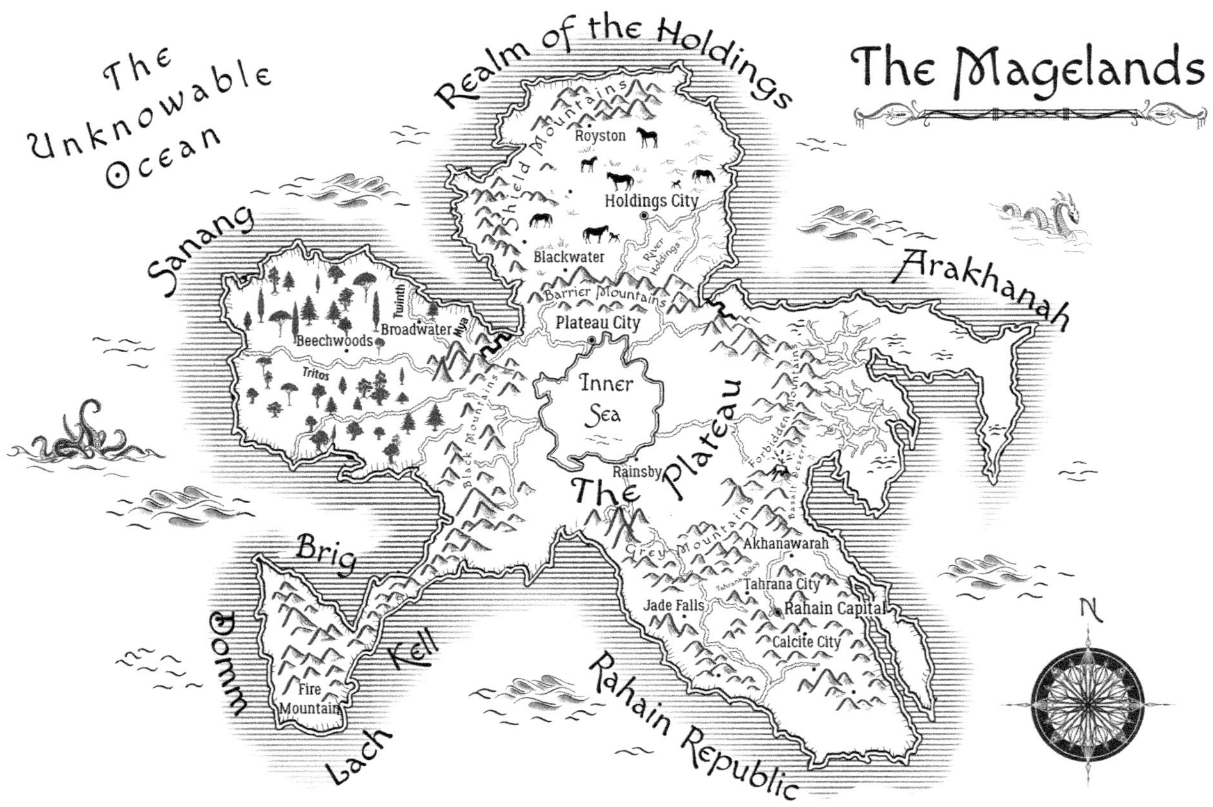
The Magelands
The Unknowable Ocean
Realm of the Holdings
Sanang
Arakhanah
Shield Mountains
Royston
Holdings City
Blackwater
River Holdings
Barrier Mountains
Plateau City
Twinth
Broadwater
Mya
Beechwoods
Tritos
Inner Sea
Black Mountains
Rainsby
The Plateau
Forbidden Mountains
Basalt Desert
Grey Mountains
Akhanawarah
Tahrana Valley
Tahrana City
Rahain Capital
Jade Falls
Calcite City
Brig
Domm
Kell
Lach
Fire Mountain
Rahain Republic
N

CHAPTER 1
CHOSEN

Plateau City, The Plateau – 9th Day, Last Third Spring 544

'I don't want to hear it,' said Kelsey. 'No happy returns, no congratulations; in fact, I'd prefer everyone to forget that I have a birthday.'

Kyra laughed. 'You can't just ignore it, Aunty.'

'Watch me.'

'Is it because you're getting old?'

Kelsey snorted. 'Thirty-four isn't old, you cheeky wee numpty. When I was your age...'

'That's the kind of thing old people say.'

'Then I'll be sure to never say it again. Anyway, I only came into the university to see how you were getting on with your new tutor.'

'He's all right, I suppose. I've only met him once.'

'Has he tried to tell you that monarchy is outdated and evil yet? I knew Achan in the City. He's what I would term a radical. He was always going on about how oppressed the Hammers were. If he says that sort of thing to you, remind him that Plateau City is not the same as the City of Salve.'

'If you don't like him, why did you bring him to the university?'

'Because he knows a lot; and who said I didn't like him? I like him enough; I just happen to disagree with his political views. Also, it's important that we have tutors and lecturers from each of the four allied worlds. Is he getting along with Professor Gallea?'

Kyra shrugged. 'I don't know. Why don't you ask them?'

'I'd rather not interfere. If you see them arguing, let me know. Right; I'm off to see Professor Ravi about something. Remember that the Empress has invited you for dinner this evening – don't be late.'

'Aye, Aunty. I remember.'

Kelsey walked off down a university corridor, and Kyra opened a door next to her and went into a classroom. Professor Elbannon glanced up at her from his desk.

'You're late,' he said.

'Sorry, sir,' said Kyra. 'Aunty Kelsey cornered me in the corridor as I was about to come in.'

Elbannon rolled his eyes. 'Do you think that being a Holdfast gives you permission to break the rules?'

Kyra glanced at the five other members of the class.

'Don't look at them when I'm talking to you, girl,' said Elbannon. 'Stay behind after classes today; you can help clean up my laboratory as a punishment.'

'Sorry, sir, but the Empress has ordered me to attend the palace for dinner this evening.'

Elbannon's eyes flashed with anger. 'Bloody Holdfasts!' he muttered. 'Well, don't just stand there. Sit.'

Kyra walked over to her desk. She placed her heavy bag onto the floor, and sat down.

Elbannon gestured towards the large blackboard attached to the wall behind him. Upon it was a diagram of the inside of a Quadrant.

'Copy that down, Holdfast,' he said. 'The others have already done so, but I'm sure they won't mind waiting for a young woman of your pedigree.'

Kyra opened a lined notebook, picked up a pencil, and started to draw what she saw on the blackboard.

Elbannon swivelled in his chair, then he raised his walking stick, and began to point at sections of the diagram.

'Write this down,' he said. 'This part here controls the *Go back* command. Its workings remain a mystery and, despite years of experimentation, no one yet understands how it operates. It would make a suitable research topic for any student who goes on to specialise in Tempest. We know that it must record the previous action, but we don't know how.' He moved his stick to another part of the diagram. 'This area of the Quadrant is also beyond our current understanding. Let's refer to it as the *Go home* command. If the Quadrant is activated here, the user will appear in the first place it was ever used. Don't ever, ever touch one of the original Quadrants in this place. If you do, then you will be whisked off to Implacatus, which, as we all know, was reduced to a cloud of dust by the Second Ascendant some ten years ago. You'll be dead before you are able to press *Go back*. Worse, your Quadrant will be lost in the void for all eternity.' He turned back to the class. 'For obvious reasons, we have not been adding these two commands to the new generation of Quadrants we have been constructing in this university.' His gaze went to Kyra. 'The esteemed Herald of the Empire, or, as Kyra calls her – Aunty Kelsey, has offered a prize of ten thousand sovereigns to anyone who can untangle the mystery of the *Go back* command.'

He pointed his walking stick at the diagram again. 'These are the wires that connect the five Serpent Jewels to the Zamatan Coils. Notice how they are linked in such a way as to render the device inoperable if even one jewel is missing. Why King Nathaniel decided that this would be a good idea is beyond anyone's guess.'

Kyra yawned.

The rest of the class held their breath as Elbannon glared at her. 'Am I boring you, Miss Holdfast?'

'I was up late studying last night, sir,' she said. 'Apologies.'

'And what were you studying?'

'Documents on steam power from the Aurelian Papers, sir.'

'Wrong answer. If you had been studying Tempest, I might have forgiven you.'

'But I don't need to know this,' said Kyra. 'Quadrants speak to me. I don't use them the same way that others use them. All I have to do is touch one, and it asks me where I want to go.'

'Showing off again, are you, Holdfast? Do I have to remind you that if you fail this class, you will not proceed into third year come autumn? You would have to re-sit the entire year and, believe me, I would not relish that prospect. Not another word, or yawn, from you; otherwise, the whole class will be doing a punishment test tomorrow.'

Elbannon gave her a cold smile, and Kyra lowered her gaze, wishing that her Aunty Sable had left the miserable old bastard in Athumia.

Two hours later, the class filed out of Professor Elbannon's classroom for lunch. They shouldered their heavy bags and trudged to the large canteen on the ground floor of the university. It overlooked the open quad in the centre of the campus, which was busy with students hurrying to join the queue for lunch. Kyra waited with her classmates as they approached the servery counter.

'Old Elbannon had it in for you today,' said Dazi, a Rakanese student.

'I shouldn't have mentioned anything about Quadrants speaking to me,' said Kyra. 'I know how he hates to hear that.'

'Nah, it wasn't that,' Dazi said. 'It's because you were late. *That's* what he hates.'

'But it wasn't my fault. My Aunt Kelsey ambushed me in the corridor. She's not just the Herald of the Empire, she's the patron of the university. Was I supposed to push her out of the way?'

'You're the most famous student here,' said Dazi. 'Who else gets personal invitations from the Empress to attend dinner, eh?'

Kyra said nothing as the queue moved forward. One of the kitchen staff handed Dazi and Kyra a plate each, and they made their way to a couple of empty seats by a table. A few of the seated students glanced in Kyra's direction, but none spoke. It had been different when Kyra had first started university, almost two years before. Back then, she had been assaulted with question after question; people asking her if the stories about her family were true; people wanting to meet the Empress; people asking for favours, as if Kyra would be able to snap her fingers and fix everything for them; and people wanting to know if her mother had really come back from the dead in a different body. Something similar had occurred when she had started her second year, and she had no doubt that it would happen again when the new first years arrived in the autumn, when Kyra would be starting third year. At least Cael would be there. Things were always easier when they were together.

'Are you looking forward to summer?' said Dazi, as they ate.

'I guess so,' said Kyra. 'Are you going back to Amatskouri to see your family?'

'Not this year,' said Dazi. 'I have an uncle and aunt in the River Holdings, so I'll be going up there. You?'

'The usual,' she said. 'Colsbury. The entire Imperial Court is going, and so I have to tag along. My brother will be there, though.'

Dazi laughed. 'And your mother.'

'Aye. But, you know, she'll be busy with her new children. She's barely looked at me or Cael since she had them.'

'How old are they?'

'Carden is two, and Caitlyn is one.'

'Then I'm not surprised that your mother is busy, Kyra.'

'I don't really mind, to be honest. The Empress has been more of a mother to me. It upsets Cael, though. He feels as though he's been abandoned; whereas, I was half-expecting it.' She leaned in closer. 'Don't tell anyone, but her new children are both going to be demigods. I mean, they are demigods. Carden and Caitlyn will be here thousands of years after we're dead, and so will my mother. Is it any surprise that she prefers them to me and Cael?'

Dazi frowned. 'It can't be that bad.'

'It is. My mother can be a selfish cow at times. She walked out on us when we were only half a year old; and she didn't come back for four years. Then, she left us again when we were eight, and didn't come back until we were ten.'

'She didn't leave you,' said Dazi. 'She was killed by the Ascendants.'

'But she still existed. She wasn't really dead. She could have spoken to us, or taken another body, but she didn't. She preferred to go off to Athumia, instead of looking after her own children. The Empress has never deserted me, not once.' She shrugged. 'It's all worked out for the best, though. I get to spend the whole year with the Empress, and I only have to see Mother every summer.'

Dazi shook her head. 'Your family's fucked up. It's amazing that you've turned out normal.' She quietened as a group of Rakanese students entered the dining hall. 'Look,' she whispered. 'It's Jano.'

Kyra glanced up, and saw the young Rakanese man that Dazi was gazing at.

'He's so gorgeous,' Dazi whispered.

'If you say so,' said Kyra. She was about to mention something about not finding the Rakanese a particularly attractive race, but thought better of it. For a start, she was a good foot taller than any of the Rakanese boys in the university, having inherited the stature of the Kellach Brigdomin from her parents. And there was something about the wide and large eyes of the Rakanese that put her off, possibly because it made them look a little childlike.

'Are you going to ask him out?' she said.

Dazi narrowed her eyes. 'No. I want him to ask me out. If I ask him, and he says no, then I'd be too ashamed to turn up for classes.'

The group of Rakanese passed by, without any of them glancing in Dazi's direction.

'You could go into his mind,' Dazi said.

Kyra laughed. 'Why in Pyre's name would I want to do that?'

'You could implant a suggestion in there, and make him ask me out.'

'You have the wrong twin for that. Cael does the *persuading*; I'm no good at it. I used to be able to do it when I was younger, but I've lost the ability, just like I lost the power to see into the future. But anyway, even if I could, I wouldn't. It's wrong to manipulate people like that.'

'How could you lose powers?'

'I don't know. Cael's lost some, too. If I wanted to, I could seal up your mind, so that no vision mage or god would be able to read your thoughts. Cael can't do that any more. Our powers grew apart when we were about fourteen. Add us both together, and you get a proper dream mage; but separately, we're like two halves of a whole.'

'Do Quadrants speak to him?'

'No; they never have. But, the Sextant speaks to him, and it doesn't work for me. I've tried a hundred times, and I get nothing. My mother is the only person alive who can do all of those things, and now she has god powers as well. She never uses them, though; they're wasted on her.'

Their lunch finished, they handed in their empty plates to the servery counter and walked out of the canteen. They went out into the large quad, and crossed to the far side, where the office of their tutor was located. They passed the milling groups of students out enjoying the late spring sunshine, and re-entered the university building. They ascended a flight of stairs, and came to where another three students were standing outside a door.

'Is he in?' said Kyra.

'Yeah,' said another Rakanese student. 'He told us to wait here until he's ready. How was your Tempest class?'

'Elbannon picked on her for the whole two hours,' said Dazi.

'I had a look at the curriculum this morning,' said Loughlin, a Kellach Brigdomin student.

'And?' said Kyra.

'It shouldn't be possible to select every course that you're doing,' Loughlin went on. 'There are waiting lists for the best courses, aye? Salve, Tempest, the Aurelian Papers, Rahain Technology – they're all over-subscribed; and yet you are in each one of those classes.'

'What's your point?' said Kyra.

'I thought it was obvious. It's favouritism. One of your aunts is the patron of the university, and another is the fucking Empress.'

'I had no say in what I studied,' said Kyra. 'I was just told to attend. If you have a problem with that, take it up with someone who gives a shit.'

The door to the office opened, and Professor Gallea walked out into the corridor. She glanced at the five students, and smiled at Kyra, then she strode away. A middle-aged man emerged from the entrance, and rubbed his hands together.

'In you come,' he said, his accent thick.

The five students walked into the small office, and the man closed the door.

'Find a seat,' the man said, as he closed the door.

All five students sat down, and the man leaned against his desk.

'My name is Mister Achan,' he said, 'a Hammer from the City; or the *City of Salve*, if you prefer. I have been asked to lecture here next year, and they wanted me to come a little early, so I can get myself settled in. For the rest of the spring term, and on into next year, I will be acting as your tutor. I assume I will be your first tutor?'

'Yes,' said Dazi. 'Students don't usually get one until third year.'

Achan nodded. 'I see. Well, I will be spending most of my time working alongside Professor Gallea, on the Aurelian Papers, but my door will always be open to the students under my tutorage. Do any of you know much about the Aurelian Papers?'

Kyra raised her hand.

'You're Kyra Holdfast, aren't you?' he said.

'Aye; that's me.'

'I was a good friend of your Uncle Corthie, many years ago,' Achan said. 'Since that time, I have been researching the discoveries made by the old Prince Aurelian – discoveries that were hidden from sight for nigh on two thousand years. Back in the City, though, we didn't have the resources to conduct any practical experiments; all we did was theory. It's a different matter here. It seems as though no expense has been spared in order to turn some of the ideas found in the Papers into reality. Kyra, why don't you tell the others some of the things discussed in the Papers?'

'Well, sir,' she said, 'the most important invention, or discovery, is steam power. The idea that steam expands, and that expansion can be used to move machinery, such as wheels, or pistons... or anything, really. I only started studying this topic at the beginning of Spring Term, so I still have much to learn about it.'

'Very good,' he said. 'Steam power has the potential to revolutionise society, but there are many other things to be found within the Papers. Machines to spin cotton, for example. This would provide cheap clothes to the poorest living among us. Now, does anyone know why these discoveries were hidden for so long?'

'Were they lost by accident, sir?' said Dazi.

'No,' said Achan. 'They were deliberately placed underground. Hundreds of scrolls, all kept in a dry, clean environment. Whoever hid them must have wanted them to be preserved, that seems clear. But why hide them at all? Let me tell you – it was to prevent the gods from destroying them. It's as simple as that. Prince Aurelian had organised a rebellion against the God-King and God-Queen of the City; a rebellion that was brutally crushed. The prince wanted to foster an atmosphere of progress, and this scared the gods. It scared them so much that they tried to wipe out every trace of the rebellion. Prince Aurelian was arrested and imprisoned in isolation for the rest of his life. I have seen the prison. Why would progress scare the gods? That's easier to answer. The gods rule by force, and the only thing that threatens their hegemony is mortals learning too much. Therefore, they suppress knowledge, rather than share power. The only reason we are allowed to study these topics, here in this university, is because the Empire is run by mortals, not gods.' He smiled. 'Knowledge allows mortals to be as powerful as gods; knowledge sets us free. Now, I am not saying that I agree with every policy undertaken by Empress Thorn, but we cannot deny that she has given us the freedom to study whatever subject we wish to examine. From salve to steam power; from Tempest to the technology used by the Rahain of old. Anyway, that's my little speech over. Now you know a little about me, and what I do. Any questions?'

Kyra raised her hand again.

'Yes?'

'Why did the Herald of the Empire refer to you as a radical, sir?'

Achan laughed. 'Is that what Kelsey called me, eh?'

'She said you were an anti-monarchist.'

'That is not true. I fully support the Aurelian monarchy currently ruling the City. King Daniel and Queen Emily have achieved great things, and the City is more fairly governed than at any time in the past. Here is what I am opposed to – hereditary sovereigns wielding unfettered power; the voices of the masses being ignored; aristocratic privilege; and, most of all – imperialism. I am not alone in seeing some of the ways that Empress Thorn has been pulling the City into her control. For a decade, the Empire has been sending aid to the City, in the form of food, mineral ores, finished goods, timber, garments, coal, oil... the list seems never-ending. As a result, the City is now completely dependent upon the Empire of the Star Continent.'

Kyra frowned. 'That makes you sound extremely ungrateful, sir. Weren't the people of the City starving? Their infrastructure was crumbling, and they had run out of natural resources. Were we supposed to let you all die? And when the City was invaded by the Ascendants, didn't we send help? I remember, because I was there.'

'Everything you say is true, Miss Holdfast,' Achan said. 'However, our survival came at a cost. The salve mine in the Eastern Mountains is now garrisoned by soldiers belonging to the Empire, and the rulers of the City are no longer free to change policies without the tacit permission of the Empress. Effectively, the City is already part of her Empire; would anyone be surprised if our King and Queen were made to bow before Empress Thorn? And where shall be next? Dragon Eyre is riven in two, with Queen Blackrose controlling the East, and Unk Tannic fanatics controlling the West. How long will it be before the Empire intervenes? And what about Athumia? Without any legal authority, the Tempest mine upon that world has been garrisoned by imperial soldiers. The Tempest you use in your classes with Professor Elbannon has been stolen from that world, without any regard given to the local inhabitants. I worry. What will be enough to satisfy the Empress? Full control of the four allied worlds? Even the word *allied* has been twisted, for what alliance has been agreed by the Dragon Dominion of Athumia? None. It is a term of convenience, used to mask the cold reality of ruthless exploitation.'

'The Empress wants what's best for the four worlds,' said Kyra, getting annoyed. 'Peace, prosperity, cooperation, progress, and a mutual defence against any attack by the gods of the Doomed Worlds.'

Achan looked her in the eye. 'Do you really believe that the gods, few as they are in number, would risk provoking the Holdfasts into another war? Sable Holdfast may be enjoying motherhood upon Dragon Eyre, and Corthie might be living the life of a farmer in Kell, but, if the Empress ordered it, the gods would be utterly annihilated. The Holdfasts have salve, Tempest, Quadrants, dream powers, the ability to be unaffected by the powers of the gods, and, young lady, they have the Sextant, the most powerful device in history.'

Kyra rolled her eyes.

Achan smiled. 'Let's leave it there for now. I must say, though, that I am looking forward to sparring with you on this subject, Miss Holdfast. Before you all go back to your classes, remember that I am here if you need anything. Don't hesitate to knock upon my door if you have a problem, or a question, or even if you just want a chat.'

The students got to their feet, and left the office. Kyra shook her head as the door was closed, and muttered, *Numpty* under her breath.

The sun was low in the western sky when Kyra arrived at the building that had housed the Ministry of the Plateau under Empress Bridget. With the new imperial palace still under construction, the Ministry had been taken over by the Imperial Court, and Thorn ruled the Empire from within its halls. Kyra had a small apartment within the Ministry, as well as her rooms on the grounds of the university, which she shared with Dazi.

A courtier met Kyra at the entrance to the building and escorted her upstairs to the private quarters of the Empress. Members of staff were everywhere, working in the various government offices, along with a small garrison of soldiers from the Imperial Guard, made up of Kellach

Brigdomin marines, warriors from Sanang, and veterans from the Banner of the Sapphire Throne. Kyra knew the way, but the courtier accompanied her to a small dining room, and presented her to the Empress, who was alone, and had been reading from a sheaf of documents.

Kyra curtsied before her Aunt Thorn, and the Empress smiled.

'Thank you for coming, Kyra,' she said. 'I always look forward to your visits. Please, be seated; dinner is about to be served.'

'Thank you, Your Majesty,' said Kyra, as she sat.

'You know the rules,' said Thorn. 'You don't need to call me that when we're alone or with family.'

The door opened, and Kelsey walked in, followed by Naxor.

'Yes,' said Naxor, 'but my dear Kelsey, things are a little more complicated than that.' He broke off to bow before the Empress. 'Your Imperial Majesty,' he said; 'you grow more regal with every passing day.'

Thorn smiled.

'Arse-licker,' Kelsey muttered.

'Lord Naxor has his ways,' said Thorn. 'Please sit.'

Kelsey and Naxor took their places at the table.

'I see our resident dream mage is present, Your Majesty,' said Naxor. 'How go your studies, Kyra?'

'They're all right,' said Kyra. 'Today, Mister Achan was telling us about how the gods of the City suppressed knowledge for thousands of years.'

Naxor slapped his thigh and laughed. 'Indeed, we did. Bear in mind, however, that the ill-fated rebellion of Prince Aurelian was a little before my time. I am old, but not *that* old. The events Achan was wittering on about occurred a thousand years before I was born.'

Kelsey narrowed her eyes. 'What else did Achan say?'

Kyra shrugged. 'He's worried that the Empire will try to swallow up the allied worlds. He thinks the Empress is an imperialist.'

'I am an imperialist,' said Thorn. 'An empire, by definition, is imperialist. The term can mean many things. At one extreme, it can mean the subjugation of conquered peoples, the stripping away of their wealth and rights. The imperialism I favour, however, is a voluntary joining of peoples who cooperate to better each other's lives. The constituent members of my empire govern themselves, do they not? In Kellach Brigdomin, the Clan Council rules; in the Holdings, a democratically-elected government holds sway. If I was attempting to play the tyrant, then I am doing a spectacularly bad job of it.'

Naxor nodded. 'Well said, Your Majesty.'

'Should I tell Achan to rein in the hyperbole, Your Majesty?' said Kelsey.

'Not at all,' said Thorn. 'What is the use of a university, if people are not allowed to speak their minds? Oh, and before I forget – happy birthday, my dear Herald.'

Kelsey mumbled something and looked away.

'Is it your birthday, Kelsey?' said Naxor. 'Why did I not know of this?'

'Because I like to keep it quiet,' said Kelsey. 'And, just maybe it's because you don't care.'

'You have me there,' said Naxor. 'Let me guess. Hmm. Thirty-nine?'

'Thirty-four, ya prick,' said Kelsey.

Naxor laughed. 'Ah, still so young. To me, it seems the merest blink of an eye since I first met you upon Lostwell. How old were you then?'

'I had just turned twenty-one.'

'Do you recall how annoying you were back then?' he said. 'What am I saying – you are just as annoying now.'

'Some people never change,' said Kelsey. 'You, for example.'

'Come now; I have been on my best behaviour for over a decade. Think back to the reasons I was truculent and mischievous – I desired power, wealth and influence. Do I not have these now in great abundance? Why would I wish to risk that? I am more than happy to serve the Holdfast Empire, because the Holdfast Empire supplies me with all that I need.'

'I have told you before, Naxor,' said Thorn; 'do not refer to the Empire by that name. It does not belong to the Holdfasts.'

'My apologies, Your Majesty,' said Naxor.

The Empress turned to Kyra. 'You will be eighteen this summer,' she said; 'and there is something that I, Kelsey and Naxor have been discussing that I felt I should let you know about.'

'What is that, Aunty?' said Kyra.

'You have shown much promise, Kyra,' Thorn said. 'In a few days, my Herald will be publishing a revised version of the Succession Law that governs who will be the next Emperor or Empress. It will still be elected, rather than hereditary, naturally, and this new law merely clarifies the rules on who should be allowed to vote. We have decided that you and your brother, along with your cousin Cole, shall become Junior Electors. You will not be able to vote until you turn twenty-one, but, as I hope to still be very much alive by then, it should not matter. What do you think about that?'

Kyra smiled. 'Thank you, Aunty. Does this mean I will help choose the next ruler of the Empire?'

'That is exactly what it means,' said Thorn. 'There is one more thing. Unlike the new law, however, this must be kept strictly between ourselves. We have also decided that you will be our favoured successor.'

'What?' said Kyra. Her eyes widened. 'Me?'

Thorn smiled at her. 'Yes, Kyra – you. We can think of no one more suitable. You have the potential to develop into an extraordinary young woman. Of course, this does not in any way guarantee that you will succeed to the throne after I pass away. There will be a vote. You may lose. What we are intending is something different. We will train you in the arts of ruling, so that you are ready when the day comes, which, I hope, will not be for quite some time yet. Once you have completed your third year at university, you will be shown all the offices of power and, slowly, you will be given more responsibility.'

Kyra felt her eyes well up, and Thorn leaned over, and placed a hand on her shoulder.

'We have faith in you, Kyra,' the Empress said. 'Of all the people, on all the worlds, we choose you.'

CHAPTER 2
ONE BIG FAMILY

Hold Fast, Republic of the Holdings – 19th Day, Last Third Spring 544

The sun shone down on the endless plains of the Holdings. With no mountains or hills in sight, the horizon shimmered in a heat haze, where the clear blue sky met the grasslands. The last of the spring flowers were wilting in the strength of the approaching summer, when the green lands would be baked to a dusty brown. Far off to the west, the Holdings grew enough food to feed the entire Star Continent, but in the lands where the great Hold Fast estate lay, the rains came seldom, and the grass began to peter out into the arid wilderness that began fifty miles to the east.

Cael adjusted the reins of his mount, as he and his cousin Cole followed a track leading to the Hold Fast mansion. Cole was on a dappled grey gelding, one of six horses that belonged to his personal stable, while Cael was astride a deep brown mare that the estate had been loaning him for spring.

They had been up since before dawn, riding out into the far pastures to the north of the estate, repairing broken fences, and retrieving part of a herd that had strayed towards the borders of Hold Fast land. They had been in no danger of being stolen, but several large predators roamed the semi-desert at the fringes of the estate, ready to pick off any straggling foals that had become separated from the herd.

Cael wiped the sweat from his brow, and moved his hat a little, so that the brim cut out more of the sun from his face. In the distance ahead of them, the whitewashed walls of the estate buildings were resolving themselves out of the haze – the mansion, the stables, the clock tower, the rows of comfortable accommodation for the hundreds of staff who worked on the estate, and the fountain in the centre of the courtyard, where the fairs, markets and festivals that marked each season took place.

'Eleven days to go,' said Cole.

Cael glanced at him, but said nothing.

'Eleven days,' Cole went on, 'and you'll be leaving again. Just in time to miss the summer heat.'

Cael suppressed an angry response that came to his lips.

'You should speak to Aunty Kelsey,' Cole continued. 'Tell her how unhappy you are with her schedule. If you don't, nothing will change.'

'I've tried telling her,' Cael said. 'She doesn't give a shit about my opinion. She moves me around the Star Continent as though I was a piece of baggage. It's for my own good, she tells me; but she never thinks to ask what I want.'

'Why you, though?' said Cole. 'Why not me or your sister? They've worked out my future – it's here, on the Hold Fast estate. They've been training me to take over the running of the estate from Aunty Celine for years; and Kyra has almost finished her second year at university – it's clear that they want her to concentrate on her studies. I can't work out why they're doing this to you, cousin. One season here, one season there. It doesn't seem fair to me.'

'Sometimes, I think they're doing it to piss me off. Just when I'm getting settled into a place, they move me again. Winter in Kell, spring here on the Holdings, summer in Colsbury, and autumn in Plateau City; I'm learning a bit of everything, but not enough about anything. By the time I come back to the Holdings next spring, I'll have forgotten what I learned this year. And what's the point of doing one term a year at the university? I spend the whole of autumn trying to catch up with everyone else.'

'Winter in Kell has to be the worst, though. Aye?'

'It's dark and cold, but Uncle Corthie is all right. He does his best to keep me busy and distracted. If we're not out rescuing sheep from a frozen river, or delivering feed in snow that comes up to your waist, he has me helping Aunty Aila in the farmhouse. They have six children now. Six. And Aunty Aila is pregnant again. It's bedlam. Then, just as spring is starting to appear, and the days are getting lighter, I'm brought here. I go from freezing my arse off to baking in the sun.'

'At least your sister will be in Colsbury.'

'Aye. Mother, too. I wonder if she'll actually notice that we're there this year. Last summer, she had just given birth to Caitlyn, and we hardly saw her. As soon as Kyra and I got to sixteen, it was as though Mother decided we were old enough to fend for ourselves; and she passed us over to Kelsey so that she could have children with Cardova. It's bullshit. Mother is a god now, and she is giving birth to immortal children.'

'Caitlyn and Carden might be immortal,' said Cole, 'but neither possess any dream mage abilities.'

'Does it matter? Mother might be producing demigods for a thousand years; why would she care about her two mortal children, even if they are dream mages?'

'Try not to fall out with her, cousin,' said Cole. 'At least you have a mother, even if she's busy with Carden and Caitlyn. I can't tell you how much I regret not seeing much of my father when he was still alive; and you have Cardova. I know he's not your real father, but he acts like one. All I have is Aunty Celine. You may hate travelling around the Star Continent, but I look forward to spring, knowing that you and Arrosa will be staying for the whole season. That reminds me, I assume you'll be coming to Arrosa's party this evening?'

'Do I have a choice?'

'Don't be so hard on her,' said Cole. 'Put yourself in her shoes. She has no real family here; her entire kin was wiped out on Athumia. All she had was your mother. Who does she have now, apart from us?'

'You don't need to make excuses for her,' said Cael. 'Arrosa is a little bitch. I can't stand her.'

'You need to make allowances. Imagine how hard it must be for her. And she's due to start university this autumn, so you should make an effort to get on with her.'

'Why? She hates me.'

'You're supposed to be her brother.'

'I'm not her fucking brother. She's just some stray that my mother picked up. If I had a Quadrant, I'd take her back to Athumia and leave her there.'

Cole shook his head.

'You're too soft on her,' Cael went on. 'You're too soft with everyone. If you try to please every person you meet, you end up pleasing no one. Look at the way Marium treats you. She's supposed to be your girlfriend, and she walks all over you. She doesn't respect you, Cole.'

Cole lowered his gaze. 'I want her to be happy.'

'What about you? Is your happiness unimportant? You're a powerful mage. You have abilities, but I've never once sensed you use them. If you went into Marium's mind, you'd soon find out the truth.'

'Have you been in her mind?' said Cole, anger flashing over his features.

'No. You made me promise not to, so I haven't. I want to, though. I don't trust her.'

'You don't trust anyone these days, cousin. You should try not to be angry all the time.'

Cael rolled his eyes. 'I have every right to be angry. So do you, but you've given up. You just accept whatever Aunty Kelsey and Aunty Celine have decided for you. You're eighteen, for fuck's sake. The family have charted out your life, and you just take it.'

'You're wrong,' said Cole. 'I want to be estate manager.'

'Aye, right. If you're not careful, you'll be married to Marium within a year or two, and you'll end up raising some other man's children.'

Cole narrowed his eyes, his features twisting with anger. Then he looked away.

Cael wondered if he had gone too far. He suspected that Marium was being unfaithful to his cousin but, without evidence, he should probably keep his mouth shut.

'I don't know why I am so angry,' he said. 'Pay no attention to anything I say, Cole. Sorry.'

'I get it,' said Cole. 'You feel abandoned, and your life has been parcelled out by Aunty Kelsey's crazy schedule. I honestly believe that if she knew how unhappy you were with being moved about every season, she would do something about it. There's no conspiracy trying to oppress you, Cael. The family are doing the best they can.'

They fell silent as they reached the first out-buildings. They dismounted, and walked their mounts through the square courtyard, stopping by the fountain to allow the two horses to drink. Cole took a brush from the saddle pack and began running it down the flank of his gelding, and Cael saw a smile appear on his face as he whispered to his mount. It was the horses of the estate that Cole truly loved; no humans came close. Cael cupped some water in his hands and splashed it over his face, feeling the cool relief of it against his burnt skin. The sunburn would fade overnight, as it always did – a consequence of his Kellach Brigdomin heritage. He and Cole had inherited the stature and build of their fathers, and they towered over the Holdings staff who worked on the estate.

Once the horses had drunk, the two cousins led them to the stables, where they passed them over to the hands who looked after Cole's mounts. Cole would normally spend a good hour with his horses after they had returned from the plains, but with Arrosa's party due to take place that evening, both cousins strode over the courtyard towards the white-washed mansion. They approached the rear porch, where Arrosa was sitting cross-legged on a swinging bench, her eyes on the pages of a book.

'Lazy little cow,' muttered Cael. 'We've been out in the baking sun all day working, and she's sipping iced tea?'

'It's her birthday,' said Cole. 'Give her a break.'

They reached the steps leading up to the porch, and Cole smiled.

'Happy birthday, cousin,' he said. He leaned over and kissed Arrosa on the cheek, and she smiled back at him.

Her gaze went to Cael, and her smile disappeared.

'What are you reading?' said Cole. 'Can I have some of that iced tea?'

'Help yourself, Cole,' said Arrosa, gesturing to a seat. 'I'm reading about the history of the Holdings. What were you boys doing today?'

Cole sat, and poured himself a glass of tea, while Cael leaned against a post.

'We were up north,' said Cole. 'A few horses had wandered into the desert. We found them, brought them back, and fixed the hole in the fence.'

'Hard work, in other words,' said Cael. 'While you've been sat on your fat arse all day.'

'Piss off, Cael,' she said. 'I have one day off in a month, and you get all uppity about it.'

'And you don't have a fat arse,' said Cole.

'I know,' said Arrosa. 'I do, however, have an arsehole for a step-brother.'

'We are not related in any way,' said Cael. 'And they're called *Thirds*, not *Months*.'

'Whatever,' said Arrosa. 'I bumped into Soula this morning, and I took the opportunity to ask her why she was wasting her time with you, Cael. You treat that girl like shit. If a boyfriend ever treated me like that, I'd turn him into glass.'

'You've never had a boyfriend,' said Cael. 'Nobody likes you.'

'That's not true,' said Cole.

'I know it isn't true,' said Arrosa. 'My head is always aching when Cael is around. He lies as easily as he breathes.'

Cael smiled. 'Grass is blue. Water is dry. The sun comes out at night.'

Arrosa winced in pain, and put a hand to her head.

'Horses have ten legs,' Cael went on.

Cole shot him a look. 'Stop it. Can't you see you're hurting her?'

Cael laughed. 'So?'

'You're a pig,' said Arrosa. 'Why can't you leave me alone?'

'I'd be more than happy to leave you alone. If you were to piss off back to Athumia, then you'd never have to see me again.'

'I have no one in Athumia; you know that.'

'You have no one here, either. Poor little Arrosa, lost and on her own.'

'Don't come to my party,' said Arrosa. 'I don't want you there.'

'That's fine by me,' said Cael. 'I'm going for a shower.'

He strode into the mansion, leaving Cole and Arrosa sitting on the porch. Cael walked through the cool hallways, passing an indoor fountain that sat in the middle of a crossroads of wide passageways. Several staff tilted their heads at him as he walked by, then he ascended to the first floor and entered his rooms. He had a bedroom, a bathroom, and a small balcony, and thick wooden shutters were covering every window, to keep out the heat and the harsh sunlight. Cael stripped off, and washed the sweat and dust from his skin in the shower, then he dressed in loose shorts and a tunic, took his cigarettes from a drawer, and went out on to his balcony. The sun was low in the western sky, and the balcony was in shade at that time of the day. He lit a cigarette, took a seat, and stared out at the view of the Holdings plains.

Part of him hated himself. Why had he said that to Arrosa, and on her birthday? Why did he hate her? Was it her, or was it what she represented? His mother had brought her back from Athumia, as though she had been planning to replace her existing children with a Gifted Gunstian waif. Cael had wanted his mother all to himself, and had been aggrieved at having another child in the house to compete for her attention and affection. None of that was Arrosa's fault, and yet he blamed her for it anyway. With the arrival of Carden and Caitlyn, Arrosa had been pushed to the side as much as Cael and Kyra had been. Kyra, of course, had taken it in her stride, but she had never enjoyed a close relationship with her mother, preferring the company of Empress

Thorn. For Cael and Arrosa, it had been a heart-wrenching experience. But, rather than their shared sense of grievance bringing them together, it had driven another wedge between them, as though they were still competing for Mother's love.

He stubbed out the cigarette and got to his feet. He wanted to apologise to Arrosa, but didn't know how. Besides, hadn't she told him that she didn't want to see him at her party? She hated him as much as he hated her, so why should he be the one to make a grovelling apology? He sat back down again, and lit another cigarette.

The sun had set by the time someone knocked and opened his door. Only one person didn't wait for a response before coming in, and Cael knew it would be his mother even before he saw her. He stood, and entered the bedroom.

'Why haven't you lit any lamps in here, Cael?' said his mother. 'I can barely see you.'

He smiled in the darkness, then he remembered why he was angry with her.

'I was on the balcony,' he said.

'I could see that,' she said. 'Why aren't you at the party? Everyone else is in the dining hall, and you are up here on your own.'

'Arrosa said she didn't want me to attend her party.'

His mother lit a lamp, and Cael almost flinched at the sight of her. In the darkness, he had been able to pretend that his mother had been in her old, familiar body, but the lamplight had dispelled the illusion.

'I need to talk to you about Arrosa, son,' she said. 'Sit down.'

Cael frowned, and remained on his feet. As a boy, he had always strained his neck to look up at his mother, but those days had long gone, and now he towered over her like a giant. She looked like an ordinary Holdings woman, rather than half-Kellach Brigdomin. He knew it was his mother on the inside, but nothing had been the same since her return from Athumia. Her new body was the reason that Carden and Caitlyn lacked any hint of dream mage abilities, even if their heritage had ensured that they would be immortal. Cael wondered how many other god powers they would develop as they grew older.

'Did you bring the children with you from Colsbury?' he said.

'Aye. Lucius is looking after them just now.'

'How are they?'

'They're well. If they fall, their bruises and cuts heal within seconds – it's an odd experience. And, they never get ill, but that was the same for you and Kyra.'

'How would you know? You weren't here when we were Carden and Caitlyn's age.'

His mother nodded. 'That's true.'

'I look almost as old as you,' he said. 'In a few years, I'll look older. In a hundred years, I'll be long dead, and you will look the same. Carden and Caitlyn will also be eternally young; forever twenty-one.'

His mother sat down on a chair. 'Are you upset with me, son?'

'Why did you have more children, when you knew they would be immortal?'

'I don't know what you want from me, Cael. Lucius and I waited until you and Kyra were old enough before trying to have a baby. My mother had four children, and I wanted the same. Was that wrong of me? If your father had lived, then it is likely that we would have had more children at some point.'

'They wouldn't have been immortal.'

'Is that the problem? I cannot help that. The body I inhabit used to belong to the granddaughter of an Ascendant, and I have inherited her powers. Should I have forsaken all hope of more children to avoid offending your sensibilities?'

Cael glared at her.

'Sit,' she said. 'I came here for Arrosa's party, and I'm missing it.'

'Then go to the party. I'm not stopping you.'

'I want to tell you something first; something about Arrosa. Sit.'

Cael sat down on the edge of his bed.

'I am aware,' his mother said, 'that you and Arrosa are not the best of friends. Partly because of that, I felt that I should say this to you first.

I haven't told anyone else yet, apart from Lucius, of course, as I wanted his agreement.'

'Are you sending her back to Athumia?'

His mother gave him a funny look. 'No. The opposite, if such a thing is possible. I intend to formally adopt her as a daughter.'

'What?'

'She deserves the rights that come with being a full Holdfast. The family has a tradition of adoption – think of your Aunty Celine, or Aunty Jemma; and, of course, there's the Empress, another adopted Holdfast. If they can do it, why can't Arrosa become one of the family?'

'No,' said Cael.

'No? I don't understand, son. It's not your decision. I am telling you as a courtesy.'

'Don't do it, Mother. Arrosa isn't a Holdfast. She isn't even from this world.'

'Neither is Lucius. Nor Aila, for that matter; yet both are Holdfasts.'

'They are married Holdfasts. It's different.'

'Perhaps, if Arrosa was to become your sister, then you might look more favourably upon her.'

Cael shuddered. 'I don't want her as my sister.'

'Why not?'

'She... she... I can't explain it. I hate her.'

'You are being childish, son. Poor Arrosa lost everything on Athumia – her family, her home. She was so kind to me when I had lost my memories; she helped me learn how to speak again, and to read and write. We had a few good years, didn't we, after I came back? Me, you, Lucius, Kyra and Arrosa – together in Colsbury. And Shella, too. We were like one big family. What went wrong, son?'

'You chose to have immortal children – that's what went wrong. As soon as Carden was born, you forgot that the rest of us were there. I think there's something left of that god in your head. You're not the same person.'

'That's not true. I look different, but I'm the same on the inside.'

'Are you? You abandoned me and Kyra twice when we were young;

and by having Carden and Caitlyn, you've abandoned us again; so maybe you're right. Maybe you haven't changed. Do you even know how I spend my time these days, Mother? Do you know what Aunty Kelsey puts me through? I live in a different place each season – Kell, the Holdings, Colsbury and Plateau City. It's driving me insane. But you don't care.'

'You are being a little melodramatic, don't you think?' she said. 'Aunty Kelsey and Aunty Thorn worked out your educational programme between them. Its purpose is to broaden your experiences, and to give you a rounded sense of life. And, you have only one more year of it to endure. You will appreciate it when you're older.'

Cael said nothing, choked by injustice and anger.

'You have been doing well in every season,' his mother went on. 'Corthie is very happy with your progress, and he enjoys the time you spend down in Kell each winter. He has been teaching you about farming, and Aila has been showing you her businesses and projects. Here, you have been learning how the Hold Fast estate is managed, and Celine has nothing but praise for the hard work you have done; and I know for a fact that Cole loves having you around. And, your lecturers in Plateau City University have tailored courses specifically to your needs. Those three seasons are hard, and that's why you have each summer off in Colsbury to relax. Frankly, I don't see the problem.'

Cael lowered his head. 'I don't have any friends.'

'You have family, son. Kelsey isn't sending you to strangers – she places you with other Holdfasts. Come downstairs, and show your face at the party. You only have to stay for ten minutes. Wish Arrosa a happy birthday, say hello to Lucius, and you can sulk in your room afterwards.'

Cael and his mother rose to their feet, and she led him out of the room. Sounds of the party filtered up from the stairs, as they descended to the ground floor. They passed servants carrying trays loaded with food and drinks, and entered the dining hall, where every lamp had been lit. Arrosa was wearing a summer dress, and she was smiling at something Celine was saying to her. Lucius was seated by a wall, with one baby on his knee, and another in a pram next to his leg. By another wall, Cole was looking sombre, as his girlfriend Marium spoke in his ear. Soula was standing by their side, and she glanced over at Cael, who ignored her. Over a dozen young members of staff had been invited to the party, the ones that Arrosa worked with on the estate, and they were laughing and chatting as they drank the wine handed out by the milling servants.

Cael walked up to Cardova. 'Hello,' he said.

'Hello, Cael,' said Cardova. 'I'm glad to see you made it down to the party. How have you been getting on in the Holdings this year?'

Cael shrugged. 'As soon as I've settled down, I'm moved on to somewhere else.'

'Well, it's Colsbury next,' said Cardova. 'We'll all be together for the summer.'

'I'd better speak to Arrosa,' Cael said.

He walked away, and approached Arrosa and Celine. The older woman was laughing, then they both noticed Cael.

'Your mother found you then?' said Celine. 'I was worried that you weren't feeling well.'

'Arrosa said she didn't want me to come to the party.'

'I was annoyed because you were lying to give me a sore head,' Arrosa said.

'Is that true, Cael?' said Celine. 'You know you shouldn't do that.'

'It was just a joke,' he said.

'It's not funny if it hurts someone.'

'That's a matter of opinion.'

Celine shook her head. 'You do a wonderful job here on the estate each spring, Cael. Please don't spoil that by being mean to your sister.'

'Arrosa is *not* my sister.'

'You know what I mean. We are all one big family.' She peered off to her right. 'Your mother is calling me over; behave yourself, Cael.'

Celine walked away, and Cael turned back to Arrosa.

'Happy birthday,' he said.

'I'm the same age as you now,' she said.

'Not for long. I'll be eighteen in summer.'

'Do you think you will have matured by then, or will you still be acting like a spoiled brat?'

'I hate you,' he said.

'The feeling's mutual, Cael. You have been an arsehole to me for years. I used to think it was something I had said or done, but I've realised that you're not a kind person. Cole is a lovely guy, but you?'

'Cole is a doormat. Look at the way Marium is speaking to him. Does he look happy to you?'

'Maybe you're right. I admit I don't particularly like Marium, but at least Cole tries. I've given up trying with you.'

'Do you think we've spoken long enough for people to see us?'

'I think so. Laugh when I stop speaking.'

She smiled, and they both laughed as though they had enjoyed a joke together.

'Don't overdo it,' she said.

'Horses lay eggs,' he said.

She flinched, and he walked away. Soula hurried over. Cael tried to avoid her, but she stood in front of him.

'Aren't you going to speak to me?' she said.

'What's the point?' he said. 'I'll be going to Colsbury in eleven days, and I won't be back in the Holdings until next spring.'

She stared at him. 'I thought you liked me. Are you breaking it off?'

'It's impossible to break off something that never started.'

'But, all those nights we...'

'I was bored, Soula, and you happened to be around.'

'But what if,' she whispered; 'what if I'm pregnant?'

'Are you?'

'I don't think so, but...'

'If you are, I'll take you to Colsbury, and you can see Shella. She's a flow mage, and she'll be able to get rid of it.'

Soula stared at him, then she slapped him across the face and ran off. Cael strode out of the hall before Celine or his mother could find him. He hadn't meant to be cruel to Soula, but it was better if she hated him. That way, she wouldn't miss him after he had left the Holdings. He would miss her, but there was no way he was going to admit that to her face. It was better if he had no friends, if he had to shuttle from one place to another every season.

He went back to his room, walked out on to the balcony, and lit a cigarette, his cheek stinging.

He had only one thing in his life that he looked forward to, and it was in Colsbury. It wasn't his family, though he would be happy to see Kyra again. No, it was something else; something he had kept secret from everyone else.

For nine thirds of the year, he was forced to be away from Colsbury, and, in eleven days, he would be back. He would wait until all of the formal parties and gatherings to mark the start of summer were in full swing, and then he would steal away to the attic in the uppermost tower of the Summer Palace. He would take his Tempest sword with him, the one he had secretly obtained in Plateau City, and activate the Sextant. With his mother busy looking after her new children, she would be too preoccupied to notice what her elder son was doing; and then Cael would have the opportunity to lose himself within the worlds he had been creating. Days spent upon one of those worlds took only minutes of real time in Colsbury, and he would be able to roam freely, tinkering with his creations, building continents, and overseeing the progress of the sub-created humans and other creatures he had brought into being.

There was no feeling like it.

He was a creator of worlds, god-like and all-powerful. It was an intoxicating mix that had utterly seduced him. Next to it, his quarrels with Arrosa and his mother faded into insignificance.

Eleven days, he said to himself; eleven days until he could be free again.

CHAPTER 3
SHADES OF IMPERIALISM

Plateau City, The Plateau – 20th Day, Last Third Spring 544

Kelsey walked into the meeting room as the last of the courtiers were leaving. As was usual for certain sessions of the Imperial Court, the Empress wanted no one present apart from the high officers of state. Kelsey closed the door, and took her seat by the right-hand side of Empress Thorn.

'Are we ready to begin, Your Majesty?' she said.

Thorn nodded. 'We are, my Herald.'

Kelsey glanced down the table at the others. On her right was Naxor, Chamberlain of the Empire, followed by Brogan, the Imperial Treasurer. Sitting across from them were Caelius, the Imperial Quartermaster, and Bedig, the Lord Marshal. There were two other members of the Imperial Court – Cardova, the High Constable, and Shella, the Imperial Chancellor, but, as they dwelt in Colsbury, sessions in Plateau City made do with a reduced number of attendees.

'We have several issues to get through this morning,' said Kelsey; 'so I will be brief. The first item is Rahain. Do we have permission to proceed with our plans, Your Majesty?'

Thorn said nothing for a moment, then she gave a slight nod.

'Yes,' she said. 'Proceed.'

'Thank you, Your Majesty,' said Kelsey. 'Bedig, issue the orders that I passed to you at the last session.'

'I will, ma'am,' said Bedig, 'but shouldn't Major General Cardova be here for all military decisions?'

'In ten days,' said Kelsey, 'we'll be seeing Lucius when we arrive in Colsbury, and he already knows the gist of the plan, and has approved it. Caelius, have the necessary provisions, weaponry and stores been prepared?'

'They have, ma'am,' said Caelius. 'Everything is ready to be moved to the borders of Rahain.'

'Then move it,' said Kelsey. 'I will visit Commander Lahnos on the frontier in a few days, to let him know our plans.'

'Invite him to Colsbury,' said Thorn. 'I wish to speak to him before the invasion begins.'

'I will, Your Majesty. Our next item is Rakana. The government of Amatskouri is agitating for a full intervention by imperial forces. How should we respond, Your Majesty?'

'The rulers of Amatskouri are always asking us to intervene in Rakana,' said Thorn. 'What makes this request any different?'

'They are stating that a severe famine is underway within the borders of Rakana, Your Majesty.'

'Does Amatskouri believe that an invasion of Rakana will solve their food problems? We must ponder our moves carefully. You all know that I yearn to see the Star Continent re-united under the Empire, but an armed intervention into Rakana would cause more problems than it would solve. I need other ideas; other solutions.'

'We could send food to relieve the famine, Your Majesty,' said Brogan. 'The treasury has a surplus that could easily cover it.'

'No,' said Thorn. 'I have lost count of the number of times we have sent aid to Rakana; it solves nothing. They never show any gratitude, and never learn from their mistakes. Fresh thinking is needed. Come up with a variety of suggestions, and we shall discuss them at the next session.'

'Very well, Your Majesty,' said Kelsey. 'The next item is Dragon Eyre.

Queen Blackrose will be here later today, and I have been informed that she wishes to discuss strengthening our alliance. The Unk Tannic are now in complete control of the Home Islands, and they have been sending agents to infiltrate the Eastern Rim. I suspect that Blackrose will formally request that we send military aid to strengthen the defences of Yearning and Haurn.'

Thorn paused again. 'Sending Banner forces back to Dragon Eyre would be a political mistake, I feel,' she said; 'and one can imagine the reaction among the Banner soldiers if we informed them that they were going back to the world from which we rescued them. I desire a strengthening of our alliance with Queen Blackrose, but we must be prudent. Let us wait until we hear her request, and then formulate our response.'

Kelsey nodded. 'The next item is the City, or the City of Salve; whatever you prefer. The annual subsidies we send there are due to expire over summer, and I have it on good authority that King Daniel and Queen Emily will be coming to Colsbury to renegotiate the terms. I assume, Your Majesty, that we shall be renewing the subsidies?'

'No,' said Thorn.

The others round the table turned to glance at the Empress.

'No, Your Majesty?' said Kelsey.

'Not without a full audit of where all of our money has gone, Herald. For ten years, we have been shipping untold amounts of goods, resources, gold and food to the City. Would I be right in saying that it costs us one-tenth of our entire annual budget?'

'Yes, Your Majesty,' said Brogan.

'That money could be put to better use,' said Thorn. 'Is Jezra not safe and prosperous? Is it not true that the City could survive on its own again?'

'They could survive, Your Majesty,' said Naxor, 'but the impact of cutting off all subsidies at once would have a serious and dramatic effect. For better or worse, the City has become dependent upon the aid we send it.'

Thorn's expression hardened a little. 'I dislike the notion that we are making the citizens of the City rich and comfortable, while many upon the Star Continent live in poverty. If the City wishes to keep their subsidies, then they must be willing to compromise on other areas. Membership of the Empire, for instance. Without an imperial bond uniting us, I see no reason to indefinitely fund the lifestyles of Evaders who refuse to work. Here then, is my proposal – we shall inform the City that the subsidies shall be reduced by a quarter every year for the next four years, unless they are willing to join the Empire as subjects of the throne. As for the salve mine in the Eastern Mountains, we shall formally annex that territory to the Empire whether the City agrees or not.'

Kelsey frowned. 'I imagine that Mister Achan will have a few things to say about this proposal, Your Majesty.'

'Too much aid has infantilised the population of the City, I fear,' said Thorn. 'Why work, when the Empire sends everything they need? Were it not for our excessive generosity, the City would be in ruins. It is time they re-learned how to stand on their own two feet. If they refuse to do so, then they are free to join the Empire.'

'How would that work in practice, Your Majesty?' said Caelius. 'What benefits would it bring to the City, and how would the Empire work with an off-world member?'

'We would establish freedom of movement, Caelius,' said Thorn. 'Citizens of the Empire are free to travel to any of its provinces. Quadrant stations will be set up, allowing set times when populations can travel back and forth. The internal laws of the City would remain under their jurisdiction, and the salve mines would pay for the City's contribution to the Empire's treasury. Their armed forces would come under our direct control, and the defence of the Great Walls would become an imperial responsibility. We would send a military governor to the Bulwark, and the Blades would swear loyalty to the Empire. Kelsey, liaise with Shella when we get to Colsbury, and have the Imperial Chancellor draw up the accession documents. Within the next year, I want the City to be a full member of the Empire, but only if they agree to our terms. We shall let them know the consequences for their refusal. They will join the Empire, or the subsidies will be cut off.'

'As you will it, Your Majesty,' said Kelsey. 'The last item on my list is the Tempest mine on Athumia. Dragons from Nom Karta have been seen in recent days, encroaching into the prohibited area around the mine, despite our warnings. The governor of the mine is worried that they might attack.'

'Is the mine adequately defended?'

'It has a garrison of four hundred Banner soldiers stationed there to protect the miners, Your Majesty. They have several batteries of ballistae, which would make any such attack a costly one. However, we should be in no doubt that, if the dragons of the Dominion decide to launch a full invasion, we would lose.'

'Could Professor Ravi's new devices assist in any way?' said Thorn.

'I can ask him, Your Majesty,' said Kelsey.

'Has Kyra been introduced to Ravi's work yet?'

'No, Your Majesty. I was saving that surprise for her third year.'

'Let her see some of his work before the end of the Spring Term,' said Thorn. 'I would be interested in gauging her response. As for Athumia, once you have spoken to Ravi, perhaps you should visit Lord Bailey upon Zamata. He might be willing to defend the Tempest mine.'

Naxor smiled. 'In the old days, we would have sent Corthie and Sable to sort out these beastly dragons.'

'Yes, but Sable has a young baby to go with her five year old. I hardly think she is likely to come out of retirement to fix our problems for us. As for Corthie, he has pledged to don his armour and pick up his Clawhammer only in the event of a direct threat to the Star Continent. A mine on another world does not qualify.'

'We have other mages at our disposal, Your Majesty,' said Naxor. 'There is Cael, Cole and Arrosa in the Holdings; as well as Kyra here in Plateau City.'

'They are all too young,' said Thorn.

'Are they, Your Majesty? Corthie was the same age as Cole when he was defending the Great Wall of the City. And Cole has battle-vision, I believe?'

'Allegedly,' said Kelsey. 'He's never used it. In fact, he seems unwilling to use any of his powers. I think he's afraid of turning into his father.'

'With good reason,' said Thorn. 'When was the last time we did a thorough census of the Star Continent's mages?'

'We have never done a full census, Your Majesty,' said Kelsey; 'primarily because we cannot access Rahain or Rakana. The Matriarch of Sanang reported that they had over a hundred hedgewitches; that was about three or four years ago, I think; and the Holdings keeps a register of all high mages. They have nine, at the last count, but that doesn't include those with battle-vision alone. As far as I know, the Clan Council doesn't count any fire mages or sparkers within Kellach Brigdomin. Should I order a census of the Plateau?'

'Yes,' said Thorn.

'What about my cousin Jade?' said Naxor. 'She has death powers and, to the best of my recollection, she is sitting idly in the Eastern Mountains with her pet dragon.'

'Are you proposing we ask her to go to Athumia?' said Thorn.

'Perhaps, Your Majesty, it might be worth our time to enquire if she is willing to work for the Empire. She and Dawnflame would wreak havoc among the dragons of the Dominion. Of course, it goes without saying that I should not be the one to ask her. Jade has never forgiven me for my indiscretions in the City during Simon's rule.'

'You're calling them *indiscretions* now, are you?' said Kelsey.

'Yes. In another decade I shall be referring to them as mere foibles.'

'Maybe you should go to Athumia. Your vision powers would give early warning of any attack by the Dominion.'

'Me, Madam Kelsey?' said Naxor, looking pained. 'As much as I would love to be posted to a volcanic wasteland, I have duties and responsibilities to which I must attend.'

'Naxor will be staying here,' said Thorn. 'Kelsey, approach the Holdings government and request that they release one of their high mages into imperial service. We shall do nothing about Lady Jade for now.'

'Aye, Your Majesty,' said Kelsey. 'That was it; Athumia was the last item on my list.'

'I had something to bring up, ma'am,' said Caelius.

'Please speak,' said Thorn.

'Thank you, Your Majesty. As Imperial Quartermaster, I am responsible for the resettlement of all personnel retiring from the Banner of the Sapphire Throne. As the average age of the Banner increases year by year, and with no fresh blood to replace those who retire, we are looking at an ever-growing number of men and women leaving the service. At the moment, all retirees have the right to resettle in the new city of Bannerton on the shores of the Inner Sea, but the site needs investment if it is to take the expected numbers. At present, twenty thousand former Banner personnel have settled there, and that will likely double over the next three years. In other words, I need an increase in my budget to cover the cost.'

'Duly noted, Caelius,' said Thorn. 'In the short term, your department can take the existing surplus from the treasury to fund building works and so on in Bannerton. Naxor, Brogan, ensure that Caelius has all that he needs. The Banner of the Sapphire Throne is dear to my heart, and I desire to see them settled in peace and prosperity. Bannerton has the potential to overtake both Westport and Rainsby as the principal trading port on the southern half of the Inner Sea, and, with a little help from us, we can ensure its success. Quartermaster, when will the last of the Banner forces be eligible for retirement?'

'They will have all reached retirement age from active service within the next ten years, Your Majesty,' said Caelius. 'The youngest among them are reaching their thirtieth year. I have produced a yearly forecast that shows the projected decline in numbers.'

'It will be a sad day when the last Banner soldier retires,' said Thorn, 'but there is no place in the future of the Empire for mercenaries. What I require is a fully-professional imperial army, one that pledges its loyalty to the throne, not to a contract. However, that does not mean I am ungrateful for all that they have achieved. When Bannerton starts to produce children, I hope that many of them will follow in their parents' footsteps, and consider a career in the imperial armed forces.'

Caelius smiled. 'I deem that very likely, Your Majesty.'

'If that's all,' said Kelsey, 'we should end the meeting. Queen Blackrose will be here soon, and I need to speak to Frostback and Halfclaw.'

'Then this meeting is adjourned,' said Thorn.

The members of the Imperial Court got to their feet, and bowed before the Empress. Kelsey remained behind when the others had left, and Thorn stepped down from her throne.

'I have some concerns about the policy regarding the City,' Kelsey said.

'I thought you might,' said Thorn. 'Do you think we should continue to fund them indefinitely?'

'No, but this seems a little like blackmail. Join us, or we cut off every luxury that makes life worth living. Sure, the City could *survive* without our subsidies, but we would be plunging them back into poverty.'

'The Empire is not a charity, Kelsey. For ten long years, we have given the City everything they need, no questions asked. At some point, if the City wishes to remain independent, it has to end. The choice is theirs. I am not forcing them into anything.'

'I'm not sure Emily and Daniel will see it that way.'

'They would remain as monarchs, were they to join the Empire.'

'But with a military governor in the Bulwark?'

'A fundamental policy of the Empire is that none of its constituent parts possesses its own armed forces. There is no Holdings army, so why should the City have an army of its own?'

Kelsey opened the door, and they strode out into a hallway, where a large number of courtiers and soldiers were waiting to accompany the Empress and her Herald. Thorn led the way, and they walked out into the large courtyard in the centre of the Ministry of the Plateau, where Frostback and Halfclaw were waiting for them on the gravel.

Kelsey smiled, and walked up to Frostback. 'How was the flight down from Colsbury?'

'The flight was pleasant, rider,' said the silver dragon; 'what I object to is being parted from you for so long. When will the imperial palace be ready? I yearn for the day when Halfclaw and I can live with you in Plateau City.'

'It will still be another couple of years,' said Kelsey, 'but work is going on there every day.'

Frostback glanced around. 'Where are your children?'

'I don't bring them to work,' said Kelsey. 'Van is looking after them in the Holdfast townhouse.'

'And doesn't Van also have to work?'

'No offence to him, but my job is more important than his.'

'A pity. I wanted to see sweet Calpurnia and little Caelius. They are seven and four, are they not?'

'That's right.'

'I have decided to train Calpurnia as my next rider,' said Frostback.

Kelsey blinked. 'What?'

'I will be alive for another four hundred years, Kelsey; did you think you would be my sole rider? You have, what – three or four decades left? I want your replacement to be kin, and I want to get started on her training soon. Calpurnia will be eight years of age this autumn. We shall begin then.'

'Uh, well, I'll ask her. Let's see what she says. I might have to run it past Van as well.'

'Why?'

'He's her father.'

'Yes, but you have a long habit of over-riding his decisions, my rider. Is your marriage in good health?'

'I suppose so. Van gets annoyed with me asking him to look after the children all the time, but, you know, that's life.'

'Perhaps you are working too hard,' said Frostback. 'You aren't neglecting Van and the children, are you?'

'I see them when I can, which, admittedly, isn't as much as I'd like.

But what can I do? I'm the Herald of the Empire. When I was young, my mother left the Hold Fast estate to become First Holder of the Holdings Republic. She was away for years, and my father looked after us.'

'I see,' said Frostback. 'And is it your ambition to repeat your mother's mistakes?'

'Why are you giving me such a hard time?'

'Frostback is upset that she hasn't seen you for a while,' said Halfclaw. 'She misses you deeply.'

'I'll be in Colsbury in ten days,' said Kelsey. 'We can have the entire summer together.'

'Apart from when you are working,' said Frostback.

'Well, aye; obviously. But that's still a lot better than me living here, and you living up there. And, when the imperial palace is finished, we will see each other every day, all year round.'

'I look forward to it,' said Frostback.

The air above the courtyard shimmered, and Blackrose appeared in the sky. She stabilised her descent, then landed in the courtyard next to the other two dragons. At this, Thorn stepped forward, and joined Kelsey, while over a dozen courtiers trailed behind.

'Welcome back to Plateau City, Your Majesty,' said Kelsey, tilting her head.

'I thank you for the welcome, Herald of the Empire,' said Blackrose; 'and I thank you for the invitation, Imperial Empress of the Star Continent.'

'It is a joy to see you again,' said Thorn.

'You may not be so joyful when I relate to you the challenges Dragon Eyre is currently facing, Empress,' said the huge black dragon; 'but, before we discuss matters of state, Maddie has requested that we fly over the city.'

'Is that alright?' said Maddie, from high up on Blackrose's shoulders. 'I would like to see the new palace, please. And, will there be a party tonight? This is the first time I've been away from the children in years, and I don't want to waste it.'

'I am never one to refuse a party,' said Thorn. 'I think I shall accompany you on the flight over the city, if, that is, Halfclaw will agree to bear me upon his shoulders.'

The green and blue dragon bowed his head. 'It would be an honour, Empress; I am at your service.'

Kelsey gestured to a couple of Kellach members of the Imperial Guard, and they escorted the Empress to Halfclaw's left flank. The dragon lowered himself, and the two soldiers helped Thorn climb up onto the harness, then they sat down on either side of her. Kelsey clambered up onto Frostback's shoulders, and then the three dragons ascended into the air. The Ministry of the Plateau occupied a central position within the city's New Town, between the market and the site of the old cathedral. The dragons banked towards the south, and Kelsey saw both the location of the Holdfast townhouse by the Sea Wall, and the tall spires of the university. Halfclaw led the way, and they soared over the aristocratic district. Ahead of them, where the Old Town walls met the old Emergency Wall, a vast building site came into view. The Great Fortress had been demolished down to its ground floor, and in its place stood the lower storeys of the new palace. At its base, it was one building, but it divided into two towers as it rose, with each tier narrower as they climbed higher into the sky. Both towers were flanked in scaffolding, and dozens of workers were toiling under the spring sunshine. Parts of the Old Town walls had been cleared away to create a larger space, and the moat installed by Bridget had been filled in and built over.

The dragons circled over the construction site for a few minutes, then Halfclaw led the others down in a slow descent. The green and blue dragon approached the northernmost of the two towers, where a great entrance had been built. He flew through it, and landed in a vast hall. The other two dragons joined him, and they settled down in the centre of the enormous space. Its walls were clad in wooden scaffolding, and its ceiling was unfinished, but the layout of the structure was clear. To the south, a bridge was being built to link the two towers together, a bridge wide and strong enough to bear the weight of several dragons.

'This is the new dragon hall,' said Kelsey, her voice loud enough for the others to hear. 'Below us are living quarters for four dragons, though six could squeeze in; or perhaps even eight. This whole tower is being built for dragons, and it will only have four levels, while the other tower is for humans, and will have twelve storeys. There will be three bridges connecting the two towers, so that both sides can be in constant communication.'

'It occupies a smaller area than I had imagined,' said Blackrose, 'but, at the same time, it is far taller.'

'We didn't want to demolish too much of the centre of the city,' said Kelsey, 'so we built upwards, instead of outwards. Even so, we've had to pare back the Old Town walls a bit, as well as the Emergency Wall, and sixty houses had to be torn down – half in the Old Town, and half in the New Town. The new palace occupies twice the area of the Great Fortress; but only a sixth of the area that Guilliam's old palace used to take up. The new palace uses granite from the Barrier Mountains, and sandstone from the Black Mountains, and bands of the exterior walls will be clad in ceramic tiles made in Amatskouri. The tiles will be glazed in cobalt blue; so we're thinking of calling it the Blue Palace. The tiles will go on last, so you can't see them yet, but the effect should be visible to sailors out on the Inner Sea. When it's finished, the towers will be twice as tall as the Great Fortress was.'

'Will it have eyries, Herald?' said Blackrose.

'Aye – two, both at the top of the dragon tower. Frostback and Halfclaw will be able to look down over the whole city from up there. The tallest of the three bridges will be at that height, allowing me or the Empress to walk over to the eyries.'

'It is a mighty achievement,' said Blackrose; 'and it stirs my heart to think how you have adapted the design to accommodate dragons. Not many humans remember to do such things. My adopted daughter and her mate will do well here, I think.'

'Indeed,' said Frostback. 'Halfclaw and I are impatient to move in. Once we are settled, then, at long last, we shall be ready to begin our own family.'

'And there will be somewhere grand for visiting dragons to stay,' said Kelsey.

'You will always be welcome here, Queen Blackrose,' said Thorn; 'our friend and ally.'

Blackrose tilted her head a fraction. 'You have my thanks, Empress. You can be sure that I shall wish to visit, once Frostback and Halfclaw have youngling dragons to look after. Now, if it not be too forward, may I tell you the reason for this current visit?'

'I urge you to do so,' said Thorn, 'and, if we can help in any way, we shall do so.'

'Dragon Eyre is divided into three parts,' said Blackrose. 'In the Eastern Rim, my rule holds sway, from Wyst in the north, to Yearning in the south. The Western Rim remains gripped by suffering and conflict. The so-called Home Islands of Na Sun Ka, Gyle and Ectus are under the control of the Unk Tannic; while Olkis has taken Alef under its wing, and has declared itself independent. With the Olkians, I have made alliance – a pact of mutual defence designed to contain the Unk Tannic threat; but our allies are under constant attack, and I find myself hardly able to fulfil the terms of the pact. Without aid, Olkis will likely fall to the Unk Tannic, and then Alef will follow. The Unk Tannic have re-learned the secrets of explosives, and the Olkians have been the victims of untold outrages – bombs in market-places, and in their harbours, and vile assassinations of their leaders. Therefore, I reluctantly call upon the alliance I have made with the Empire of the Star Continent. As we came to your aid when Edmond assaulted this world, and as we have aided the City of Salve by sending volunteers to guard Jezra; may we now request reciprocal aid? What say you, Empress?'

'We shall not stint in our support of your realm,' said Thorn; 'name what you need, Queen Blackrose, and you shall have it.'

'Your reputation for honour and friendship has not been overstated, Empress,' said Blackrose. 'Let us return to your temporary palace, and I shall supply you with every detail.'

Kelsey suppressed a frown as the three dragons made their way to the hall's entrance and took to the skies. With everything that was going on, she felt as though she was juggling a dozen balls at once – Rakana, Rahain, the Tempest mine on Athumia, the City – each one had the potential to become a full blown crisis, and the resources of the Empire were starting to stretch a little.

Add Dragon Eyre to the list, she thought. One more ball to keep aloft.

CHAPTER 4
GARRISON DUTY

Grey Mountains, Rahain – 22nd Day, Last Third Spring 544

The silvery-green dragon soared high over the mountains. Summer had almost arrived, but it was bitterly cold at that altitude, and Lahnos wrapped his fleece-lined coat tightly round his shoulders. He glanced down from the dragon harness at the valleys spread out beneath them.

'The pass seems clear, my friend,' said the dragon.

'The pass is always clear these days, Sigum,' said Lahnos. 'The Rahain raiding parties know that we're here, and none of them risk trying to cross into the Plateau this way any more. We've been so effective that the job's becoming boring.'

'That feeling will pass soon enough, if the rumours are to be believed. I shall take us back to camp.'

Sigum banked to the right, and began heading north. After a few minutes, they approached a wide, flat valley trapped between two high mountain ridges. A stream ran down one flank, and a fortress had been constructed by the cliffs on the northern side of the valley. By the base of the fortress, a military camp took up a large section of the valley; while a paved road ran from one entrance of the Great Tunnel, to another. The two entrances appeared as dark holes in the sides of the cliffs opposite each other, and wide ramps led up to them from the valley floor.

When Lahnos had first been asked to guard the Great Tunnel between Rahain and the Plateau, he had envisioned one, long, continuous stretch, when, in reality, the tunnel was divided into several parts. It would emerge from the side of a ridge, and the pass would continue overland for a while, before it followed another section of tunnel. Imperial forces were occupying its entire length, from the Plateau all the way to the fortress at the Rahain end. There were several other routes through the Grey Mountains, however, and raiding parties of Rahain had often crossed into the Plateau to rob and pillage the homesteads and farms between the mountains and the port of Rainsby. The arrival of Lahnos and Sigum had put an end to that.

The silvery-green dragon soared down towards the gates of the camp. Its four sides were protected by a high palisade wall, and a full regiment of soldiers from the Imperial Army was stationed there. The Bullan who had accompanied Lahnos to the Star Continent were also there, but they did not live within the camp. Instead, they, Lahnos and the dragon resided inside the southern entrance to the Great Tunnel. Apartments, shops and offices had been hewn out of the rock on either side of the wide tunnel by its original builders, and they had been turned into living quarters for Lahnos and the Bullan, while Sigum slept within the main tunnel. It was cold in winter, but the tunnel was dry, and gave shelter from the storms.

Smoke was rising from a few fires dotted around the camp, while several soldiers were collecting water from the stream. A few looked up as Sigum started his descent, and Lahnos raised his hand in greeting. The dragon landed on a wide sward of grass, close to the ramp that led up to the tunnel entrance where he lived. Lahnos unbuckled the straps keeping him to the harness, and climbed down to the ground. He stretched his arms and legs, then he followed Sigum up the ramp. Three of the seven Bullan were sitting by the entrance to the tunnel, and they got to their feet as the dragon approached.

'My lords,' said Corporal Gaddiz, 'welcome back. Is there anything to report?'

'The pass is quiet,' said the dragon; 'we saw no sign of any Rahain trying to reach the Plateau.'

Lahnos reached the mouth of the tunnel, and took an offered mug of water from one of the Bullan. In the eight years they had spent on the Star Continent, only one of the soldiers – the corporal – had shared his name with Lahnos; the six privates had remained anonymous to him, despite the level of trust that existed among them.

The dragon entered the tunnel, and began to eat from a long trough.

'I almost miss the days when we used to catch Rahain raiders regularly,' Lahnos said.

'Crime in the southern Plateau has fallen significantly since we were stationed here, sir,' said Gaddiz. 'The farmers are able to live without the fear of being raided. This is a worthy task, and I am proud of what we have achieved.'

'We could be doing more,' Lahnos said. 'We've been guarding the pass for three years, and for the last two, we've had nothing to do but go on patrol.'

'Yes, sir,' said Gaddiz, 'but, if the rumours we are hearing from the Imperial Army have any truth to them, we may soon be called into action.'

'Have you heard anything else, corporal?'

'Not today, sir, but that young lieutenant from the army is approaching. She might know more.'

Without turning, Lahnos knew exactly to whom the Bullan was referring. He took a long breath to prepare himself.

'Commander Lahnos!' a voice cried out.

Lahnos fixed a smile to his face and turned. 'Lieutenant Dolwyn,' he said.

The Kellach woman strode up to the entrance to the tunnel, a cocky smile on her face. Like every soldier from Kellach Brigdomin, she was taller than those from the various other elements of the army, from

Holdings cavalry to Banner infantry, and Dolwyn was only a few inches shorter than the top of Lahnos's horns. At first, he had been bemused by how many Kellach women served in the armed forces of the Empire, but after having seen them in action, any doubts about their abilities had been laid to rest. Regardless, he felt awkward in the lieutenant's presence, as she had told him frankly several times that she was interested in him. Each time, he had politely refused her advances, but she hadn't seemed remotely put out.

'Did you see anything interesting on your patrol today, Commander?' she said.

'Nothing,' he said. 'The pass is quiet.'

'Not for much longer, though, eh?' she said. 'We're expecting the orders to come through any day now.'

'What have you heard?'

'A portal opened up by the northern end of the tunnel this morning,' she said, 'and five thousand soldiers walked through. More are coming tomorrow, by all accounts. The invasion is happening; the Empress wouldn't be sending all those soldiers through to sit on their arses all day.'

'You sound as though you're looking forward to it, Lieutenant.'

'Call me Dolwyn, sir. And aye; I'm raring to go. Imperial soldiers have been guarding the Great Tunnel for over seventeen years; it's time we brought order back to Rahain.'

'Why?'

Dolwyn raised an eyebrow. 'The poor wee lizard bastards have suffered enough, no? They're living like animals, in complete squalor; and the strong ones steal whatever they like from the weak. It's hard to believe that they used to be an advanced civilisation.'

'Why can't we leave them to sort out their own problems?'

'That's exactly what we've been doing for nearly two decades, sir. Has it worked?'

'Invasions are... messy. As far as I know, Rahain doesn't have an organised army, so who would we be fighting? Are we supposed to be a police force? What if the locals object to our presence?'

'The Empire is strong enough to deal with any threats,' she said.

'Is Rahain a threat? Are we going in as conquerors, or liberators, freeing them from the rule of the warlords and gangs? The problem is, how will we distinguish between gang members and ordinary civilians? Do we wait until they attack us?'

Dolwyn laughed. 'You worry too much. Under the first emperor, the entire Star Continent was united. Why can't it be united again?'

'I don't know much about the history of the Star Continent, but I've been part of an invasion force, and I've seen my own homeland invaded by various enemies. I know what it feels like to be on both sides.'

'Aye? I'm too young to have taken part in the last war, when the Ascendants got their arses handed to them; and there's been no fighting in the Star Continent since then. Many of the lads and lassies in the regiment are itching to get some action. Well, except for the old Banner veterans. They talk a bit like you, sir – all caution and doubt.'

'And what does that tell you, Lieutenant?'

'I told you – call me Dolwyn. The way I see it, sir, is that the old guys in the Banner have managed to survive until now, and they don't want to stick their heads above the parapet again, eh? Half of them are near retirement age, and they just want to play it safe. Young guys like you should be keen to get stuck in.'

Lahnos shook his head. 'I'm twenty-nine, Dolwyn – eight years older than you. I'm not a wide-eyed *young guy*.'

Dolwyn smiled. 'There's no way you're twenty-nine.'

Sigum turned his head. 'Are you calling my rider a liar, soldier?'

'I didn't know you were listening, my lord,' said Dolwyn. 'I was just having a wee joke with the commander; I didn't mean any offence. Is he really twenty-nine? He looks... the same age as me.'

'I can vouch for his age,' said Sigum. 'Was there anything else you wanted?'

'Aye, there was,' she said. 'Commander Lahnos, sir, I was wondering if you wanted to join me this evening? A crate of the new whisky from Lach has arrived, and I need some assistance to drink a bottle or two. Are you up for it?'

'Thank you,' Lahnos said, 'but I'm tired, and I need to keep a clear head, in case any orders arrive.'

Dolwyn shrugged. 'I'll wear you down one of these days, sir. See you later.'

She turned, and strode away down the ramp towards the camp nestled in the valley.

'Kellach women,' Lahnos said, shaking his head.

'I assume by that remark that you do not like her, Lahnos?' said Sigum.

'No, I like her,' he said, 'but her main interests appear to be swearing, fighting, alcohol and trying to get me into bed. Maybe I should do it. She might leave me alone after she's satisfied her curiosity.'

'Or she might wish to marry you.'

'I somehow doubt that. She's just a bored soldier, fed up with garrison duty. It's the horns. They make me irresistible to women.'

'At some point, Lahnos,' said the dragon, 'you will have to tell the others about your self-healing abilities. With every year that passes, the incongruence between your age and your youthful looks grows ever wider. Will you be believed when you are forty? Fifty? You look the same as the day you killed Lord Arden.'

'I don't want them to treat me differently.'

'You have horns, and you ride upon my back – you are already different.'

'I think I'll get something to eat.'

'Dinner has been prepared for you, sir,' said one of the Bullan. 'Will you take it in your room?'

'Yes, thanks,' Lahnos said.

He followed the Bullan soldier into the tunnel, and they entered a network of chambers to the right. They had once been shopfronts, with storage areas behind, and the Bullan had converted them into their living quarters. The Bullan soldier went into the kitchen, and Lahnos continued onwards to his room – a square, windowless chamber cut from the rock. He lit a lamp, then he pulled off his fleeced coat, untied the laces on his boots, and sank into a comfortable chair.

As soon as his body was still, he began to think over his life on the Star Continent. The first few years had been spent in listless indolence; the effects of Leona's death, his manipulation by Athyro, and the carnage upon Elidus had stayed with him for a long time, sapping his will to do anything productive or useful. The Holdfasts had been patient and understanding, allowing him, Sigum and the seven Bullan to live in Colsbury without asking for anything in return. In that time, he had made friends with Shella, the custodian of the small isle, and he had seen Karalyn, Cardova and Arrosa every day, as well as Karalyn's twins. Every summer, the Imperial Court would transfer itself from Plateau City to Colsbury, but Lahnos had tended to stay out of everyone's way, in the same manner that Karalyn also did when the Empress was on the isle.

It had taken the Bullan to force a change in Lahnos's attitude. They had grown fond of the Empress, and were intrinsically attracted to the concept of one vast Empire looking after the united peoples of the Star Continent. It seemed to be part of their nature to admire order and progress, and they had developed a deep loyalty to Thorn and her ideals. Above all else, though, the Bullan had wanted to return to being soldiers. It had been their constant pestering that had persuaded Lahnos to offer his services to the Empress, and she had accepted without hesitation. With a few words uttered by Her Imperial Majesty, Lahnos had been promoted to a commander in the Imperial Army, Lord Sigum had become an Imperial Dragon, and the Bullan were assigned to cater to their needs. In many ways, the Bullan were more devoted to the imperial cause than either Lahnos or Sigum. More than that, they seemed to truly believe in the Empire, as though it had replaced the Dominion in their affections.

His door opened, and the Bullan soldier brought in a tray of food for Lahnos. He set it down on a low table, saluted, and left the chamber.

Lahnos glanced at the food, then he picked up a knife, and ran the edge of the blade down his arm, piercing his skin. He watched as the wound healed within seconds, then he wiped the blood away. He had got into the habit of checking that his self-healing was still working every now and again. When he had used the Thirteenth Gift to kill a dragon, the powers he had inherited had worn off over time, but nothing seemed to have changed since he had taken Arden's life. Had Karalyn been right – was he as immortal as any god? Would he live forever? Lahnos lowered his gaze. He tried to imagine still looking twenty-one after a thousand years had elapsed. Some people would see it as a dream come true, to be eternally youthful, but it made Lahnos feel sad. Would he have to watch his friends grow old and die? Would he end up as arrogant and self-centred as Arden had been, with no room in his heart for compassion? Karalyn had also told him that, due to the way his Gift worked, he wouldn't pass on his self-healing abilities to any children he might father. He wasn't a genuine immortal, she had said to him; instead, he had acquired the ability from Arden. That knowledge was worse than imagining his friends dying, and he had resolved to himself that he would remain childless.

His thoughts wandered to Dolwyn. She was a good-looking young woman, even if she was a little tall for him, and, after eight years of enforced celibacy, he missed the company of women. Would it be so bad to submit to her wishes?

He put the thought out of his mind, and ate in silence.

An hour later, one of the Bullan knocked on his door.

'Sir,' he said, 'the first soldiers that came through the portal have arrived at the camp.'

'Banner?'

'No, sir, a mixture of Holdings and Sanang.'

'Sanang?' said Lahnos. 'Shit. I suppose I'd better go and see them.'

He got to his feet, and followed the soldier to the tunnel entrance. On the opposite cliffside, columns of soldiers were issuing from the tunnel that led directly to the Plateau. Holdings infantry armed with crossbows marched in formation, alternating with companies of armoured Sanang heavy infantry. They were walking down the ramp, and setting up tents by the camp's palisade wall.

Lahnos gestured to Efizel. 'Let's go down and introduce ourselves to their officers, sergeant major.'

Efizel frowned.

'Yes, I know,' said Lahnos, 'but they would take it as an insult if we ignore them.'

'Yes, sir,' said Efizel.

The two men walked down the ramp leading from the tunnel entrance. They were halfway down when they were noticed by the Sanang warriors, who turned to stare at them. A few pointed, while others made horn signs over their heads and started to laugh. By the time Lahnos and Efizel had reached the bottom of the ramp, all semblance of order among the Sanang had dissipated, and they hurried over to stare at the part-Bullan and his sergeant major.

'Laugh all you like, Sanang bastards,' Lahnos said.

Lieutenant Dolwyn walked over, accompanied by a few other Kellach soldiers. The noise among the Sanang continued to increase, despite the efforts of their officers to calm them down.

Dolwyn frowned, and put her hands on her hips. 'What's all this fuss about?'

'It's the horns,' said Lahnos.

'What about them?' said Dolwyn.

'In Sanang culture,' Lahnos said, 'a man with horns is a cuckold. I guess they find it amusing.'

'I didn't know that,' said Dolwyn. She narrowed her eyes. 'How do you know it, sir?'

'There were plenty of Sanang stationed in Colsbury every summer,' he said. 'I've heard everything they have to say on the topic.'

Dolwyn gestured to one of the Sanang officers. 'Get these numpties under control. This is a military camp, not a fucking playground.'

The Sanang officer stared at her, then he pointed at Lahnos and Efizel. 'It's them. Get them out of here. My men have never seen folk with horns before.'

Dolwyn narrowed her eyes. 'That's Commander Lahnos you're talking about, and no, I will not be asking him to move.'

Several Sanang shouted abuse at Lahnos and Efizel in their own language, while others kept laughing.

Lahnos took a few steps forward. 'Take a good look, arseholes,' he said. 'By the dragon spirits, you Sanang are the ugliest bunch of bastards I've ever seen.'

'Don't antagonise them, sir,' said Efizel.

Lahnos raised his right hand. 'Maybe I should give them a taste of the Gift of Pain.'

'That will not be necessary,' said a booming voice behind them.

Lahnos turned, and saw Lord Sigum walking down the ramp. The Sanang quietened, and began to back away, as sparks flashed round the dragon's jaws.

'Does anyone here wish to insult my rider?' Sigum roared out to the crowd of Sanang. 'I know what you all think of his horns – I met many of your kind upon the isle of Colsbury. Allies or not, I will kill the first Sanang that angers me.'

More Kellach soldiers were spilling out from the camp to see what was causing the uproar, and they gathered behind Lahnos and the dragon, making it clear whose side they would take in any confrontation with the Sanang.

'Move back!' shouted the Sanang officer to his men. 'Move back, or there will be no rum allowance for the rest of the third!'

The Sanang began to disperse, and more officers appeared to guide them to where they were to pitch their tents.

Lahnos laughed.

'You're taking it well, sir,' said Dolwyn. 'I know a few men who would consider that to be a mortal insult.'

Lahnos eyed her. 'I've been called every name you can imagine because of these horns. It didn't bother me then; it doesn't bother me now. The one thing I will not do, though, is run away and hide in shame. I'm proud of these damn horns.'

'As you should be, sir.'

Lahnos turned to Sigum. 'I had the situation under control.'

'Did you, indeed?' said the dragon. 'You have never lost the ability to get into trouble, my rider, regardless of which world we happen to be upon. I shall return to the tunnel now, as the Sanang seemed to have learned their lesson.'

'Yeah, until the next time,' said Lahnos.

Sigum gazed at Lahnos, then he walked back up the ramp.

'The excitement appears to be over,' said Dolwyn.

'Have you opened the whisky yet, Lieutenant?' said Lahnos.

'No, sir. Why? Are you interested in joining me for a drink?'

'I might be,' he said. 'No, I am interested.'

Dolwyn laughed. 'You don't need to prove anything to me, sir. I know you're not a cuckold.'

'Are you turning down my offer?'

'Certainly not, sir. If it's whisky you want, it's whisky you'll get.'

Two hours later, Lahnos reclined on Dolwyn's bed, the sheets wrapped around their legs. Dolwyn leaned over to the bedside table, then she filled two glasses and lit a cigarette. She passed one of the glasses to Lahnos.

'Smoke?' she said.

'No,' said Lahnos. 'I've never smoked one of those things.'

'What about weed? You tried that?'

Lahnos shook his head. 'Unlike the Kellach Brigdomin, I don't feel the need to drink and smoke myself into oblivion.'

'Don't knock it until you've tried it.'

She leaned back against a wall, and sipped from her glass.

'Pyre's cock,' she said. 'Severton's got a fucking battle on its hands; this Lach stuff's as smooth as a bairn's arse.'

Lahnos laughed. 'I didn't understand most of what you just said.'

'That's fine,' she said. 'I usually talk a load of shite anyway. Can I tell everyone that I fucked the dragon rider?'

'Is that why you wanted to get me into bed?'

'Naw, it's because I like you. I'm not into having a relationship, but;

just a bit of fun on the side. So, you're really twenty-nine, aye? You ever been married?'

'No. The last two girlfriends I had were murdered by angry mobs. After that, I stayed clear of women.'

She smiled. 'Until me?'

'Yeah. Until you.'

'I knew I'd wear you down.'

'What part of Kellach Brigdomin are you from?'

She laughed. 'By that very question, I now know how clueless you are about my folk. What's my name?'

'Dolwyn.'

'Aye – so, therefore, that's means I'm a Domm, right? All Domm names start with the same letter. Just like folk from Brig – such as Bridget. Or Kell – like Corthie Holdfast.'

'That's just about the most stupid naming system I've heard in my life.'

'I didn't make the rules. But anyway, the truth is that I've never been to Domm, or any part of Kellach Brigdomin. I'm from Plateau City. My ma and da were in the army, so me and my twin brother joined up as soon as we were old enough. We both went to the academy, to learn how to be officers. This is my first posting.'

'I've been here for three years,' he said. 'Before that, Sigum and I patrolled the Rakanese frontier for a while. Did you know that, every night, hundreds of Rakanese refugees try to sneak over the wall that runs along the border?'

'And did you have to stop them, aye?'

'No, we were under orders to help them. If they were being chased by Rakanese soldiers, we would intervene to scare them away, to allow the refugees to enter the Plateau. People from Amatskouri would be there, to give the refugees food and blankets. After a couple of years of that, we were sent here to suppress the Rahain raiding parties.'

'Aye, I heard. It's your fault, apparently, that this posting has been so dull. You've driven all the raiding parties away. None of them try to cross the mountains this way any more – they all go the Long Way Round. The pass is as quiet as it's been for twenty years.'

He sipped from his glass.

'What do you think?' said Dolwyn.

'It's all right, I guess.'

She rolled her eyes. 'If you can't appreciate that, there's no hope for you.' She nudged him. 'Are you ready for another go?'

'All right,' he said, 'but I'm going on top this time.'

They reached for each other and kissed, then a loud banging came from the door.

'Fuck off!' Dolwyn cried. 'We're busy.'

'Lieutenant!' shouted a voice from the other side of the door. 'The Herald of the Empire is here to see Commander Lahnos.'

'Pyre's tits,' Dolwyn cried. 'Lahnos, get yer clothes on.'

They rolled out of bed and scrambled to dress themselves.

'Just a minute!' Dolwyn shouted.

Lahnos threw on his clothes, then pushed his feet into his boots. He started to laugh, then he lifted his glass of whisky and drained it. Dolwyn opened the door. Standing outside was an embarrassed-looking Holdings corporal.

'Where's the Herald?' said Lahnos.

'I'm here,' said Kelsey, as she walked down the corridor of the old fortress towards them. She eyed Dolwyn for a second, a slight smile on her lips, then she turned to Lahnos. 'It's nice to see you've settled in well with the Kellach contingent here, Commander.'

Lahnos saluted. 'Ma'am.'

Kelsey glanced at the insignia on Dolwyn's uniform. 'A lieutenant?'

'Aye, ma'am,' said Dolwyn.

'Haven't you got any work you need to be doing, Lieutenant?'

'I do, ma'am.'

'Then you'd best get on with it.'

Dolwyn saluted. 'Understood, ma'am.'

'You clear off, too,' Kelsey said to the Holdings corporal.

Lahnos and Kelsey watched as the two soldiers hurried away.

Kelsey raised an eyebrow. 'Didn't you tell me that you'd sworn off women, Lahnos?'

'That's right, ma'am.'

'You can quit saying *ma'am* every two seconds. I'm here to tell you two things; no – three things. The first is that the Empress has invited you and Lord Sigum to Colsbury for Summer's Day. Be ready at noon, and I'll come here and collect you both. The second thing is – a Kellach Brigdomin woman? Really? Do you understand half of what she's saying?'

'Half would be about right.'

'Well, good luck with that, I suppose. It's better than moping about on your own.'

'Was there a third thing, ma'am?'

'Aye, there is. Keep this to yourself for now, Commander; the invasion of Rahain has been approved by the Empress – and you'll be leading it.'

CHAPTER 5
SCORCHED EARTH

Hold Fast, Republic of the Holdings – 27th Day, Last Third Spring 544

'I can't,' said Cole. 'I have too much work to do here.'

'That can wait,' said Cael. 'Why don't you go for the First Third of Summer, and then you can come back here?'

'Summer is a busy time on the estate, and Celine needs me.'

'But everyone goes to Colsbury for the Empress's birthday,' Cael went on. 'There will be parties, and plays, and music.'

'Not everyone goes. I've never seen Uncle Corthie there on Summer's Day. Or Aunty Celine or Aunty Sable. And, Cael, you know that the Empress has a low opinion of me. I think she sees my father whenever she looks in my direction. I remind her of him, and it makes her uncomfortable. It gets awkward, and I'd rather avoid all that, if possible.'

Cael frowned, then he raised a water skin to his lips and drank. The heat was intense, almost unbearable, and the two young men were taking their break in the thick shadows of the largest stables on the Hold Fast estate – a horseshoe-shaped curve of stalls that surrounded the parade ground. The odour of straw and manure hung in the air, and Cael's clothes stank of horses.

'You can't stay here all summer,' he said. 'The heat will kill you.'

Cole laughed. 'I'm used to it. I've lived in the Holdings all my life. I'll miss you when you go, cousin. It's been good having you here. I'll miss Arrosa, too.'

'That's another reason you should come to Colsbury, to keep that little bitch away from me.'

Cole narrowed his eyes. 'Why do you have to call her that?'

'She says worse about me.'

'I know she does. You're as bad as each other. Every spring, I look forward to both of you coming, but you can't stand the sight of her, and she can't stand the sight of you. I get stuck in the middle. You moan to me about her; she moans to me about you, and so it goes on, for the entire spring. I don't understand it. You're both angry at the world, and you blame each other.'

Cael pulled a half-crushed packet of cigarettes from his pocket, and lit one.

'Pyre's arse,' he muttered. 'It's almost too hot to smoke.'

'Then don't do it. Aunty Shella says it's bad for your health.'

Cael laughed. 'Since when do we take health advice from Aunty Shella? She drinks whisky like a Kellach, and smokes weed like a Sanang. The only reason she's still alive is because the Empress heals her regularly.'

A side door leading into the stables opened, and a group of young women emerged from the interior. Most were Holdings, but Arrosa stood among them, her overalls spattered with mud and horse manure. They huddled together in the shade of the building, and most of them lit up cigarettes.

Cole raised his hand. 'Morning, girls.'

'Morning, boys,' said one of the women.

A few walked over to where Cael and Cole were sitting.

'Are you looking forward to going to Colsbury, Cael?' said one.

He shrugged. 'I guess so. It's getting too hot for me here.'

'We shouldn't be speaking to you,' said another. 'We know what you said to Soula. Everybody knows.'

'Why were you so cruel to her?' said a third.

'Because he's an arsehole,' said Arrosa. 'Isn't that right, Cael?'

Cael ignored her, and gazed at the heat haze shimmering over the white-washed buildings.

'Where's Marium?' said Cole. 'Is she not coming out for her morning break?'

'I saw her earlier,' said one of the young women, 'but I don't know where she is now. Are you going to Colsbury this year?'

Cole shook his head. 'I have too much to do here. The herds from the north-west will be coming down, ready to be sent to the cavalry training grounds in Holdings City. I might go for the twin's birthday at the end of summer, once the busy period has calmed down a bit.'

'I'd love to go to Colsbury for the summer,' said one of the women, her eyes gazing off into the distance. 'Imagine going to one of the Empress's formal balls, with the candles and lanterns, and the dancing, and with everyone all dressed up. And the dragons; I'd love to see them.'

'I'd be happy to see mountains for a change,' said another.

'Why don't you take Marium?' said a third. 'She'd love to attend a fancy ball.'

'Would she?' said Cole.

'You mean you've never asked her?'

'She's never brought it up.'

A few of the women laughed. 'You're hopeless, Cole,' said one. 'I've heard Marium drop hints all spring.'

'Poor Soula thought she was going to be invited this year,' said another. 'You broke her heart, Cael.'

'She'll get over it,' Cael muttered.

He stubbed out his cigarette and stood, moving slowly in the blistering heat. Upright, he was head and shoulders over the young Holdings women, and a few had to crane their necks to peer up at him.

'Everyone told me that you've got a mean streak,' said one, 'but I didn't believe it until I heard what you did to Soula. You'll be lucky if any of the girls speak to you next spring.'

'I'm sure I'll survive,' he said.

'You're all lucky he's leaving,' said Arrosa. 'I have to go to Colsbury, and then I'll have to spend the entire summer with him; and autumn, too. I'm starting university this year.'

'Aye,' said Cael, 'but you won't be in the same classes as me. And I don't want you following me around campus like a lost little puppy.'

Arrosa put a hand to her heart. 'Oh no,' she said, feigning hurt. 'How will I manage without you, Cael? You've been such a great friend to me.'

'Fuck off, you little Gunstian bitch.'

Several of the women took a step back, their eyes narrowing.

'Stop fighting,' said Cole, as he got to his feet. 'I'm tired of hearing you both attacking each other.'

'Stay out of it,' said Cael. 'This is none of your business.'

Anger passed over Cole's face, then he looked away.

'There's no point talking to him when he's like this, Cole,' said Arrosa. 'Cael's heart has nothing but bitterness in it. He thinks he's hard done by, because the Holdfasts move him around every few thirds. Well, guess what, Cael – they move me around, too. Do you think I have any say in where I go from season to season? You don't hear me complaining about it, but you think you're being persecuted. Is it any surprise that you don't have friends? Cole tolerates you, but he's your cousin – he has to.'

'That's not true,' said Cole. 'I...'

'Shut up, Cole,' said Arrosa. 'You're so weak. You agree with me when we talk about Cael, but as soon as he's here, you let him walk all over you. Why don't you stand up for yourself? Stop trying to please everybody – some people aren't worth it.'

'Who's walking over him now?' said Cael. 'You don't even see it, do you? You act like a bitch, then you pretend that you're the injured party. I wish you'd fuck off back to Athumia.'

Arrosa's eyes darkened, and she stared at Cael. She prodded a finger in his chest.

'You'd love that, wouldn't you?' she said. 'You've always hated me.

Why? What did I ever do to you, Cael?' Her voice almost broke with emotion, then her gaze hardened again. 'I tried to be friends when I arrived on this world. I tried my best, but you never gave me a chance. For years, you've looked at me as though I was a demon. I had no one. I lost everything.'

'Don't exaggerate,' he said. 'You came to this world with nothing, and my family gave you everything you needed. You've lived like a princess, thanks to the Holdfasts. You don't deserve everything that my family has done for you. My mother never loved you – she felt sorry for you; and I'm sick of your poor-little-orphan-girl bullshit.'

'If it wasn't for Karalyn, I'd turn you to glass for that. How dare you say that to me? My parents were murdered by dragons...'

'It's a pity they didn't kill you, too.'

A tear rolled down her cheek as she stared at him, then she turned and hurried away. Cael glanced around, but everyone else had gone. He frowned. He had been so wrapped up in arguing with Arrosa that he hadn't noticed the others leaving. He lowered his gaze as a wave of regret passed through him. His mind had seemed like a bewildered bystander, as his mouth had formed words aimed to injure Arrosa.

He slumped back down to the dusty ground, and leaned against the wall of the stables, his head in his hands.

Was it any wonder he had no friends, Arrosa had said to him. She was right. It was no surprise, because he kept everyone at arm's length, offering them nothing but hard words and cold glances. He did it to protect himself, but to others, he knew he appeared selfish and uncaring.

He started to sob. He had no friends, and his mother cared more about her new children than she did about him or Kyra. He had built a wall around him, to shield himself from harm, but in doing so, he had made himself unlikeable. He was alone in the world, and he deserved the contempt of others.

'And another thing,' cried Arrosa. 'Don't think for one minute that I...'

She paused, and Cael kept his head down, trying to hide his tears.

'Are you crying?' she said.

'Go ahead and mock me,' he said. 'I don't care what you think.'

Arrosa remained silent for a few moments, then she crouched next to him and put a hand on his shoulder.

'Leave me alone,' he said. 'I don't want your fucking sympathy.'

'You do this to yourself,' she whispered. 'You can stop it, if you want. We don't have to hate each other, Cael.'

'I can't help it,' he said. 'I feel angry every time I look at you.'

'Why? Please tell me, Cael; I don't understand.'

'Neither do I.'

He pushed her hand off his shoulder, got to his feet, and walked away.

Two hours later, Cael was sitting on the top storey of the tall clock tower, as the midday sun beat down upon the Hold Fast estate. Over a dozen cigarette butts were on the floor next to him, some in the shade of the wooden roof, others lying out in the light. Cael gazed down at the white-washed buildings and the surrounding plains, as sweat kept his tunic stuck to his back.

Three more days, then Kelsey would be arriving to take him and Arrosa to Colsbury. The Herald of the Empire would no doubt ask Cole and Celine if they wanted to come, but that was done out of politeness, as neither ever showed much enthusiasm for joining the Imperial Court for the summer thirds.

'I have been looking for you for over an hour,' said a voice.

Cael turned, and saw his Aunt Celine standing by the stairs that led down to the ground.

'What are you doing up here?' she said. 'You are supposed to be working in the stables. Cole says he hasn't seen you since you had your morning break.'

'I needed to get away from the others,' he said.

'Away from Arrosa, you mean? Oh, Cael, it pains me that you and Arrosa seem to loathe the sight of each other. What would your mother think? What will she say if the two of you argue in Colsbury, the way you've been arguing here?'

'I doubt Mother will notice.'

Celine frowned. 'Self-pity is not your most attractive feature, Cael.' She walked over and sat down next to him. She groaned. 'I'm too old for this. I remember I used to come up here when I was younger, to look out over the estate, and, sometimes, when I wanted to be alone. Your great-grandmother Rosalind didn't think much of me. She didn't like me before I married into the Holdfasts, and when my husband died? She chastised me daily. She thought I wasn't sufficiently mournful. I don't know what she was expecting. I was only twenty-one when Vince died. For thirty-eight years, I have lived as a widow, but I don't regret not re-marrying. Vince was the only man I ever loved. What I am trying to say to you, Cael, is that time passes, whether you like it or not. Some of the things that are upsetting you now will seem silly in years to come.'

Cael said nothing.

'Your mother will always love you,' Celine went on. 'And you have Kyra. You two were the closest brother and sister I'd ever seen; you did everything together.' She smiled. 'Perhaps it's the Kellach blood; I know how important twins are to that folk. I wanted to say that you have done a great job here this spring. You've worked hard, and you have learned a lot about how the estate is managed. Please don't spoil it. Whatever problem you have with Arrosa, couldn't you try to see past it?'

'Did she tell you that we argued today?'

'No. She didn't say a thing.'

'She hates me.'

'I don't believe that, Cael. She defends herself, because you are always attacking her. She has a sharp tongue; that I will not deny, but you give her plenty of cause to use it. And poor Cole – stuck between the two of you. He can't win. If he picks a side, the other one will turn on him, and so he tries to stay friends with you both. In some ways, he might be relieved when you and Arrosa leave for Colsbury, for then he won't have to choose between you.'

Cael felt his eyes well. 'Why do I feel sad all of the time, Aunty?'

'I don't know, Cael. I know these last few years have been hard on you. No, your whole life has been hard. Being a Holdfast is a blessing, but it's also a curse. You saw things when you were young that no child should ever have to see. Greenhides, Ascendants, wars and death. You were passed around between your mother and Empress Thorn, never having time to settle anywhere. And, Cael, you watched your mother be killed in front of you. I can't imagine the impact that has had upon your life.'

'Cole also saw his mother die.'

'I know. Cole suffers, too, but he does it in a different way. With you, it comes out as anger. With him, well, he tries to make everyone like him, and for that he is accused of being too soft. He isn't soft, though. I know him better than anyone else, and I can see his strength. It is easy to be angry and spiteful; it takes courage to be as gentle and kind as he is. That is another lesson you will learn as you grow older.'

'How do I stop feeling this way?'

'I don't know. I wish I could give you a piece of advice that would fix everything, but life doesn't work that way. Perhaps you could start by trying to stop yourself from pushing everyone away? I think I know why you're doing it. You are moved from one location to another every season, and so you don't want to get too close to anyone, because if you do, you will be hurt when you have to move on to the next place. Take Soula, for example. I saw you together at the beginning of spring; you seemed to be having a great time in each other's company. You laughed at each other's jokes, and I could see the real you emerge from behind your defences, if only for a short while. And then, when the time drew near for you to go to Colsbury, you broke it off with her in the most hurtful way imaginable.'

'I'm sorry.'

'There's no use in telling me that; you should say it to her.'

'I can't. It's better that she hates me. It'll make it easier for her.'

'That's a cruel logic; cruel to you, and cruel to her. And Arrosa? Tell me, Cael; why do your eyes flash with such anger whenever she opens her mouth? Is there something I don't know about? Did she hurt you deeply in some way?'

'She's a cuckoo in the nest.'

Celine sighed. 'That comment was beneath you, Cael. Where is your compassion? That girl was all alone until your mother took her in.'

'But why did she have to take her in? I wanted my mother to come back, but when she finally did, she brought Arrosa with her, as though... as though she was replacing me and Kyra. All I wanted was my mother. Why did I have to share her with a stranger?'

'It sounds as though your anger is really directed at your mother, Cael. If that's true, why are you taking it out on Arrosa?'

Cael said nothing.

'Lunch is being served in the staff dining hall,' Celine said. 'You should eat something. After that, you can take the rest of the day off. You can pack your things, so that you are ready to go to Colsbury when Kelsey gets here. Will you help me stand?'

Cael got to his feet, then he extended a hand. Celine took it, and he pulled her up.

'Thank you,' she said. 'You know, Cael, I firmly believe that there's a good man somewhere inside you, buried beneath all that anger and bitterness. Go on; get yourself down to the dining hall.'

Cael avoided her gaze, and walked to the stairs. He descended to the ground floor, and strode out into the baking heat. He felt stupid for having shed a few tears in front of his great aunt, but that was nothing compared to the embarrassment he felt at Arrosa having witnessed him cry. He had no doubt that she was telling everyone about it, and laughing at him for his weakness.

He turned a corner, and ran into Marium.

'Hey, Cael,' she said. 'I want to have a word with you.'

'I'm not in the mood,' he said.

'I don't care. I just wanted to say that I think you're a complete arsehole for what you did to Soula.'

'Fuck off.'

'You can't speak to me like that.'

'I'll speak to you any way I like. While I've got your attention, can I say something? If I find out that you've been a bitch to Cole, I'll end you. Do you hear me?'

Marium snorted. 'You hypocrite. You dare to accuse me of treating Cole badly, after what you did to Soula? I can't wait until you leave the Holdings. If I had one wish, it would be that you never came back. No one here likes you, Cael – did you know that? Everyone thinks you're a selfish, arrogant dickhead.'

Cael laughed and walked away; then he stopped. He turned, and saw that Marium was glaring at him. He remembered his promise to Cole. The powers of the younger Holdfasts had been kept secret from the staff on the estate, and it was unlikely that Marium knew what he could do.

'Yes?' said Marium, as he stared at her. 'Do you have something else to say?'

Cael unleashed his powers, and drove them into her mind. He made sure she wouldn't be aware of what he was doing, then he ransacked her recent memories. He saw Soula in tears, then he saw Marium berating Cole for some perceived fault. Cael dug deeper. He discovered her real feelings towards Cole – that he was a pushover, that he would do or say anything to avoid angering her, and she loathed him for it. She was with him due to his family name, and for no other reason. And there was someone else – a young man, who worked on the estate in the blacksmith's forge. Tarrun. Marium loved Tarrun, and the pair had been conducting a secret relationship behind Cole's back.

Cael broke off the link.

'Why are you staring at me?' she said. 'Go away.'

Cael gave her a mock bow, then he walked off. Rather than head towards the dining hall, he walked in the direction of the forge. He heard the noise of metal striking metal coming from it before he saw it. A thin column of dark smoke was rising from the out-buildings where the forge lay, staining the clear blue sky. Cael strode down a small alleyway between two storehouses and emerged in front of the forge. At least a dozen Holdings folk were working there, repairing bucket-loads of horseshoes. Cael scanned their faces, dipping into their minds until he found the one named Tarrun.

'Do you want something, Master Holdfast?' said one of the smiths. 'Is there anything you need?'

'I want to speak to Tarrun,' he said.

Tarrun glanced up, and a nervous gleam appeared in his eyes. 'What is it?' he said.

'Nothing important,' said Cael. 'Have you got a moment?'

'No, sorry,' said Tarrun. 'I'm busy.'

'That's not what you say to a Holdfast, lad,' said the smith. 'Take a short break. We'll cope without you for a few minutes.'

Tarrun set down his hammer, and walked out of the forge. He glanced around, but didn't look into Cael's eyes.

Cael wasted no time. He pushed his powers into Tarrun's mind, and confirmed that Marium's memories matched his.

'I need you to do something for me,' Cael said.

'Yeah?'

Cael readied his powers of persuasion.

Confess your relationship with Marium to Cole Holdfast, he said in Tarrun's mind.

Tarrun blinked, and took a step back.

Cole is in the dining hall. Do it there, in front of everyone. You have no choice.

Tarrun swallowed.

'Will you walk with me to the dining hall?' said Cael.

'All right.'

The two young men walked side by side towards the large stables. The staff dining hall was close to one end of the horseshoe-shaped building, and they entered through a side door. Inside, most tables were busy, with staff from the estate eating the subsidised food prepared by a large kitchen. Cael saw Cole sitting with Marium and Arrosa, and he guided Tarrun over to the table where they were seated. Marium glanced up, saw Cael and Tarrun, and her eyes widened. Arrosa also looked up, but her expression gave nothing away.

'There you are, cousin,' said Cole. 'Aunt Celine was looking for you.'

'She found me,' said Cael. 'Tarrun has something he wants to say to you.'

'No, he doesn't,' said Marium. 'Go back to work, Tarrun. It's not your lunchtime.'

Tarrun swallowed again, his hands trembling. 'I... uh, I...'

Cole laughed. 'Are you all right, Tarrun?'

'Marium and I have been seeing each other behind your back,' Tarrun went on. He blinked, as though he could barely believe what he had just said.

'Is this a joke?' said Cole.

'Yes,' said Marium. 'A stupid joke. Stop bothering us, Tarrun.'

Cael kept his grip on Tarrun's mind.

Apologise to Cole.

Tarrun lowered his gaze. 'I'm sorry, Cole.'

Tell Cole what Marium really thinks of him.

'Marium laughs at you behind your back,' Tarrun said. 'We both do. We've been seeing each other for thirds. She thinks you're a fool; a gullible fool.'

Marium got to her feet. 'Stop,' she cried, gaining the attention of most of the people in the hall. 'It's not true, Cole. He's lying.'

Arrosa flinched. 'No, Marium,' she said. 'It's you that's lying. Tarrun spoke the truth.'

Cole stared at Arrosa. Like Cael, Cole knew of Arrosa's ability to detect when lies were spoken.

'I'm sorry, Cole,' said Arrosa. 'Your girlfriend's been cheating on you.'

Cole stood up slowly, then he ran from the dining hall, as everyone stared.

Cael released Tarrun's mind from his grip, and the young man sagged, his eyes distraught.

'Why, Tarrun?' Marium said. 'Why would you do that?'

Tarrun shook his head. 'I don't know.'

Marium hurried from the hall, and Tarrun went after her. Cael walked round the table, and sat down in the seat where Cole had been. He kept his gaze away from Arrosa, and began to eat.

'I'm not stupid, you know,' Arrosa said. 'I can guess what just happened.'

Cael said nothing.

'I know what your mother can do,' Arrosa went on. 'I saw her do it a few times on Athumia. Sable can do it, too, can't she? And you?'

'I don't know what the fuck you're talking about,' said Cael.

Arrosa laughed.

'Do you think what's happened to Cole is funny?' he said.

'I wasn't laughing at that. I know when you're lying, Cael. You knew exactly what I was talking about. You used your weird Holdfast powers on Tarrun, to force him to confess.'

'I've been wanting to read Marium's mind all spring,' he said.

'Maybe you should have done it a bit sooner, and saved Cole a ton of pain.'

'Cole made me promise not to.'

'Oh. That means he probably suspected.'

'Did you?'

She shrugged. 'I thought there was something funny going on, but no – I didn't know about Tarrun.'

Cael put down his fork. 'I'm going to find Cole.'

'I'll come with you.'

'I'd rather you didn't.'

'I don't care.'

They both stood, then they made their way out of the dining hall. Over to their left, Marium and Tarrun were engaged in a ferocious argument, and Cael smiled.

'I'm glad you did what you did,' said Arrosa, as they walked towards the mansion.

'Then it's a shame that your opinion means nothing to me.'

Arrosa exhaled. 'For a few moments there, we were talking as though we didn't hate each other. I should have guessed that you'd ruin it.'

'Horses can fly.'

Arrosa grimaced. 'Bastard,' she whispered.

They entered the mansion, and climbed the stairs to Cole's small apartment. Cael knocked on the door, then he pushed it open.

'Cole?' he said.

'Are you all right?' said Arrosa.

They walked into the apartment, and found Cole lying on his bed, weeping. Arrosa hurried over to him. She sat on the edge of the bed, and put a hand on Cole's shoulder.

'You're better off without her,' said Cael.

'We're here for you, Cole,' said Arrosa. 'You can talk to us. I know this must be hard; it's awful. Can we help?'

Cole sat up, but kept his face covered with his hands. Arrosa reached out, and pulled his hands away.

'I am completely humiliated,' Cole said, as tears fell down his cheeks. 'What did I do wrong? I tried to make her happy. I did everything she suggested. Am I not good enough?'

'You're too good,' said Cael. 'Too trusting. Don't trust anyone.'

'Don't listen to him,' said Arrosa. 'You can trust us.'

'How can I show my face on the estate after this?' said Cole. 'Everyone will be laughing at me.'

'No, they won't,' said Arrosa. 'Everyone will blame Marium and Tarrun.'

'They'll still laugh at me. I'm such a fool.'

'Don't say that,' she said. 'Is there anything we can do?'

Cole said nothing for a while, then he nodded. 'Take me with you to Colsbury.'

CHAPTER 6
THE FORTY-EIGHTERS

Plateau City, The Plateau – 28th Day, Last Third Spring 544

'And remember, class,' said Professor Gallea, 'your end-of-year assignment is due to be handed in tomorrow. I know that you have all been working very hard on them, and I am looking forward to reading them over summer.'

The small class rose to their feet, and filed out of the room, passing the large model of a rudimentary steam engine by the doorway.

'What do you have next?' said Dazi.

'Salve,' said Kyra. 'Shall I meet you at lunch?'

'See?' said Loughlin, as he emerged from the classroom. 'She gets to study all the best subjects. It's blatant favouritism. The Holdfasts think they can do whatever they like.'

'I know,' said Kyra. 'It's almost as if they run the Empire. Oh, wait – they do.'

Loughlin muttered something, and wandered off.

'I won't be joining you in Elbannon's class after lunch,' Kyra said, as she and Dazi walked along the corridor.

'Why not?'

'My Aunt Kelsey is coming to collect me.'

Dazi frowned. 'I thought you weren't going to Colsbury until Summer's Day.'

'She's not taking me to Colsbury. She said she wants to show me something. Could you tell Elbannon for me?'

'All right,' said Dazi, 'but you know what he's like. You're lucky we sat our spring examination on Tempest a few days ago; otherwise, he'd use this as an excuse to mark you down.'

'Maybe we should get him a new dog,' said Kyra; 'as a present, you know? It might make him less miserable.'

'I can't believe we only have two days left of second year,' Dazi said. 'What am I going to do for three thirds without you, Kyra?'

Kyra smiled. 'I'm sure you'll cope.'

'I will miss you, though. Is it all right if I tell my folks that my best friend is a Holdfast?'

'If you like. But don't make them any promises that I can't keep. I'm just a student; I don't have any authority to change the law, or anything like that.'

Dazi laughed. 'I know.'

They came to a junction.

'See you at lunch,' said Kyra.

They went their separate ways, and Kyra ascended a flight of stairs to the third floor of the university. She passed a few students in the corridor, and walked into a laboratory. The teacher glanced over from a workbench.

'Could you close the door, Kyra?'

'Aye, ma'am.'

Kyra shut the door, and walked over to an empty desk.

The teacher smiled. 'A Holdfast calling me *ma'am*. You're much politer than your Aunt Kelsey. Did you know that she consistently refused to address Queen Emily by her proper title? For years, she used to call her *Queenie*. I don't know how she got away with it.'

'What was she like back then, ma'am?'

'Am I allowed to be honest? Will I get into trouble if I speak the truth?'

Kyra smiled. 'I won't say anything, ma'am. I promise.'

The teacher took a seat. 'All right. Kelsey was rude to pretty much everybody she met. She didn't care if they were a god, demigod, king, queen – it didn't matter. She was especially rude to Van Logos, or so I heard. I was living next to the salve mine in the Eastern Mountains when Kelsey and Van got together. I guess that's why I became an expert on salve. Before that, the only things that interested me were catapults and ballistae. When I was fourteen, I built a ballista on the roof of my parent's house.'

Kyra laughed.

'My sister thought I was crazy,' the teacher went on, then she came to an abrupt stop as the door opened. A young army officer walked into the laboratory.

'Sorry I'm late, Professor Jackdaw,' he said, closing the door.

'That's all right,' said the teacher. 'Take a seat.'

The soldier sat down at a workbench along from where Kyra was sitting.

'Let's go over the usual formalities before we begin,' said the teacher. 'Nothing that is said or done in this laboratory may be shared with anyone else. All aspects of salve studies are covered by the Imperial Secrets Act, and you may be prosecuted if you are found to be in breach of these regulations. People think this course is over-subscribed, but the truth is that only a select few are permitted to learn what goes on in here. All right? Let me hear your agreement.'

'Aye, ma'am,' said Kyra.

The young officer nodded. 'Understood, ma'am.'

'Thank you. During our last lessons together, you learned the process of refining raw salve into the product that is used to heal injuries, and today we are going to look at another aspect of salve. Have either of you heard of a god called Prince Montieth?'

'I have heard the name, ma'am,' said Kyra.

'Prince Montieth was easily the greatest authority on salve who has ever lived,' said the teacher. 'For almost one and a half millennia, he studied the properties of salve in a large laboratory that he had constructed in the basement of his palace in the City. There, he carried out a multitude of experiments. Some of those experiments were cruel in the extreme. He used mortal captives to test out his ideas, and the numbers that he murdered over the centuries probably runs into the thousands. He was a dreadful man, in other words. Luckily for everyone, he's dead. His achievements, however, live on. Can anyone tell me how the traitor dream mage known as Daimon lost his life?'

Kyra put her hand up. 'Lord Naxor killed him, ma'am.'

'That's right; but how?' She held up a vial of red liquid. 'This is how – anti-salve. Prince Montieth invented this substance a long time ago.' She smiled. 'Put on your protective gloves because, today, I am going to show you both how to make it.'

Two hours later, Kyra and the Holdings officer emerged from the laboratory.

'That was one of the best classes I've ever had,' said the young officer. 'I want to go back to the barracks and tell everyone about it, but I can't.' He glanced at Kyra. 'The only person I can talk to about it is you, Miss Holdfast.'

She eyed him.

'So, uh, what I was trying to say,' he went on, 'is I was wondering if you would like to join me for a drink some evening?'

'We barely know each other,' said Kyra. 'We've shared a total of four classes together.'

'Precisely, and with summer approaching, miss, we won't be sharing any more classes until autumn.'

'I go to Colsbury every summer,' she said. 'Don't take this personally, but there's little point in us seeing each other if I'll be leaving the city in a couple of days. Besides, I'm still only seventeen; did you know that?'

'No. I didn't. You act older.'

'You don't want to get involved with a Holdfast,' she said; 'but, if you're still interested come autumn, let me know. I'll be eighteen by then.'

The young officer tilted his head. 'I hope you have a pleasant summer, miss.'

Kyra smiled as the young officer strode away. She went downstairs to the canteen, and queued for five minutes to collect her tray. She scanned the hall, and saw Dazi at a table, eating while reading a book. Kyra walked over to her, and sat down.

'I just got asked out by an army officer,' she said.

Dazi turned her head. 'What did you say to him?'

'I told him I was going to Colsbury, and that I was too young for him.'

Dazi shook her head. 'Another opportunity spurned. You get asked out all the time, and you always say no. Was he handsome?'

'He was Holdings.'

'And?'

'Too short for me.'

'Everyone's too short for you.'

'Everyone except the Kellach Brigdomin.'

'You don't say yes to them, either, when they ask you out.'

'That's because most of them are in the student bar every night. I will not go out with a drunkard. What are you reading?'

Dazi showed her the spine of the book – it was a large volume on Holdings literature.

'Any good?' said Kyra.

'I have to read it for my language exam tomorrow. When it's over, I might join the Kellach in the bar and get completely drunk. An end-of-term party has been arranged; do you want to go?'

'I'd like to, but I don't think it's a good idea.'

Dazi smiled. 'Do you think the Empress would disown you if you drank too much in public?'

'I don't want to embarrass her.'

Loughlin strode over to their table. He was holding a sheet of paper in his hand.

'Have you seen this?' he said to Kyra and Dazi.

He set the paper down in front of them.

'There's a whole pile of these at the reception,' Loughlin went on. 'It's an Imperial Proclamation, setting out the new rules for the succession. Your name's on it, Kyra.'

Kyra's gaze went to the paper. She read through the printed text of the new proclamation, regarding the formal procedures for electing a new emperor or empress. At the bottom was the list of eligible electors. The familiar names were there – Kelsey, Karalyn, Corthie, Sable and Shella, then underneath were the Empress's additions – the Matriarch of Sanang, the First Holder of the Holdings Republic, and the Clan Council of Kellach Brigdomin; followed by Queen Blackrose of the Eastern Rim, and Emily and Daniel of the City. Next came the list of junior electors – Cael, Cole and Kyra, who would not be eligible to vote until they had passed their twenty-first birthdays.

'Count the Holdfasts,' said Loughlin. 'The Empress must think we're stupid. Thirteen Electors, and over half of them are from her own fucking family.'

'Every Holdfast on the list is a high mage,' said Kyra.

'The whole system's rigged,' said Loughlin. 'Mister Achan is right. The powerful are only interested in retaining all authority for themselves.'

'Don't talk shite,' said Kyra. 'Three of the Holdfasts are Ascendant-killers, and another is Herald of the Empire.'

'Fair enough,' said Loughlin. 'That's four. What have the three junior electors ever done? Why are you on the list? You haven't earned the right to decide who the next emperor or empress should be. This is an inherited privilege.'

'You don't know what you're talking about,' she said. 'Cael, Cole and I were there, when the Ascendants tried to kill us all in Clackenbaird. We risked our lives to help.'

Loughlin laughed. 'You were wee bairns back then, and you're taking credit for defeating the Ascendants? And who ever said the Holdfasts were arrogant, eh?'

Anger surged within Kyra, as a storm of buried memories and emotions burst through her trained sense of composure; and her right fist clenched involuntarily. Loughlin must have perceived the change in her demeanour, as his eyes narrowed, and he took a half-step back.

'I saw friends and family butchered that day,' Kyra cried. 'My grandmother, my Aunty Jemma, my mother... The Empress and Uncle Corthie would have died if I hadn't...' She took a breath, seeing that several students in the hall had turned to see what the shouting was about. 'Forget it. Whatever I say, it will only sound as though I'm boasting, and I did nothing to boast about. I did my best, that's all.'

'The Holdfasts think the Empire belongs to them,' said Loughlin. 'Thorn stole the throne from Bridget's family – a Kellach Brigdomin family; and we don't forget.'

'Aye, Bryce was a great emperor, right up until he sold us out to the Ascendants.'

'That's what the Holdfasts say, but why should we believe them? How do we know it wasn't your family who invited Edmond to the Star Continent?'

'Maybe because it was my family who defeated Edmond?'

'There you go – taking all the credit again. Thousands of soldiers fought the Ascendants' army, along with dragons; have you forgotten about them?'

Kyra shook her head. 'I'm not going to argue with you, Loughlin. Believe whatever you like, but do it somewhere else. I'm trying to eat my lunch.'

Loughlin smiled down at her as though he had emerged victorious, then he turned and strode away.

'I really thought you were going to hit him,' Dazi whispered.

Kyra glanced down at her tray, but her appetite had gone.

'I'd better go to the reception,' she said. 'My aunt will be arriving soon.'

'Okay,' said Dazi. 'I'll see you when you get back, yeah?'

'Aye.'

Kyra took her tray to the servery counter, and set it down. She noticed a few students glancing in her direction. Copies of the proclamation were lying on several tables, and Kyra knew they would be gossiping about her as soon as she left. She walked from the hall, and went out into the large quad. Summer was in the air, and the sky above Plateau City was a deep and cloudless blue. A carriage was parked outside the university reception, and four soldiers were standing next to it. The carriage door opened, and Kelsey peered out. She gestured towards Kyra, then beckoned her towards the carriage.

Kyra crossed the quad, then she climbed up into the carriage.

'Let's go, lads,' said Kelsey, and a soldier closed the door. Kyra sat back on her seat, her arms folded across her chest.

'Bad day?' said Kelsey.

'The new Succession Proclamation caused a few comments,' Kyra said. 'Not all of them were favourable.'

Kelsey chuckled. 'Pay no attention.'

'Why are seven out of the thirteen Electors Holdfasts?'

'We earned it,' said Kelsey. 'That's it – it's as simple as that. Our family saved the allied worlds from the Ascendants. You, personally, saved the lives of the Empress, Corthie, Aila, and her children. If you hadn't done that, Corthie wouldn't have killed Edmond.'

'Naxor killed Daimon. Why isn't he on the list?'

'He doesn't want a vote. He said he would resign if he was forced to become an Elector. Naxor enjoys the power and privilege his position gives him, but he doesn't want to stand out in the eye of the public. I think he made the right decision. There are many people, especially in the City, who remember how he behaved when Simon tried to take over.'

The carriage was pulled out of the quad by two horses, and they set off north, towards the aristocratic district.

'Are we going to the townhouse?' said Kyra.

'No. I'm going to be honest with you – this was the Empress's idea. If it had been up to me, I would have held this visit back until the start of the Autumn Term.' She gazed out of the window. 'Are you still enjoying university?'

'Most of the time,' Kyra said. 'I don't like the attention, though. Everyone knows I'm a Holdfast.'

'That's part of the entire point of you attending.'

'What's that supposed to mean?'

'Once you leave university,' said Kelsey, 'you will become part of the imperial government. From that moment onwards, you will move among the high and mighty – the Empress, ministers, ambassadors, courtiers – all of that is about as far away from real life as you could imagine. You need to spend a few years living with the folk that you might one day rule. In some ways, that's more important than anything the professors can teach you. Bridget forgot that part when she was training Bryce to be her successor – he was a good man, at first, but he had no idea how the people of the Empire lived. With your Aunty Thorn, it was different. She spent years working in hospitals, then she had experience in Rainsby, and in running the Hold Fast estate. In other words – she had a well-rounded, practical education. That's what we're trying to achieve with you, and with Cael. We didn't want to smother you in aristocratic privilege. That's why you don't have guards or servants. That's why we don't monitor what friends you make, or who you speak to. You need space to be able to make your own mistakes, and to learn from them.'

'I don't think Cael would agree with you.'

Kelsey frowned. 'From what I'm hearing, you might be right. When we get to Colsbury, find out just how unhappy he actually is with his schedule. Your Aunty Celine and Uncle Corthie have been telling me that he's been miserable; that he thinks he's a victim of a conspiracy to break his spirit. He doesn't seem to understand that we're trying our best for him. Can I ask you – what do you think of Arrosa?'

Kyra shrugged. 'She's all right, I guess. We were never all that close. Does my brother still hate her?'

'With a passion, it seems. I might have to separate them, if it gets worse. The last thing we need is for Cael to be turned into glass.'

'He's jealous.'

'Of what?'

'He thinks Arrosa stole the love and attention he reckons he was due from our mother. It was Cael who never lost hope that Mother would return. He talked about it all the time, and he was right. Bringing her home was the most important thing in his life, but when it happened, Mother wasn't alone. She had Arrosa with her, and she treated her as though she were her real daughter. Cael didn't take it well.'

'You seemed to deal with it without any problem.'

'I guess I had a more realistic view of our mother's faults. I expected less than Cael, and so I wasn't disappointed.'

'That's harsh, Kyra. Karalyn went through a lot.'

'I know she did.'

'And yet you've never really forgiven her, have you?'

'Did you get along with your mother, Aunty?'

Kelsey narrowed her eyes. 'You know the answer to that question. My mother was completely different to Karalyn. She never stopped criticising me, for a start. Nothing I did was ever good enough. Karalyn isn't like that.'

'No, she's the opposite. She focuses on one thing, and ignores everything else that's happening in the world around her. At the moment, she's focussing on her two new children, and it's as though me, Cael and Arrosa have ceased to exist. She's oblivious to other people's feelings. I would be happy if she criticised me, for it would mean that she actually remembered I was there.'

'You're overstating it, I think. Aye, I know Karalyn can be single-minded, and she sometimes forgets to look up and see what's happening right next to her, but she will always love you and your brother. You have to remember that she missed seeing your first few years. Is it strange that she would want to relish every moment with Carden and Caitlyn?'

'As I said, I wasn't surprised by what happened. It's Cael you should be speaking to. I've made my peace with the situation.'

The carriage pulled up in front of a terraced row of elegant houses.

'We shall continue this later,' said Kelsey. 'We're here. Take a look out of the window. Do you see those houses? No one lives there, and the interior walls have been knocked through, to create one large laboratory and production facility. What goes on inside is an imperial secret, and you mustn't tell anyone. Do you agree?'

Kyra frowned as she gazed at the houses. They looked normal – the curtains were drawn, and the flowerboxes were well-tended.

'Aye,' she said. 'You know I can keep a secret.'

Kelsey opened the side door, and a soldier helped her step down to the roadside. Kyra left the carriage next, and Kelsey escorted her up to the front door of one of the houses. She knocked, and the door opened a minute later.

'Herald,' said a man, bowing his head. 'Please come in.'

'This is my niece Kyra Holdfast,' Kelsey said, as they walked into an entrance hall. 'The Empress has given her permission for Kyra to see the facility.'

'Very good, ma'am,' said the doorman. He pulled on a rope, and a bell sounded.

A soldier wearing a Banner uniform entered the hall.

'Good afternoon, ma'am,' he said.

'Is Professor Ravi busy?' said Kelsey.

'I will take you to him, ma'am,' said the soldier.

He led them through another doorway, and they entered a long corridor that stretched the entire distance of the row of houses. Large rooms opened up on either side, though several had doors that were securely locked, and were guarded by other soldiers. They went into a chamber, where a middle-aged Rakanese man was sitting at a workbench, reading from notes as he assembled a metallic object.

'Afternoon, Ravi,' said Kelsey.

The man turned. 'Hi, Kelsey. What can I do for you?'

'This is Kyra, Karalyn's daughter,' Kelsey said. 'She's been given permission to see what you do here. Could you give her a quick summary, and then a tour?'

Ravi wiped his hands on a rag, then he got up from his seat and walked towards them.

'Nice to meet you, Kyra,' he said, looking up at her. 'Where do I begin? Right. Technically, this facility is part of the university, so Kelsey is our patron. She's my boss, basically. The staff are managed by me. Most of them are Banner personnel; experts and so on. What we do here is simple – we design and build explosives for the Imperial Army.'

Kyra narrowed her eyes.

'The original technology comes from Dragon Eyre,' Ravi went on. 'Both sides used it in the war there. I think it was discovered by an earlier version of the Unk Tannic, but the Banner occupation forces refined the process, and made a few advances. As you might know, Sable destroyed the manufacturing centres on the island of Ectus, and by doing so, she killed off most of the people who knew how to build bombs. She didn't kill them all, though. After surveying the entire Banner of the Sapphire Throne, we found half a dozen officers who had some experience of producing explosives, and we hired them all to work here. That was about eight years ago. I was picked to head the department, as I had managed to reverse-engineer a few of the explosives Sable had brought over from Dragon Eyre.' He smiled. 'I'm quite proud of that.' He gestured towards a stack of shelves, upon which lay a collection of objects. 'The ones on the lower shelf are original Dragon Eyre bombs. They called them pisspots, if you can believe that; I guess because they look a little bit like chamber pots. They would launch them from catapults, and any direct hit would sink a ship. They have detonators at the pointy end, that set off the explosion if struck. And when they fly through the air, they rotate themselves, so that the pointy end always strikes the target first. Any questions so far?'

'Aye,' said Kyra. 'Why are we doing this?'

Ravi laughed. 'That'll be a political question, so you'd better ask Kelsey.'

'Explosives give our armed forces a great advantage,' said Kelsey. 'They save the lives of our soldiers. Well, they have the potential to do that; we haven't actually used them in combat yet. The last ten years have been peaceful, but it's better to be prepared for the worst.'

'Come and see our latest developments,' said Ravi.

He led them out into the corridor, then he unlocked a door, and they walked into a large storeroom, which was lined with shelves and crates of equipment. Ravi walked over to a small catapult.

'This is a model Forty-Eighter,' Ravi said. 'It's called that because the basket can fit forty-eight anti-personnel explosives.' He reached into a crate and withdrew an orange-sized metallic object. 'In other words, forty-eight of these. There are no timers or fuses – if one is launched, it will detonate upon impact. Imagine you are facing a large and hostile enemy force. Put forty-eight of these little bastards into the basket, set off the catapult, and the enemy's entire front ranks get blown to pieces. Ten catapults, and the battle's over before it can start. Of course, soldiers can throw them, too. They just need to twist the top half, to make it live, and then they can hurl it towards the enemy. Each little bomb contains metal shards that will rip through armour.'

He walked over to another crate, and withdrew a leather pouch. 'In here,' he said, 'is the secret ingredient that powers the explosives. We call it Ectus Powder. It's different from the compound I came up with for Sable. It's better. What goes into it is a military secret. If working flat out, this facility can produce tons of the stuff every third, enough to arm thousands of explosive devices.' He smiled again, oblivious to the deepening frown on Kyra's face. 'But how, I hear you ask, would we use Ectus Powder to knock down a castle wall? Good question. The forty-eights are great at killing soldiers, but they're no good against walls. For that, we need a new way of thinking. What if we don't launch the bombs at an enemy, but, instead, we use the powder to launch something massive – something that could make a great big hole in the strongest wall? That's the project we're working on at the moment, but we haven't cracked it yet.' He walked to another crate. 'Here's a primitive prototype.' He picked up a long metal tube, and cradled it in both arms. 'Put a ballista bolt in one end, and a little bit of Ectus Powder in the other; light the powder, and bang! The ballista bolt comes shooting out of the tube at an incredible velocity, far faster than any normal ballista can manage. Put forty of them along the side of a warship, or along the top of a castle wall, and you're going to turn the enemy into minced meat.

But, as I said, we're still experimenting, and we have a long way to go.' He placed the tube back into the crate.

'This is going to revolutionise warfare as we know it,' he went on. 'No army in its right mind is going to march across a field in battle order if the other side has Forty-Eighters. Castle walls will become obsolete overnight when we're able to pound them into rubble. But, I guess that's a problem for the tacticians.'

'They may even prevent war,' said Kelsey. 'The Empire could use them defensively, as a deterrent.'

'This is obscene,' said Kyra. 'I feel sick. How much money has the Empire spent on devising crueller ways to murder people?'

'Is it crueller than shooting someone with a crossbow?' said Kelsey. 'Crueller than stabbing them with a spear or a sword?'

'You're building machines capable of mass murder.'

'What is a dragon, or a flow mage, if not a being capable of mass murder? If Ravi's work makes our enemies consider the price they will pay for aggression, these devices will be worth every penny we've spent on them. We have enemies who want to destroy us, and I will not hesitate to develop better weapons to protect ourselves.'

'Do you swear that they will only be used to deter an attack, Aunty? Do you swear that the Empire will never use them to invade another's territory?'

'I could swear any oath you like,' Kelsey said, 'but I'm not the Empress.'

'Can we leave now?' said Kyra. 'I've seen enough.'

Kelsey nodded, then she glanced at Ravi. 'Thanks for the tour.'

'No problem, Kelsey,' he said.

Kelsey accompanied Kyra to the front door, which the doorman on duty opened for them. They stepped back out into the sunlight, and Kyra walked in silence to the carriage. They boarded, and the carriage got underway.

'I wish I'd never seen any of that,' Kyra said.

'Do you think it's wrong?'

'Of course it's wrong, Aunty! And Ravi seemed so excited by what he's making. I wanted to grab him by the shoulders and shake him.'

'I understand your reaction. Now, I would like you to imagine something for me. Pretend for a moment that you are the Empress. You know the dangers that surround the Empire – Rakana, Rahain, the Unk Tannic, the greenhides, the Doomed Worlds, the Dragon Dominion. Each one of them would love to bring us down. As Empress, your main responsibility is to defend the people. You have at your disposal a technology that would almost guarantee the defeat of any hostile force. Would you shun it, because it would cause casualties among those trying to kill us?'

Kyra said nothing.

'The Empress does not love war, Kyra. She does not crave the deaths of those opposed to her rule. She is a healer who loves her people. She also loves the men and women who serve in our armed forces – the armed forces that defend our borders. If these weapons can deter an invasion, then can you blame her for spending money on their development?'

'You make it sound simple, but it's not.'

'Two days from now, you will be with the Empress in Colsbury,' said Kelsey. 'Talk to her about what you have seen. Let her explain her reasons to you.'

'Oh, I will, Aunty,' said Kyra. 'You can be sure about that.'

CHAPTER 7
THE GALA

Plateau City, The Plateau – Summer's Day 544

'Shift your arse, Van,' said Kelsey; 'we need to leave.'

'I'm coming,' he said, as he struggled down the stairs of the town-house with armfuls of luggage. Little Caelius was shrieking and running around the hallway on the ground floor, while Calpurnia was skipping with excitement.

'Can we go swimming in the lake?' Calpurnia said. 'And will Frost-back fly us over the mountains?'

'I'm sure we can do all those things,' said Kelsey. 'We'll be there for the entire summer, as usual.'

Van reached the ground floor, and grunted under the weight of what he was carrying.

'Do we really need to bring all that stuff with us?' said Kelsey.

'Almost none of it's mine,' Van said. 'Most of the bags are full of the kids' clothes.'

'Caelius, be quiet,' Kelsey cried. 'I can't hear myself think. Van, did you pack the kids' shoes?'

'Yes.'

'And a dress for when Calpurnia attends court?'

'Yes.'

'Are you sure? The red one?'

'Yes.'

'And did you remember Caelius's white shirt?'

'I'd be more than happy to let you help me pack,' he said. 'In fact, you were supposed to help me last night, but you were working, again.'

'I had to organise the transfer of the entire Imperial Court to Colsbury,' she said; 'and you're complaining about having to pack a few bags?'

'I'm not complaining; but if you ask me to do something, then you'll have to trust that I get it right. Everything that was on the list is in the bags. Open them and check if you don't believe me.'

'I don't have time for that,' she said. 'Caelius, stop shrieking like a greenhide. Tell him, Van.'

'Let's just go,' said Van.

'We're going to be late if we take a carriage,' she said. She took out her Quadrant, and swiped her fingers over it. The air shimmered, and they appeared in the central courtyard of the Ministry of the Plateau.

'I didn't lock up the house,' said Van.

'Shit; why didn't you tell me?'

'I didn't have a chance to tell you.'

'Well, it's too late now. We'll just have to hope we aren't robbed.'

'Ah, marital bliss,' said Naxor, who was standing by a doorway.

'Shut up, Naxor,' said Kelsey. 'Is the Empress ready?'

'She is,' said Naxor. 'Wait here, and I'll fetch Her Majesty.'

Naxor disappeared into the building, and Kelsey activated the Quadrant again. She, Van, and their two children appeared in the large forecourt in front of the Summer Palace on Colsbury.

'Take Calpurnia and Caelius to our rooms, then fetch Cardova and Shella. I'll see you soon,' Kelsey said, then she swiped the Quadrant and returned to Plateau City.

She savoured the peace and quiet of the courtyard. She had a slight headache from the noise Caelius had been making, and she knew she was only at the beginning of what would be a long day. Over the years, the Empress's parties on Summer's Day had become ever more elaborate and expensive affairs, with teams of actors, musicians, singers, florists, chefs, butlers, and countless other trades being transported to Colsbury. The Empress expected it all to run smoothly, and had left Kelsey in charge of the organising. And Van was complaining about having to pack a few bags? Did he have any conception of the stress she was under?

Naxor emerged from the building, with the Empress next to him. Behind them stood Brogan and Kyra, followed by over a dozen courtiers, all bearing luggage.

Kelsey bowed her head. 'Happy birthday, Your Majesty. Shall I take you to the Summer Palace?'

'Thank you, Herald,' said Thorn. 'Caelius and Bedig have volunteered to remain behind this year to watch over Plateau City, but we shall be bringing Brogan.'

Kelsey smothered a curse.

'Is that all right?' said Brogan.

'Aye, it's fine,' said Kelsey. 'I may need to switch about some accommodation, but it's no problem. Would everyone please stand in the middle of the courtyard?'

The small crowd moved into position around Kelsey, and she activated the Quadrant. They appeared in front of the Summer Palace, where Cardova and Shella were waiting for them.

'Welcome back to Colsbury, Your Majesty,' said Cardova, bowing low. 'Many happy returns.'

'Yeah,' said Shella. 'Back for another summer, eh? Disturbing my tranquillity. The palace is ready for you, Your Majesty, and the Sanang Imperial Guard have arrived; they got here yesterday.'

Thorn smiled as she gazed around. 'It's good to be back. Are the gardens ready for today's gala?'

'Kelsey sorted all that out, Your Majesty,' said Shella. 'She's been back and forth, running about like a demented donkey.'

'Everything has been prepared, Your Majesty,' said Kelsey. 'The stage has been erected, and enough food and drink has been brought in to keep an army happy.'

'I will escort you to your quarters, Your Majesty,' said Cardova, 'and then the gala can begin.'

Thorn walked with Cardova into the palace, trailed by Naxor, Brogan and the courtiers.

Shella laughed. 'Let the chaos commence, eh? You look a little stressed there, Kelsey.'

'Aye? I have another twenty trips back to Plateau City to take care of, and then I have to go to the Hold Fast estate to collect Cael and Arrosa. After that, I have to head down the Rahain border. I'll be happy when I can sit down and relax for a minute.'

'Why would you be going to the Rahain border?' said Kyra.

'To pick up a couple of extra guests,' she said.

'I have a Quadrant,' said Kyra, 'I can help you.'

'No, it's fine. This is your holiday, Kyra. I'm not going to ask you to work. Go inside and say hello to your mother.'

Kyra nodded, then she walked into the palace.

'She's grown another foot, I see,' said Shella.

'You're looking well,' said Kelsey.

'For someone my age, you mean?'

'For someone who hasn't received a healing since last summer.'

'I take a bit of salve now and again,' Shella said. 'I pour a teaspoon of it into my whisky.'

'Where did you find some salve?'

'Did I tell you that Olo'osso lives here now? He brought some with him when he arrived.'

'What? And how did he...? Never mind; I don't want to know. Just don't give any to Van, alright? How's Karalyn? I noticed that she didn't bother her arse to come down to greet the Empress.'

'She's probably forgotten what day it is,' said Shella. 'And with two small children; well, you know how it is. She's so busy some days that she forgets to eat. And I'm too old for babysitting duties. I told her to hire a maid, but she wasn't interested; she wants to do it all herself. She's making up for lost time.'

'I'd better get back to work. I have a hundred boxes filled with government business to ferry here, along with dozens of staff, officers and more courtiers.'

Shella chuckled. 'Then you'd best get on with it, eh?'

Kelsey frowned, then she swiped her fingers over her Quadrant.

Kelsey worked as quickly as she could for the next two hours, bringing people, luggage and crates stuffed with documents from Plateau City to Colsbury. She saw Frostback briefly when she delivered the army chiefs to the Summer Palace, but then she was off again. When everything had been transferred, she swiped the Quadrant, and appeared by the rear porch of the mansion on the Hold Fast estate. She almost staggered from the heat and, at once, memories of her childhood flooded back. She gazed out over the vast grasslands, and saw a few herds moving across the plains amid the haze.

She turned, and saw Celine sitting on the porch.

'Do you have time for an iced tea?' said Celine.

'Aye, please,' said Kelsey.

She walked up the steps and sat down next to Celine.

'You were never as polite as a girl,' Celine said.

'So I've been told.'

Celine handed her a glass, and Kelsey took a long drink.

'Cole will be going to Colsbury this year,' Celine said.

'Aye? Why? He doesn't usually come.'

'He fell out with his girlfriend.'

'He had a girlfriend?'

'Yes. Be kind to him, Kelsey; she was seeing someone else behind his back. He's a little upset about it.'

'I'm not surprised. Well, he's more than welcome to join us. Are Cael and Arrosa still trying to kill each other?'

'No change there, I'm afraid.'

'I don't understand it. Kyra was trying to tell me that Cael's jealous of the attention Karalyn gave to Arrosa; but I think there's more to it.'

'There is more to it,' said Celine. 'He's angry about getting moved from place to place every season.'

'It's for his own good.'

'He doesn't believe that. Maybe you should re-think his schedule.'

'How's his work been? Has he been idle?'

'No. He has worked very hard this spring; so has Arrosa. You know, I think she would like to be Cael's friend. If only he would treat her better, then she would stop fighting with him immediately. There might even be something else going on beneath the surface.'

'Like what?'

'You might think I'm foolish for saying it.'

'Tell me, and I'll be the judge of that.'

'All right. Don't laugh, but I think that, deep down, they might actually like each other quite a lot, if you know what I mean.'

Kelsey laughed. 'No way. Cael loathes her.'

'I know, but there can be a thin line between love and hate. I've watched them together all spring, and I can't shake the feeling off. The intensity, no – the passion with which they fight swallows them both up. I might be wrong, but it would explain why Cael is so utterly opposed to Arrosa being adopted as his sister.'

'I can think of a few reasons why he's opposed, but fancying her isn't one of them.'

'That was just my impression,' Celine said, as she got to her feet. 'I will go inside and fetch them.'

Kelsey sat back and relaxed as Celine disappeared into the mansion. She sipped her iced tea, and thought about what Celine had said. She dismissed the notion that Cael and Arrosa were in any conceivable way attracted to each other, and wondered where she would put Cole.

A few moments later, Celine led Cael, Cole and Arrosa out onto the porch. They were each carrying a small bag, and none looked happy.

Kelsey stood. 'Are we all set?'

'Do we have a choice?' said Cael.

Kelsey ignored the comment. She glanced at Cole. 'You're going to have a good time in Colsbury this summer, Cole,' she said. 'It'll take your mind off things.'

'Thanks for letting me tag along, Aunty,' he said. 'Do you think the Empress will mind?'

'Her Majesty will be glad to see you. She will be glad to see you all. Celine has told me how hard you've been working. This will be your last time in the Holdings for a while, Arrosa. Are you looking forward to starting university?'

'Yes,' she said. 'It will be nice to stay in the same place for nine months.'

'Thirds,' said Cael. 'I assume I'll be back here next year?'

'That's the plan,' said Kelsey. 'One more year of spending a season in each place, and then you will be a free man, Cael.'

Cael frowned and looked away.

'What would you rather be doing?' said Kelsey. 'Be honest with me, Cael; what would you choose to do if it were up to you?'

'But it's not up to me, is it?'

'That's no way to answer the question.'

'Fine. I'd rather do what Arrosa's doing, and stay at the university all year. Why is she allowed to do it, while I'll be dragged off to Kell for winter again?'

Kelsey said nothing for a moment.

'Will you answer my question?' Cael said. 'I answered yours.'

'Aye. I will,' she said. 'Look; if this isn't working out, I mean, if your schedule is making you miserable, then we can discuss it. Before we go, I have a little announcement that affects you and Cole. The Empress has decided to make you both Electors. That means you will have the right to vote for the next emperor or empress, but not until you've passed your twenty-first birthdays. I'll give you each a copy of the proclamation later. Remind me if I forget.'

'Is Kyra an Elector, too?' said Cael.

'Aye.'

'What about Arrosa?' said Cole.

Cael shook his head. 'Why would Arrosa be an Elector? She's not a Holdfast; she's not even from this world.'

'I don't mind,' said Arrosa.

'No one asked for your opinion,' said Cael.

'Nobody asked for yours, either,' said Arrosa, 'but that doesn't stop you from opening your mouth.'

Kelsey watched as Cael and Arrosa narrowed their eyes at each other. Both looked as though they would happily rip the other's head off with their bare hands, and Kelsey dismissed Celine's idea.

'Have you stopped?' Kelsey said. 'Neither of you want to get one last insult in before we go to Colsbury?' She turned to Cole. 'How have you managed to put up with this shite all spring?'

Cole shrugged.

'And now you want to spend the summer with them, too?' she went on. 'I'll tell you what, Cole; if these two get too much for you, let me know, and I'll whisk you off somewhere else – Corthie's place in Kell, for instance.'

'I'll be all right, Aunty,' Cole said.

'Take care, you three,' said Celine. She hugged Cael and Arrosa, but she reserved the longest embrace for Cole. 'Look after yourself, Cole, and I'll see you when you get back.'

'I love you, Aunty,' he said.

Celine smiled. 'I love you, too.'

Kelsey gave Celine a nod, then she swiped her fingers over the surface of her Quadrant. The air shimmered, and they appeared in the forecourt of Colsbury. Sanang soldiers were marching through from the gatehouse, and they and the Kellach from the Imperial Guard were taking up their positions by the palace.

Cael closed his eyes. 'Out of the fucking heat at last.'

'Hey,' said Kelsey; 'none of that language here. At least, not in front of me.'

'Are we in our usual rooms?' said Arrosa.

'Aye,' said Kelsey. 'For the moment, Cole can share with Cael. After the gala, things will calm down a bit, and hundreds of folk will be heading back to Plateau City. I'll find you a room of your own then, Cole; all right?'

'When does the gala begin?' said Cole.

'At noon,' said Kelsey. 'We're all going to watch a play, and then there will be food and music. It'll be in the gardens, as usual.'

'Do we have to come?' said Cael.

'Aye, you do,' said Kelsey; 'but you don't have to stay for long. Just make sure you wish the Empress a happy birthday, and mingle for an hour or so. Deal?'

The three teenagers nodded.

'Off you go, then,' said Kelsey. 'And remember – this is a holiday. You're here to relax and have fun.'

Kelsey watched them enter the palace, then she set off for the gardens. She reached the end of the forecourt and turned right, her route taking her past the harbour. She heard laughter coming from the pier, and saw Shella and Olo'osso sitting by a small yacht. Kelsey approached them, and they glanced up at her.

'If it's not the almighty Herald,' cried Olo'osso. He got to his feet, took Kelsey's hand, and kissed it. 'I give thanks to the gods for providing us with such beautiful and powerful women. I confess that my heart, my lady, has been utterly captured.'

Kelsey frowned. 'Not by me, I hope?'

Olo'osso laughed. 'No, my fair lady, by the sweet Princess Shellakanawara, whose kisses I crave, and whose very breath I worship.'

'Except when I've been eating cheese,' said Shella.

'Yes, well, apart from that,' said Olo'osso.

'And, uh, is this feeling reciprocated?' said Kelsey.

'Don't look so surprised,' said Shella. 'Yeah, okay – we're a pair of old bastards, but even old bastards are allowed to have fun.'

'Is this your yacht, Olo'osso?'

'It is, my lady. I had it transported here from the shores of the Inner Sea. I sat upon its deck for the duration of the journey, in order to be able to say that I sailed all the way to Colsbury.'

Shella cackled with laughter.

'Are you both drunk?' said Kelsey.

'Exceptionally,' said Olo'osso.

'You were sober when I last saw you, Shella.'

'That was two hours ago!' said Shella. 'It's Summer's Day.'

'Well, try not to fall into the lake.'

Kelsey left the harbourside, and carried on towards the entrance to the gardens. She passed under the brick arch, and followed a path towards the centre of the gardens. Lanterns had been strung from the branches of the trees, and staff were busy applying the finishing touches to the wooden stage. Dozens of chairs had been set out on the lawn in front of the stage, with several ornate throne-like chairs in the centre of the front row for the Empress and her closest family and advisors.

Kelsey walked up to the actors' manager, who was overseeing some last-minute adjustments to the wooden scenery. He saw her approach, and bowed.

Kelsey held out her hand. 'Script.'

'Of course, ma'am,' he said. He beckoned one of the actors over, and snatched the script from his hands. He passed it to Kelsey, who flicked through the pages.

'What's it about?' she said.

'It is a romance, and a comedy, ma'am,' he said; 'with three songs and some dancing.'

'Nothing too lewd, I hope.'

'Certainly not, ma'am. One would not wish to offend Her Most Imperial Majesty.'

'One would not. Happy ending?'

'The happiest, ma'am.'

'Length?'

The man raised his palms. 'Under two hours, or thereabouts.'

'Do you know what to do if the Empress yawns?'

'We wrap it up in five minutes, ma'am.'

Kelsey passed the script back to him. 'Carry on, and good luck.'

The man bowed. 'You are most gracious, Madam Herald.'

Kelsey turned from the stage, and walked between the rows of chairs. In another clearing, the tables for the feast that would follow the play were being laid, and a large group of waiters was being briefed by the head steward of the Imperial Household. The steward caught Kelsey's gaze for a moment, but he was a man she trusted, and she gave him the briefest of nods before continuing down the path. She came to the apple orchard and paused. As she had predicted to herself, Karalyn was standing by the graves in the small cemetery. She was re-arranging the flowers by Lennox's headstone, a baby in her arms, and a small toddler sitting on the grass next to her. It had been eight years since she had returned from Athumia, and her new appearance never failed to surprise Kelsey.

'Sister,' she said.

Karalyn turned. 'Kelsey.'

'We are here to ruin your peace and quiet for another three thirds.'

'Aye.'

'Your children are here. Your other children. Arrosa, too.'

'I'll see them a little later.'

'Cael is unhappy.'

'Why?'

'Several reasons. One of them is that he thinks you're neglecting him.'

Karalyn shook her head. 'He's almost eighteen.'

'He's a boy who misses his mother.'

'He's almost a man.' She stood. 'Caitlyn has just turned one, and Carden was two at the end of winter. Cael and Kyra are old enough to look after themselves; it's these two that I need to be concentrating on. I told Cael that I was planning to adopt Arrosa.'

'I know.'

'His response did not impress me.'

'You and I need to sit down with him, and discuss his life. He thinks we're treating him unfairly.'

'He told me about that,' said Karalyn. 'His schedule is your responsibility, Kelsey. I'm too busy to plan out the next few years of his life.'

'I was thinking that, if he's really unhappy, then I might let him stay at university for all three terms next year. Then he'd have his sister for company, instead of going to Kell and the Holdings again.'

'It's up to you.'

'Pyre's tits, Karalyn; is that all I'm getting out of you today? Your children are not my problem. I have a million things to deal with right now; is it too much to expect a little assistance?'

'I'm sorry, Kelsey; I'm too tired to think. You must remember what it's like to have two young children. It's exhausting.'

'Then get some help. Hire a maid, or a nanny. You're part of the richest family on the Star Continent; surely you can afford a maid.'

'No. I am going to do this on my own. Letting someone else care for my children was how I lost Kyra to Thorn. That won't be happening again.'

'Fine. I'll fucking fix it, then; just like I fix everything else.'

Karalyn nodded. 'Thank you.'

Kelsey rolled her eyes and strode away. She passed under the two keeps, and emerged from the tunnel into the forecourt in front of the Summer Palace. Its pink and peach façade was looking resplendent in the bright sunshine, like an iced wedding cake. Several grand carriages had arrived in the time it had taken her to walk round the island, and richly-robed members of the Holdings aristocracy were stepping down to the flagstones. Kelsey ducked into the shadows of the Great Keep, knowing that if she were seen, she would be dragged into a dozen conversations.

'Hey, this is my hiding place,' said Cardova.

Kelsey glanced at him, and laughed.

He smiled back at her. 'Let's wait until they've all been escorted to the gardens, and then we'll run into the palace before anyone else can arrive.'

'You must hate this,' she said. 'A thousand people descend on your home every Summer's Day.'

'No, I like it,' he said. 'It's Karalyn who hates it.' He lit a cigarette. 'For me,' he went on, 'it's one of the highlights of the year. The theatre comes to us, along with dancing, and feasts, and new people to talk to. The Empress certainly knows how to throw a party. Colsbury is too quiet for the rest of the year.'

'I wish your wife felt the same way.'

'Despite her outward appearance, Karalyn remains the same person she always was. She would rather live in a kind of solitude. I'm more of a city boy at heart.'

'Then you picked the wrong sister.'

'I didn't realise I had a choice. How's Van?'

'The same. A bit older, a bit grumpier.'

'Are you still leaving him to look after the children?'

'What else am I supposed to do? I can't neglect my duties; and I have hundreds of them. Have you had a chance to look at the detailed plans for Rahain yet?'

'You only got here a couple of hours ago, Kelsey. I'll read them over tomorrow.'

'Lazy bastard.'

'Nagging shrew.'

'Don't you miss the time when life was simple?'

He laughed. 'When, exactly, was that?'

'Probably never. I feel like I can't slow down. I rush from one place to another, ticking off my mental list of everything I need to do each day. Like this gala – I've been planning it for four thirds. You said that the Empress knew how to throw a party, but it's me who organises everything.'

'That's what the Herald does. You turn the Empress's ideas into reality. If you don't like it, you could always resign.'

'Aye, right. I hate it, but I love it, too. If I wasn't busy all the time, I'd be bored. You should try to make some time for Cael.'

'That's who I was about to visit,' he said. 'I'm going to do my best to persuade him to watch the play with me. Will you be escorting the Empress to the gardens?'

'Naxor volunteered to do it this year. I just have to be there.'

'Listen,' said Cardova; 'do you think the two of us could spend some time with Cael, going over his various complaints? Maybe we shouldn't send him back to Kell this winter. It might be good for him to stay at university for the entire year. We could ask him what he wants to do.'

She glanced down and shook her head.

'What is it?' he said.

'You're more of a parent to that boy than his own mother.'

'That's unfair. Karalyn wants to focus on Caitlyn and Carden just now, and I respect her decision. All the same, I love the twins, and I'll try to do my best for them, even if neither of them particularly sees me as their father.'

'That's not through want of trying, Lucius. I know the effort you've put in over the years. They're lucky to have you.'

Cardova gestured towards the forecourt. 'I think it's safe to emerge from the shadows. Come on.'

They hurried across the forecourt towards the palace. They were about to reach the main entrance, when Van appeared, along with Calpurnia and little Caelius.

A broad smile came over the faces of the two men, and they embraced.

'It's good to see you, Van,' said Cardova.

'And you, Lucius.'

Kelsey glanced at her two children. 'Thanks, Van, for getting them ready for the gala. You even did Calpurnia's hair. I owe you one.'

'One?' he said. 'I think you might owe me more than that by now.'

Cardova laughed, and Kelsey shook her head.

'Fair enough,' she said. 'I'll take that one on the chin.'

'I'll go inside, and see if Cael, Kyra and Arrosa want to come to the play,' said Cardova.

'And Cole,' said Kelsey. 'He's come this year. His girlfriend was cheating on him, so be nice.'

Cardova saluted. 'Understood, ma'am.'

He entered the palace, and disappeared from sight.

Kelsey smiled at her husband and children. 'Shall we get our seats for the play?'

The children beamed back at her, then Van took her hand, and they walked towards the gardens.

CHAPTER 8
INVASION ORDERS

Grey Mountains, Rahain – Summer's Day 544

'Frostback and Halfclaw are the only other dragons upon this world,' said Sigum. 'They are pleasant enough, and they made me feel welcome when we dwelt in Colsbury.'

'Colsbury is just a name to me,' said Dolwyn. 'It's a wee island, isn't it?'

'It is.'

'And the Empress spends every summer on it with her friends?'

'She moves the entire government there for the season.'

'So, it's not all parties, balls and gowns?'

'It is not, though there are an abundance of those,' said the dragon. He gazed out over the green valley. 'The Empress enjoys hosting the world, and many visit Her Majesty in her Summer Palace – Holdfasts, dignitaries, officers and ambassadors. It feels like a three-month-long party.'

'He means thirds,' said Lahnos. 'They're called *months* on the other worlds. They mean the same thing.'

'I'm jealous,' said Dolwyn. 'Not everybody gets invited to Colsbury for Summer's Day.'

'Have you ever worn a ball gown?' said Lahnos.

'I've never even worn a skirt,' she said. 'My ma and da were getting me ready for the army since I could crawl. When other bairns got dolls, I was given a toy sword and shown how to take a defensive stance.' She laughed. 'I wasnae the only girl in my tenement who had army parents; we used to drill in Duncan Gardens when the sun was out, and have mock battles by the Auld Rampart.'

Sigum gazed up at the sky. 'The sun is halfway down,' he said. 'The Herald is officially late.'

'She was vague with her timing,' said Lahnos. 'We could be waiting here for a while yet.' He glanced at Dolwyn. 'You can go back to the fortress. You don't have to sit with us on the ramp all afternoon.'

'Are you trying to get rid of me?' she said.

'No. But if you're bored…'

'I'm all right,' she said.

Sigum glanced down. 'I think she might be hoping that you will invite her to Colsbury, my rider.'

'Really?' he said.

Dolwyn narrowed her eyes. 'Are you reading my mind, Sigum?'

'I cannot read minds,' said the dragon. 'Your innermost thoughts are concealed to me; but I remain a good judge of human nature, and I couldn't help but notice that you have brought a small bag with you – one that I assume contains spare clothes? Are you going to invite her, Lahnos?'

Lahnos turned to the young Kellach officer. 'Do you want to come to Colsbury with us?'

'Would that be all right?' she said. 'I don't want to get in the way.'

'There might be meetings that you're not allowed to attend,' he said. 'Sigum and I haven't been summoned just so we can enjoy ourselves. And I don't know how long we'll be there; but, if you want to come, and if it's all right with your superior officers, then I'll tell the Herald to bring you, too.'

'*You* are my superior officer, sir,' she said.

Lahnos frowned. 'I feel a bit bad about that. It's against army regulations for an officer to embark upon a relationship with someone under their command.'

'Is that what we're doing?' she said. 'I thought we were just having a bit of fun.'

'It's been fun,' he said, 'but others might think I'm taking advantage of you.'

She laughed. 'It was me who approached you,' she said, 'not the other way around. You're too considerate to take advantage of me, sir. By the way, I accept your invitation. We'll just have to wait to see what the Herald says. By the way, how many times have you met the Empress?'

Lahnos paused for a moment. 'Four times? We lived on Colsbury for two years, so she was there every summer. The last time I talked to her was when we volunteered for active service; that was about five or six years ago. I've met the Herald a lot more. And I used to see Karalyn Holdfast pretty much every day.'

'What's she like?'

'That's a good question,' he said. 'When I first met her, she had lost her memories, and she was in a different body.'

'So the stories are true? She can move from body to body? If she dies, she can take another one?'

'I don't know how it works. At the beginning, she was just a voice in my head, giving me advice. We called her the *Demon Witch*. If she desired power, she could take it; but all she wants is a quiet life. She used to get annoyed every summer when the Empress and her court turned up in Colsbury, as if they were invading her home. She has new children, or so I heard.'

'These people are just myths to me. The Holdfasts. The Empress. I can still remember when Bridget was in charge. She seemed normal, as though an ordinary person had managed to climb to the top. If she could do it, I used to think, then anybody could. But Thorn? She's different. It's like she was born to be Empress. Does she really only ever wear blue?'

Lahnos nodded. 'And no one else is allowed to wear that colour in her presence. Well, no woman, at any rate. I once saw Corthie in blue armour, and she didn't seem to mind.'

'You've met Corthie?'

'I have. He seemed like a nice guy. Down to earth. And I've met Sable a few times, too.'

'Pyre's tits. If Corthie and Sable are there, I might pee my pants.'

'They probably won't be,' he said. 'They don't usually go to Colsbury for Summer's Day.' He smiled. 'If those two are there when we arrive, then I'll start to worry.'

The air shimmered a few yards away on the ramp, and Kelsey Holdfast appeared.

Lahnos tilted his head. 'Herald.'

'Hey, Lahnos,' said Kelsey. 'Are you ready to go?'

'Can Dolwyn come with us?'

Kelsey eyed the young Kellach officer. 'Why?'

'She's never been to Colsbury before.'

'Most people have never been to Colsbury.'

'But I'm asking.'

Kelsey shrugged. 'Whatever. She won't be allowed to sit in at the strategy meetings, but she can mingle at the party.'

'Thanks, Herald,' said Dolwyn. 'This is a great honour for me. I'll be on my best behaviour.'

'Just make sure you're around when I bring Lahnos and Sigum back here.'

'And when will that be, Herald?'

'Tomorrow morning; nice and early. Hangover or no hangover, you'd better be ready.'

'Aye, ma'am,' she said.

'Have you got your best dress uniform, Lahnos?'

'All packed up and attached to Sigum's harness, ma'am.'

'You've missed the play,' Kelsey said. 'Dinner was about to be served when I left to come here. Lahnos – you have a space reserved for you at the Empress's table. Sigum – you'll be eating with Halfclaw, Frostback and Blackrose.'

'Queen Blackrose is present in Colsbury?' said the silvery-green dragon.

'Aye. She arrived halfway through the play.'

'I look forward to meeting her.'

'Have you never met her before?'

'I have not,' he said.

A slight frown creased Kelsey's face. 'Well, be prepared.'

'For what?' said Lahnos.

'Blackrose has a low opinion of dragons from Athumia,' she said. 'That was Sable's doing. She told the queen that Athumian dragons routinely lie and cheat, and Blackrose took offence. She may decide to make a few comments.' She glanced down at the Quadrant in her left hand. 'What was your name again, Lieutenant?'

'Dolwyn, ma'am.'

'Do I need to find you separate accommodation?'

'She can stay with me,' said Lahnos.

'That's what I thought,' said Kelsey, 'but there was no harm in checking. Right; let's go.'

She brushed her fingers over the Quadrant, and they appeared in the large forecourt of Colsbury. It was packed with people. Soldiers were guarding the entrances to the Summer Palace and the Great Keep, while a few dozen market stalls were selling everything from hot food to flowers and clothing. Families from the local village were mingling with ladies and gentlemen of the Imperial Court, and music could be heard floating up from the area behind the two keeps where the gardens lay. The arrival of Lord Sigum in the middle of the forecourt had caused most people to turn to look at the huge dragon. After that, their gazes went to the horns on Lahnos's head

'Pyre's unholy tits,' muttered Dolwyn, as she gazed up at the palace. 'If I lived here, I wouldnae bother going back to Plateau City.'

'My sister would agree with you,' said Kelsey. 'She hasn't left Colsbury in years. Come on; follow me.'

The crowds parted for the silvery-green dragon, and Kelsey led the way past the harbour and into the gardens. Musicians were performing on a wide stage, entertaining the people seated at over a dozen long tables set out amid the trees.

'What do you do if it's raining?' said Dolwyn.

'We hang tarpaulin sheets from the branches of the trees,' said Kelsey, as she glanced up at the clouds in the sky. 'Why? Do you think it's going to rain?'

'No. I was just wondering.'

'Well, stop giving me something else to worry about, and find yourself a place at one of the tables by the apple trees. Lahnos – you're at the Empress's table with me.'

'I'll walk Sigum over to the other dragons first,' he said. 'I want to see if the great and mighty Blackrose tries to insult him.'

Kelsey frowned. 'You've only been here two minutes, and you're looking to cause trouble with Blackrose?'

'I'm not causing trouble. I'll be polite if Blackrose is polite.'

'Then I'd better come with you both.'

Dolwyn walked off towards another set of tables, then Kelsey led Sigum and Lahnos to the northern edge of the gardens, where there was a large clearing next to the banks of the lake. Lahnos saw Frostback and Halfclaw, the two young dragons he had known when he had lived in Colsbury. Next to them was a large dragon, as large as Lord Sigum. Her scales were jet black, and her eyes glowed red.

Frostback caught sight of the approaching group.

'Son of Sigel,' she called out; 'how goes it with you?'

'Life is treating me well, daughter of Deathfang,' he said. 'My cordial greetings to you and the noble Halfclaw.'

'It is good to see you again,' said Halfclaw; 'and you, Lahnos of the Horns.'

'It's good to be back,' said Lahnos; 'although we're only here until tomorrow morning.'

Blackrose waited, her eyes taking in the size and bearing of Sigum.

'I shall make the introductions,' said Halfclaw. 'Lord Sigum, this is Queen Blackrose of Dragon Eyre, liberator of Ulna, and monarch of the Eastern Rim.'

Sigum tilted his head. 'It is truly an honour and a privilege to meet you, Your Majesty.'

'Queen Blackrose,' Halfclaw went on, 'this is Lord Sigum Mon Sigel of Athumia. We befriended him when...'

'Athumia?' cried Blackrose, her eyes like burning coals. 'The home of ignoble dragons who lie and break their oaths? I have heard of this place, and what I heard fills me with disgust. Even the worst of our kind on Dragon Eyre would not stoop so low as to knowingly utter falsehoods. Let him not speak to me; for I will be unable to judge whether his words are false.'

Sigum kept his head tilted, but said nothing.

'Lord Sigum is honourable,' said Halfclaw. 'He was always true in his dealings with us.'

'You are young, Halfclaw,' said Blackrose, 'so I will forgive your mistake. No dragon who lies is honourable; it is an impossibility.'

'He is here as our guest,' said Kelsey.

'Then I must also fault your judgement, Herald. Please do not tell me that you have given any position of trust or responsibility to this disgrace to the name of dragons.'

Lahnos shook his head, and put his hands on his hips. 'You arrogant piece of shit,' he said. 'How dare you speak those words about someone of whom you know nothing? I've heard great things about you, Blackrose, but no one told me how stupid you were.'

Sparks flashed across Blackrose's jaws, and she moved closer to Lahnos.

'Only respect for the Empress is preventing me from ripping your head off, horned creature,' she spat.

'If you did so, Your Majesty,' said Sigum, 'I would fight you to the death. I can accept insults against my own person, but I will not stand by while my rider is being threatened.'

'Any fight between us would be mercifully short,' said Blackrose. 'Your throat would give way to my jaws, and your neck would snap like a rotten branch. I would throw your body to the dirt for the worms and rats to devour, and then your name would be utterly forgotten.'

Kelsey raised her hands. 'Stop! Lahnos, keep your damn mouth shut from now on. And Blackrose, you don't even know Sigum. Do you think every dragon on Athumia is the same?'

'The dragons upon my world are descended from Dragon Eyre,' Sigum said. 'Unfortunately, our ways and traditions were usurped by a human god in dragon-form. I abhor the falsehoods disseminated by my kin, and have never broken an oath once sworn. By these habits, and by taking a rider, I am shunned by the dragons of Athumia. But I feel no shame, for I have done no wrong. Perhaps it is you who should be ashamed, mighty and renowned Blackrose, for your intemperate words. I shall take my leave, lest you are further tainted by my presence. Come, Lahnos; let us go where we are welcome.'

Blackrose edged back a step, confusion and suspicion on her features. Sigum turned, and walked away. Lahnos went with him, while Kelsey remained behind. As they re-entered the orchard, Lahnos could hear Kelsey's voice, but he couldn't make out the words.

'I think I shall fly while you dine at the Empress's table,' the silvery-green dragon said. 'I have no appetite after that encounter, and I long to see the familiar mountains around Colsbury.'

'Are you angry?' Lahnos said.

'No. I am a little aggrieved to have been so pre-judged, but Blackrose is merely mistaken. I shall readily forgive her when she sees fit to apologise.'

'You may be waiting a while for that.'

'We shall see. I suspect Kelsey Holdfast is gently reprimanding her as we speak.' He turned his long neck to gaze down at Lahnos. 'Stay out of trouble, my rider,' he said. 'I will return after nightfall.'

He extended his wings and soared into the blue sky. He circled once above Colsbury, then flew over the lake towards the mountains. Kelsey joined Lahnos as he was watching the shape of the dragon fade into the distance.

'Sorry about that,' she said. 'That was completely uncalled for. But you didn't help. I doubt anyone has ever told Blackrose that she was stupid to her face and lived to tell the tale.'

'I was standing up for my dragon,' he said. 'Sigum is too considerate to stand up for himself.'

'As you might have gathered, Blackrose hates liars, which is quite amusing, actually, seeing how she and Sable are such good friends. They used to hate each other; well, no – Blackrose used to hate Sable. My aunt had to liberate Dragon Eyre before Blackrose would overlook her lies.'

'Why didn't Frostback and Halfclaw intervene?' he said. 'I thought they were Sigum's friends.'

'They are,' said Kelsey; 'but Frostback is Blackrose's adopted daughter, and Halfclaw is Frostback's mate, which sort of makes Blackrose his mother, too. It's dragon politics. Neither Frostback nor Halfclaw can contradict Blackrose, at least not in public. I'll speak to Frostback about this later, when she and I are alone. As for now, I'm starving, and our food will be getting cold.'

They walked through the gardens until they reached the high table, where the Empress sat at one end. Lahnos glanced at the people down each side of the long table. He gave a brief nod to Karalyn and Cardova, then he performed a deep bow before Empress Thorn, who gave him a smile in return. Kelsey showed him to his seat. On his left was Arrosa, and he smiled when he saw her.

'My favourite demon,' said Arrosa.

'It's good to see you,' he said, as he sat down.

'You've missed the first three courses,' she said, 'but there's plenty more to come. I hope you're hungry.'

'I would have been on time, if Blackrose hadn't behaved like an insufferable arsehole.'

'Hey!' said the woman seated to Lahnos's right. 'Don't speak about my dragon like that.'

Lahnos glanced at her. 'Your dragon insulted mine.'

'Then your dragon must have done something bad.'

'He didn't. Blackrose took exception to his place of birth, as though he had any control over that.'

'Eh?'

'Lahnos's dragon is from Athumia,' said Arrosa. 'Just like me and Lahnos.'

The woman grimaced. 'Oh. Well, uh... I remember Blackrose getting very upset, when Sable told her she'd met a dragon from Athumia who had broken an oath. Was she rude?'

'Very,' said Lahnos.

'Oops. Sorry. My name's Maddie, by the way. Maddie Jackdaw. I'm from the City.'

'Which one?'

'She means the City of Salve,' said Cael, who was sitting opposite Lahnos.

Lahnos nodded. 'How have you been, Cael? I heard you were at university.'

Cael gestured towards his twin sister, who was sitting at the other end of the table from the Empress, just to Arrosa's left.

'Kyra goes to university,' Cael said. 'I get sent all over the place.'

'And he loves to complain about it,' said Arrosa.

'Piss off,' said Cael.

'Watch your mouth,' said Lahnos. 'Don't speak to Arrosa like that.'

Cael shrugged. 'I'll say whatever I like to her.'

'You're a big lad, Cael, but I've knocked down bigger. If you can't be civil, say nothing.'

'It's all right,' said Arrosa. 'Cael and I are always teasing each other. It's just a bit of fun. Don't read anything into it.'

'Fair enough,' said Lahnos. 'If that's all it is, then I'll back off. No hard feelings, Cael?'

'I'm fucking sick of this shit,' said Cael, getting to his feet. He turned and strode away, heading in the direction of the palace.

'Damn it,' muttered Lahnos. 'Sorry about that, everybody.'

'It's not your fault,' said Kyra. 'I don't know what's wrong with my brother. He's been in a terrible mood since we arrived in Colsbury.'

'He's been in a terrible mood for thirds,' said Cole, who was sitting to Kyra's left, opposite Arrosa. 'He's tired of being sent to a different place each season; and Arrosa was lying. They weren't teasing each other. They've been fighting all spring.'

'I've tried hard to be friends with him,' said Arrosa. 'Haven't I tried, Cole?'

'Yeah. All right – you've tried.'

'But Cael just throws it back in my face,' she went on. 'I swear to you, if he stopped, then I'd stop, too. I don't want to be his enemy, but I have to stick up for myself.'

Maddie nudged Lahnos. 'Why are we stuck down here with the teenagers?' she whispered.

Lahnos laughed. 'Probably because our family name isn't Holdfast.'

'Yeah, that'll be it,' she said. 'I am sorry about what Blackrose said to your dragon, you know. But is it true? Are there dragons on Athumia who can lie?'

'For sure,' he said. 'Most of them are devious and crooked. Sigum is an exception.'

'Were you trained to be his rider?'

'No. As far as I'm aware, he's the only Athumian dragon to have a rider.'

'Wow. That's odd. Do the dragons there not have humans running around looking after them?'

'They do, but none are riders. Most would take great offence if you suggested it to them. The first time I asked Sigum if I could climb on his back, I thought he might eat me.'

'Really?'

'No, I'm joking. He was fine about it. The monks in the monastery were outraged, though. They thought it was blasphemous. Dragons are worshipped by many humans on Athumia.'

'But not by the Gunstians,' said Arrosa. 'We consider them to be demonic.'

Lahnos gave her a look. 'Your people also consider me to be demonic.'

'True.'

'Is that because of the horns?' said Maddie. 'Is it rude to talk about them? You're the first person I've ever seen with horns. Have you ever accidentally stabbed someone with them?'

'Not accidentally.'

'They make you look quite ferocious. Are they sharp?'

'Touch them and find out.'

'Ooh, can I?' Maddie reached out with a finger, and tapped one of his horns. 'Are you always destroying pillows? What happens if you go through a doorway and forget they're there? And I take it that hats are out of the question?'

'I suppose I could pull a hat down, and make two holes in it.'

'I'd like to see that. Where do you live?'

'I'm currently posted on the frontier with Rahain. We patrol the mountains, and keep a look out for raiders.'

'That's exciting. Do you have a girlfriend?'

'Why? Are you asking me out, Maddie?'

Her face went red. 'I'm married! I have two children. I was only asking.'

'I was joking with you. Yes, I have a girlfriend. She's Kellach Brigdomin.'

'Malik's ass. You're going out with a giant? Do you not mind that she's taller than you?'

'Why would I care about that?'

'I wasn't saying you should care; only that some men might. And some women wouldn't be interested in going out with a shorter man. Are you older than her?'

'Yes, by eight years.'

Maddie screwed up her face. 'What? But... that would make her about twelve.'

'She's twenty-one.'

'No. Are you joking with me again? There's no way you're almost thirty. I'm thirty-two, so I should know.'

'You look mid-twenties to me.'

'That's sweet of you, but I know you're lying.'

Cardova walked by. 'Where's Cael?' he said.

'He wasn't hungry,' said Kyra.

Cardova narrowed his eyes for a moment, then he glanced at Lahnos. 'Are you free to discuss something?'

Lahnos got to his feet and saluted. 'Yes, sir.'

'This is informal, Lahnos. No need for salutes. Come on; we'll go for a walk.'

Lahnos walked round to the other side of the table, then he and Cardova strode towards the small harbour.

'I was going to leave this until later,' Cardova said, 'but Kelsey told me that you are returning to the Rahain frontier first thing in the morning.'

'So I believe, sir.'

'I read the plan for Rahain over dinner,' Cardova went on.

'Then you're one step ahead of me, sir.'

'I'll make sure a detailed copy is given to you before you leave. It's going to be a full scale invasion, but its initial aims are limited to Tahrana City. Once you get there, you shall pacify the city, dig in, and wait.'

'Are we not going to the Rahain Capital, sir?'

'No. It's going to be one city at a time. The army will not move on to another city until the one they are in has been completely subdued. The Empress has made it clear that she's prepared to take decades to fully occupy Rahain. It is the Empress's desire that Rahain is absorbed into the Empire, no matter how long it takes. Understood?'

'Yes, sir. I am not a policeman, though, and this sounds like a policing operation.'

'I know exactly what you mean. You and Lord Sigum will be required for the initial advances, and to cover the Imperial Army from the air. When Tahrana City is in our hands, you will be deployed elsewhere.'

'Do you know where, sir?

'I do, but I'm not at liberty to tell you. Several plans are in motion, of which Rahain is only one.'

They reached the harbour, and walked along the narrow pier. The sun had set behind the mountains to the west, but the sky remained blue. A hundred yards away, out in the lake, a sleek yacht was taking advantage of the breeze, and Lahnos could see a man and a woman by the tall white sail.

Lahnos narrowed his eyes. 'Is that Shella I can see out there, sir?'

Cardova smiled. 'Yes. She remains remarkably sprightly for an elderly princess, and boating is her new passion. I've told her a hundred times that she shouldn't go sailing when she's drunk, but she never listens to a word I say.'

'How do you know she's drunk, sir?'

'I saw her an hour ago. She could barely walk.

They watched the yacht for a few moments, then Cardova turned to Lahnos. 'Your Gift of Pain will come in useful in the invasion; I'm sure of that,' he said. 'It sounds ideal for non-lethal crowd suppression. Use it to subdue any angry mobs.'

'Do we anticipate many of those, sir?'

'The Empire has invaded Rahain before, several decades ago, under the first Emperor. The invasion was a great success, but the occupation which followed was a complete disaster. Rahain descended into a barbarous civil war, from which they have never fully emerged. Empress Thorn is determined not to repeat those mistakes. Ten full regiments of the Imperial Army will be deployed to Tahrana City, along with a division of Sanang warriors, who will be the first to enter the caverns.'

'What kind of armed opposition can we expect, sir?'

'The gangs and warlords currently in control of Rahain are well-armed, but badly-supplied. Those with food hoard it, and guard it from everyone else. Fresh water is also becoming scarcer. The Empress's priority for Tahrana City is to repair its infrastructure, and make it habitable again – schools, hospitals, roads, lighting and heating, agriculture, trade. We won't win by terrorising the locals; we have to show them that they would be better off inside the Empire. At first, though, show no mercy. Overwhelm them with superior force, and annihilate any armed opposition. High casualties among the Rahain gangs will be regrettable, but justified. As soon as Tahrana City has been pacified, the rebuilding will begin.'

'Annihilate, sir? Are we taking no prisoners?'

'Those are your orders, Commander. We go in hard, so that we can ease up later. It sounds ruthless, and it is; but it's the only way to restore Rahain to its former glory, as part of the Empire. If any Rahain are armed, the Sanang are under orders to kill them. Any questions?'

'No, that was quite clear, sir. Might I ask you something, man to man?'

'Go ahead.'

'That wasn't your plan, was it, Major General? This has come from the Empress.'

Cardova said nothing for a while, then he nodded. 'We serve the Empire, Lahnos. The Empress believes that this approach will save lives in the long run, and we have to trust that she will be proved right.' He eyed Lahnos. 'Let's go back to the gardens; it's almost time to get ready for this evening's ball. Will you be coming?'

'Yes, sir.'

One hour later, Lahnos was seated in his chambers within the Summer Palace, with his eyes closed.

'All right,' said Dolwyn. 'You can look.'

Lahnos opened his eyes, and saw Dolwyn wearing an elegant, dark green ball gown edged with silver thread.

'What do you think?' she said. 'It matches Sigum's colours. Five seamstresses helped get it ready for me.'

He got up from the couch. 'You look beautiful.'

'I cannae believe this is really happening,' she said. 'A ball, with the Empress and the entire Imperial Court.'

'There has to be some benefits of going out with the commander,' he said. 'I didn't mean that. We're not going out; we're just having a bit of fun.'

Dolwyn shrugged. 'I don't mind if you call me yer girlfriend in front of other people.'

'Good, because I've been doing it since we got here.'

'Yer looking very handsome in that uniform. I could eat you.'

'Maybe later; we have a ball to attend.'

She put a hand on his arm. 'Are you all right? You've been quiet since ye went off for that walk with Major General Cardova.'

'I'm fine,' he said.

'Did he say anything that worried you?'

'Not at all. He was just wishing me good luck for the invasion.'

She nodded. 'All right. Shall we?'

They linked arms, and strode towards the front door of the quarters they were sharing.

'And if we see Blackrose?' she said, as they walked out into the corridor of the Summer Palace.

'I will definitely not tell her that I think she's a rude, useless lizard.'

'Excellent,' she said. 'There's hope for ye yet, sir.'

CHAPTER 9
WORLD THREE

Colsbury Castle, the Holdings – 7th Day, First Third Summer 544

Cael gazed down at the vast jungle-covered mountain range. Only the naked stone peaks were poking up through the sea of green. Far to the south, the ocean was crashing against a ragged coastline, but everywhere else was ruled by silence.

'Where are all the people?' said Cael. 'There should be people living here.'

There are eight hundred and fifty-two humans within a twenty-mile radius, said the Sextant.

'Is that all? There should be more of them. Why are there no towns or cities? I left them alone for five hundred years, aye?

That is correct, Cael Holdfast.

'Then they've done nothing in five centuries?

It can take thousands of years for civilisations to emerge.

'I've already given them several millennia; and I made sure they had plenty of wood, coal and oil to get them started.'

There are many factors that contribute...

'Aye, I know. I just get so impatient. I want to go down there, and walk around, but I can't do that until I align the time; and I don't want to align the time while my sub-created humans are still living like savages. Show me the coast again; I want to see if there are any boats, or if anyone's fishing.'

The scene before him changed, and the Sextant bore his vision south, to where the high waves of the ocean were battering the shore.

'This is no good,' said Cael. 'The water's too wild. Take me to where a river enters the ocean.'

The view changed again, as the Sextant raced his vision along the coast. They came to a region where the mountains had petered out, and Cael saw a wide river course meandering lazily through a broad plain. It split into a hundred channels as it reached the ocean, depositing millions of tons of mud and silt, which coloured the waters of the ocean brown for miles around. Cael stared down at the large delta. Between the sluggish channels was nothing but uninhabitable marshlands, but there were long-limbed birds, too, the first signs of wildlife that he had seen.

'This,' he said, 'is... disappointing. The geography's all wrong.'

Your instructions were carried out exactly, said the Sextant.

'Follow the river inland, slowly,' Cael said. 'If there are any settlements on this continent, they'll be close to fresh water.'

The Sextant did as it was bade, and Cael watched as the dozens of small channels consolidated into one wide river. The land rose a little, and parts of it dried out into patches of forest and tall grasses. More birds were seen, which was a good sign, Cael thought. Birds signified that an important era of development had passed, but he couldn't remember the details. Grass was good, too, for it presaged the cultivation of crops, and allowed for the grazing of animals. He noticed a rocky escarpment by a bend in the river, and saw a few thin tendrils of smoke rising from its summit.

'There!' he cried. 'Move in closer.'

The Sextant lowered his vision towards the top of the rocky hill. A crude wall of large boulders had been constructed around the lip of the summit, and a single path that wound its way up the slope passed through the wall to reach the top. A collection of wooden structures had been built within the defensive circle of stone, and a few half-naked humans were gathered by a small fire.

Cael watched them for a while in silence. His humans – his creation. Had it not been for his deliberate choices, none of the people he was looking at would be alive. He had brought them into being; he had given them existence.

There was a rumbling noise, and the humans in the small settlement cried out in terror. The ground by the river buckled and moved, and water poured into a crevice that opened up. The ground settled again after a few moments, the river taking a slightly different course from before. Up on the escarpment, the humans were lying prostrate upon the ground, their voices calling out in prayer or supplication.

'What was that?' said Cael.

An earthquake.

'I know it was a fucking earthquake,' he said; 'but why? The ground is supposed to be stable.'

The plates underpinning this continent are unstable. There are no stable regions upon this world.

'Fix it,' said Cael.

It is too late. The plates are in place, and undoing them would destroy all life upon the continents.

'But you were supposed to make the continents solid and stable.'

Your instructions were followed precisely.

'Then I must have made a mistake somewhere. Shit. I've fucked it up again. Three worlds, three disasters. Where did I go wrong?'

I follow instructions. I do not offer advice.

'Did you offer advice to my mother when she used the Sextant?'

You are not your mother, Cael Holdfast. There is no one like your mother.

'You helped her ascend into godhood, didn't you? It was you, Sextant. You did it to her.'

It was a unique combination of her powers and my abilities, Cael. You do not possess the same powers. No one possesses the same powers as Karalyn.

'I wish I had someone to teach me how to create worlds properly.

I'm not giving up, though. I'll get it right in the end, even if it takes me a hundred attempts.

Do you wish to create a new world?

'No, not yet. I want to learn what I did wrong with this one, first. Can you show me some of the humans to whom I gave death powers?'

There are none left alive.

'What happened to them?

They died.

Cael was about to lose his temper with the Sextant when he felt another presence push its way into his mind.

What are you doing, brother? cried Kyra. *Aunty Kelsey and the Empress are going to lose their damn minds when they find out that you've been messing around with the Sextant again.*

Cael lifted his hand from the device. Standing next to him in the shadows of the palace attic was his sister, her hands on her hips as she glared at him.

'So this is where you've been hiding?' she said. 'You promised that you wouldn't do this any more. The Sextant is not a toy.'

'You're just jealous that it won't speak to you.'

'Jealous? What are you talking about? Lucius Cardova has been looking for you, and I covered for your absence, again. I told him you had gone out to the village for a walk. And how did you get the Weathervane? It's locked up in a secret location in Plateau City, to stop you from doing this.'

Cael said nothing.

Kyra walked up to the Sextant. She reached out to grip the sword that had been inserted into its flank, then she hesitated.

'This isn't the Weathervane,' she said.

'I know.'

'It isn't one of the Fated Blades, either.'

'Aye. I know.'

'Where did you find another Tempest sword?'

'I stole it from an imperial armoury.'

Kyra narrowed her eyes. 'What? But... I thought...'

'You thought what?'

'I thought we were only using Tempest for armour, not weapons.'

'That's mostly true,' he said, 'but I found a few dozen experimental axes and swords. There was only one blade that would fit the Sextant, so I took it.'

'How did you know where to find it?'

'I read the minds of over twenty officers in the Imperial Army, starting with Caelius Logos. As Imperial Quartermaster, it made sense to read his mind first. What else was I supposed to do? After I was caught last summer, I knew that Cardova and the others would place the Weathervane out of my reach.'

'When did you steal this sword?'

'Last autumn, when we were in Plateau City. I hid it here, and then I had to wait for summer to come round again.'

'This has become an obsession, brother.'

'That's easy for you to say. Quadrants talk to you; the Sextant talks to me. You would become obsessed if you weren't allowed to ever touch a Quadrant again. But that's not how things work. You are allowed as many Quadrants as you like, while I'm forbidden from even being in the same room as the Sextant. Is that fair? Why should you be able to use your powers, while I am denied the same thing?'

'Quadrants cannot obliterate entire worlds, Cael. There is no comparison.'

'I'm not interested in destruction. I want to create something new; something beautiful and wonderful. A world that belongs to me, where I can walk amid forests and mountains, and see the stars shine down from the sky each night.'

Kyra frowned, and folded her arms across her chest. Cael took out his cigarettes. He offered one to his sister.

'I don't smoke any more,' she said. 'I gave up in winter.'

'You never really liked it, anyway.'

'Which is why I gave it up.'

Cael struck a match, and lit his cigarette.

'How many worlds have you created?' she said.

'Three. Could you see the one I was looking at?'

'Aye. I saw it through your eyes.'

'That's World Three.'

'Is that what you're calling it?'

'I didn't want to give it a proper name until I have aligned the time.'

'And when will that be?'

'I don't know. It's not ready. It might never be ready. I keep making mistakes. World One is a barren, waterless desert. World Two is just as bad. There, the seas swallowed up the few landmasses I'd created, and now the entire world is nothing but ocean. I thought I'd cracked it with World Three, but it's still not quite right. There's something wrong with the plates that support the continents; they're unstable. And, for some reason, my sub-created humans are still living like savages. I might give them another thousand years, and see what they look like then.'

'I don't really understand what all that means,' said Kyra. 'Is someone showing you what to do?'

'Who?' said Cael. 'No one knows how to create worlds. I'm learning by trial and error. Don't worry about it. I'll tidy up my errors. I'll destroy any world that's not quite right.'

'But you've created humans?'

'Aye. They're sub-created, you know? They're not... real.'

'Cael, we are sub-created, or had you forgotten? Nathaniel made us. Theodora made Arrosa. Simon made Blackrose. Are we not real?'

'That's completely different. My humans will only become real if I align the time. Before that, they might as well be figments of my imagination.'

'But they do exist? I mean, somewhere, out there, they live and breathe?'

'Aye, but only within their own time. I can spend several thirds inside World Three, but only a few minutes would have elapsed in Colsbury. When I went in today, for example, I told the Sextant to move time forward by five hundred years, so that I could look for any new developments. The people who lived and died during those five centuries didn't really exist, did they? They only exist when I'm looking at them.'

'There's something troubling about this, brother. You shouldn't play with people's lives like that. It seems wrong.'

'If it's wrong, then all worlds created by the Sextant are equally wrong, and that includes this world.'

'Why don't you create a beautiful world where no humans live?' she said. 'Then, we could visit it, and perhaps even colonise it.'

'Where's the fun in that? I want to create humans with powers; I want to create mighty dragons, and other animals that can talk. There are a million possibilities. If Nathaniel hadn't been curious and wise, there would be no Kellach Brigdomin, and no dream mages.'

'This world caused the death of Nathaniel. He over-reached, and became trapped here.'

'Aye, I know. I won't try to create dream mages; I promise.'

Kyra stared at the wooden floorboards of the dark attic. 'I shall have to tell Aunty Kelsey about this.'

'No,' said Cael. 'Please, Kyra; don't tell her.'

'I have to. What you are doing is not only callous, it is extremely dangerous. I'm sorry, Cael, but they hid the Weathervane for a good reason.'

'Wait! What if I destroy the three worlds I've created?'

'I can't believe you're saying this. You would murder the humans on World Three?'

'Their time isn't fucking aligned!'

'Are they alive, or are they not, Cael? Men, women, children? Mother can transport them all here, and then *she* can destroy your worlds.'

Kyra reached out to grab the hilt of the Tempest sword, and Cael pushed her back.

'Let me take the sword, Cael.'

'No. You have no right to do this. The Sextant is all that I have. Have you any idea how unhappy I've been? You and Cole get exactly what you want. You're allowed to spend your time at university, and Cole gets to live on the estate. What about me? I can't take it any more. I fucking hate this place, and I hate the life I've been told to lead. While you're sitting with your friends in Plateau City, I'm wading through mud and snow in Kell, or roasting my arse off in the Holdings. Did I do something to offend the Empress?'

Kyra took a step back. 'Calm down.'

'I will not. If you try to take away the one thing in life that I actually enjoy, I will never forgive you, sister.'

Kyra placed a hand into her pocket. The air shimmered, and they appeared on the middle balcony of the Summer Palace, close to a table where Cole and Arrosa were sitting. Kyra looked into Cael's eyes for a moment, then she shook her head and vanished.

'Fucking bitch!' Cael cried. He clenched his fists, looking for something to hit, then he realised that the courtiers and staff on the balcony had turned to stare at him.

Arrosa got to her feet. 'What's wrong?' she said.

'Like you give a shit,' he said.

'Sit down,' said Cole. 'Take a moment.'

Cael fell into a seat and put his head in his hands. 'I don't have a moment. Right now, my fucking sister is telling Aunty Kelsey what I've been doing.'

'What have you been doing?' said Cole.

Cael said nothing as Arrosa re-took her seat. She sipped from her tall glass of iced tea.

'Commander Cardova was looking for you,' Cole said.

'I know.'

'Are you going to tell us what you've been doing?' said Arrosa. 'We've seen less of you here than we did on the Hold Fast estate.'

'It's none of your business.'

'Are you in trouble?' she said.

'Fuck off.'

'We can help,' said Cole. 'Is there anything we can do to help?'

'There's no point in talking to him when he's like this,' said Arrosa.

'We should still try,' he said. 'Give it a go.'

Arrosa shrugged, then she put down her iced tea and turned to Cael. 'I know we've had our problems,' she said, 'but I don't hate you, Cael. I know how you feel, because I feel it, too. You're not the only one who gets moved around every season.'

'They're letting you stay at university all year,' he said.

'Yes, I know. But they've moved me around for the last two years, just like they've moved you around. And you were staying with family. I... No. I'm not going to sit here and complain. I know how lucky I am.'

'She's right,' said Cole. 'Everything that you complain about, Cael; the same thing has happened to Arrosa. The difference is that she tries to make the best of it. Is it perfect? No. Is it forever? Also no.'

Cael glanced over at the entrance to the balcony, but there was no sign of Kyra or Kelsey. A wild hope came into his mind. Perhaps Kelsey was too busy to speak to Kyra; perhaps that meant he had a little time left.

He got to his feet.

'Where are you going?' said Cole.

'For a walk,' he said.

'Can we come?' said Arrosa.

'No,' he said, then he paused. Maybe it would look less suspicious if he had Cole and Arrosa with him. 'I've changed my mind,' he went on. 'You can come, if you like.'

Cole and Arrosa finished their drinks and got to their feet.

'We should go to the gardens,' said Cole, 'or perhaps Olo'osso might take us out on the lake.'

Arrosa pulled a face. 'What, and run the risk that he and Shella get all frisky in front of us, when we're stuck in a boat with nowhere to escape to?'

Cole laughed. 'What do you suggest?'

'I have an idea,' said Cael. 'I want to show you both something.'

'What?' said Arrosa.

'It's a surprise.'

He glanced towards the balcony entrance again, and sent out a short burst of vision to ensure that the way ahead was clear. He strode into the palace, with Cole and Arrosa close behind, then they took a flight of stairs that ascended up to the private living quarters of the Empress and her closest staff.

'Where are we going?' said Arrosa. 'I haven't been up here for ages.'

'I found a secret way to the top of the tower,' said Cael. 'You can see for miles up there.'

They passed a few courtiers, who bowed or curtsied in the presence of the two Holdfast boys, then Cael opened a door that led into a grand, but empty throne room. The hall took up most of that floor of the palace, and had long curved windows that overlooked the rest of the island. Cael led Arrosa and Cole to the rear of the tall throne, and they came to a series of concealed doorways.

'That door goes up to Aunty Kelsey's personal rooms,' Cael said, pointing. 'The next one goes up to the Empress's quarters, and the third goes straight to a guard room on this floor.' He pointed to a fourth door. 'This one goes directly up, bypassing the rooms on the floor above.' He took out a key. 'Don't ask me where I got this.'

'I wouldn't dream of it,' said Arrosa.

Cael unlocked the door, and they passed through into the bottom of a stairwell. A worn old set of stone steps went up in a spiral, which was dimly lit by a few narrow openings in the outer wall of the palace. Cael led the way up, with the others following, and he started to doubt the wisdom of his actions. He had intended to hide the Sextant, but Arrosa was bound to tell Kyra and the others, even if Cole could be trusted to keep his mouth shut. They tramped up the stairs for several minutes, passing the levels where the Empress lived, until they reached a door at the top. Cael opened it, and they walked out into the attic where the Sextant lay.

Cole groaned. 'I might have guessed. Didn't you get into trouble for messing about with the Sextant last summer?'

'Ahh, so this is the Sextant?' said Arrosa.

'Have you never seen it before?' said Cole.

'I knew it was here, somewhere; but I was told that it wouldn't work without a special sword.'

'A Tempest sword,' said Cael.

'Well, a Tempest alloy,' said Arrosa. 'There needs to be some iron in the mixture. One part in ten.'

Cael pointed to the hilt of the blade that was embedded into the side of the huge device. 'Like that one.'

Cole peered at it. 'Is that the Weathervane?'

'No, it's not. The Weathervane is locked up somewhere, to stop me getting my hands on it. They underestimated my determination.'

'Well, I guess this explains what you've been doing,' said Arrosa. 'Have you been pretending to be a god?'

'I have been creating new worlds.'

'That's what I meant,' she said. 'But it must feel like being a god. You have ultimate power over an entire world; you could create any type of animal imaginable; like a giant dog, or a talking horse; or a flying, talking horse.'

Cael shook his head at her. 'I'm still trying to get the basics right. I... I have not been all that successful.'

Arrosa gazed at the Sextant. 'It's hard for me to see this, and to know that Chadura used it to make me. She really was our creator god.'

Cael laughed. 'Theodora didn't make you personally,' he said. 'She would have made your ancestors – humans that lived thousands of years ago.'

'I know,' said Arrosa. 'This device also made you.'

'And now I'm using it to make new worlds,' he said. 'Well, I was. No doubt Kyra will be telling Aunty Kelsey all about this.'

'Your sister caught you, did she?' said Cole.

Cael nodded.

'Why are you not supposed to use it?' said Arrosa.

'They think it's too dangerous,' said Cael. 'They're right, in a way. If I wanted to, I could command the Sextant to destroy Athumia, or Dragon Eyre, or even the Star Continent, and it would obey me. Within a few seconds, the world would be completely obliterated. I could also use it to transfer populations around. I could tell it to move every human from the City of Salve, and put them in Kellach Brigdomin, for example. Or, I could order the Sextant to move every dragon from Athumia, and place them at the bottom of the ocean, or inside the heart of a volcano.'

Arrosa laughed. 'That's the kind of thing I would do. Who else knows how to use it?'

'Just me, my mother, and Sable.'

'What about Bailey? He might know. It was his sister who built it, after all.'

'It's possible, I suppose,' said Cael. 'I've never met Bailey, so I don't know.'

Cole smiled. 'Listen to you two. You're talking without arguing.'

'Then why did you have to mention it?' said Arrosa.

Cael glanced away. 'You two should leave. I'm going to do something that will definitely get me into trouble.'

'Like what?' said Cole.

'If I don't tell you, then you can't be held responsible. Go back down the way we came.'

'No,' said Arrosa. 'We're in this together.'

'We are not,' said Cael.

'What do you intend to do?' said Cole. 'If it's bad, then we should probably try to stop you.'

'You wouldn't be able to stop me,' said Cael. 'If you tried, I would go into your minds and blank out your memories of this conversation. By the time you woke up, I'd be long gone.'

Arrosa narrowed her eyes. 'Would you really do that to us?'

'Aye.'

'You arsehole,' she said. 'I could tell you weren't lying. Cole and I are the closest thing you have to friends.'

Cael laughed. 'You are not my friend, Arrosa. I fucking hate you.'

Arrosa grimaced, then she smiled. '*That* was a lie. Did you hear that, Cole? He doesn't actually hate me. Take us with you, Cael. I'm already bored of Colsbury, and I'm sure Cole would enjoy going on a little trip.'

'What?' said Cole. 'No, thanks.'

'We could visit any world ever created,' said Arrosa.

'But then my mother would find us,' said Cael. 'She's linked to the Sextant. If we travel to a world that she's previously sensed, she'll know about it.'

'Bullshit,' said Arrosa.

'It's not. All she would have to do is wait for one of us to use our powers, and then it would be like an alarm bell going off in her head.'

'Then we don't use our powers.'

'What if we're attacked by a flying, talking horse?'

'What if we disable the Sextant? We could take the sword out when we arrive. '

'That makes sense. We should only need to re-activate the Sextant to get back.'

'Shut up, you two,' said Cole. 'We're going nowhere.'

'Tell me, Cole,' said Arrosa; 'are you looking forward to going back to the Hold Fast estate, knowing that Marium will be there?'

'He's not going to take us anywhere,' said Cole. 'We're going to go back downstairs, and tell Aunty Kelsey everything, before Kyra has a chance to. That's the best thing to do. Admit it, and ask for forgiveness.'

'Maybe you're right,' said Arrosa. 'Cael isn't brave enough to defy the Empress; and he certainly isn't brave enough to take us with him.'

'Don't tempt me,' Cael said.

'If you take us to one of the worlds that you've created,' she said, 'then Karalyn won't be able to find us – is that right?'

'Aye, that's right.'

'Then I'm not tempting you, Cael,' she said. 'I'm *daring* you to do it.'

'Shut up,' said Cole.

'Calm down,' said Arrosa. 'He doesn't have the balls to do it.'

'We'll fucking see about that,' said Cael. He walked up to the Sextant, and placed his right palm onto its smooth surface.

What is your desire, Cael?

'It is possible to move the Sextant, and us three standing here, to World Three?'

It is possible, once the time has been aligned.

'World Three?' said Arrosa. 'What a stupid name. Have you no imagination?'

'What would you call it – Arrosa-land?'

'That would be better than World Three.'

Cael turned back to the Sextant. 'Align the time on World Three. Do it now.'

The time has been aligned.

'The joke's over, guys,' said Cole. 'Let's go back downstairs.'

'We can't,' said Cael. 'Arrosa dared me to do it. I'm not backing down.'

Arrosa smiled. 'Maybe you do possess a backbone.'

He gazed down at her face for a moment, unsure whether he would rather slap her or kiss her. *Kiss her?* What was he thinking? Arrosa was the most annoying girl he had ever known. Why would he ever want to kiss her? He shuddered.

'He's getting cold feet,' said Arrosa.

'Thank Pyre for that,' said Cole. 'Can we go now?'

'Aye,' said Cael. 'You're right. Let's go.'

He closed his eyes. *Transport me, Arrosa, Cole and the Sextant to the river plain upon World Three. Do it now.*

The air in the palace attic crackled and spat. Arrosa shrieked, then they fell through the air under the light of a ferociously-hot sun. They landed in a vast marshland. Cole fell headfirst into one of the many water channels, then Arrosa and Cael struck the mud of a huge swamp. Next to them, the great bulk of the Sextant began to sink into the thick mire.

'Help!' Arrosa cried, as she began to sink into the sea of mud.

Cael ignored her, and crawled towards the Sextant. He reached it just before it disappeared, and forced his hand down onto its surface.

What is your desire, Cael?

'Transport us to higher ground,' he yelled. He glanced around. 'That hillock, to my left. Do it now!'

The air crackled again, then he, Arrosa, Cole, and the Sextant appeared on the grassy brow of the small slope. Cole got to his knees, and vomited up water onto the dry ground. Arrosa groaned, her clothes and skin smeared with dark mud. Cael gasped in relief, and leaned back against the reassuring solidity of the Sextant.

Arrosa started to laugh. 'That was fun.'

'Are you out of your mind?' said Cole. 'Why did you have to dare him?'

'It's done,' said Cael; 'we're here. Welcome to World Three.'

CHAPTER 10
TAKING THE BLAME

Colsbury Castle, the Holdings – 8th Day, First Third Summer 544

Kyra yawned and stretched her arms. Sunlight was entering her bedroom through the narrow slits in her shutters, and she could already feel its warmth. It was going to be another hot summer's day in Colsbury, and she was looking forward to what had become her favourite new ritual – breakfast with the Empress on the upper balcony. She got out of bed, and walked into her private bathroom. She washed, then she returned to the bedroom and got dressed, picking a dark red dress. It had an inside pocket sewn into the folds of its skirt that was large enough to hide her Quadrant. She daydreamed for a while as she brushed her hair, wondering if she would ever be in a position to choose her own personal colour to wear, just as the Empress had long before selected blue. It was a conceit, but Kyra didn't care. The problem was that there weren't many other suitable colours to pick. Black would be too oppressive and sombre, pink too frivolous for an Empress, red too suggestive of blood, yellow too relentlessly cheerful, and white too innocent. That left green, purple, orange and brown, but none of them particularly appealed to her.

The bedroom door opened, and Kyra bit back a frown.

'Good morning, Mother,' she said. 'Don't you ever knock?'

'Where's your brother?' she said.

'How should I know? We haven't shared a room since we were ten.'

'Have you seen Arrosa?'

'Why don't you check under the bed?' Kyra said. 'She might be hiding there.'

'I don't have time for this nonsense,' said Karalyn. 'I need to speak to them both, and I can't find either of them.'

'Well, they may have murdered each other, I suppose.'

Karalyn frowned at her. 'Do you have any objections to my plan?'

'What plan?'

'My plan to adopt Arrosa into the family. She would become your sister.'

'Why would I object to that?'

'Cael objected.'

'I am not Cael. My only surprise is that you didn't do it years ago.'

'I wanted to wait until she was old enough to truly understand the implications,' said Karalyn. 'Becoming a Holdfast brings its own problems. They might treat her differently at university, for example.'

'Aye, I can vouch for that.'

'So you haven't seen them?'

'I have just got out of bed.'

'What about yesterday?'

'I saw them both on the middle balcony yesterday afternoon. They were with Cole.'

'I can't find Cole, either.'

Kyra narrowed her eyes.

'Cael was supposed to meet Lucius and me for dinner last night,' her mother said, 'but he didn't turn up. I was angry but, against my better judgement, Lucius persuaded me not to look for him. When you saw him yesterday, what kind of mood was he in?'

'Let me finish putting my make up on, and I'll help you look for him.'

'I notice you didn't answer my question.'

'He was in a terrible mood,' said Kyra.

'You don't need to put any make up on. You're only seventeen. Who are you trying to impress?'

'Go away, Mother.'

'Ah, so you do remember who I am? Sometimes, I think you forget.'

'I will help you when I am ready. Go away.'

Karalyn glared at her daughter for a moment, then she walked out of the bedroom. Kyra turned back to the mirror, the tranquillity of her morning already soured. She thought back to her conversation with Cael on the previous afternoon. She had given him a good scare by threatening to tell Kelsey about his use of the Sextant, but she hadn't followed through on her promise. Cael just needed some time to reflect upon his actions; he would calm down once he realised that she hadn't told anyone about what she had seen, and then he might be willing to compromise. She wondered where he had gone, but she didn't worry. If Cole and Arrosa were with him, then they would stop him from doing anything too reckless or stupid.

She applied less make up than usual, and walked out of her quarters. Four courtiers bowed low.

'How may we assist you today, ma'am?' said one.

'Perhaps you could look for my brother,' Kyra said.

'The isle of Colsbury has already been thoroughly searched, ma'am,' said the courtier. 'Cael Holdfast was not to be found.'

'Who requested the search?'

'Your noble mother, ma'am. She has had soldiers and courtiers out looking from dawn this morning. The search has moved to the mainland, as far as I am aware.'

'What about Cole and Arrosa?'

'They are also missing, ma'am.'

'None of them are on the island?'

'That is correct, ma'am.'

'Are any Quadrants missing?'

'All Quadrants are accounted for, ma'am. Do you have yours in your possession?'

Kyra tapped her dress. 'Aye. I have mine.' A dire thought occurred to her. 'I think I might have forgotten something,' she said, then she walked back into her bedroom.

A sickly feeling of panic began to arise in the pit of her stomach. She lowered her hand, and pushed a finger through the tiny hole in the folds of her dress that gave access to her Quadrant.

Attic. Go.

The air shimmered, and she appeared in the attic above the Empress's quarters. The space where the Sextant had lain was empty.

'Shit,' she muttered. 'Oh Cael, what have you done?'

Twenty minutes later, Kyra was sitting in a small meeting room with the Empress, her mother, Kelsey, Naxor and Cardova.

'I can't believe I am hearing this,' cried her mother. 'You knew what he was doing, and you didn't tell anyone?'

'I realise now that I made a mistake,' said Kyra. 'I'm sorry. I didn't think he would run away with the Sextant.'

'You told him that you were going to tell me?' said Kelsey.

'Aye.'

'Then why didn't you?'

'I didn't want him to get into trouble,' she said. 'I was trying to scare him. I was going to speak to him about it today.'

'Pyre's arse,' said Kelsey. 'Karalyn, are you not linked to the Sextant? Can you tell where it is?'

'I will need time to search,' Karalyn said. 'He could be on any of the worlds created by the Sextant, or he might be just a few miles away. This could be an elaborate hoax. He could be sitting on the Hold Fast estate with Cole and Arrosa drinking iced tea.'

'How easy will it be to find them?' said the Empress.

'That depends,' said Karalyn. 'If they are together, and any one of them uses their powers, then I will be able to locate them a lot quicker. But, Cael knows this, and if he doesn't want to be found, he will have told the others not to use any of their abilities.'

'We should assume that they are together,' said Cardova. 'Witnesses saw the three of them leaving the middle balcony in each other's company, then other witnesses saw them walking towards the upper throne room. The stairs in the back of that chamber lead up to the attic.'

'That door was locked,' said Kelsey.

'If Cael could steal a Tempest sword,' said Karalyn, 'then stealing a key wouldn't have caused him any difficulties. I'd better begin the search. Wherever he is, I'll find him.'

Naxor raised his palms. 'Are you absolutely sure about that, Karalyn? I have some experience of deception, and if I were Cael, and I wished to both steal the Sextant, and to remain undiscovered, I would have examined every possibility. Is there anywhere he could hide that is beyond your sight?'

'No,' said Karalyn. 'I haven't been directly connected to the Sextant for several years, but I became aware of every world it had created.'

'What if he removes the Tempest sword from the device?'

'He has already removed it from the device,' said Karalyn. 'I could sense that when I first heard what had happened. However, I no longer need the Sextant to be active to detect the other worlds. I learned that lesson after my first, accidental trip to Athumia.'

'And if he doesn't use his powers?'

'Then it will take longer, but I will still be able to manage it.'

'Naxor might be right,' said Kyra. 'Cael has created three new worlds. What if he's gone to one of them?'

Karalyn fell silent.

'Would you be able to sense him upon a world that was not in existence when you last connected to the Sextant?' said the Empress.

Karalyn raised a hand to her face.

'I think that's your answer, Your Majesty,' said Kelsey.

'This is all my fault,' said Kyra.

'Aye,' said Karalyn. 'It is.'

'Let us not rush too swiftly to judgement,' said the Empress. 'Not one of us sitting here has led a life free of mistakes; and I deem it more important to learn lessons, rather than to apportion blame.'

Karalyn stared at the Empress, then she walked from the room.

'I'd better go, too, Your Majesty,' said Cardova. 'I will look after Carden and Caitlyn while Karalyn begins her search. I will keep you posted of any developments.'

'Thank you, Lucius,' said the Empress.

Cardova bowed, then he followed his wife out of the chamber.

The Empress turned to Naxor. 'What is the worst scenario we are facing?'

'The worst, Your Majesty?' said Naxor. 'That would be if the Sextant falls into the hands of our enemies. Lord Elmhirst and some of the other surviving Ancients may possess the ability to activate the Sextant. If that occurs, they would be able to annihilate the entire Star Continent.'

The Empress nodded. 'Herald, pay a visit to Lord Bailey upon Athumia, and ask him if he knows of any Ancients with the power to use the Sextant. I would rather he did not learn the reason for this question, however.'

'Understood, Your Majesty,' said Kelsey. 'I am scheduled to visit Zamata in a few days; I will ask him then.'

'Naxor,' said the Empress, 'I want you to spread the story that Cael, Arrosa and Cole have decided to return to the Hold Fast estate. Reassure the courtiers, staff and soldiers that nothing is wrong. If you hear any rumours regarding the Sextant, quash them. It is not beyond the realms of possibility that spies from the Doomed Worlds are at large upon the Star Continent, and it is imperative that they do not learn of our current misfortune.'

Naxor bowed low. 'I shall take care of it, Your Majesty.'

Kelsey and Naxor walked out of the room and closed the door, leaving only Kyra and the Empress remaining.

'What do you think you will learn from this, Kyra?' said the Empress.

'That I should always follow through on my threats, Your Majesty?'

'Perhaps. In this case, however, it might have been better not to have made any threats at all. If you had merely nodded along with what Cael was doing, then he would not have suspected your true feelings. That would have given you time to tell me or Kelsey without him panicking.'

'Do you think I should have lied to my own brother, Your Majesty?'

'You did lie to him, Kyra. You told him that you were going to inform Kelsey, when you had no intention of doing so. You were trying to scare him, when mollifying him would have resulted in a more successful outcome. I love your brother, but he has become a little distant over the last few years. I judge that his mistake will prove to be far greater than yours.'

'You must think I'm such an idiot, Your Majesty.'

'Of course not. Kelsey and I decided years ago that we would give the children plenty of space to make their own mistakes. Now that you and Cael, along with Arrosa and Cole, have indeed made mistakes, it would be churlish of me to complain about it. Tell me; why do you think Cole and Arrosa are a part of this? Did they choose to go, or is there a chance that Cael took them against their will?'

'I don't know either of them that well. Cole seemed to be unhappy about his girlfriend on the estate. She was cheating on him, or so I believe. Therefore, he might have gone willingly, if only to avoid the prospect of seeing her again. Arrosa is more difficult to judge. Does she hate Cael, or is there something else going on? I should have read her mind, but it didn't occur to me.'

'Cael and Arrosa fight like lovers.'

Kyra's eyes widened. 'Excuse me, your Majesty?'

'It is merely an observation,' said the Empress. 'They argue with passion, as if no one else is watching; as if no one else exists. Has that thought never crossed your mind?'

'I hadn't seen Cael or Arrosa since the end of autumn last year, Your Majesty. I suppose that the intensity of their arguments has increased since then. But passion? No. I cannot believe it. Well, I could believe that Arrosa likes Cael; but the other way around? He's hated her for years.'

'Let us return to our present problem,' said the Empress. 'Let us imagine that your suspicions are correct, and that Cael has taken the

Sextant, along with Arrosa and Cole, to one of the worlds he has created. It is possible, of course, that they could return at any moment. But if they don't, and if Karalyn is unable to locate them, then what options do we have?'

'If we don't have the Sextant, then we might never find them, Your Majesty.'

'That is unacceptable. I refuse to countenance the idea that Cael, Cole and Arrosa are lost to us forever. Is there any other way the Sextant could be found?'

'If there were, the Ascendants would have found it on Lostwell long before Uncle Corthie did.'

'The Ascendants did not know that the Weathervane was required to activate the Sextant,' said the Empress. 'Belinda was able to carry it without them suspecting a thing. Therefore, one might conclude that the Ascendants did not know all there is to know about the Sextant.'

'With the exception of Nathaniel, Theodora and Simon, Your Majesty?'

'That's right. Only three Ascendants understood much about the Sextant; the others appear to have been ignorant. It would seem safe to deduce that this is the reason they were unable to locate it upon Lostwell. Furthermore, we have an advantage the Ascendants lacked – access to Tempest. We also have Professor Elbannon, an acclaimed expert on Tempest. Do you see where I am leading?'

'We could use Tempest to create something; something that could find the Sextant?'

'I have no idea if it's possible, of course.'

'But it's worth investigating, Your Majesty.'

'Indeed. Kyra, would you be offended if I asked you to keep this discussion private for now? There is a reason I waited until we were alone before bringing it up. Do not tell anyone about our little plan, not even your mother.'

Kyra frowned. 'Why not, Your Majesty?'

'Because, if we are successful, this new device might be exceedingly dangerous, were it to fall into the wrong hands. We do not understand the extent of its implications. It may share some features with the Sextant itself, including its destructive capability. Professor Elbannon is an exception to this rule, of course; you will have to speak to him regarding it. Are you willing to take on this task for me?'

'Aye, Your Majesty. Thank you for placing your trust in me.'

Thorn smiled. 'I happen to know that Professor Elbannon spends his summers with Professor Gallea in a little Rakanese fishing village called Alatsuraga Bay. It lies on the shores of the Inner Sea, some forty miles to the south-east of Amatskouri. If you look into my mind, you will see its location.'

Kyra pushed her powers into the mind of the Empress, and garnered the position of the village from her thoughts.

'Should I go now, Your Majesty?' she said.

'That would be wise, I think. Pack for a short stay, and ask Naxor for five thousand gold sovereigns before you go. Travelling expenses.'

Kyra got to her feet and curtsied. 'Thank you, Your Majesty.'

She walked out of the room, and hurried down one flight of stairs to her quarters. On the way, it occurred to her that the Empress had chosen her partly because it had been her fault in the first place. She was being given a chance to redeem herself; and to show her mother that she was more than capable of fixing her mistakes. At that moment, Kyra loved the Empress more than ever. She had understood how painful it had been to hear Karalyn agree that her daughter was at fault, and so she had given her the opportunity to make up for it.

She packed a bag, then she changed into more informal clothes for travelling. While she was doing so, she sent out her powers and summoned Naxor to her quarters, telling him to bring the gold. Ten minutes later, as Kyra was tying her hair back, Naxor knocked at the door.

'It's open,' she said.

Naxor strode in, a large leather pouch in his right hand.

'Leave it on the table,' she said.

'Certainly, Miss Holdfast,' said Naxor. He smiled. 'Are you also running away?'

'I know that you've spoken to the Empress, Naxor.'

'I felt I should, if only to confirm that Her Majesty was willing to part with five thousand gold sovereigns. It is her money, after all. I am merely its custodian.'

'I'm not going to tell you where I'm going.'

'Can I guess?'

She smiled, as she began lacing up her boots. 'You can try.'

'Let's see. You wish to buy a ship? Can you sail?'

She laughed. 'No.'

'You wish to purchase salve? There is a god with whom you have fallen hopelessly in love, but he is looking a little haggard, and you wish to restore the beauty of his youth?'

'That's right, Naxor! However did you guess?'

'I sense you mock me.'

'You make it too easy.'

'I do. Did you know that I have divided the Holdfasts into two groups?'

'The ones you have mortally offended, and those you have yet to offend?'

'I fear there are very few left in the latter category. My division is based on ruthlessness. There are those who possess the calm determination to do what has to be done, no matter the damage to their reputations; and there are those who lack this quality. Empress Thorn, for example, is most definitely in the first category; whereas, your noble mother falls into the second. I am, naturally, drawn to those who share my own sense of ruthlessness.'

'And where do I fit into this scheme?'

'I thought you'd never ask. Cole is certainly in the second group, while I sense Arrosa and Cael are inching towards the first, but we shall have to wait and see. You, I am undecided on. Sometimes, I think you are sailing towards the Empress's group, while on other occasions I sense the hesitation and squeamishness of your mother about you.'

'My mother has killed hundreds of thousands of people.'

'That is true, but she has acted in that manner only in moments of extreme duress. If some villain were to murder her young children, for instance, then I firmly believe we would see the vengeful Karalyn make her appearance again. The Empress, on the other hand, is capable of commissioning acts of great violence while enjoying her morning cup of tea.'

Kyra waved him away. 'You're talking nonsense.'

Naxor smiled. 'I am sure you are right, Miss Holdfast. Have a wonderful day.'

Kyra narrowed her eyes as Naxor strode away. She knew all the stories about him, but she also knew how useful he was to the Empress. Had he been toying with her? Or was there a hidden meaning to his words?

She placed her Quadrant into the inside pocket of her travelling coat, and touched her finger against its surface.

Alatsuraga Bay. Go.

The air shimmered, and she appeared in a village by the shores of the Inner Sea. Several fishing boats had been dragged up onto a nearby beach, and small groups of Rakanese fishermen and women were sitting repairing nets out in the sunshine next to a row of boat sheds, all of which had seen better days. A few had noticed Kyra's appearance, and they quietened as she approached.

'We don't get many Kellach down here,' said one. 'Can we help you?'

'I'm looking for the two old professors,' she said. 'You know, the ones from the university? I'm a student.'

'They'll be in the cafeteria at this time of the day,' said another, 'drinking coffee, eating breakfast, and telling tall tales. Head into the village and take a left at the crossroads.'

'Thank you.'

Kyra walked along the paved track, between houses painted in various pale shades of blue, green and pink. She saw the cafeteria by the left of the crossroads, and entered, the door catching a bell, which alerted the serving staff to her presence.

'Are you looking for a table, miss?' said a waitress.

'I'm actually looking for the two professors,' she said.

'May curses rain down upon us!' cried a voice. 'Gallea, we have been discovered. Nowhere is safe from the blasted students, I tell you – nowhere!'

Kyra turned, and saw Gallea laughing, as Elbannon shook his fist at the sky. They were seated at a corner table, their table covered in a great variety of dishes containing bread, olives and seafood, and a tall pot of coffee sat in the centre.

'Have a seat, Kyra,' said Gallea. 'Coffee?'

'Yes, please,' said Kyra.

She sat down opposite the two old professors as Gallea filled a cup with coffee.

'Now,' said Gallea, 'as only one or two people in the entire Empire happen to know where Elbannon and I spend each summer, I must assume that you are here on official business?'

'Official, and secret,' said Kyra.

'They want us to work,' muttered Elbannon. 'We've been here for eight days, and already they have found work for us to do.'

'I'm afraid so,' said Kyra, 'though it's Tempest related, so the work is for you, Elbannon.'

'Has some fool broken their Quadrant?' he said. 'Well, you can tell whoever it is that they'll have to wait. I am not an on-call Quadrant repairman.'

'You must promise not to react when I tell you the next thing,' Kyra said. 'And by react, I mean, no shouting, gesticulating, cursing or otherwise drawing attention to yourself. Something dreadfully unfortunate has happened.'

'Then you will need to give me a moment to compose myself,' said Elbannon. 'I am still suffering from the shock of seeing you walk through that door, Miss Holdfast.'

'I hope no one has died,' said Gallea.

'It's not that,' said Kyra. 'The Sextant has been stolen.'

Elbannon spat out his coffee, spraying a section of the table, then he started to cough and wheeze.

Kyra frowned.

'I don't think that's what Kyra meant by not drawing attention to yourself,' said Gallea. She turned to Kyra. 'I thought your mother had the ability to locate the Sextant?'

'Under normal circumstances, she does,' said Kyra. 'However, in this case, we believe that the Sextant has been taken to a newly-created world; one beyond my mother's abilities.'

Elbannon wiped his chin with a napkin. 'This is dreadful news, but what does it have to do with me?'

'The Sextant contains a great amount of Tempest, does it not?'

'Of course, yes.'

'Is there any possible way to detect that source of Tempest from a distance?'

'No, there isn't. You would need a Sextant to track down a Sextant.'

'Then, can you build a Sextant that could do this?'

Elbannon started to laugh. He slapped his thigh, then he began to rock back and forth in his chair, as Kyra and Gallea watched.

'It wouldn't have to do anything other than find our Sextant,' Kyra went on. 'It doesn't need to create worlds, or anything like that.'

'Oh, that's a relief,' he said, still laughing. 'It doesn't have to create worlds, eh? Just all the other stuff that it took Theodora centuries to invent.'

'You don't know how long it took her to make it. You can have unlimited money, and unlimited Tempest.'

'Unlimited money?' he said. 'In that case, I accept. It will take me at least ten years, and I'll need to live in a palace with a hundred extremely attractive concubines to cater to my needs.'

'I don't think you're taking this very seriously,' said Gallea.

'I am giving her request the level of seriousness it deserves.'

'So you cannot do it?' said Kyra. 'You cannot build a tracking device? That's all you had to say.'

'Frankly, girl, I have no idea if it could be done,' he said. 'Why would I have ever thought to aim my experiments in this direction? I have never needed to *track* Tempest. And how would I possibly test any such device? Imagine that I created something that looked similar to a compass. Let's say that you had some Tempest hidden in your bag. You would expect the needle to point in that direction, yes? So far, so good. But what if the Tempest is on another world? Which way should the needle point?'

'I have abilities, too, when it comes to Tempest,' she said. 'It talks to me, just as it talks to my mother. Do you know how I got here? I touched the Quadrant in my inside pocket, and said *Alatsuraga Bay. Go.* That's it. That's all I did. If you make the compass, and I am able to speak to it, it would tell me where the Sextant is located.'

Elbannon shrugged. 'In theory. But we have no proof that Tempest is remotely traceable.'

Gallea smiled. 'Come now, my old friend; does this project not spark a little professional curiosity within you?'

'I have already achieved my life's dream by constructing a working Quadrant,' he said. 'All else is vanity.'

'Vanity, and five thousand gold sovereigns,' said Kyra; 'along with the undying respect and gratitude of the Empire. We do very much want to get our Sextant back.'

'Who stole it, if I might ask?' said Gallea.

'I cannot tell you that,' said Kyra. 'I have already told you everything that I'm allowed to say. Moreover, you would not be allowed to speak about any aspect of this work to anyone until imperial permission is granted. At this stage, we cannot allow the gods of the Doomed Worlds to know what has occurred.'

'Then one must assume that they were not behind the theft,' said Elbannon. 'Was it Bailey?'

'No. It wasn't Bailey.'

Elbannon sighed. 'Give me some time to think it over,' he said. 'I will ponder the possibilities. You may leave us now, Holdfast girl. Come back in a few days, and, if I accept, I will present you with a list of my requirements.'

'She brought a bag with her,' said Gallea. 'I think she was hoping to stay with us for a day or so.'

'Am I supposed to care?' he said. 'I shall need peace and quiet to think, and I cannot do that if a Holdfast is looking over my shoulder.'

Kyra got to her feet. 'I will come back to see you both in a few days,' she said. 'Now, watch carefully, Professor Elbannon.'

She smiled at him, and placed a fingertip against the surface of the Quadrant.

My room, Colsbury. Go.

CHAPTER 11
THE HIDDEN COST

Colsbury Castle, the Holdings – 20th Day, First Third Summer 544

'Once the business with Emily and Daniel is over, Your Majesty,' said Kelsey, 'Van wants to go back to the City with them for a few thirds.'

'To do his job, presumably?' said the Empress.

'Aye. He doesn't seem to understand that his job amounts to keeping greenhides away from a single wall, while I... Well, I don't want to boast, but you know the work I do for the Empire, Your Majesty.'

'I am perfectly aware of the work you do, Herald. We are a team, you and I, and if I haven't already thanked you today for what you do for me, then I do so now. As for Van, what else can you do but let him go to the City, if that is what he desires?'

'But he wants to take the children with him,' Kelsey said.

'I see. I assume that you are opposed to this?'

'Aye. Most definitely. But if I insist that he leaves the children here, then I'd have to find someone to look after them. Van's arguing that, because his job only takes up a few hours each day, he'd be able to look after them far better than I would. And, do you know what – the bastard's right. If Calpurnia and Caelius stay here with me, I'd barely see them.'

'This is my fault,' said the Empress. 'Because you are so competent in your post, I pile responsibility after responsibility upon your shoulders. I will of course pay for anything you require – nannies, accommodation, servants; but I cannot give you a leave of absence, not at present. There are too many difficult decisions that lie ahead, and too much to do.'

'I know, Your Majesty. I wasn't going to ask for any leave; I just needed someone to talk to.'

'I am always here for that, Kelsey. You are my closest and dearest friend.'

'Do you know what scares me?' she said. 'One day, Van might decide that he's had enough, and he gives me an ultimatum – to choose between him and my job. I would choose being the Herald, and he knows it. I love Van, but my job is more important than my marriage. It breaks my heart to say it, but it's true.'

The air shimmered in the corner of the room, and Kyra appeared.

Thorn smiled. 'Welcome back,' she said. 'Does Professor Elbannon have any progress to report?'

Kyra curtsied. 'I'm afraid not, Your Majesty,' she said. 'He still doesn't know if it's possible to track Tempest. He's been consulting his old books from Tell Hoard, searching for any mention of the subject, but with no luck so far. The good news is that he has begun practical experiments. I helped him set up a small laboratory in an out-building next to the house where he and Professor Gallea are staying, and I have equipped it according to his specifications.'

Kelsey narrowed her eyes. 'Twelve days, and he's only just getting round to setting up a laboratory? It would have been better if he'd gone back to the university.'

'He is refusing to leave Alatsuraga Bay, Aunty. He knows that I don't possess the authority to order him back to Plateau City.'

Kelsey glanced at the Empress. 'Should I go?'

'Leave him where he is for the moment,' said the Empress. 'He will only dig his heels in if we force him back to the city. We need him to remain willing and eager to carry out his task.'

'He is both of those things, Your Majesty,' said Kyra. 'The prospect of inventing a compass intrigues him.'

'Is that what we're calling it?' said Kelsey.

'It's Professor Elbannon's term, Aunty,' said Kyra. 'Instead of pointing north, it will point towards the presence of Tempest, if it works. It remains conjecture at this point.'

'With Karalyn unable to locate either the children or the Sextant, the Compass is our best hope of finding them,' said the Empress. 'Unless, of course, they decide to come home of their own accord.'

'There's every chance of that, Your Majesty,' said Kelsey. 'We might just have to wait until they're bored, or they run out of food. At least the Sextant is out of the reach of the gods of the Doomed Worlds. If we can't find it, they'll have no chance.'

'Let us hope they remain unaware that we have misplaced it,' said the Empress.

'Alatsuraga Bay seems a little vulnerable, Your Majesty,' said Kyra. 'A few fisher folk would not be able to protect the professors if our enemies discovered their presence there.'

The Empress smiled. 'I am glad you believe that, Kyra, for it means that the professors likely consider it to be the case. The truth, however, is that Alatsuraga Bay is surrounded, at a discreet distance, by elite forces from the Imperial Marines. The majority of those humble fisher folk you mentioned are in fact imperial agents and soldiers, there to protect Elbannon. I did not want to risk such an important asset, but I also wished to grant him the illusion of a peaceful place to spend his summers with Gallea.'

Kyra frowned. 'But... no one in the village has ever mentioned this fact to me.'

'They have been instructed to maintain the act when visitors arrive,' said Kelsey. 'Did anyone bat an eye when you arrived by Quadrant?'

'Eh... no. They acted as though it was normal.'

'They know who you are,' Kelsey went on. 'Had you been a stranger to them, they would have detained you.'

'I feel a little embarrassed,' said Kyra. 'I have been speaking to the villagers as though they were... real villagers. What happens to the village each autumn and winter?'

'The soldiers are sent back to barracks,' said Kelsey. 'They return to Alatsuraga Bay in the middle of spring, to get the place ready for the arrival of the professors.' She laughed. 'For the first couple of years, they were too efficient. They re-painted every house, paved the road, repaired the fishing fleet, and started work on a new jetty. We had to tell them to scale it back. The village is supposed to look slightly dilapidated; it's part of the illusion.'

'It is an illusion that must be maintained, Kyra,' said the Empress. 'Do not reveal the truth to either professor. It is important to me that they enjoy their summers.'

'I will not utter a word to them regarding this, Your Majesty.'

Kelsey glanced out of a window. 'It's time,' she said. 'Any moment now...'

Someone knocked on the door.

'Your timing is impeccable, Herald,' said the Empress. 'Enter.'

Naxor strode into the room and bowed. 'I have brought the King and Queen of the City to Colsbury, Your Imperial Majesty. Shall I show them into your presence?'

'Please do,' said Thorn.

Naxor retired from the chamber, then he returned a few moments later with King Daniel, Queen Emily, and two courtiers from the City.

The monarchs of the City tilted their heads slightly.

'Good morning, Your Majesties,' said the Empress. 'How lovely it is to see you again.'

'And you, Your Majesty,' said Daniel.

'How are your children?'

'They are both well, Your Majesty,' said Emily.

'Excellent. Shall we move ourselves out on to the upper balcony? An early lunch has been prepared for us, and we can discuss business while we eat.'

'That would be delightful, Your Majesty,' said Daniel.

'Should I come?' said Kyra.

'Most certainly,' said the Empress.

Thorn stepped down from her throne, and then Naxor led the way out through a doorway. They ascended a flight of stairs, and emerged out on to the Empress's private balcony, where a table had been set out with food and drink. Naxor pulled out a chair for the Empress, and she sat at the head of the table. Naxor did the same for Queen Emily, and she sat to Thorn's left, while Kelsey and Kyra took their places to the right of the Empress. Daniel and Naxor also sat, and a few courtiers opened a bottle of wine and uncovered the selection of dishes.

They ate for a few minutes, then Daniel gestured to one of his courtiers.

'We have the annual report ready for your inspection, Your Majesty,' the King said.

'Please give it to Lord Naxor,' said the Empress.

Daniel nodded to the courtier, who pulled a large envelope from his robes and handed it over to Naxor. The demigod broke the royal seal, withdrew a sheaf of documents, and began to read.

'How are the dragons faring in Jezra this year?' said Kelsey.

'They destroyed another small greenhide nest a few days ago,' said Emily. 'We think that means that the last of the greenhide queens on the Western Bank has been killed. Work is continuing on the town's permanent defences without any interruptions. Altogether, it has been a resounding success, and we owe our thanks to Queen Blackrose for providing so many volunteers over the years.'

'We also owe many thanks to the Empire, of course,' said Daniel. 'The City is recovering well from the losses we sustained during the crisis years.'

'I am very pleased to hear that,' said the Empress. 'Before we move on to the re-negotiation of our existing obligations, I wanted to ask about the status of the various immortals dwelling within the City.'

'Lady Jade is still dwelling out by the salve mine, Your Majesty,' said Emily, 'while Maxwell has reached his tenth year and is attending school in Pella. It remains too early to tell if he will develop the same death powers as his mother possessed.'

'Is he aware of his parentage?'

'He is. Kagan has told him all about his mother. Well, he told him the parts he wanted the boy to know – that Amalia was the founder of the City, and that she gave up her life to save her friend. The next few years may be more difficult for Maxwell, as the other students at the school know who he is. It is likely that his fellow students will inform him about some of the less reputable actions of his mother. If his situation becomes desperately unhappy, would the Empire be prepared to offer him an education upon the Star Continent?'

'Of course,' said Kelsey. 'Just let us know, and we will relocate the boy and his father to Plateau City.'

'Thank you, Kelsey,' said Emily. 'Lady Lydia has offered to house the boy in Port Sanders, but we feel that it might be better to remove him from the City entirely, especially if he turns out to have death powers.'

'And how is Lady Lydia?' said the Empress.

'The same as ever,' said Emily. 'Lady Doria is still living with her in Tonetti Palace.'

'And the... other one? The one whose name we do not mention?'

'He remains blissfully unaware of his true heritage, Your Majesty,' said Daniel. 'We found him a job in Jezra, and are keeping a close eye on him.'

'He's completely harmless,' said Kyra. 'His memories have gone forever, and only my mother, brother or I would be able to restore his powers.'

'He's met someone,' said Emily. 'A young Reaper woman. They started a relationship a few months ago.'

'Ah,' said the Empress. 'I feared this would happen. Why has it taken so long?'

'He spent several years unable to read or write, and behaving immaturely,' said Daniel, 'and he has only become what I would call socially well-adjusted in the last year or so.'

'Do we know if his powers will pass on to any children he may father? Kyra, what is your opinion on this?'

'I would have to go into his mind to be sure,' said Kyra, 'but I deem it highly likely that his powers, though blocked, would pass on to his children.'

'I sometimes wish Karalyn had executed him,' said the Empress, 'but she didn't, and now he is blameless. All the same, it would seem imprudent, not to say negligent, to allow him to father a large brood of children. The first time one of them exhibited self-healing powers, his true nature would be revealed to him. Has he shown any curiosity about his past?'

'Not for a while, Your Majesty,' said Emily. 'He has accepted the story that we prepared for him; that he is a Roser who lost his memories while fighting the Ascendants. He is also aging very slowly, even though his self-healing abilities have been blocked. We suspect that this is due to the salve he consumed in his previous life.'

'Let us know at once if the Reaper girl becomes pregnant,' said the Empress.

'We shall,' said Daniel.

The Empress glanced at Naxor. 'Are you still reading that report?'

'I have almost finished, Your Majesty,' said Naxor. 'I read slower when I am listening at the same time.'

'Have you drawn any conclusions?'

'The finances of the City appear to be in order, Your Majesty,' he said.

'Are we ready to discuss the renewal of the treaty, Your Majesty?' said Daniel. 'For our part, we would be satisfied if the terms were to continue as they are for another year.'

The Empress smiled. 'Would you say that the aid granted by the Empire to the City over the last ten years has been beneficial?'

'Of course,' said Emily. 'More than beneficial, and we are extremely grateful. Ten years ago, the City was ravaged by war and famine, Jezra was almost unsustainable, our town centres were in ruins, and our infrastructure was falling to pieces. You have been a most gracious and generous ally, Your Majesty.'

'Your kind words please me,' said Thorn. 'It is now my duty to announce that the aid we have been sending to the City is to discontinue.'

Emily and Daniel stared at the Empress, their mouths slightly open.

'It shall not cease all at once,' the Empress went on. 'Instead, it shall be reduced by a quarter every year. This year, you shall receive three-quarters of the entire sum; next year a half, then a quarter, and in the year following that, you shall receive nothing. We are happy that we have been able to get the City back onto its feet, and we look forward to a long and prosperous relationship between our two sovereign nations.'

Emily and Daniel continued to sit in silence.

'Our defensive alliance is, naturally, unaffected by this,' the Empress said. She waited for a moment, but neither of the monarchs from the City spoke. 'Come now,' she went on; 'you didn't expect that this one-sided bargain would continue indefinitely, did you? If you like, I can have Naxor recite from memory all of the aid, item by item, that we have supplied to the City over the last decade, free of charge, and with no questions asked. We are friends, and we acted as any friend should to help others in their time of need.'

'But, Your Majesty,' said Daniel, 'there are several long-term building projects underway in the City that depend upon the aid we receive from the Empire. There is a huge project to refurbish the sewer network under Pella, for example, that remains unfinished.'

'That is a domestic issue,' said the Empress. 'The City is an independent, sovereign nation. I would not presume to bore you with details of the Empire's domestic programme.'

Daniel's eyes flashed with anger. 'Did you know about this, Naxor? Did you bring us here in the full knowledge that we were about to be ambushed?'

Naxor's shoulders shrugged. 'I am the Chamberlain of the Empire, King Daniel Aurelian. My allegiance is to the Empress.'

'We should consider our words carefully,' said Kelsey. 'This is not an *ambush*. We are all friends here. Think of it this way – the Empire has a responsibility to serve its own people, before it serves the citizens of a foreign nation. The City is our ally and friend, but it is also a sovereign, independent, and aye, foreign state. Reapers, Evaders and the rest are not citizens of the Empire; they are subjects of the City. Your subjects, Daniel. For ten years, we have been supplying one tenth of our entire budget to the needs of a foreign people. We did this gladly, because you are our friends. Thanks to our generosity, some of our own citizens are now poorer than the people who dwell in the City. Is that fair? Don't the citizens of the Empire deserve to be treated with the same dignity as the subjects of the City?'

'I can barely believe you are saying this, Kelsey,' said Daniel. 'You, who lived in the City for years. You were one of us, were you not? How soon you forget.'

'Please do not insult my Herald,' said the Empress. 'Kelsey has suffered over this change in policy more than anyone else in the Imperial Court. She dearly loves the City, but she also understands that the duty of the Empire is to its own citizens. How could it be otherwise? What nation, state, realm or empire could survive if it neglected its own people? We shall not be squandering the money we stop sending to the City – we shall be using it to invest in the poorer regions of the Empire, regions we have recently neglected because of our policy to favour the City. You have done very well out of this arrangement, and I am not going to apologise for our change of stance.'

'I remain grateful for everything you have done for us, Your Majesty,' said Emily, 'but I suspect that there is something you are not telling us. I further suspect that you are waiting for us to bring it up, to save you from having to make the suggestion.'

The Empress smiled. 'Whatever do you mean, Emily?'

'Your favoured solution seems obvious to me,' the Queen of the City said; 'but I shall spell it out so there is no room for doubt – you desire the City to join the Empire. That is where your talk of sovereign realms, and the duty towards your citizens leads me. If the City were a part of the Empire, its people would become your people, and the aid would continue to flow. Pella would receive its new sewer system, because it would become *your* domestic issue.'

'This is outrageous,' said Daniel.

'Hush, darling,' said Emily. 'Let us listen to the proposal before we condemn it out of hand. I assume that you have a proposal ready for us, Thorn?'

The Empress gestured to Kelsey.

'It's quite simple,' Kelsey said. 'If you join the Empire, you would be entitled to the same treatment as any other province. You would keep your own form of government, but the Empire would take control of your armed forces. You would receive one vote as an Elector, to assist in the selection of the next emperor or empress. There would be freedom of movement between the City and every other province of the Empire. The City would be obliged to obey any emergency decrees issued from the throne in a time of crisis. You would pay an annual imperial tax, which would be taken from the profits of the salve mine in the Eastern Mountains. Said salve mine would remain under the military jurisdiction of the Empire in perpetuity. One palace in the City would be set aside as a residence for the Empress to accommodate her Imperial Majesty on her visits to the province. The Empire would cover the expenses for this palace's refurbishment. And, finally, you would be required to swear an oath of allegiance to the Empire, and to the Empress.'

A wry smile crept over Emily's face. 'The City has been independent for three and half thousand years,' she said. 'It has taken only ten for us to become dependent upon the Empire, after Emperor Bryce revealed our location to the Ascendants.' She glanced at Daniel. 'We are undone, darling. If we wish to keep our freedom, our people will have to return to eating seaweed three times a day.'

'This is blackmail,' said Daniel.

'It is not,' said Naxor. 'Such language ill-becomes you, King Aurelian. Have you become so used to receiving the generous aid that the Empress has provided, that you cannot see the simple truth? If you wish to remain independent, then remain independent. No one is holding a knife to your throat. Joining the Empire is a free choice, one that you may accept or refuse. But you cannot expect us to fund you indefinitely if you decide to cling on to your sovereignty.'

'Do what is right for the City,' said Kelsey. 'Do what is right for your people.'

'Do you have a copy of the details that we could read?' said Emily.

Naxor took a sheaf of papers from his robes and passed it to the Queen of the City. 'The terms have been drawn up by Chancellor Shellakanawara,' he said.

Emily passed the documents to one of her courtiers.

'Thank you,' she said. 'Would someone please take us back to Ooste? My husband and I have much to discuss privately.'

'I will take you,' said Naxor, 'and then I shall organise the transport of this year's aid – three-quarters of the previous total, as Her Imperial Majesty has stated.'

Emily and Daniel got to their feet, their features ashen, then Naxor led them and the two courtiers from the balcony.

Kelsey exhaled. 'Pyre's arse,' she muttered. 'That was painful.'

'You did wonderfully, Herald,' said the Empress. 'Thank you. I know that you did not necessarily agree with what had to be done, but you did your duty to the Empire.' She turned to Kyra. 'What have you learned from this?'

'That I should never accept aid that I cannot live without,' the girl said.

'Well said.'

'Was this your plan all along, Your Majesty?' Kyra went on.

'It was,' said the Empress. 'I could have annexed the City by force ten years ago, but that is not how one treats one's friends. Instead, I allowed them to take whatever they needed from us, year after year, until they could no longer thrive without our help. If they choose to join the Empire, they will be in a far better condition than they were in all those years ago.'

'What if they refuse?'

'That is their right,' said the Empress. 'Our defensive alliance shall continue, as will our occupation of the salve mine. I shall request the presence of a permanent embassy upon their soil, and ask that they send ambassadors to join the Imperial Court. Life will go on.'

'Can I ask why, Your Majesty? Why do you want the City to be absorbed into the Empire?'

'For our mutual benefit,' said Thorn. 'We are stronger, and more prosperous, together. It is not about power, as I shall seek no control over the daily lives of the people who dwell there. I worry that it might be vanity, my vanity, but I try to look at it objectively. One day, you may be in the same position, Kyra. You will need to judge between your own desires, and what is best for the Empire as a whole.'

Kelsey glanced up. 'May I be excused from duties for a couple of hours, Your Majesty? I need to tell Van what transpired here this day. As major general of the Banner of the Lostwell Exiles, he has a right to know.'

'You are excused, Herald,' said the Empress. 'Kyra, remain here with me a little longer, so that we can talk about your future.'

Kelsey got to her feet. She bowed, then she strode from the chamber. She went up a flight of stairs to her private quarters, and entered through the front door. Inside, Van was pacing the floorboards of their living room, a piece of paper in his left hand, and an expression of fury on his face.

He saw Kelsey come in, and he turned towards her.

'How could you do this?' he cried. 'You delivered an ultimatum to the King and Queen of the City as though they were disobedient schoolchildren.'

'Ah, so you already know?' she said.

'Queen Emily slipped me a note before Naxor took her and King Daniel back to the City,' he said. 'You will cut off all aid unless they join the Empire? I'm disgusted. And you didn't even tell me what you were planning to do. My own wife. Do you care so little for me?'

'It was right that the King and Queen heard it first.'

'I am the City's most senior military officer,' he said. He held up the note. 'And this is how I find out? You and your damn Empress are blackmailing us. Ten years of friendship, thrown away in fifteen minutes.'

'Ten years of unlimited aid.'

'Only now do we see the hidden cost. Do you realise that, if the King and Queen agree to these terms, then I will become a servant of the Empire?'

'Where are the children?'

'I asked two of the ladies-in-waiting to take them for a while. I was too angry to think straight, and I didn't want them to see their father so enraged. And I didn't want them to hear me accuse my wife of betrayal.'

'I haven't betrayed you, Van.'

'I feel sick looking at you,' he said. 'Once again, you have chosen her over me. Does our marriage mean nothing to you? You have stabbed me in the back.'

He walked towards the door.

'Where are you going?' she said.

'To fetch the children, and then you will take us to Ooste. I need to be in the City, and the children are coming with me.'

'No,' she said. 'I will take you, but the children shall be staying here.'

'And who's going to look after them? You? I'm surprised you even remember their names at times. Do you know what they like to eat for breakfast? Do you know what stories are Caelius's favourites? When's the last time you tucked your daughter into bed? Did you know that Calpurnia is frightened of the dark?' He broke down in tears. 'I love you, Kelsey, but I cannot live like this. The children need at least one parent who is always there for them, and that parent is not you. It's never been you.'

'I will not take the children to the City, Van. I can change. I can be better. Will you give me a chance?'

'If you refuse to take the children, then I will have to remain here,' he said. He wiped his eyes. 'Caelius and Calpurnia are more important than my position as major general of the Banner. They matter more to me than my job. I wish you were able to say the same, Kelsey. Can you?'

'The children are more important than my job,' she said.

'Do you believe it?'

'I want to believe it.'

'I need some time to think, on my own,' he said. 'I don't want you to come back to our quarters tonight. Can you give me one day? Let's meet for breakfast, and see if we can work out our future, if we have one.'

'I don't want a divorce, Van.'

'Neither do I, but that's where we're headed, if nothing changes.'

'I'll sleep in Cael's apartment tonight,' she said. 'Can I see the children?'

Van nodded, then he led her to the rear of their quarters, and opened a door. Inside, two elegantly-dressed ladies-in-waiting were sitting on a long couch. One was reading to Caelius, while the other was braiding Calpurnia's long brown hair.

Kelsey and Van affixed smiles to their faces.

'Hello, children,' said Kelsey, as she walked in. She crouched by Caelius, and he gave his mother a hug. Kelsey closed her eyes, then she released the boy, and embraced her daughter.

'I love you, mummy,' said the girl.

'I just came in to say hello,' said Kelsey. 'I need to go back to work now, but your father will look after you for the rest of today.'

She got back to her feet, smiled at the children, then strode from the apartment. She walked along the corridors of the palace, until she reached the door that led to Cael's empty quarters. She let herself in, and sat down on a chair by the window. She glanced at the view for a moment, then began to weep.

CHAPTER 12
THE ROAD TO TAHRANA CITY

Grey Mountains, Rahain – 21st Day, First Third Summer 544

Dolwyn shook Lahnos's shoulder. 'Time to get up. Ye've got a big day ahead of you, and you'll need some breakfast inside ye before you kill any Rahain raiders.'

Lahnos opened his eyes. The dawn light was streaming in through the open window in Dolwyn's room within the stone fortress. Down on the floor of the valley, hundreds of soldiers were dismantling part of the camp, and columns were marching through the entrance of the Great Tunnel that led south, towards Rahain.

'Have I overslept?' he said.

'Nah,' she said. 'That lot had early orders to get to the front. You've still got an hour before you're due to leave.'

She turned back to the small stove, and carried on preparing their breakfast.

'I'd rather have sex than eat,' he said.

She laughed. 'Tough shit; I'm starving.'

'I could order you into bed.'

'I'd mutiny. Was last night not enough for ye? You werenae this insatiable when we first started sleeping together.'

'It's the thought of imminent violence.'

She pulled a face. 'And that gets ye in the mood?'

'That's not what I meant. I... I want to feel alive before I have to confront death.'

'Just make sure ye come back to me tonight,' she said.

He watched her as she piled a large assortment of fried food onto two plates. She then filled four mugs – two with ale, and two with coffee. Lahnos swung his legs out of bed, then he pulled on his uniform and laced up his boots. He stood up, and wrapped his arms around her. He kissed her neck, then he moved a hand under her shirt, and she yelped.

'Yer hands are fucking freezing,' she said. 'Sit down, and behave.'

'Yes, ma'am,' he said, taking a seat.

She placed the plates and mugs onto the table, then she sat down opposite him.

'Eggs, bacon, blood pudding, fried bread and mushrooms,' she said; 'and don't be expecting this quality of service every day. I'm doing it because you're off to war this morning; I'm not yer fucking servant.'

'I appreciate it,' he said. 'I've not had a cooked breakfast since we were in Colsbury.'

They ate for a few minutes, and Lahnos sipped from both the ale and coffee mugs. The ale was strong, and the coffee stronger, and he felt himself start to wake up.

'Are we still just having a bit of fun?' he said.

'And why would ye want to bring that up, on today of all days?'

'I don't know. It's just... forget it. There are things I want to say to you, but I don't think I should.'

'Then don't,' she said.

'Do you wish you were taking part in the attack?'

She shrugged. 'I'm not bothered one way or the other. Rahain is unlikely to be conquered in one day, so I'm sure I'll get a chance to join in.'

'I won't be in any real danger,' he said.

She glanced at him.

'I won't,' he said. 'I'll be on Sigum's back, looking down at the Rahain. It's the safest place in the entire invasion.'

'What will yer Bullan be doing?'

'They'll be staying here. When this is over, I think I might go back to Athumia.'

'Eh?'

'Just for a visit,' he said. 'I have a brother and three sisters that I haven't seen in eight years.'

'In all the time we've been together,' she said, 'this is the first you've mentioned yer family.'

'We're not particularly close.'

'No kidding. Did ye have a big falling out with them?'

'I ran away from my village when my horns began to grow. My mother's father was a Bullan soldier, and sometimes their children or grandchildren have horns, or even tails. People like me were... unpopular.'

'What about yer ma and da?'

'Both dead.'

'Sorry to hear that, Lahnos.'

'I was an angry young man.'

'I'm not surprised. Is there any particular reason that ye've decided to open up to me this morning?'

'Do you think I'm doing the right thing? Athumia's not part of the Empire, and the Rahain have never done anything to me. I don't have to be here. I could resign my commission and live in comfort and security in Colsbury.'

'Then why are ye here?'

'Because I thought I should be doing something useful with my life, and I don't know how to do anything else. I never wanted to be a soldier, but the island where I lived was attacked by two different empires, who both wanted to control it, and I had no choice. I ended up ruling that island for a while, but everyone hated me, and I had to leave.'

'And that was all because of your horns?'

'They hated me for other reasons by that point. I've told you about the Gift of Pain, yeah?'

She nodded.

'There's more. I can kill people by touching them. I pull out their memories; I re-live them, in a way, and when that stops, the other person's dead.'

Dolwyn said nothing.

'That's not all,' he said.

He picked up a knife, and stabbed it down into his left arm. Dolwyn jumped out of her seat and backed away, her eyes wide.

Lahnos pulled the knife out, and held up the wound for her to see. His self-healing got to work, numbing the pain as the wound closed up. He wiped away the blood, and showed her the smooth, unblemished skin on his arm.

'I'm not going to die today,' he said. 'I might never die.'

'You... you're a demigod?'

'I don't know what I am. Before... whatever we have goes any further,' he said, 'you should know these things about me. I owe you the truth.'

Dolwyn re-took her seat, and stared at him in silence.

'If you want to break it off, I'll understand,' he went on. 'I come with a lot of excess baggage.'

'Is that why you look so young?' she said.

'Yes. I really am twenty-nine. I stopped aging when I was twenty-one, after I stole the memories of a powerful god. I didn't know it at the time, but I also stole that god's ability to self-heal. In forty years from now, I'll look the same.'

'I won't,' she said. 'Forty years from now, I'll be in my early sixties, if I make it that far.'

'I don't want to have children. Ever. I couldn't bear the thought of them growing old and dying, while I'll linger on for centuries, looking exactly the same.'

Dolwyn glanced down. 'I want to have children some day.'

'I understand. I'm sorry, Dolwyn; this is why I had to tell you, before things got too serious between us. I like you, a lot, and I don't want to hurt you.'

She smiled sadly at him. 'It might be too late for that.'

Lahnos got to his feet, then he leaned down and kissed her forehead. 'Take care, Dolwyn.'

He walked out of her room and closed the door. He leaned against the wall of the corridor for a few moments, wishing he had kept his mouth shut. He had been building up to that conversation for a few days, trying to pick his moment, as he had realised that he was becoming ever more attached to her. He hoped she wasn't in love with him. He had seen a few glimpses of what might have been developing into a more serious relationship, and so he had decided to kill it before it had a chance to thrive. It was better that way, he told himself. At least she knew the truth about him.

Lahnos took a deep breath, and walked out of the fortress. Sigum and the Bullan had been asked to leave the entrance of the Great Tunnel, to allow the flow of soldiers to march south, and they had gathered over by the small stream. Lahnos jumped down off the elevated road, and tramped through the long grass towards them.

'Greetings, rider,' said Sigum. 'You look well-fed this morning. Has your Kellach woman been good to you?'

'She cooked breakfast for me,' he said, 'and then I broke it off with her.'

'Sir?' said Efizel. 'Why would you do that? As far as I could see, she made you happy.'

'She did make me happy,' he said, 'and that's why I broke it off. I told her about the self-healing. I told her that I never wanted children. I had to be honest with her. I couldn't let her live in hope of a life I could never give her.'

'You seem to be an expert in squandering every chance of happiness, rider,' said the dragon. 'What did Lieutenant Dolwyn say when you presented her with every reason why she should not be with you?'

Lahnos glanced up at the sky. 'Let's change the subject. I have to lead several divisions of Her Majesty's finest into battle today, and I can't do that if we're standing here discussing my love life. Are you ready to fly south, Sigum?'

'I am.'

One of the Bullan handed him a thick, fleece-lined coat, and a war axe. Lahnos attached the leather loop of the war axe to his belt, then he pulled the coat over his shoulders.

'We'll probably be back a few hours after nightfall,' he said to the Bullan arrayed before him. 'This will remain our base until we've secured a corridor through Tahrana Valley, but it'd probably be wise to start packing up our things here, ready for the move south.'

'I shall miss this valley,' said Sigum. 'It has been a pleasant home.'

'Good luck, sir,' said Efizel. 'We shall be waiting for your return.'

Lahnos nodded at the Bullan, then he pulled himself up onto Sigum's harness. He placed his feet in the stirrups, and buckled the belt round his waist.

Sigum turned his long neck to look at him. 'Are you ready?'

'Yes.'

'Then let us proceed to war.'

The silvery-green dragon extended his wings and launched himself into the sky. He circled over the fortress and camp, then soared over the mountains to the south. They had flown that route dozens of times before, and Lahnos knew the way well. He settled into the harness with the thick coat wrapped round him, and he narrowed his eyes to shield them from the biting wind.

It was a two-hour flight to the huge fortress that marked the southern end of the Great Tunnel, and Lahnos had seen imperial troops marching south wherever the route passed overland. Thousands of soldiers had assembled within the area to the rear of the fortress, ready for the command to invade Rahain. Most of the troops positioned to spearhead the attack were from Sanang, though a few companies of Kellach marines were among them. That combination represented the toughest forces under the Empire's control, and there was great rivalry between the two factions, but also much hard-won respect.

On the southern side of the fortress stretched the Tahrana Valley – a wide plain that separated the Grey Mountains from the highlands, where the majority of the Rahain cities were clustered. Lahnos had made sure to fly that way often with Sigum, so that the Rahain down in the valley would become accustomed to his presence, and he hoped they wouldn't be alarmed by the sight of him that morning. Along the road that led south to Tahrana City, large encampments of Rahain raiders had been established, from where attacks upon the Plateau would be launched. With Sigum's arrival in the mountains, those attacks had petered out, but the camps remained in place, and they would be that day's main target.

A junior officer from the Holdings was standing upon the upper battlements of the fortress when Sigum began his descent. He raised a green flag, and the dragon lowered himself down onto the flat roof. The officer ran over to him.

'Commander Lahnos!' he cried. 'The leaders of the invasion force have gathered in the hall below us, and are awaiting your instructions.'

Lahnos frowned down from the harness. 'Are you just going to ignore the massive dragon standing next to you?'

'Sir? Uh… greetings, Lord Sigum. My apologies.'

'That is quite all right,' said the dragon.

Lahnos unbuckled the strap securing him to the harness and climbed down to the roof.

'Sigum is not my beast of burden,' he said to the young officer. 'I expect him to be shown respect.'

'Yes, sir. Sorry, sir.'

Lahnos gestured to the stairs, and the officer led him down to where the main hall of the fortress was located. Lahnos strode into the packed room, and walked up to the platform that lay at one end. He gazed out over the crowd. He could see officers from Sanang, Kellach Brigdomin, the Holdings, and a few who had to be Banner veterans.

'Who is this young pup?' cried a Sanang captain. 'We were led to believe that a mighty commander was going to lead us into battle today. This is a boy with horns!'

Several Sanang started to laugh, but Lahnos remained silent as he scanned the crowd.

A few Kellach officers shouted at the laughing Sanang, telling them to shut up, but Lahnos continued to say nothing, as murmurs of complaint and dissension rippled through the hall. After a few long, painful minutes, the crowd began to quiet.

'My name is Lahnos Laimos,' he said, 'and I am in command of the invasion. I will pacify the entire road across the Tahrana Valley, and your job is to secure the terrain in my wake. The Sanang divisions will be at the centre, with the Imperial Marines protecting their flanks. All Rahain encampments along the road are to be destroyed. At sunset, you will dig in, and we shall do the same thing tomorrow, and for as many days as it takes us to reach Tahrana City. When you see flames come down from the sky, that will be your signal to open the gates of the fortress and begin the assault.' He paused for a moment, as they stared at him. 'Take no prisoners.'

He stepped down from the platform, and pushed his way through the crowd. He left the hall, and ascended the stairs back to the roof.

'That was remarkably brief,' said Sigum.

'I told them all they needed to know,' said Lahnos. 'I don't have time for small talk, and I'm not here to make friends.' He glanced up at the dragon. 'Are you ready?'

'I am.'

'Are you sure? Do you understand exactly what we'll be doing today?'

'You are talking to a dragon, Lahnos. Did I hesitate when we annihilated the Gunstian Fleet? Fire and pain; pain and fire. We are built for war, the two of us.'

Lahnos climbed up onto the harness, and strapped himself in. Sigum stretched his wings out, and they rose into the air, as hundreds of soldiers down by the fortress gates gazed up at them. Sigum soared south, and they passed over the high outer walls of the large fortification. It was less than a mile to the first Rahain encampment, and Sigum sped towards it. Dozens of Rahain scrambled to get their weapons in order, but they had no ballistae or catapults. A few crossbows were loosed up at them, then Sigum opened his jaws. Flames ripped down from the dragon, enveloping the ramparts of the encampment, and incinerating every Rahain who had been standing there. At that, whistles and horns blew out from the fortress behind them, and the gates opened. Sanang soldiers emerged at a steady trot, their upper bodies protected by breastplates, and then companies of Kellach marines fanned out to either side.

Sigum made another pass over the Rahain camp, spreading flames to every corner, then he hovered above it for a few moments, ensuring that nothing was left alive. With the camp in flames, the dragon soared off to the south. He ignored a small number of Rahain who had fled from the slaughter, and made for the next encampment. The Rahain there had seen what had happened to the first camp, and were better prepared, but the result was the same, and in less than five minutes it, too, was ablaze from end to end.

Lahnos gazed down at the carnage. The Rahain had nothing with which to counter the dragon attacks, and he almost felt sorry for them.

'Move on to the next camp,' he said.

'There are still a few stragglers at this one, Lahnos.'

'Leave them for the Sanang.'

Sigum broke off the assault on the second camp, and they soared to the south, as smoke filled the sky behind them.

Sigum and Lahnos killed Rahain until the sun started to set. They had covered eighty miles on the first day, far out-pacing the divisions of imperial soldiers on foot advancing to their rear. As they flew back north, they passed over the front lines of the Sanang, who were building a temporary camp for the night on top of the ruins of a Rahain encampment. The Sanang raised their weapons and cheered at the sight of the dragon. The bodies of the slaughtered Rahain had been thrown onto several large mounds to the west of the road, and more charred corpses were being added to the piles. Sigum circled over a command centre that was being erected to the north of the front line, then he landed by the road. Sanang and Kellach officers emerged from a large tent, as Lahnos climbed down to the ground.

'Well done, Commander,' said a Kellach captain.

Lahnos glanced at the assembled officers. 'Is this everyone?'

'Yes, sir,' said the captain.

'Lord Sigum and I have cleared every camp to a distance of sixty miles south of here,' he said, 'so you should be in no danger of being attacked overnight. Push south at first light tomorrow, and cover as many miles as you can. Sigum and I will patrol overhead.'

'Did you say sixty miles, sir?' said another Kellach officer.

'I did.'

'Including the twenty miles that we have covered today, that's almost half the distance to Tahrana City, sir.'

'I know.'

'How many lizards did you and your dragon kill, Commander?' said a Sanang officer.

'Several thousand. I wasn't keeping count.'

'I was one of those who laughed at you this morning, sir,' the Sanang officer went on. 'For that, I apologise.'

'I took no offence,' said Lahnos. He glanced at the other officers. 'If we keep this up, we will be in Tahrana City within ten days. As you might have guessed by now, the underground cities of the Rahain are no place for a dragon to operate. As soon as we near the city, I shall lead, on foot, while Sigum patrols the skies to protect our lines of communication. I want the best-performing Sanang regiment by my side when we enter the city. You have ten days to work out which regiment that will be.'

A Sanang colonel raised his battle mace. 'To Lahnos, Sigum, and the Empire!'

'To the Empire,' the other officers cried.

'I will see you officers tomorrow,' said Lahnos. 'Even dragons need to get their sleep.'

Lahnos walked back to Sigum, and climbed up to the harness.

'Take us back to our little green valley,' Lahnos said.

Sigum tilted his head. 'As you will, Commander.'

It was dark by the time they reached the valley. Lamps had been lit by the small fortress, and most of the garrison was out, waiting for the dragon's return. Sigum circled once, then he landed in the space between the two ramps, on the valley floor.

The Holdings colonel in charge of the garrison stepped forward.

'Welcome back, Lord Sigum, and welcome back, Commander,' he said.

Lahnos climbed down to the ground. He went to speak to the colonel, when he noticed that Kelsey Holdfast was standing next to him.

He tilted his head. 'Herald.'

'Lahnos,' she said. 'What news of the invasion?'

'Our army has advanced twenty miles down the road that leads to Tahrana City,' he said; 'and Sigum and I cleared another sixty miles beyond that. Nearly two dozen Rahain encampments have been destroyed. Surprise was complete. They weren't expecting us, and they had nothing to counter a dragon attack. I have ordered the army to resume their advance at dawn tomorrow.'

'Good work, Commander,' said Kelsey, though she remained unsmiling. 'Any casualties on our side?'

'None that I saw or had reported to me, ma'am.'

'What about on their side?'

'I didn't take a count, ma'am.'

'I did,' said the silvery-green dragon. 'Would you like to hear my estimate, Madam Herald?'

'I would, Lord Sigum,' she said.

'I incinerated around eight and a half thousand Rahain on the valley road,' said Sigum. 'I left close to two thousand alive in the northernmost camps that we destroyed, and the Sanang had disposed of them by the time we returned north. Therefore, I would estimate that ten thousand or so enemies of the Empire met their deaths this day. There were no wounded, and no prisoners were taken.'

There were a few suppressed gasps from the soldiers who had gathered in front of Sigum and Lahnos, but Kelsey kept her features expressionless.

'As I mentioned,' said Lahnos, 'the Rahain had no way to fight back against a dragon descending from the skies. Unless they manage to invent ballistae in the next few days, then we should be able to reach the outskirts of Tahrana City in the same manner.'

'The Rahain used to have the best artillery on the Star Continent,' said Kelsey, 'but those days have long since passed. Well done, Commander, and well done, Lord Sigum. I will report your words to the Empress this evening; Her Majesty is eager to hear what has occurred.'

She nodded to the colonel of the garrison, then she took out her Quadrant, brushed her fingers over its surface, and vanished.

'Back to your posts,' the colonel shouted at the soldiers. 'Let Lord Sigum rest.'

The gathering began to disperse, and Lahnos caught sight of Efizel, who was standing on the ramp. He walked forward and embraced the Bullan sergeant major.

'We have prepared food for you and Sigum in the tunnel entrance,' Efizel said.

'Thanks,' said Lahnos. 'And I could do with a hot bath.'

'The water is currently being heated, sir. Would you prefer to eat or bathe first?'

'Eat.'

'I concur,' said Sigum. 'Let us eat.'

The dragon led the way up the ramp, while Lahnos and Efizel followed. They entered the Great Tunnel, where the other Bullan were busy filling Sigum's food trough until it was overflowing with the fresh carcases of goats and mountain deer. A large tub of cool water from the stream was sitting next to it, and the dragon took a long drink, then he began to eat. Lahnos and Efizel went through to a side chamber, where a table sat. It was large enough to seat Lahnos and the Bullan, but only one place had been set, at the head of the table.

Lahnos sat.

'It was a slaughter then, sir?' said Efizel, as he uncovered the dishes that lay on the table.

'Yes,' said Lahnos. 'They weren't civilians. I saw large amounts of weapons in each camp. And there were no children.'

'Will you be doing the same tomorrow, sir?'

'I don't think those conditions will arise again. A few hundred Rahain managed to get away, and the smoke would have been visible for miles. If I was a Rahain raider sitting in one of the remaining camps, I'd be running south by now. I'll probably be spending the next few days shadowing the army's advance. I want to reach Tahrana City without incurring any casualties.'

'Was it difficult to find the reserves of ruthlessness required, sir?'

'No. Sigum and I were doing what the Empress pays us to do.'

'Then you should have no trouble sleeping tonight, sir.'

His thoughts went to Dolwyn, and how he would miss her presence next to him in bed.

'I recognise that look, sir,' said Efizel. 'What are our orders if a certain young lieutenant walks up the ramp this evening?'

Lahnos said nothing for a moment, then he picked up a fork. 'Ask me if it happens.'

An hour later, Lahnos was climbing out of the bath tub, his body scrubbed clean of sweat and dust. He felt no aches or pains from having sat upon the harness for over twelve hours that day, but he knew that was due to his self-healing abilities. He dried himself with a towel, and pulled on a clean uniform. He went into his bedroom and lit a couple of small lamps, then he went out in to the Bullan's common area, where the soldiers were relaxing. They made space for him at their table, and he sat.

'Whisky, sir?' said the corporal.

'A small one, thanks,' he said.

He glanced at Efizel, who gave him a subtle shake of the head.

The corporal handed him a glass of whisky, and Lahnos took a sip. The taste had been growing on him over the summer, but it brought back recent memories of Dolwyn. He glanced at the doorway, but no one was there.

Hiding his disappointment, he talked with the Bullan for twenty minutes, then he made his excuses and went back to his bedroom. He lay on the bed, and folded his arms behind his head.

Part of him had expected Dolwyn to come to the tunnel that evening, and he felt foolish for his presumption. Of course she wasn't going to come – he had made it clear that their relationship was over. Was he expecting her to beg? She had more pride than that, and anyway, she was probably relieved to be rid of him after he had told her his secrets. Regret washed over him. Could he not have remained selfish for another few nights?

He undressed, slipped between the sheets, and then, for the first time in over twenty days, he tried to get to sleep on his own.

CHAPTER 13
AN IMPERFECT CREATION

World Three – (24th Day, Second Third Summer 544)

Wearing nothing but a pair of shorts, Cael lay upon the grass by the entrance to the cave, as the sun warmed his skin. It wasn't as hot as the Holdings had been, but it was more humid, and after an hour or so he would need to go for a swim in the nearby river. He heard a fly buzzing over his head, then the sounds of birds calling out from the forest's edge reached him. They had seen very little wildlife since arriving, and there had been no sign of any humans for miles around.

It had been idyllic. Peace, quiet, and no one ordering him about. He felt safe, and out of reach.

Footsteps approached, and he opened his eyes.

Cole looked down at him. 'We're running out of food.'

'There are orange groves by the forest,' said Cael.

'We can't eat nothing but oranges, and that's all we have left. Arrosa and I have scoured the land around here for miles; there's nothing else to eat.'

'Catch a fish.'

'How? With a sharpened stick? We have no rods or twine. Listen, Cael; perhaps it's time we went home.'

'You say that every day.'

'I know, but this time I mean it. Our clothes are becoming ragged, and we have nothing else to wear. We've been here for...' He paused, as his glance went to a series of marks scratched onto the stone by the entrance to their cave. 'It's forty-seven days,' he said. 'Shit. Forty-seven days, Cael. Surely, that's enough? You've made your point.'

Cael sat up. 'I didn't come here to make a point. I did it to escape for a while.'

'Forty-seven days *is* a while. Half the summer has passed.'

'So? It's perfect here, Cole. We have clean water, and sunshine; and there's plenty of food if you look hard enough. We have a comfortable cave, where we can sit by a little fire each night and look at the stars. I'm not going anywhere.'

'We're living like savages.'

'We've stripped life back to its bare essentials,' said Cael. 'What does a human really need to survive – food, water, shelter? We have all those things.'

The sound of splashing came from the nearby bank of the river.

'Arrosa's taking a swim,' said Cole.

'See? At least she knows how to enjoy herself.'

'She fell into a bog, and she's washing off the mud. I should warn you – she's pissed off. She spent hours yesterday cleaning her only set of clothes, and they're all muddy again.'

Cael laughed.

'She threatened to glass you if you make fun of her appearance,' said Cole. 'Please don't say anything when she comes up to the cave.'

Arrosa appeared at that moment, striding up the bank towards the cave. Her dress was ripped and torn at the hem and shoulders, and it was dripping water onto the ground. Her hair was also soaking wet, and was hanging down her back. She was holding a battered pair of shoes in her hand, and her eyes were glowing with anger.

She came to a halt in front of Cael, and glared down at him.

'Take me home,' she said. 'I'm done. I want to go back to civilisation.'

'I want to stay here,' said Cael.

'Then you are holding us here against our will. Beat him up, Cole.'

Cole laughed nervously, and glanced away.

'You'll dry out in ten minutes,' said Cael. 'Sit down and relax.'

'Relax?' she said. 'This is harder work than being on the Hold Fast estate. We spend hour after hour each day looking for food, and then we have to prepare it, and find wood for the fire to cook it. And what about our clothes? I've scrubbed this dress so many times it's falling apart. And my hair... Why didn't we bring a bar of fucking soap with us?'

'You've had fun here; admit it.'

'All right. The first twenty days were fun. You have me there, Cael; I admit it. The next twenty days were harder; a lot harder, and now? I'm fed up, and Cole's fed up, too.'

'But this place is beautiful,' said Cael. 'Look at the river, and the mountains, and the forest...'

'Yes, it's beautiful,' said Arrosa, 'but what about the insects? They bite my legs every night.'

'You should sit closer to the fire.'

'But then I stink of smoke.'

'We can all agree that World Three is beautiful,' said Cole, 'but imagine if we went home – we could return here better prepared, with tents, and trunks full of clothes, and soap, and fishing rods...'

'And blankets, hairbrushes, proper boots...' said Arrosa.

'And even a few ales,' said Cole. 'But to do all that, we have to go home first.'

'You both know that's never going to happen,' said Cael. 'As soon as we go back, the Sextant will be taken away from me, forever. I'll never be allowed to go near it again. This is our only chance. If we return, it's over.'

'Then give us a date,' said Cole. 'Tell us when we'll be going home. If you want another day or two, then fine.'

'I was planning on staying for the entire summer.'

Arrosa stared at him. 'That's another forty days away.'

'If we go back before I turn eighteen, I'll be at their mercy,' said

Cael. 'If I'm eighteen, then I'll be an adult, and they won't be able to order me around.'

'It doesn't matter what age you are when you get back,' Arrosa cried; 'your mother's going to kill you. She's going to kill us all!'

'You dared me to bring us all here.'

'That was when I thought we'd be away for a couple of days! If we'd gone back after two days, Cael, then we could have weathered the storm. I would have taken the blame. I would have told Kelsey that it was my idea. But now? We've been gone for fifty days, Cael!'

'Forty-seven,' he muttered. 'Do you have any idea what we've achieved? My mother probably assumed that she'd be able to find us easily. We've remained hidden from the most powerful mage-god in all existence. Who else could have done it? Nobody, that's who. Not even Kyra.'

'They will be worried sick,' said Cole.

'I fucking hope so,' said Cael.

'Now we learn the truth,' said Arrosa. 'We're here, Cole, because Cael wants attention from his mummy. We're playing an elaborate game of hide and seek. *Bet you can't find me, Mama.*'

Cole laughed, until a look from Cael silenced him.

'I'm right, though,' Arrosa went on. 'This has all been one final, desperate plea for attention. Karalyn has barely looked at us since Carden and Caitlyn were born, so Cael needed to do something dramatic. Well, you've certainly succeeded.'

'For Pyre's sake, Arrosa,' said Cael, 'why can't you just shut the fuck up for once?'

'You have all the power, Cael,' she said. 'Only you can operate the Sextant. Cole and I have nothing but our voices, and I will not be silent. We are asking you to take us home. Please. I dare you to take us home.'

'That won't work this time,' he said. 'We're not leaving, because I'm not ready to face the consequences of what I've done. There will be punishments, lectures, people telling me how disappointed they are... Worse, I will never be allowed to create another world.'

'Maybe you could use the Sextant to send our family a message,' said Cole; 'just to let them know that we're all right; that we're still alive.'

'Can the Sextant do that?' said Arrosa.

'Aye,' said Cael. 'I would have to find the Star Continent, and then home in on Colsbury. My mother's more in tune with the Sextant, but I could probably work out a way to talk to my sister.'

'Then we could negotiate our return,' said Arrosa. 'That was a good idea, Cole. We could tell Karalyn and the others that we want to come back, but only on our terms. Well, your terms; I don't really give a shit. Come up with a list of conditions, Cael. You could tell them that you'll bring the Sextant back, but only if you're allowed to use it. They could hardly refuse.'

'It's worth a try,' said Cole.

Cael frowned. 'Maybe. I need to think about it.'

Cole and Arrosa glanced at each other, but neither spoke.

Cael picked up his shirt, and pulled it over his head. It was rough against his skin from having dried out in the sun, and it was fraying at the edges, but it was all he had. He stood, and stretched his arms.

'I'm going to find some food,' he said.

Arrosa snorted. 'Good luck with that, unless you fancy another orange.'

'There are probably bananas left.'

'Just the green ones,' she said. 'We've eaten every yellow banana.'

'I'm three-quarters Kellach Brigdomin,' he said. 'I can eat things that would turn your stomach.'

'Great. That means I'll be the first to starve,' she said.

He stared down at her. Despite her anger, despite her bedraggled appearance, there was something about her face that drew him in. For someone so annoying, he couldn't deny that she was beautiful. Her eyes... He shook himself, slightly bewildered that he had allowed his thoughts to wander in that direction.

'If you get really hungry,' he said, 'you can eat Cole.'

Arrosa raised an eyebrow, then she glanced at Cole. 'There's enough of him to keep us going for a few days, I suppose. I wonder what human tastes like.'

'Ha ha,' said Cole.

Cael set off towards the forest. He walked down the slope to the side of the river, and strode along its banks. The air was warm and fresh, and everything seemed to be at peace. He passed a few bushes that had been picked clean of their berries, then the sweet aroma of ripe oranges reached his nose, a smell that had become a little sickly to all three of them in recent days. He passed through the wild grove, and entered the forest. Tall trees towered over him, but none of them bore any food. His stomach rumbled as he headed deeper into the forest. He had been hiding it before, but he was just as hungry as Cole and Arrosa, and just as bored with berries, nuts and oranges. He saw a few mushrooms, and crouched down to inspect them. He sniffed a handful. He and Cole would probably be able to eat them without too many ill effects, but they might well prove fatal to Arrosa and her frail constitution. Irritating as she was, he didn't wish to inadvertently poison her. He thought about her face again. It wasn't just her eyes that attracted him – it was every part of her. It was because she was the only girl his age in the vicinity, he told himself, and they had spent so much time in each other's company that his feelings were natural, possibly inevitable. He shook his head. How she would mock him if she ever guessed what he had been thinking at that moment. If she ever became his sister, then all such thoughts would have to come to an immediate and abrupt end, and never again would he be able to look at her the way he had looked at her before he had begun his search for food.

He was going mad – it was the only explanation. He hated Arrosa. And yet. If he hated her, then why had he brought her along? It wasn't as though she would have been any use to Karalyn in finding him, but he hadn't wanted to leave her behind. A perverse part of him sometimes enjoyed their raging arguments, as though fighting had brought them closer in some way. She didn't argue with that intensity with anyone else, and neither did he.

He searched the forest for an hour, and found nothing. Every source of nuts and berries had been exhausted, and the few ripe bananas that remained were too high for him to reach. The next time he built a world, he decided, he would populate it with large, slow-moving animals packed with meat; ones that were trusting and easy to catch. He was about to turn round and head back to the cave, when the ground began to move beneath his bare feet. It was a gentle sway at first, then the earth buckled and twisted, and Cael was thrown to the ground. Trees to his left and right were uprooted and came crashing down, and he had to scramble clear to avoid being struck by a heavy branch. The ground shook again, and then fell still. The next noise Cael heard was from the startled birds, which were squawking and circling above the forest in great numbers. Cael rose to his feet, and brushed the dirt and leaves from his clothes. He was disorientated, and couldn't remember the way back to the cave. He almost panicked, then he glanced up at the sky. His immediate surroundings had been altered by the earthquake, but the sun was exactly where it should be, and he used its position to set off in the right direction.

The way back was beset with challenges. Fallen trees and displaced boulders were blocking many of the routes to the river, and his arms and legs were scratched as he clambered over rocks and trunks. He broke into a run when he reached the wild orange grove, and raced along the bank of the river. He looked up, and almost cried out in relief when he saw that the cave was still intact. Cole and Arrosa came rushing down the slope to meet him, then Cael put his hands on his knees, panting and gasping for breath,

'Are you all right?' said Cole.

'Aye. You?'

'We're fine,' he said. 'We were sitting on the river bank when the earthquake struck. We could see the trees in the forest fall over, and we didn't know what to do. Arrosa wanted to go looking for you, but I thought it would be better to stay here, in case we got lost.'

Cael straightened his back, and gazed down at Arrosa. She looked frightened, her usually-cocky demeanour absent from her features.

'Please take us home, Cael,' she said.

'Will the Sextant be all right?' said Cole. 'Maybe the earthquake damaged it.'

'The Sextant is indestructible,' said Cael. 'It would take a lot more than an earthquake to scratch it.'

'Does that mean that you'll take us home?' said Arrosa.

'I don't know.'

'Is it likely that there will be more earthquakes?' said Cole.

'Maybe. The Sextant said that the continental plates aren't completely stable.'

'And you knew this?' cried Arrosa. 'You knew there might be earthquakes?'

'There have been no earthquakes since we got here,' he said. 'It seemed safe enough.'

He walked up to the entrance of the cave, and the others followed him. They went inside. Several rocks had fallen from the ceiling of the cavern, and one had landed on the spot where Arrosa slept each night. She muttered a curse under her breath.

'Fine,' said Cael. 'You win.'

'If the earthquake had happened at night...' Cole said.

'I get it,' said Cael. 'You don't need to fucking spell it out to me. I'll collect the sword, and we'll get out of here.'

He walked to the rear of the cavern, and moved the pile of leaves where he had hidden his Tempest sword. He picked it up by the hilt, and they left the cave.

'I'm not going back in there again,' said Arrosa.

'You won't have to,' said Cael. 'We'll be in Colsbury in a few minutes.'

They set off together down the slope, then they followed the river downstream, away from the forest. The Sextant was sitting where they had left it, on a flat, rocky ledge by the base of the hill. Part of the ledge had cracked down one side, but the Sextant looked intact.

Cael gazed at the large device. 'This feels like giving up.'

'You're welcome to come back here on your own,' said Arrosa. 'Just drop me and Cole off in Colsbury, and you can have the entire world to yourself.'

'My mother... she...'

'We'll stick together,' said Cole.

'I'll take the blame,' said Arrosa. 'We'll tell them that I badgered you into doing it.'

'I can't let you do that,' said Cael.

'Why not?'

'Because it isn't true.'

He walked up to the side of the Sextant, gripped the sword, and inserted it into its correct slot.

Nothing happened.

Cael adjusted the sword, partly-withdrawing it, and re-inserting it more firmly, but the Sextant did not respond.

'Is something wrong?' said Cole.

'Maybe it's in the wrong hole,' said Arrosa. 'There are plenty of places a sword could fit.'

'I think I know which slot it's supposed to go into,' yelled Cael. 'It's not working. I don't understand. Why isn't it working?'

He placed a palm onto the flat surface of the Sextant, but heard no voice emanating from its depths.

'Fuck!' he cried.

Arrosa came round to where he was standing. She glanced down at the hilt of the sword.

'Are you definitely sure it's in the right place?'

'Of course I'm fucking sure!'

'Don't shout. Stay calm. We can fix this.'

'How?'

'Can I have a look at the sword?'

He stared at her. She seemed to take that as a yes, so she took hold of the hilt, and pulled the sword out of the side of the Sextant.

'It's the same sword that brought us here,' he said. 'Looking at it isn't going to change that.'

'What's this?' she said.

'What's what?'

She traced a finger down the edge of the black blade. 'There's a crack. Do you see it?'

Cael took the sword from her and peered at where she had been pointing.

'There's a fine crack,' she went on. 'About three inches long.'

'That wasn't there before,' he said.

'The colouring of the blade looks a little off as well,' she said. 'Where did you get this sword, Cael?'

'I stole it from an imperial armoury. '

'Did you have it checked, to make sure the alloy didn't contain any imperfections?'

'What?'

'It needs to be perfect,' she said. 'Nine parts Tempest, and one part iron. If there's anything else in there – lead, tin... carbon... the alloy would behave differently.'

'It was working perfectly well whenever I used it before we came here.'

'But it had no crack then? Are you sure?'

'Certain. There was no crack in it before we came to World Three.'

'Could the journey here have caused the crack to appear, if the alloy wasn't pure?'

'I... have no idea. I only had a couple of Tempest classes at university last autumn.'

'I might be able to fix it,' she said, 'if we had tools and a forge.'

'Well, that's fine then. All we need is a forge and some tools to appear out of nowhere.'

'Think for a moment, Cael,' she said. 'You have been observing this world, yes? Did you ever see any signs of human habitation? Might it be possible that a forge exists somewhere? Is there iron on this world?'

'Aye, but the humans I saw were too primitive to have developed much in the way of technology.'

'Do you remember where these human live?'

'Further up the river. Much further.'

Arrosa nodded. 'In the absence of any alternatives, we shall have to visit them.'

'Try it again,' said Cole. 'Stick the damn sword in, and try it again.'

Arrosa handed the sword to Cael, who gently pushed it into place. The Sextant remained dormant.

'What about a Quadrant?' said Cole. 'Don't Quadrants sometimes get inserted? There might be one embedded into either side of the Sextant.'

'There's no point,' said Cael. 'None of us know how to use a Quadrant.'

'Let's look, anyway,' said Arrosa.

Cael, Cole and Arrosa scrambled round the flanks of the Sextant, searching every available slot in vain for a Quadrant. Cole groaned aloud, then he sat down on the rocky ledge with his head in his hands.

'Don't despair,' said Arrosa. 'We still have the Tempest contained within the sword.'

Cael lowered his gaze. 'Thank you.'

'For what?' she said.

'Right now, you have every right to be angry with me; you have every right to scream abuse at me for this, and I would deserve it. I've trapped us here, and all you're doing is trying to think of a way to get us home.'

'I would enjoy shouting at you,' she said, 'but that isn't going to help us.'

'Here's what we'll do,' said Cael. 'We'll follow Arrosa's plan, and walk upstream by the river until we find one of the hilltop settlements that I saw from the Sextant. There was smoke rising from the summit of one, so we know that the natives have discovered fire at least. When we find them, we'll ask for help.'

'It might be simpler to scare them away,' said Arrosa. 'You two are mages, and I'm Gifted. And what if they don't speak any language we understand?'

'We're going to die here,' said Cole.

Arrosa laughed. 'We might. But if we do, I first intend to rule this world as queen. You two can be my loyal courtiers.'

'No way,' said Cael. 'I'll be king, and you can be my servant.'

Arrosa smiled, then she glanced at Cole. 'There's no point in sitting there feeling miserable, Cole. We have to make the best of it. We have a Tempest sword, and I know how to repair it. It might take us days, or months, but if there's any way to get off this world, we'll find it.'

They went back to the cave, and gathered up their meagre possessions. Cael found his boots, which he hadn't worn for many days, and pulled them on. With no means to attach the sword to his belt, he had little choice but to carry it in his right hand.

'Make sure you don't lose it,' said Arrosa. Her dress had dried out in the sunshine, and her good cheer contrasted with the sullen misery that had descended upon Cole. Cael eyed his cousin, but Cole refused to meet his glance.

They set off when they were ready, staying close to the river bank as they walked upstream.

By late afternoon, they had ranged far further than any of them had previously gone. The availability of food increased a little, and they found a few bushes which had enough berries to satisfy them. They ate until their tongues were blue from the juice, then they carried on, climbing steadily as the height of the land increased. They entered a forest, and were passing through it when Arrosa came to a halt. She gestured to a wide tree trunk. A yard from the ground, a small wooden implement of some kind had been driven into the side of the tree.

'Look at that,' she said. 'There's a little groove in it, to collect the sap.'

'There's no way that's natural,' said Cael. 'Humans.'

'That's exactly what I was thinking,' she said; 'but look at the way the bark is growing back around it. It hasn't been used in a while.'

They gazed around, but the forest seemed empty and still.

They carried on, following the river as it began to narrow.

'How far is this village, do you think?' said Arrosa, as they trudged along.

'It might be two or three days' walk from here,' Cael said.

'It will be getting dark soon. Should we look for somewhere to sleep?'

Cael nodded, then he raised a hand, and crouched down.

Arrosa leaned in. 'What is it?' she whispered.

'I thought I saw someone, on the track ahead,' he whispered back. 'Maybe it's just the fading light, playing tricks on my eyes. Hold on, and I'll use my vision to check.'

'What about your mother sensing your powers?'

He raised an eyebrow at her. 'I think we might be beyond that stage now. Maybe we should all use our powers. Why the fuck didn't I think of this down by the Sextant? Cole, use your vision, and I'll use mine. Arrosa, turn something into glass.'

'Like what?'

'Whatever you like.'

Cael sent out his vision powers. He hadn't used them since they had arrived on World Three, to avoid being detected by his mother, and it felt good to push his vision above the tops of the trees. He gazed around in the last light of the day, as the sun neared the horizon to his left. He looked down at the river, and at the track that ran next to it – another sign that his sub-created humans had been in the area. He was about to look in a different direction, when Cole shook his shoulder. Cael pulled his vision back to his body, and turned to his cousin.

'Did you see it?' said Cole, his eyes wide.

'See what?' said Cael.

'At the top of the hillside – a village.'

'A village?' said Arrosa. 'Are there people there?'

Cole stared at her, as though he was on the verge of panic. 'No. Not any more.'

Cael got to his feet, and he hurried up the track with Arrosa, as Cole lagged behind. They came to a more level stretch of ground, and Cael almost ran into a wooden post that had been hammered into the ground. A severed human head was sitting on the top of the post, its flesh rotting, and parts of the skull visible amid a swarm of insects.

Cael backed away. 'That's what I must have seen before, when I thought I'd seen someone.'

Arrosa touched his arm, then she pointed. Cael turned away from the head on the post, and saw the village laid out to their right. A dozen wooden huts were laid out in a circle, and in the middle of that circle was a mound of decapitated bodies – men, women and children.

'I tried to tell you,' said Cole, as he reached Cael and Arrosa. 'This is what I saw.'

Arrosa put a hand to her mouth.

'This happened a few days ago,' said Cael, 'while we were sunbathing and swimming by the cave.'

'Why?' said Arrosa.

'I don't know. Why have humans ever killed each other?'

'They're your humans,' said Cole. 'Your creation did this.' He walked closer to the pile of headless bodies. 'Most of the bodies have been mutilated,' he said.

'I don't want to hear about it, Cole,' said Arrosa.

'Burn them,' said Cael. 'Use your fire powers, Cole, and burn them all.'

'It's nearly dark,' said Cole. 'The fire will be seen from miles around.'

'We'll be long gone by then,' said Cael. 'We'll leave as soon as the flames take hold.'

'Where will we go?' said Arrosa.

'Deep into the forest,' said Cael, 'where we'll hide until it gets light. We'll take turns to stay awake, just in case, and Cole and I will scan the area with our vision.'

'I'll need one of you to generate a spark for me,' Cole said. 'I can't summon fire from nothing.'

Cael and Arrosa got to work. They gathered a small collection of stones, then they sat and began striking the rocks together, as Cole crouched next to them, his right hand raised and ready. Cael cracked one stone against another, and a large spark flashed. Cole's powers caught it, and he sent it into the thick thatch of a village hut. Smoke and flames began to rise from the roof, and Cole moved his fingers. He aimed the flames at the mound of bodies, and they shot away from the thatched roof, and exploded onto the mound. Cole raised his right hand higher, and the fire swept over the mound, until the flames were leaping up into the darkening sky. Thick coils of pungent smoke billowed out from the inferno Cole had created. He, Cael and Arrosa stared at the bonfire for a moment, then they turned, and fled into the forest.

CHAPTER 14
OF UNCERTAIN PARENTAGE

Alatsuraga Bay, the Plateau – 26th Day, Second Third Summer 544

Professor Gallea poured coffee into two delicate cups.

'He has become quite obsessed, Kyra,' she said. 'I suppose I shouldn't be surprised. After eight years of teaching students and repairing broken Quadrants, he was probably in need of another little project to occupy his mind.'

'It's not just a *little project*, ma'am,' said Kyra. 'It is work of the utmost importance.'

'You are a very earnest young lady,' said Gallea, 'and I don't mean that as a criticism. Too many girls your age spend all their time chasing boys, or worrying about their hair. It is refreshing to find one so serious.'

Kyra frowned. 'You think I'm too serious?'

'You are an exceptional student, and it is clear that you are a young woman with a great future ahead of her. You are a Junior Elector, are you not? That is a singular honour. Your vote will help decide the future of the entire Empire; although, of course, I hope that day is very far from now. Empress Thorn is only in her thirties, is she not?'

'Late thirties.'

'Then one would expect her reign to last several more decades. You might be well into your middle age before you get a chance to exercise your vote. In other words, you should perhaps consider enjoying yourself a little more while you are still young. It passes all too quickly, believe me.'

'I'm not really interested in boys, or drinking and going to parties. I would rather stay in and read a good book.'

'Oh yes? And what do you like to read?'

'History, politics... that's it, really. History and politics.'

Gallea smiled. 'You would have made an excellent acolyte in Tell Hoard. I gave forty years of my life to that place. In order to further my studies, I had to make several sacrifices. No marriage, no children, no normal family life. Everyone who lived in Tell Hoard had to do the same; it wasn't just me. I do not regret any of it, but I sometimes wonder what my life would have been like had I chosen a different course. My family was quite rich, you see, and so I had a few paths open to me when I was your age. My nephew ended up inheriting the family wealth that was originally due to come to me. I don't think my parents ever quite understood the choice I made to go to Tell Hoard, but they didn't try to stop me. What do you see yourself doing after university, Kyra?'

'I want to go into government.'

'Spoken like a true Holdfast. No, don't take offence. I meant that you possess the easy assurance and wilful self-confidence that have seen the Holdfasts rise to the top. One does not rule an empire by being meek and humble. One has to be bold, and be prepared to make terrible mistakes. But try to leave a little space in your life for enjoyment.'

Elbannon limped into the kitchen, his apron and gloves soiled and filthy.

'I am a genius,' he said.

'Have you made a breakthrough, my old friend?' said Gallea.

'Not in the slightest,' he said, sitting down. 'I have absolutely no progress to report. Every experiment has been a disaster. My only achievement is that I can rule out every idea that has so far occurred to me. I now know much more than I did about what doesn't work.'

He pulled his gloves off and poured himself a coffee.

'I was thinking about our missing Sextant,' he said. 'It dawned on me this morning that, whoever has it, clearly does not wish to destroy us all; or, if they do, then they lack the knowledge or skills to do it. If it had been stolen by an enemy with dark designs, then the Star Continent would already be nothing more than a cloud of vapour and dust. Then I wondered if the thief had used a Quadrant to steal it. If that was the case, then they would lack the requisite Tempest sword to activate it. I trust that the Weathervane and the two Fated Blades are safe and accounted for?'

'Aye,' said Kyra; 'as far as I know.'

'Was it stolen by use of a Quadrant? Does it remain inactive?'

'Is this relevant to your project, Professor?'

'It might be. If I knew for certain that the Sextant is inactive, then its Tempest signal would be weaker, and therefore harder to detect from afar.'

'The thief stole a Tempest sword to activate it. There was no Quadrant involved.'

Elbannon narrowed his eyes. 'Excuse me? They *stole a Tempest sword*? Is that what you said? Impossible. There are no Tempest swords worthy of the name, apart from those I have already mentioned.'

'It was stolen from an imperial armoury.'

Elbannon stared at her.

'I'm only telling you what I know,' she said. 'The thief stole the only Tempest sword that would fit the Sextant, and they stole it from an imperial armoury.'

'Oh.'

'What is that supposed to mean?'

'I think I know the sword in question. I supervised the forging of those weapons a few years ago, as a favour to Caelius Logos, the Quartermaster. I ensured that, uh, well... I made sure that they were of exceedingly low quality. I didn't want my Tempest turned into weapons, so I added lead to the alloy.'

'You did what?' said Gallea.

'I sabotaged my own work, to offer proof to Caelius that Tempest was an unsuitable material for constructing weapons. Tempest should not be used to kill, Gallea. Are you saying, Kyra, that one of my contaminated swords was placed into the Sextant... and the Sextant became operational?'

'It was definitely operational,' she said. 'I saw it being used with my own eyes. Therefore, even though it contained lead, it still worked.'

'Not for long, I fear,' he said. 'That alloy is inherently unstable. I wanted my Tempest swords to snap, you see, and the lead provided the critical weakness. Put it under any kind of pressure, and it will crack or break. In fact, the stress involved in transporting the Sextant to another place may have already damaged it. This is useful information. I shall proceed under the assumption that the Sextant is currently unusable.' He smiled. 'I suppose that explains why no worlds have yet been destroyed – the Sextant is a useless heap of junk at the moment. My sabotage has sabotaged the thief. You see, Gallea; I am a genius.'

Kyra got to her feet. 'Thank you for the coffee, and the company,' she said. 'I should return to Colsbury. My Aunty Sable is due to arrive this afternoon. It's her birthday.'

Elbannon laughed. 'The killer of three Ascendants, eh? Though not the important ones, of course. Be sure to tell her I said that.'

'What do you mean, *not the important ones*?' said Kyra. 'Sable killed Belinda; didn't you know that?'

The smile vanished from Elbannon's face. 'I didn't know that. I thought Edmond killed Belinda.'

'No, it was Sable. Though, in her defence, she had no control over her actions at the time. Do you still want me to pass on your message?'

'Eh, no. Probably best not to.'

'Just pass on our regards,' said Gallea.

'Thank you, Professor; I shall.'

Kyra touched the Quadrant concealed in her coat.

Middle balcony, Colsbury. Go.

The air shimmered, and she appeared in the centre of the wide middle balcony. She took a moment to gaze out over the lake, which was glistening in the summer sunshine, then she looked around for Kelsey. She found her aunt seated next to Naxor and Cardova, and she walked over.

'Take a seat,' said Cardova.

Kyra sat down.

'How's the miserable old bastard doing today?' said Kelsey.

'He has no progress to report,' said Kyra, 'but he is certainly busy.'

'Aye,' said Kelsey; 'busy spending our money.'

'Do you remember the sword that Cael stole from the armoury?'

'Aye.'

'Elbannon deliberately added lead to the alloy, to weaken it. Tempest does not react well with lead. It causes the alloy to become brittle and unstable. He believes that the movement from here to Cael's new world has most likely broken it.'

Kelsey looked up at the sky and emitted a loud groan of frustration.

'You sound like an animal that should be put out of its misery,' said Naxor.

'Did Elbannon say why he had done this?' said Cardova.

'He was trying to prove to Caelius Logos that Tempest was an unsuitable material from which to fashion weapons.'

'That sly old bastard,' said Cardova. 'The entire weapons programme was altered after those experiments. We had originally planned to create thousands of Tempest weapons – swords, axes, maces – you name it. Wait until Caelius finds out. I am going to authorise an immediate re-start of the Tempest weapons project; this time, without Elbannon's oversight.'

'Did you miss the other part, Lucius?' said Kelsey. 'The part about how Cael, Cole and Arrosa are probably stranded on that world?'

Cardova narrowed his eyes. 'Could you repeat that part for me?'

'Elbannon thinks that the brittleness of the sword has probably resulted in it being damaged,' said Kyra. 'If that is true, then the Sextant will be inoperable.'

'Inoperable,' said Naxor, 'and forever out of reach. Without wishing to sound callous, in the grand, and long-term, scheme of things, the loss of the Sextant will indubitably prove to be of far greater consequence than the loss of any three people, no matter how dear they are to us. One thousand years from now, the Sextant will still be missed. I shall certainly still miss it.'

Kelsey shook her head at him. 'Do not repeat that comment in front of Karalyn or the Empress. It's bad enough that you say those kinds of things to us. Kyra is Cael's sister, for Pyre's sake.'

'I was making a philosophical point,' said Naxor. 'The loss of the Sextant means no more new worlds, ever. It also means that no existing worlds can ever be arbitrarily destroyed. These are profound matters of consequence.'

'Elbannon might be a numpty,' said Kelsey, 'but he's our best hope of finding the Sextant, and the three reprobates who stole it. Don't anyone mention this news to the Empress. I will inform her later this evening, after Sable gets here.'

'I will have to tell Karalyn,' said Cardova.

'That's fine,' said Kelsey. 'It's highly unlikely that she'll speak to the Empress about it.'

'I want to ask about the Quartermaster's experiments,' said Kyra. 'I remember being told years ago that Tempest would not be used to create weapons. I thought the Empire was taking the moral high ground; that wasn't true, was it?'

'It was never true,' said Cardova. 'We stopped building weapons with Tempest because we believed, wrongly, it seems, that the alloy was unsuited for that purpose. If Tempest turns out to have military applications, then we will be taking advantage of them.'

'Why?'

'Because Tempest might turn out to be much better than steel.'

'Better at what – killing people?'

Cardova glanced at Kelsey, who smiled back at him.

'I recall having a similar conversation with Kyra when we visited Ravi's facility,' she said.

Cardova nodded, then he turned back to Kyra. 'War is awful; no one needs to explain that. We all know it. The only thing worse than preparing for war, is not preparing. The job of Imperial Constable is to make sure we are ready, just in case; and I will use every advantage at my disposal to defend the Empire.'

Kyra frowned, but fell silent.

A courtier approached the table and bowed low.

'Madam Herald,' she said, 'the delegation from Amatskouri is insisting that they be allowed to speak to you before they leave Colsbury.'

'Oh, they're insisting, are they? Didn't you speak to them after breakfast, Naxor?'

'I did,' said the demigod. 'It was the usual tirade of complaints about the government of Rakana. I told them that we would consider their words carefully. I thought they had already left Colsbury.'

Three Rakanese hurried onto the balcony. Cardova got up from his seat and placed a hand on the hilt of his sword, ensuring that he was between the Rakanese and the table, while the courtier raised his hands and tried to push them back.

'You are not allowed on to this balcony without express permission,' the courtier called out.

More soldiers appeared, and they cornered the three Rakanese by the balcony doors. The Rakanese fell to their knees, and lifted their arms in supplication.

'We beg you,' one cried, 'forgive us this indiscretion, but we must talk to the Herald of the Empire.'

Naxor chuckled. 'One has to admire their persistence, at least.'

Kelsey sighed and shook her head. 'If they promise to leave Colsbury, I'll allow them to speak. Two minutes – that's all you got.'

'Thank you, oh gracious Herald,' said one of the Rakanese. 'The government of Amatskouri, your faithful Rakanese allies within the Empire, have sent us here to implore you to beg the Empress to directly intervene to overthrow the wicked regime oppressing our brothers and sisters in the Republic of Rakana. After decades of corruption and misrule, our people on the other side of the frontier are suffering the worst famine in a century, worse even than in the dark days following the Migration. Only the Empire has the force and the will necessary to remove the regime that has caused this famine. Deploy the Imperial Army into Rakana as liberators, and the Rakanese people everywhere will rejoice and give thanks to the blessed Empress. Save our brothers and sisters from starvation, and you will forever earn our loyalty and gratitude.'

'That's your two minutes,' said Kelsey. 'Be assured that I will raise this topic with Her Majesty. Soldiers, please escort the delegation gently but firmly to their carriages, and ensure that they leave the island.'

The soldiers of the Imperial Guard hauled the three Rakanese to their feet, and escorted them from the balcony.

The courtier bowed low. 'My humble apologies that they managed to reach the balcony, ma'am. They promised me that they would remain at the top of the stairs, where I left them.'

Kelsey waved her away. 'It's fine. They're harmless.'

'Thank you, ma'am.'

The courtier bowed again, and hurried away.

'Do they actually want us to invade their homeland?' said Kyra.

'They've been asking us to invade Rakana for years,' said Kelsey. 'Did you know that Amatskouri might have a larger population than the whole of Rakana? And it's a damn sight more prosperous. I say *might*, because the Rakanese government never supplies us with any information about what goes on within their borders.'

'Then how do the Amatskourians know there's a famine?'

'They send spies over the mountains.'

Kyra glanced at the others sitting by the table. 'Are we going to invade?'

Cardova laughed. 'Not a chance,' he said. 'There would be

carnage – pointless, expensive, and tragic. Our troops would reach the centre of Arakhanah City, and inherit nothing but a violent, chaotic mess. Our presence there would make things worse, not better.'

'Then how can we help the Rakanese?'

'The Imperial Court is examining a range of options,' said Kelsey.

Kyra opened her mouth to ask another question, but the air shimmered a few yards away before she could get the words out. Sable appeared, cradling a young infant in her left arm. Next to her was Lara, who was holding the hand of a small boy. Kyra smiled and rose from the table. She extended her arms to embrace her aunt, and Sable handed her the baby.

'That's not what I meant, Aunty, but all right,' Kyra said.

Sable embraced her niece. 'That's little Lindi Holdfast you've got there,' she said. 'Try not to drop her.'

'Happy birthday, Aunty,' said Kelsey.

'Thank you,' said Sable. 'Here we are, in Colsbury once again.' She glanced out over the balcony. 'Nothing appears to have burnt down since this time last year. Is that Shella I can see on that yacht?'

'Aye,' said Kelsey. 'Olo'osso lives here now. He brought the yacht up from the Inner Sea.'

'My father's in Colsbury?' said Lara.

'He's been here for around five thirds or so,' said Cardova. 'He and Shella... have become close companions.'

Kelsey laughed. 'That's the polite way to put it.'

Lara walked over to the edge of the balcony. 'That randy old bastard.'

'Which one are we talking about?' said Kelsey. 'Shella or your father?'

'Both,' said Lara. 'Well, at least Anaj'osso will get to see his granddad while we're here. I wonder why Maddie didn't tell us.'

'She probably didn't notice,' said Sable. She turned to Kelsey. 'Blackrose was a little upset when she returned to Dragon Eyre. She was happy you had reached an agreement over the Unk Tannic, but that wasn't what was occupying her thoughts. I understand that she was exceedingly rude to Lord Sigum.'

'She was,' said Kelsey. 'At one point, I thought it might jeopardise the talks. She was deeply insulting.'

'And then Lahnos insulted her?' said Sable.

'Aye. He called her stupid to her face.'

Sable sat down at the table and lit a cigarette. 'This is partly my fault. Eight years ago, I told Blackrose that I'd met a dragon on Athumia who'd broken a vow. But – I also told her that Lord Sigum was honourable. I think she remembered the first part and forgot the second. When I reminded her of this, she got quite defensive. All the same, I believe that, deep down, she knows that what she did was wrong. It might take her a long time to admit it, though.'

'And even longer to get a bleeding apology,' said Lara. 'The yacht has just berthed alongside the jetty. I might take Joss and Lindi down to see my father.'

'Are you sure?' said Sable. 'You don't mind taking both children for a while?'

'I'll take 'em for the whole bleeding day, Sable,' said Lara. 'This is your birthday. Spend it with your family, and I'll take care of the tiddlers.' She took the baby from Kyra's arms. 'I'll be seeing you all later, eh? Are our quarters in the same place as usual?'

'Aye,' said Kelsey. 'They've been laid out just how you like them.'

'Thanks, Kelsey,' said Lara. She kissed Sable, then strode off, a baby in one arm, and her grip firmly on the boy's hand.

Sable watched them leave, then she turned to the others. 'I intend to get drunk tonight.'

'You get inebriated every time you come here for your birthday, Sable,' said Naxor.

'Yeah, because I spend the rest of the year sober. Believe it or not, I am a responsible parent. And, I didn't get drunk last year, because Lindi was only a month old. There's nothing worse than looking after a baby when you've got a raging hangover.'

'I think I might have blotted out your last birthday from my memory,' said Naxor. 'All that crying and wailing; and that was just you. The baby was even worse.'

'Giving birth to Lindi nearly broke me,' Sable said. 'Joss was bad enough, but Lindi? I'm not having any more; that's for certain.'

'Is it time to play *Guess the father*?' said Naxor. 'Or should we wait until you've had a few drinks?'

'Either way, I won't be telling you.'

'It seems clear to me that you employed a Kellach Brigdomin to father Joss,' Naxor said. 'His stature gives it away. As for Lindi, it is too early to tell. At the moment, she looks just like her mother.'

'You'll never guess,' said Sable; 'and it's none of your business, anyway.' She glanced around. 'Where's Cael? He's usually here to see me.'

No one spoke, and Sable narrowed her eyes.

'Oh dear,' said Sable. 'Tell me everything.'

Two hours later, Sable and Kyra were in the gardens, strolling through the orchard in the summer sunshine.

'I'll do it,' said Sable. 'If Elbannon creates his Compass, and it works, then I will fetch Cael and the others from his world.'

'No, Aunty,' said Kyra. 'I will do it.'

'I can't let you take the risk,' said Sable. 'This is what I do.'

'It's what you used to do. You have two young children to look after.'

'And you have your whole life ahead of you.'

'It was partly my fault that he stole the Sextant and ran away. I need this chance to redeem myself.'

'That's the voice of pride, Kyra,' said Sable. 'Don't let pride govern your decisions.'

'It's not just pride. I can hear Tempest whenever I touch a Quadrant. The Compass might only work for me.'

'But I can hear the voice of the Sextant,' said Sable. 'It might only work for me.'

They reached the gravestones.

'I was hoping your mother would be here,' said Sable.

'I'm behind you,' said Karalyn.

Kyra and Sable turned. Karalyn was pushing a pram containing her two infant children. She parked it by Lennox's headstone, and embraced Sable.

'Keeping busy, I see?' said Sable.

'Aye,' said Karalyn. 'I noticed the presence of a new god on Colsbury a few hours ago.'

'A new god?' said Kyra. 'Who?'

'Why don't you let Aunty Sable explain? Sable?'

Kyra's aunt narrowed her eyes.

'You didn't think you could hide it from me, did you?' said Karalyn.

Sable shook her head. 'Your mother is talking about Lindi, Kyra. Lindi's father was a god.'

'He is an exceptionally powerful god,' said Karalyn. 'I hope you know what you're doing.'

'You're a fine one to talk,' said Sable. 'You have two demigods in that pram.'

'The Holdfast gods are multiplying,' said Karalyn. 'Corthie has six, soon to be seven; I have two, and you have one, Sable.'

'Why did you choose a god, Aunty?' said Kyra.

'Partly through vanity, I suppose,' she said. 'I want my legacy to live on forever. Also, I never have to worry about Lindi falling ill, or getting hurt in an accident. It takes quite a weight off the mind.'

'It does,' said Karalyn, 'but we should try to consider the long-term consequences.'

'That's easy for you to say,' said Sable. 'You are also immortal. I am most definitely not.'

Karalyn knelt down by the gravestone, and re-arranged the flowers. 'I heard what you were saying about the Compass,' she said. 'You can talk to Quadrants, Kyra, and you can talk to the Sextant, Sable. Only I can talk to both. I will do it.'

Kyra folded her arms across her chest. 'Have you finally noticed that Cael is missing? He'll be pleased.'

Karalyn gave her daughter a look of confusion.

'Are you coming to the party tonight?' said Sable.

'No,' said Karalyn. 'Lucius wants to go, so I will be looking after Carden and Caitlyn. Would you do me a favour while you're there, Sable?'

'Sure.'

'Kelsey's marriage is in trouble, and she's...'

'Is it?' said Kyra.

'Aye, it is,' said her mother. 'Kelsey and Van hide it well, but they're close to getting divorced. I've tried to speak to Kelsey about it, but I'm not very good at that sort of thing. She needs a sympathetic ear, Sable.'

'And I will supply it. Thanks for letting me know.'

'Aunty Kelsey has never mentioned anything about this to me,' said Kyra.

'There's a lot she keeps from you,' said Karalyn. 'Did you know, for example, that over forty thousand Rahain have been killed so far in the invasion?'

Kyra blinked. 'What?'

'Did you even know that an invasion of Rahain was underway, Kyra? You're so blinded by the imaginary ideal of Thorn's Empire, that you overlook the brutal reality. Lahnos Laimos's dragon, along with battalions of Sanang warriors deranged on their own bloodlust, have been burning and slaughtering their way through Tahrana City. Why don't you ask your beloved Thorn about it? You can also ask her about the shipments of explosives that she's been sending to Dragon Eyre, in order to blow up the Unk Tannic. Why do you think Blackrose keeps visiting? They're arranging a military alliance.'

Kyra glanced at Sable. 'Is this all true?'

'I keep clear of politics these days,' said Sable, 'but I knew that Blackrose was in talks with the Empress.'

'Did you hear about the ultimatum Thorn gave to the City of Salve?' said Karalyn.

Sable shook her head.

'She told Emily and Daniel that if they didn't join the Empire, all aid would be cut off.'

'It was more complicated than that!' said Kyra.

A faint smile appeared on her mother's lips. 'Was it? I thought I'd accurately summed it up.'

'It has been clear to me for some time, Mother,' said Kyra, 'that you will say anything to make the Empress appear in a bad light. No matter what Her Majesty decides, you will find a way to denigrate it.'

'Maybe,' said Karalyn, 'but in this case, she's making it easy for me. Rahain, Dragon Eyre, the City... where shall be next? Rakana? Athumia? Thorn's imperial fantasies are limitless. Anyone with half a brain could have told you that twenty years ago.'

'I doubt your husband would agree.'

'You're right about that, Kyra,' said Karalyn. 'Lucius is a good husband, and a good father, but we don't share the same opinions regarding Thorn. His heart is in the right place, though. Lucius cares deeply about the people of the Empire, and that's good enough for me. His advice tempers some of Thorn and Kelsey's more extreme ideas.'

'I think I might get ready for the party,' said Sable. 'It's my birthday and, no offence, I would rather not spend it discussing the rights and wrongs of imperialism.'

Karalyn smiled. 'I understand, Sable. Have a good evening.'

Sable strode away, and Kyra hurried after her. They left the gardens via the lamplit tunnel that went under the two keeps, and emerged into the main forecourt in front of the Summer Palace.

'My mother's wrong,' Kyra said. 'She seems to think...'

Sable raised a hand. 'I'm not getting involved in an argument between you and your mother.'

'Did you notice that she didn't even once express any concern about Cael or Arrosa?'

'What did I just say, Kyra? I love you, but I also love your mother. I think Thorn is a good Empress, but I also happen to believe that she is not without her flaws. There you have it. That is my opinion. I will not be drawn into criticising either woman. No one is perfect, least of all me.'

'I don't know about that, Aunty; you're pretty close.'

Sable smiled. 'I know, Kyra, but one shouldn't boast. Let's go into the palace, and find our best dresses to wear for tonight. I'll do your hair, if you'll let me. And I might have to borrow some of your make up. If I'm going to get blind drunk, I might as well look good.'

CHAPTER 15
ADMISSION OF DEFEAT

Colsbury Castle, the Holdings – 27th Day, Second Third Summer 544

An enormous purple dragon descended over the burning city, its huge wings silhouetted by the flames. It landed upon a line of tall battlements, and turned its gaze towards a young woman standing by the parapet.

'You know what to do,' said the woman, her eyes reflecting the raging fires. 'Kill them all.'

Kelsey's eyes opened, and she shuddered as a wave of nausea rippled through her guts. She leaned over, then fell out of bed, landing on the polished wooden floor. She crawled to the bathroom, and threw up into the toilet. She leaned back against the bathtub, her hands shaking, as sweat appeared on her forehead.

'Pyre's cock,' she mumbled.

She glanced down. She was still wearing the same clothes she had been in the night before, when she and Sable had worked their way through far too much whisky. They had been trying to work out which was better – the usual whisky from Severton, or the new varieties emerging from Aila Holdfast's distilleries in Lach; but after several glasses, Kelsey had been unable to tell the difference.

Her dream about the purple dragon came back to her, and then, with a sudden realisation, she knew that it hadn't been merely a dream. She wondered which city had been burning. Kelsey hadn't recognised the young woman who had appeared in the vision, and so she filed it away with the other useless prophecies over which she had no control. It occurred to her that she must have been present by the battlements; it had been her own eyes that she had been looking through, and that gave her some comfort, as it meant that she wasn't about to die any time soon.

She gripped on to the side of the bath and pulled herself to her feet. She washed her face with cold water, and stumbled back into the bedroom of Cael's quarters. Sable was lying on the room's only couch, her black dress still on, while several bottles, glasses, and a couple of full ashtrays were sitting on the floor. Kelsey almost gagged from the smell of stale smoke, and she staggered over to a window, and opened it wide. Sunlight flooded into the room, and Kelsey turned away, her sight dazzled.

Sable groaned from the couch.

'Serves you right,' muttered Kelsey, as she fell into a chair.

Sable opened her eyes. 'Are we dead?'

'If we are, then this is a very disappointing afterlife.'

'Who won – Severton or Lachellan?'

'Either way, we lost. I'm, eh... sorry about all the crying.'

'I only wish I could have been more use, niece.'

'It helped just having someone to talk to,' said Kelsey. 'I don't know what I'm going to do. Van's acting as though I'm holding him here under duress, because I won't let him take the children to the City. Maybe I should admit defeat.'

Sable swung her legs off the couch and sat upright. 'Maybe you should,' she said. 'You should probably do what's best for Calpurnia and Caelius.' She reached into a small, hidden pocket, and pulled out a tiny vial.

'What do you think you're doing?' said Kelsey.

'What does it look like?' said Sable. 'I'm going to take some salve to cure my hangover.'

'How often do you take it?'

'Whenever I have a hangover, which, at this rate, is about once a year.'

'You're not addicted, then?'

'I have no time in my life for a full-blown salve addiction, Kelsey. I'll save that for when Joss and Lindi are older.'

She took a small sip, and her appearance and posture immediately improved. She stretched, and a big smile spread over her face.

'That's better,' she said. 'Do you want some?'

Kelsey shook her head.

'Is this because Van used to be addicted?'

'Salve nearly killed him,' said Kelsey. 'It killed Bridget.'

'Bridget was trying to re-grow an eye,' said Sable. 'I'm not. See – I'm putting the lid back on, and I won't be having any more.'

'Do you feel an urge to take more?'

'I always feel the urge to take more – be it alcohol, weed or salve. I've learned how to say no to myself. I have to put Lara and the children first. Life is a compromise, isn't it?'

'That feels as though it was aimed at me,' said Kelsey. 'Do you think I should compromise with Van? Are you saying that I don't put him and the children first? I'm sorry, Sable, but I'm the Herald of the Empire. I don't think I have any room to compromise, not without giving up my position.'

'Do you enjoy being Herald?'

'Are you joking? I fucking love it. At the end of this year, I will have been Herald for a decade, but sometimes I feel as though I'm just getting started.'

'It sounds as if you've already made your mind up about Van. Here's a suggestion – allow him to take the children to the City for a short period, until the end of summer, say; then see how you feel when he comes back.'

'You think I'm a terrible mother, don't you?'

'Men can get away with it far more easily, Kelsey. Some folk expect a man to concentrate on his career, but when a woman does it, they complain that she's not a good mother. You can't win – that's the honest truth, so you might as well pick your side and get on with it.' She got to her feet, and began to pull back her hair. 'I picked my side,' she went on, 'when I decided to have children. I don't regret it, even though I sometimes miss the craziness of my old life. With any luck, I'll impart some of that craziness into Joss and Lindi. Do you have a hair band?'

'These are Cael's quarters,' Kelsey said. 'I've never seen him wear a hair band, so the answer's probably no.'

'He might have had a girlfriend.'

'Not in Colsbury. He had one on the Hold Fast estate, before he brutally dumped her.'

'Whatever happened to the sweet little Cael we used to know?'

'He grew up.'

'Kyra seems well-balanced.'

'Aye, but I worry about her, too. She seems to be developing… pacifist tendencies.'

'You mean she has a conscience?'

'A naïve sense of idealism, more like.'

Sable gave up trying to put her hair into order. She crouched down by an ashtray, and rummaged around until she found a cigarette that had been only half-smoked.

Kelsey grimaced. 'That's vile.'

'Former smokers are always the most judgmental.'

Kelsey watched as Sable lit the half cigarette with her metal lighter. 'I suppose we should announce to the world that we're still alive. Are you coming back for the twins' birthday this year?'

'Do you think I should?' said Sable. 'If Cael and the others haven't been found by then, it might be quite a sombre affair. I wouldn't want to intrude.'

'If Cael hasn't been found, then Kyra will need her Aunty Sable.'

'Then I'll be here.'

Sable stubbed out her cigarette, then she extended a hand, and pulled Kelsey to her feet.

'I'll tidy this later,' Kelsey said.

They left the apartment, and started walking through the corridors of the palace. Their party dresses raised a few eyebrows among the courtiers and soldiers they passed, but none dared make a comment. They reached the quarters where Sable and Lara stayed when in Colsbury, and Sable opened the door.

Lara was feeding Lindi in a chair, and she laughed when she saw the two women by the door.

'Have a good night, did you, girls?' she said. 'Check the bleeding state of you.'

Joss ran through from the bedroom, and Sable crouched down to give him a hug.

'I'll leave you to it,' said Kelsey. 'I'm off to lie down in a dark room.'

'Did Sable not give you any of her salve?' said Lara. 'It works a treat.'

'Salve's the last thing I need, Lara,' said Kelsey. 'I'll see you all later.'

Kelsey closed the door. She took a flight of stairs up to the floor where her own quarters lay, and entered her living room. Van, Calpurnia and Caelius were dressed and up, and Van was readying the children to go down for breakfast.

Van glanced up at her, but said nothing.

'I'm not going to die for a few years,' said Kelsey. 'I don't know why I just said that.'

'Because you're still drunk?' said Van.

'Aye. Maybe. I need to have a bath, and I need to get ready for today. Envoys from the Republic of Rakana are arriving at noon.'

Van nodded. 'I have received an urgent summons to return to the Royal Palace in Ooste; a summons I can't ignore.'

'From whom?' said Kelsey. 'I mean, it's usually me who travels back and forth between here and the City. Who gave you the summons?'

'Naxor. He was in the City briefly yesterday, and he gave me the news last night.'

'What do Emily and Daniel want you for?'

'City business.'

'So you're not going to tell me?'

'That's right. The City, as has been pointed out, is an independent sovereign realm, and I am not at liberty to discuss its internal affairs with a politician of a foreign entity.'

Kelsey smiled. 'You've been waiting to spring that line on me for a while, haven't you?'

'It's the truth. I'm going to ask you this question only once – will you allow me to take the children with me when I leave?'

'When would you be back?'

'I don't know. It might just be a couple of days, it might be longer.'

'Then no.'

'Then I have nothing more to say to you, Kelsey. Come on, children; let's go to breakfast while mummy has a bath. You'll see her later.'

Kelsey stood to the side in silence as Van led the children out of the apartment. When the door was closed, Kelsey went round from room to room, closing the shutters, then she went to the bathroom, and filled the tub with scalding-hot water.

By noon, Kelsey was ready to resume her duties as Herald. Sable, Lara, and their two children had gone back to Dragon Eyre after breakfast; and Van had taken Calpurnia and Caelius out on Olo'osso's yacht so they could sail around the lake. From the middle balcony of the palace, Kelsey watched the small craft slip away from the side of the jetty, then she strode into the main reception room on that level, where the Empress, Naxor, Shella, Cardova and Brogan had gathered.

'Good morning, Herald,' said the Empress, who was seated upon her throne. 'This meeting shouldn't last too long, but I would like to request that no one loses their temper with the Rakanese officials, even if we are severely provoked. Is that understood?'

The others murmured their agreement.

Kelsey walked up to Naxor. 'Why were you in the City yesterday?'

'I was arranging the last of this year's aid shipment,' said Naxor.

'Some coal was late to arrive from Northern Kell, and I wanted to give the City no reason to complain about our tardiness. Van told you about the summons, did he?'

'Has Van been summoned to the City?' said Cardova.

'He has,' said Naxor. 'King Daniel told me it was urgent.'

'They'll moan, and they'll complain,' said Shella, 'but there's little they can do. They either accept our deal, or they don't.'

'If they accept,' said Brogan, 'and they formally become part of the Empire, should the full allotment of aid be reconstituted?'

'Yes,' said the Empress. 'It may well decline over the coming years, as needs vary across the provinces of the Empire, but it would be wise to remain generous if they accede to our offer. It will allow them to save face, and to claim a victory among the people of the City. I did not set out to insult the King and Queen, but I fear they have taken this badly. Naxor, what is the general atmosphere like in Ooste at present?'

'To be frank, Your Majesty,' he said, 'there is a climate of raw anger and feral terror. The upper echelons of City society are extremely fearful that they will lose the generous subsidies they receive from the Empire; and many are urging the King and Queen to accept the terms of annexation. It would be different, I feel, if any large number of Rosers were still alive, but most perished at the hands of the Ascendants. The Rosers would have been strenuously opposed to any loss of independence. The other tribes are not as... patriotic, shall we say.'

'You also mentioned anger.'

'Yes, Your Majesty – great currents of anger. Some is being directed towards the King and Queen, for having led the City into this precarious situation; and some, it is true, is being directed at us. Some see the Empire as callous and cynical, taking advantage of the poor little City, as though we were cast as the schoolyard bully, stealing sweets from an innocent child.'

'That analogy is all wrong,' said Brogan, 'for we have been supplying them with the best sweets money can buy for ten years.'

'Indeed; but now we are threatening to take them away. At any rate,

I am reporting what I have heard, not how I personally feel about the matter.'

The main set of double doors opened, and several courtiers bowed and entered.

'The officials from the government of the Republic of Rakana are here, your Imperial Majesty,' said one.

'Please show them in,' said Kelsey.

The courtier bowed again, then he gestured towards the entrance, and four Rakanese strode into the hall – two men, and two women.

'Greetings,' said Kelsey. 'How may we help you this beautiful summer's day?'

'We are not here to exchange pleasantries, Herald,' said one of the Rakanese men.

'Why are you here?' said Kelsey. 'We have often sent invitations to your government to meet with us, yet we are always rebuffed.'

'We are here to counter the false and dangerous arguments made by the delegates from Amatskouri, Herald. It has come to our attention that several delegations from that corrupt and greedy city have been attending this court, telling ignorant and fabricated claims of famine.'

'Do you deny these claims?' said Kelsey.

'What goes on behind the border of Rakana is of no concern to the Empire. We are here to ensure that you take no heed of the desperate pleas of the Amatskourians.'

'If your business is private, then so is ours,' said Kelsey. 'You would be aggrieved if we presumed to offer you advice; therefore, I see no reason why we should accept yours.'

'I will give you a reason, Herald,' said the envoy. 'If a single imperial soldier crosses the frontier between the Empire and the Republic of Rakana, there will be a catastrophe of devastating proportions. We are equipped and prepared for war, and we are ready to resist any imperial aggression emanating from the so-called Sapphire Throne. We know what you are doing in Rahain – a nation that presents no threat to the Empire; and we know that Empress Thorn has long cast her avaricious eye upon Rakana. Yes – I see you up there upon your throne, Empress.

Too timid to talk to us? So timid that you let your Herald speak for you? You pack your court with untrustworthy demigods, foreigners, and...' – he glanced at Shella – 'traitors. This is the last warning you shall receive from the Republic of Rakana. Cross our borders, and you may consider war to have been declared. Good day.'

The four envoys turned and strode out of the hall.

'Thank you, everyone, for remaining silent during that little tirade,' said the Empress. 'It was more or less exactly what we expected. This audience is now at an end – we will continue our discussions on the Rakanese problem at the next session of the Imperial Court. Cardova and Shella, would you please remain behind, as I have something I wish to discuss with you both?'

Kelsey, Naxor and Brogan bowed, and left the hall. Kelsey made her excuses, then she walked off in the direction of the middle balcony, where she had arranged to meet Kyra for lunch. The sun was out, and Kelsey watched the Rakanese envoys get into their carriages in the forecourt below. If they ever got the Sextant back, she thought, she might ask Sable to transfer the entire population of Rakana to a desert in the middle of Athumia. She turned as soon as the two carriages disappeared through the gatehouse, and saw Kyra sitting at a table, waiting for her.

'Hello, Aunty,' she said.

Kelsey sat. 'Have you ordered?'

'Not yet.'

Kelsey raised a hand to attract the attention of a waiter. 'Coffee, please,' she said, 'and some pastries, the ones with the raisins.'

The waiter bowed, and Kelsey turned back to Kyra.

'You look a little rough, Aunty,' Kyra said. 'Did you have a late night with Aunty Sable?'

'Very late. How have you been? You said you wanted to talk to me.'

'Aye. Is it true that forty thousand Rahain have been killed in the invasion?'

'It's hard to get an exact figure.'

'But forty thousand would be a good estimate?'

'Aye. About that. Why?'

'Isn't it obvious, Aunty? Forty thousand dead Rahain? Why are we slaughtering them? You told me we were entering Rahain to restore law and order, not to wipe them out.'

'We're hardly wiping them out. At least three million people live in Rahain. We're targeting the gangs who have terrorised the Rahain cities for decades. Brutal, violent gangs, who think nothing of enslaving their own folk, and who have run Rahain into the ground. If we don't tackle them, we'll never restore order.'

'Are you saying that every single death is justified? All forty thousand were active members of a violent gang? I find that hard to believe.'

Kelsey said nothing in reply, as their waiter approached with a tray. He set down a coffee pot, two mugs, milk, sugar, and a large plate of pastries.

'Thank you,' said Kelsey.

The waiter bowed, and strode away.

'Well?' said Kyra.

'There are bound to have been a few civilian casualties,' Kelsey said. 'Unfortunately, it's unavoidable, despite our best efforts to target only the gangs. In the long run, however, a tough approach at the start will pay dividends later. Once order has been fully restored in Tahrana City, we can start to rebuild.'

'Rebuild what you have just destroyed?'

'Rebuild decades of neglect and decay.'

'This is not rule by consent. This is rule by dragon fire and the sword.'

'Lahnos and Sigum will be redeployed once Tahrana City calms down.'

Kelsey poured coffee into the two mugs, as Kyra narrowed her eyes.

'Rahain was never going to be easy,' Kelsey went on. 'For ten years, we have sat back and watched in dismay as conditions in Rahain kept getting worse and worse; and they were already bad enough when Thorn became Empress. Agatha and her little band of gods stripped the place bare to fund their invasion of the Empire. If we had continued to do nothing, would not we share part of the responsibility for the suffering endured by the people of Rahain?'

'No. I don't think that has anything to do with us.'

'Are you sure? The Empire has the resources, the strength and the wealth to intervene, in an attempt to make their lives better. Do we not then have a responsibility to intervene?'

'Tell me the truth, Aunty – does the Empress want Rahain to become part of the Empire? Is that why she has unleashed the Imperial Army upon Tahrana City?'

'The Empress *does* want Rahain to become part of the Empire, but that desire has not affected Her Majesty's judgement. Left alone, Rahain is a danger to our southern borders; what they lack in Rahain, the gangs try to steal from the Plateau. Over a thousand citizens of the Empire have been killed in the last decade by raiders operating out of Rahain. We cannot allow that to happen. Our first duty is to protect the people we govern. Pacifying Rahain will put an end to the raids, forever. And, in time, Rahain will retake its place among the normal, sanely-run nations of this world. Eventually, it will prosper again.'

'They kill one thousand of our people, so we kill forty thousand of theirs?'

'That is a gross simplification, Kyra. The world is a dangerous place. We have had peace for ten years, but there is no guarantee that it will continue. In the event of another calamity, we cannot afford to have a rogue and hostile nation to our south; along with another rogue and hostile nation to our east.'

Kyra's eyes flashed. 'So you *are* thinking of invading Rakana?'

'Do not put words into my mouth, Kyra. Any decision concerning the future of Rakana will be made by the Imperial Court. You seem to think that the Empress and I are engaged in a grand conspiracy; that we're trying to devour all of the known worlds and peoples. It simply isn't true. Of course there are difficult decisions that have to be taken, and we agonise over any that might lead to violence or the loss of life. As far as Rahain goes, we judged that a tough initial approach would save lives in the long run. That still holds true.'

Kyra lowered her gaze.

'I welcome your questions,' Kelsey went on, 'and I welcome any dissent. We are not perfect; we all make mistakes. But believe me, Kyra, we are trying to do what is best for the Empire as a whole, and its people.'

'I miss my brother.'

'I miss him, too; and Cole and Arrosa. Colsbury in summer isn't the same without them.'

'Thank you for talking to me.'

'Keep questioning everything. Poke our arguments; look for flaws and errors; and never be afraid to speak up. I'd better go. I saw the yacht berth at the jetty, and I need to speak to Van.'

'Is your marriage in trouble, Aunty?'

Kelsey frowned. 'Who told you that?'

'Mother.'

'Let's just say that it's not in the best of health. I'll see you later.'

Kelsey got up from her chair, then she went into the palace and ascended to her own quarters. She walked into the living room. The shutters had been opened but there was no sign of Van or the children. She went into the bedroom shared by Calpurnia and Caelius. Everything seemed to be in order, then she noticed that one of the wardrobes was slightly open. Kelsey went to close it, and her eyes narrowed. The wardrobe was empty. Kelsey walked over to a chest of drawers and opened one. Also empty. A cold fear rippled down her back. She ran into the bedroom that she and Van shared. All of his clothes were gone.

Kelsey raced out of her quarters and ran to the meeting room used by Naxor and Brogan when they were discussing matters related to the Imperial Treasury. She opened the door without knocking, and found Brogan at her desk, being attended by several treasury clerks and officials.

'Have you seen Naxor?' she said.

'He's gone back to the City, ma'am,' said Brogan. 'He had a delivery of Kellach coal to supervise.'

Kelsey swore under her breath, and rushed back out into the hallway. She ran along the corridor, and collided with Naxor as he ascended a flight of stairs.

'Steady on there,' said Naxor. 'Everything's fine. I transported Van and the children to Ooste, just as you requested.'

'What are you talking about?' Kelsey cried. 'I didn't request that.'

Naxor withdrew an envelope from a pocket. 'Is that not the seal of the Herald?'

Kelsey snatched it from his hands and stared at it.

'Van gave it to me earlier,' Naxor went on. 'He said that you had given permission for the children to travel to the City. Was I mistaken?'

'You were tricked. Shit. I'll strangle that bastard. Van must have stolen my seal when I was sleeping. Where did you leave them?'

'On the steps of the Royal Palace in Ooste.' He pulled out his Quadrant. 'Let us return forthwith. I take grievous exception to having been deceived in this manner.'

Kelsey nodded. 'Do it.'

Naxor brushed his fingers over the surface of the Quadrant, and they appeared in the large plaza in front of the Royal Palace in Ooste. Overhead, the sky was a deep shade of peach, and the air held the warmth of the last days of the City's summer. Kelsey raced up the steps of the palace towards its gleaming white façade, then several soldiers from the Banner of the Lostwell Exiles stepped out to block her way.

'Let me through!' Kelsey yelled. 'Van has my children.'

The soldiers eyed her.

'Do you have an appointment, miss?' said a sergeant.

'Of course I don't have a fucking appointment!' Kelsey shouted. 'Did you not hear me? Van has my children.'

'There is no admittance without an appointment, miss,' said the sergeant; 'not even to politicians of a foreign state.'

'Especially not to politicians of a foreign state,' said another soldier.

'This is quite out of order,' said Naxor, as he reached the top of the steps.

'Is that so?' said the sergeant. 'If you would like to submit a complaint, my commanding officer is stationed in Pella. I'm sure he'd be delighted to see you both.'

'Naxor,' said Kelsey, 'use your Quadrant to get us inside the palace.'

'I would advise against that course of action,' said the sergeant. 'We have been ordered to treat any breach of palace security with the utmost force at our disposal. If you enter the palace without permission, you will be detained and charged with espionage.'

Kelsey lashed out with a fist, and Naxor pulled her back, as the sergeant ducked.

'Violence will not help your case,' Naxor hissed in her ear.

'I want my children back!'

'Think, Kelsey,' said Naxor. 'Do you want your children to see you fight their father? Van has won this round; accept defeat, lick your wounds, and plan for the next battle. You will gain nothing by being arrested. Use your brain, not your fists.'

Kelsey stopped struggling, and Naxor released her.

'Tell my husband that I was here,' she said to the soldiers. 'Tell him that this isn't over. If he wants a war, he's got one.'

The sergeant smiled. 'I'll be sure to pass on your message to the major general, miss.'

Kelsey glanced at Naxor, and he activated the *Go back* command on his Quadrant. The air shimmered, and they appeared in the same hallway in the Summer Palace from where they had left.

Kelsey's shoulders sagged, and she stared at the floor.

'I am at your service, ma'am,' said Naxor. 'In my opinion, Van has behaved despicably. How can I help?'

'Could you tell the Empress what has happened?'

'Certainly. Where will you be?'

'In my quarters. I need time to think.'

'The Empress and I will look at the diplomatic options,' said Naxor. 'We will also examine a few of the undiplomatic ones, in case they are required.'

Kelsey nodded, and Naxor strode away. She stood there in silence for a few moments, her feet frozen to the floor, then she slowly walked to her quarters. She found her Quadrant, and thanked Pyre that Van hadn't discovered where she kept it hidden. She sat on the large bed, and began to think of revenge. She could ask Sable to intervene. Or Corthie. She imagined them storming the Royal Palace in Ooste to rescue her children. She started to cry. She wouldn't be rescuing them; she would be snatching them from the arms of their father, a father who had done more to look after them than she ever had.

She thought back to the last time she had seen them that day, when she had returned from Cael's quarters hungover and needing a bath. She had stood in silence and watched as Van had led Calpurnia and Caelius out. If she had known what was going to happen, she would have grabbed on to them and never let go. But no matter how much she longed to see her children, one fact shone clearer in her mind than all the others.

Her marriage was over.

CHAPTER 16
DANGEROUS ALLIES

Tahrana City, Rahain – 11th Day, Last Third Summer 544

'I fucking hate this shithole,' said the Sanang colonel. 'What kind of people live underground, as though they were rats?' He glanced at Lahnos. 'The Rahain aren't people; that's the answer. Look at their eyes, and their tongues, and the way the lamplight catches off their scaly skin. They're lizards, Horned Chief. The Empress is dreaming if she thinks they can be civilised.'

'The evidence of my eyes would seem to contradict that theory, Colonel D'Rangalecht,' said Efizel, who was sitting to Lahnos's right. 'The civilisation of the Rahain may have fallen, but whoever delved these magnificent caverns was clearly advanced.' He pointed up into the centre of the vast underground space. 'Look at that bridge, the one that spans the gap between the spiralling towers – it's as thin as a few sheets of paper, and yet it can carry the weight of dozens. Elegance, beauty and strength, all in proportion.'

D'Rangalecht waved away the Bullan's opinion with a hand. 'I'm not saying that they didn't used to be great – that's obvious; but they have fallen so low that they will never again reach their previous heights. Four decades have passed since the first emperor sent his armies to conquer Rahain. The natives of this city have no memory of what life was like back then, and they have no conception of how to return to their previous status.' He smiled. 'Forty years ago, Sanang was the backward nation of this continent; while the Rahain were the most advanced. Emperor Guilliam had to unite the other peoples in order to defeat Rahain – Holdings, Kellach, Sanang; even the feeble Rakanese were involved.'

Lahnos gazed out at the interior of the enormous cavern. The grandeur of the place was undeniable. Tall structures clung on to the sides, and buildings designed to look like stalagmites and stalactites rose from the floor or hung down from the ceiling. Sanang soldiers and Kellach marines were patrolling the lower levels, where great heaps of refuse lay unattended by the sides of the roads. Everything movable had long before been looted and stripped from the cavern, and the smell of decay lingered everywhere. 'What went wrong?' he said.

'What was that, Horned Chief?'

'If the old emperor conquered Rahain, why didn't it stay in the Empire? Why did it fall into this... squalor?'

'Religion,' said D'Rangalecht. 'The same religion the Holdings imported from their own lands was the unmaking of Rahain. The Holdings folk were in the process of abandoning that religion at the very moment they invaded, passing it onto the lizards here was as though they'd cursed them. Under the grip of religious fervour, the Rahain refused to cooperate with the rest of the Empire, and then, twenty years ago, they invaded us. Hundreds of thousands of Rahain soldiers flooded the Plateau, trying to spread their faith, but Empress Bridget stopped them at Rainsby. The slaughter that went on there sapped both sides. The Rahain eventually made it as far as Plateau City, and then...'

'Yes?' said Efizel.

'The Holdfast witch annihilated them,' said the Sanang colonel.

Lahnos narrowed his eyes. 'Which one?'

'Karalyn. If the stories are true, she *willed* their deaths. A hundred thousand Rahain soldiers, dead in the blink of an eye.'

The three men sat on the balcony in silence for a while.

'Can I ask something else, Colonel?' said Efizel.

D'Rangalecht nodded. 'Of course you may, sergeant major.'

'What was the Sanang army doing when the Rahain invaded the Plateau? Were their armed forces defeated?'

The Sanang colonel snorted. 'By the lizards? Don't insult me, Bullan. No Rahain army has ever defeated the Sanang in battle, and they never will. Sanang was going through the Dearth at the time – we had no army, because we had no men.'

'What happened to the men of Sanang?' said Lahnos.

'Emperor Guilliam killed them all,' said D'Rangalecht. 'We had tired of the Empire, and the Fire Witch led a rebellion. We invaded the Plateau, and... we lost. That's how the first Matriarch took power – there were no men left. It's taken us forty years to recover.' He laughed. 'Now, the new Matriarch thinks there are too many men in Sanang. Well, too many men of the wrong sort. Did you never wonder why so many Sanang soldiers in the Imperial Army are former criminals? It's the Matriarch's way of getting rid of violent men. Send them to the army! Then they become Empress Thorn's problem.'

Lahnos glanced at him.

'Yes,' said D'Rangalecht, 'I was a criminal in Sanang. I led a few raiding parties in the south, back when I was in my twenties, and when we were rounded up, we were given a choice – the noose or the Imperial Army. That was eight years ago. Now, I'm leading raiding parties again, only this time, the Empire rewards me for it.'

'Here come more regular units of the army, sir,' said Efizel.

Lahnos gazed down into the cavern, and saw a regiment of Holdings soldiers entering under a massive archway. Their officer strode over to where a group of Kellach marines was standing, as the new arrivals stared up into the vastness of the interior.

'It'll soon be time for the Sanang lads to leave this shithole,' said D'Rangalecht. 'We've done our job; Tahrana City is ours. The Holdings can take care of the occupation; they're welcome to it.'

'Sigum, the Bullan and I will be getting redeployed as well, I imagine,' said Lahnos.

'I fucking hope so,' said the colonel. 'I'm expecting to see you and your dragon in the skies above us when we attack the Rahain Capital. We can get back to killing again, instead of pretending to be police officers. The Sanang have no patience with that sort of work, and the Empress knows it. She's one of us, isn't she? She understands our strengths, and our limitations. That's why she uses us as assault troops, and then brings in the Holdings when the fighting is over. I don't envy them. Trying to govern a mass of uncivilised lizards will be a thankless task. I don't know why we don't just kill them all.'

'The Empire is thinking about the long-term,' said Lahnos. 'It might take decades to bring Rahain back up to a decent level of living conditions. The fighting of the last month... I mean third, has been to subdue the natives, so that the rebuilding can begin.'

D'Rangalecht laughed. 'Well, that's the plan. We killed what? – sixty thousand Rahain taking this city? And it'll probably be more when we assault their capital. It still won't be enough. If we truly wanted to pacify Rahain, we'd do to them what Emperor Guilliam did to us, and annihilate their menfolk. Butcher every man over the age of fourteen; that would knock the fight out of them. Let them experience their own Dearth. A Rahain that consisted of only women and children would be easy to control.'

'It would also mean the murder of over a million people,' said Lahnos.

'Are they really people?' said D'Rangalecht. 'They're reptiles. Snakes.'

'They're people,' said Lahnos. 'Where I come from, folk said the same kind of things about people who look like me. They said that we have no souls, and some called us demons.'

'You are a demon, Horned Chief,' said the colonel. 'What of it? You and your dragon slaughtered thousands of Rahain on our way to this city and, by doing so, you've endeared yourself to every Sanang serving in the Imperial Army. If you're a demon, then you're our fucking demon.'

Lahnos was considering his response when two Kellach marines stepped on to the balcony.

'Commander Laimos, sir,' said one, 'a riot has broken out in one of the eastern caverns over a food convoy, and our major sent us here to ask for your assistance.'

Lahnos and Efizel got to their feet.

'Have fun, Horned Chief,' said D'Rangalecht.

'I will see you later, Colonel,' said Lahnos.

He and Efizel walked off the balcony with the two marines, and entered the huge building complex where the Imperial Army had set up its headquarters in the heart of Tahrana City.

Lahnos eyed the tall marines as they descended a well-lit staircase. 'What do the Kellach think of their Sanang colleagues?'

The two marines glanced at each other.

'It's not a trick question,' said Lahnos. 'I'm interested in hearing your opinion.'

'They are fine fighters, sir,' said one.

'Do they ever give you any problems?'

'No, sir.'

'The Sanang respect the Kellach Brigdomin, sir,' said the other marine. 'We know where we stand with them.'

'Colonel D'Rangalecht was trying to persuade me that it would be better if we killed every Rahain male over the age of fourteen. Do you agree?'

'No, sir; I do not,' said the first marine.

They came into the ground floor of the massive building, and strode through a large entrance hall, where a mixture of Sanang, Kellach and Holdings soldiers and marines were on duty. Many turned to stare at the arrival of Lahnos and Efizel. It was the same wherever they went in Tahrana City, their horns making them as notorious as they had been on Zamata. Most of them could probably guess what Lahnos was about to do; and why he had been called for by the marines. A few of the Sanang bowed their heads out of respect, while others cheered at the sight of him.

'Make those lizards suffer!' shouted one.

Lahnos ignored the stares and the comments. His experiences on the Serpent Isle had inured him to the opinions of others, and he had lost the ability to care what anyone thought of him. Perversely, his nonchalant attitude had made the soldiers and the marines of the invasion force like him all the more.

He and Efizel stepped outside into the vast cavern, while the two marines went off to fetch a carriage.

'I heard you talking to the Kellach marines, sir,' said Efizel. 'Were you expecting to hear them criticise the Sanang?'

'I don't know what I was expecting.'

'The marines are too professional to deride their colleagues in front of a senior officer, sir, no matter their personal feelings. It would be like asking the Bullan what they thought of the Aucterians.'

Lahnos shook his head. 'Look at this place. Could you have ever imagined that such underground cities could exist? The people who fashioned this place were among the greatest architects and builders on any world. I can't help but respect that.'

'I was told that slaves carried out most of the work, sir,' said Efizel. 'The old Rahain Republic enslaved many of its own people.'

'Is that right?'

'And, of course, sir, they had stone mages to help.'

An unmarked carriage pulled up in front of them. The two Kellach marines were up on the driver's bench, and they gestured for Lahnos and Efizel to board.

'It's a fifteen minute journey to the location of the riot, sir,' said one. 'The major shall brief you upon arrival.'

Efizel opened the side door, and then he and Lahnos climbed into the carriage. Efizel closed the door, and the carriage set off, its wheels clattering over the recently-repaired road. Lahnos gazed out of the window as the carriage moved through the cavern towards a wide tunnel. The centre of Tahrana City consisted of three vast, inter-linked caverns formed into a triangle, from where the city had been governed in the days of the republic. Despite decades of neglect, those three caverns had retained traces of their original splendour, but beyond, the rest of the city was in a dire situation. The lighting and heating systems hadn't functioned for years, and the water supply and sewer pipes were in a worse condition. The invading army had restored lighting to the central caverns, and along the main routes that led from the centre to the outside world, but the majority of the city lay in almost perpetual darkness, illuminated only by piles of burning refuse.

They travelled along a well-lit tunnel boulevard, then slowed when they reached a series of side tunnels branching off to the left. One of the tunnels had been blocked by thick ranks of Kellach marines, who were holding large shields to prevent the riot from spreading. The carriage came to a halt, and Lahnos stepped down to the floor of the tunnel.

An officer had been waiting for him, and approached.

'Commander Lahnos,' he said, 'thank you for coming.'

'How many Rahain are rioting this time, Major?' said Lahnos.

'About three hundred, sir. Trouble was ignited when a food convoy began distributing supplies to the Rahain civilians.'

Lahnos gazed at the blocked tunnel. The sounds of violence could be heard coming from beyond the lines of marines. Stones were battering off the large shields, but none of the marines took a step backwards.

'Do you require some armour, sir?' said the Kellach major.

Lahnos shook his head. 'Tell the marines to stand aside.'

'Aye, sir.'

The major walked over to the tunnel entrance.

'Remain where you are but listen carefully,' he said to the marines blocking the tunnel. 'Commander Laimos has arrived, and he will be taking over. On the count of three, you will withdraw from the entrance, keeping your shields up at all times. Is that understood?'

'Aye, sir,' came the response from the marines.

'One, two... three.'

The marines split into two groups, and peeled away to the left and the right. A stone was hurled through the gap that opened, and it landed close to Lahnos's feet. Then the rioting Rahain saw his horns, and the screaming began. Before Lahnos could even lift his hand, many of the Rahain packing the tunnel were already trying to flee. Lahnos raised his right arm, and filled the tunnel with the Gift of Pain. As the marines watched from either flank, hundreds of Rahain fell to the tunnel floor, writhing and howling in agony. Lahnos gazed at them, seeing their yellow eyes stare at him as he sent Pain into each of their bodies.

Within a minute, every Rahain in the tunnel was on the ground, incapacitated. Lahnos walked into the tunnel. Ahead of him was an abandoned wagon. Its two ponies had been killed by the rioters, and its cargo was strewn over the tunnel – boxes of food, and sacks of grain lay discarded and opened amid the writhing bodies. One of the Rahain stared up at Lahnos with his vertical pupils, then he plunged a knife into the side of Lahnos's left leg. Lahnos gazed down at him, then he stamped a boot onto the Rahain's arm, and the knife fell from his grasp. Behind him, none of the Kellach marines reacted. Every soldier and marine in the invasion force had learned by then that Lahnos could not be injured, and he knew that many of them believed him to be a demigod.

He gave the tunnel one more blast of Pain, and the last of the movement stopped.

'Retrieve the wagon,' said the major, 'and arrest all Rahain of fighting age.'

The marines piled into the tunnel, and began dragging the bodies of the unconscious Rahain out. Several went to the wagon. They gazed at the two dead ponies with anger on their faces, but did not retaliate against the Rahain civilians.

'Why do the Sanang never police these riots, Major?' said Lahnos.

The officer glanced at him. 'Well, sir, the Sanang are sometimes a little more enthusiastic than they need to be in these situations. How is the leg?'

'It's fine. I'm handing control of the tunnel back to you.'

'Thank you, sir, and thank you for the timely intervention.'

Lahnos walked back to where Efizel was waiting for him.

'The sooner we are out of here, the better,' he said to the Bullan.

'I agree, sir.'

'I was thinking this morning about how much I miss Dolwyn,' Lahnos went on, 'but I'm glad she isn't here to witness what it is that I do every day.'

'I didn't know you were still thinking about her, sir.'

'I'm thinking about her, and wishing I'd kept my big mouth shut. The next time I try to sabotage my own happiness, do me a favour and slap me across the face.'

'Shall we return to the city centre, sir?'

Lahnos half-smiled. 'Why, so we can continue our productive conversation with the charming Colonel D'Rangalecht?'

'We need to remain where we can be easily found, sir. And, if I may say so, I do not think the colonel is a good representation of the Sanang. Not all of his people feel the same way that he does.'

'No, just the ones in the Imperial Army. Knowing that most of them are former criminals explains a lot about their behaviour. Can you imagine them being tolerated by the Dominion army?'

'No, sir. However, they have their uses as assault troops. Their courage is undeniable.'

'So is their disregard for life and the civilised rules of warfare. Still, who am I to judge them? Sigum and I are responsible for many of the deaths that have taken place since the invasion began. That's why the Sanang have decided to admire me. And if they like me, what does that say about me? It sounds as though the Dearth was a good thing for this world, if it meant that there were no Sanang men for a generation.'

'Before you say any more about the Sanang, sir, perhaps you should remember that the Empress is one.'

'Shit. I'd forgotten that. Come on; let's get back to our balcony.'

Four hours later, Lahnos and Efizel were ascending a narrow staircase that cut through the side of the mountain beneath which lay Tahrana City. Two Holdings soldiers from the regular Imperial Army were holding lanterns to light their way as they climbed ever higher. At the top of the stairs, the passageway opened out onto the flank of the mountain, and Lahnos relished the fresh air. A chill wind was blowing over the barren summit, and Lahnos gazed around at the view. To the north lay the road across the Tahrana Valley to the start of the Great Tunnel. Since Lahnos had been stationed down in the city, it had been Sigum's task to patrol the road every day, and the silvery-green dragon was waiting for Lahnos by the entrance to the stairs.

'You reek of the underground,' the dragon said. 'I do not like it.'

'You're not the only one,' said Lahnos. 'Living in a cavern is not for me. Am I early?'

'You are on time,' said Sigum. 'Our visitors are late.'

'How far is the Rahain Capital from here?' said Efizel.

'It takes me four hours to fly there,' said Sigum, 'and I cover fifty miles every hour, when I am not pushing myself. Is that to be our next target?'

'I'll guess we'll find out when the others get here,' said Lahnos.

The air shimmered a few yards away, and Kelsey Holdfast appeared with Lucius Cardova and a handful of other officers. As soon as their feet were on the ground, Kelsey said something to Cardova and strode away on her own, her eyes heavy and red.

Cardova walked over to Lahnos, Efizel and the dragon.

'Good afternoon,' he said. 'Please excuse the Herald. She needs a moment to gather her thoughts.'

'She looks upset about something,' said Lahnos.

Cardova said nothing.

'How is life in Colsbury, Constable?' said Sigum.

'This summer has been a little more fraught than usual,' Cardova said. 'There is still no sign of Cael, Cole and Arrosa.'

'What's Karalyn doing about it?' said Lahnos.

'What can she do? Without the Sextant, she has no way of locating the missing children. Our hopes are pinned on Professor Elbannon's ability to invent something that might be able to help.'

Kelsey walked over to join them. 'Any changes in Tahrana City to report?' she said.

'No, ma'am,' said Lahnos. 'The situation remains volatile. When will the Sanang be leaving?'

Kelsey narrowed her eyes. 'Soon. We are transferring several divisions of the regular army to take over the running of the city. The Sanang, and most of the marines, will be redeployed to take up positions closer to the Rahain Capital. That's why we're here. Lord Sigum, would you please carry me and Lucius south, so that we can take a look at the terrain between here and the Rahain Capital?'

'I would be honoured,' said the dragon. 'I assume Lahnos will also be coming?'

'Aye,' said Kelsey.

'I shall wait here for your return,' said Efizel. 'There are only three spaces upon Lord Sigum's harness.'

Cardova gestured to his aides, who handed him and Kelsey thick winter overcoats, along with gloves. They pulled them on, then they and Lahnos climbed up onto the dragon's shoulders.

'Could you please take us by the roads our forces will use, Lord Sigum?' said Cardova.

'Certainly,' said the dragon.

Sigum extended his wings and ascended into the cold air.

'It's freezing up here,' said Kelsey.

'If we intend to assault the Rahain Capital this year, ma'am,' said Cardova, 'then we will have to do it before winter begins.'

They soared over the enormous mountain range that covered the centre of Rahain. Some of the peaks were as tall as any in the Grey Mountains, and the fertile valleys that lay around Tahrana City were being patrolled by imperial soldiers. Old and derelict farms were being brought back into operation but, as it was already autumn, there would be little produced there until the following year.

Lahnos waited for an hour to pass before he turned to Kelsey.

'Is everything all right, ma'am?' he said.

Kelsey frowned. 'What? I'm fine. The harness is a little uncomfortable, but I'll cope.'

'I wasn't talking about the journey, ma'am,' he said. 'I was talking about the look on your face when you arrived.'

'What business is that of yours?'

'Probably none,' he said.

'Then do me a favour and shut the fuck up.'

The dragon turned his head. 'I take exception to you insulting my rider, Herald. Remember that I am loyal to Lahnos before I am loyal to the Empire. If you wish me to continue to help you with this invasion, then I recommend that you apologise.'

'Pyre's arse,' muttered Kelsey. 'There's a chain of command for a reason.'

'That does not excuse your words, Herald,' said Sigum. 'I await your apology.'

'Fine,' Kelsey cried. 'Lahnos, I'm sorry I told you to shut the fuck up. Next time, I'll add a *please* to the end. I haven't seen my children for fourteen days, so forgive me if I'm a little tetchy.'

'Why haven't you seen your children for fourteen days?' said Lahnos.

'Because my husband took them to the City of Salve, and he won't let me see them.'

'I can think of a few solutions to that. Sending Sable with a Quadrant to bring them back would be my first suggestion.'

'I've already asked the Empress to do exactly that,' said Kelsey. 'She refused, because the City is threatening to break off all diplomatic relations with us if we interfere with their laws. I even asked Karalyn if she would do it, but she thinks I should sit down with Van and talk through our problems.'

'Is Van offering to speak to you?'

'Lucius is supposed to be meeting him tomorrow. Are you content now, Lahnos? Are you happy that you managed to squeeze my misery out of me? On top of all that, I still have to deal with the invasion of Rahain, the growing crisis at the Rakanese border, and the stubborn bastards in charge of the City. Not to mention Cael and the damn Sextant.'

Lahnos glanced at Cardova. 'Why are you meeting her husband, sir?'

'You are too forward for a subordinate,' said Cardova. 'I respect your abilities, but the personal lives of the Holdfasts are none of your business.'

'You may as well tell him,' said Kelsey. 'We need to keep Lahnos and his dragon happy.'

Cardova frowned. 'Very well. Van and I are old friends, and I am hoping to talk some sense into him. I know he has been angry and frustrated, but there is no excusing what he did.' He gazed at Kelsey. 'I will do what I can, ma'am. I will try my best to arrange a reunion between you and your children.'

'I know you will, Lucius.'

'We are approaching the forward positions of the Imperial Marines,' said the dragon. 'You can see their camps to our left.'

Lahnos and the others looked down. The main road that led from Tahrana City to the Rahain Capital ran along the bottom of a wide valley that the marines had blocked from end to end. A few of them gazed up at the dragon and waved.

'Every other main road leading to the Rahain Capital has been blocked in the same manner,' said Sigum. 'Are we to infer that the assault upon the city is imminent?'

'I thought we were going to wait until Tahrana City had been completely pacified,' said Lahnos.

'No final decision has yet been taken,' said Cardova, 'which is one of the reasons the Herald and I are here today.'

'Aye,' said Kelsey, 'but if we don't deploy the Sanang assault divisions down here soon, we'll have to move them back to their barracks in the Plateau. We can't keep them in Tahrana City; they're doing more harm than good.'

'Are you aware of their behaviour, ma'am?' said Lahnos.

'Of course I'm aware. Have you any idea of the number of complaints I've had about them? An army of Sanang criminals is great for throwing into the initial assaults, but they're no good for anything else. Tahrana City will never settle down if we try to use them for peace-keeping duties.' She glanced at Cardova. 'I'm going to recommend to the Empress that the assault on the Rahain Capital goes ahead.'

'It's earlier than I had hoped for, ma'am,' said Cardova, 'but it would be wise to keep the Sanang busy in active operations. We'll send them in first, and keep the marines in reserve.'

'We've seen enough, Lord Sigum,' said Kelsey. 'Take us back to Tahrana City.'

'As you will, Herald,' said the dragon.

Sigum banked in the air, and turned for the north. They crossed over the lines of Imperial Marines encamped by the main road, and Lahnos waved down to them.

'Is there a risk, ma'am,' he said to Kelsey, 'that we might be creating a battle-hardened division of Sanang veterans who will never adjust back into civilian life?'

'That will never happen, Lahnos,' she said.

'Why not?'

'The Sanang regiments will never be returning to civilian life,' she said. 'There will always be one more war for them to fight; and if there isn't, we will find one for them.'

CHAPTER 17
FORAGING

World Three – (30th Day, Last Third Summer 544)

'I don't remember much about my father,' said Cole. 'Just a few, fleeting images.'

Arrosa leaned back against the wall of the cave, the light coming through the waterfall shimmering over her face.

'What age were you when he died?' she said.

'Nine,' he said.

'I was eight when my parents were killed,' she said, 'and I remember them well. We had a little house in a place called Kaugatz, and I have several memories of being with them.'

'My mother died at the same time as my father,' said Cole, 'and I can remember her without any difficulty. The reason I don't have many memories of my father is that... well, he was never there. He left my mother when she was pregnant with me, and got married to Thorn, long before she became the Empress. It was my mother who looked after me for the first nine years of my life. My parents were too young to be having children; that's what Aunty Celine told me. They were only sixteen.'

'How did they die?' she said.

'My father died a hero, fighting an Ascendant. I've heard about other things he did before that – things that didn't make him very popular with the rest of the family; but his death redeemed him in the eyes of most of the Holdfasts. I wish I had known him better, but I don't think he was interested in being a father. I didn't see what happened to him, but I watched my mother die. It's the worst memory of my life. A god killed her. Cael was there, too.'

Arrosa glanced over at where Cael was sitting in the shadows of the cave.

'That day in Kell...' Cole went on. 'I've never seen so much blood. We were in the bedroom that Empress Thorn had been using, and...'

'I don't want to hear about it,' said Cael. 'Can we talk about something else?'

'Can we talk about your father, Cael?' she said.

'There's nothing to know,' said Cael. 'He died when I was a baby. I don't have any memories of him.'

'He was a fire mage, wasn't he?'

'Aye.'

'Why aren't you a fire mage?'

'Why are you asking me? I don't know.'

'Don't get angry,' she said.

'This is a morbid topic,' said Cael. 'We're orphans – so what? Do we have to discuss every last detail?'

'You're not an orphan,' said Cole. 'Your mother came back.'

'That was more fucked up than losing her in the first place,' he said. 'When everyone was mourning the death of my mother, I was clinging on to the belief that she was still alive. I didn't grieve. Instead, I sometimes thought I might be going mad, and I was angry that no one believed me.'

'Sable believed you,' said Arrosa.

'Aye, eventually. And then, when she did come back, she looked different. I knew it was her on the inside, but everything changed again.'

'Those were good years,' said Arrosa. 'For me, it was like having a new family in Colsbury.'

'You were oblivious to what was going on underneath,' said Cael. 'My sister... she... well, I think she preferred it when Thorn was looking after us. She was always Thorn's favourite, and Kyra adored her. I was the opposite; I didn't get along with Thorn because I wanted my mother back, at any cost.' He narrowed his eyes at Arrosa. 'And then I had to share her with you. Kyra lost Thorn, which made her as unhappy as I was. You did well out of the arrangement, but neither Kyra nor I got what we wanted.'

'Is that why you were always angry with me?' she said. 'I was just happy to be loved. I ignored everything else. I knew that Kyra was always fighting with your mother; and I knew that you were angry, but none of that mattered to me. Colsbury felt like home; and for the first couple of years, Lahnos was there, too, and I could speak to him if the arguments got too heated. Lahnos was like a big brother to me. I missed him when he left Colsbury. That was when I realised how much you hated me, Cael.'

'This is all in the past,' said Cole. 'You two have no reason to hate each other any more.'

'Tell that to him,' said Arrosa. 'I know I can be a bitch at times, but I would stop if Cael didn't act like an arsehole towards me.'

'That's right,' said Cael; 'blame me for everything.'

'I don't blame you for everything,' she said, 'just for being an insufferable bully.'

'I might go and look for some food,' said Cole. 'I'm sick of hearing you argue.'

'There's no food out there,' said Cael. 'We've taken everything there is to eat for miles around. We're going to have to move again; we have no choice.'

'But I like it here,' said Arrosa. 'It feels safe. No one can see us through the waterfall.'

'Then stay here and starve to death on your own,' said Cael.

'What about the town I saw?' said Cole. 'Should we risk it? The people there will have food.'

'If we go there, we should have a plan,' said Arrosa. 'We can't just walk in and expect them to help us. We might even have to fight. What exactly did you see?'

'I told you,' said Cole; 'it's a small town, in a cleared part of the forest, surrounded by a wooden fence. It's about six miles away.'

'Six miles isn't far,' said Arrosa. 'I wonder if they already suspect that we're here. They might have noticed the footprints we've been making when we go out to look for food. It's a pity neither of you have battle-vision. And it's a pity I don't have the Gift of Pain. Still, at least none of the people living here have any powers or Gifts.'

'That might not be completely true,' said Cael.

The others looked at him.

'I tried to give my sub-created humans mage powers,' Cael said, 'but I don't think it worked. When I asked the Sextant to show me people with death powers, it told me that they had died out.'

'You gave them powers?' said Cole.

'I tried to.'

'Isn't that dangerous? Isn't that how Nathaniel got trapped on the Star Continent? What other powers did you try to give them?'

'The whole range, but don't worry – it was far too complicated, and the Sextant couldn't or wouldn't do as I asked. I was treating World Three as a place to experiment. I also tried to create Tempest and salve, and that didn't work, either.'

'It probably took the Ascendants centuries to learn how to properly create worlds,' said Arrosa, 'let alone the more complex stuff like powers and Tempest. And you thought you could do it on your third attempt?'

'I was enjoying myself,' said Cael. 'I was seeing what would work, and what wouldn't. I didn't think we'd end up stuck here.'

'I don't suppose the Tempest worked?' said Cole. 'If it did, then we might be able to find some, and make a new sword.'

Cael laughed. 'It would be that easy, aye? We just dig up some ore, refine it, melt it down, and forge a sword? It would take years.'

'Then it takes years,' said Cole. 'I don't want to die here.'

'The Tempest didn't work,' said Cael. 'When I asked the Sextant about it, it told me that there wasn't any on this world. I don't know what I did wrong.'

'Did you study the composition of Tempest first?' said Arrosa.

Cael shrugged.

'And salve – do you understand how it is made?'

'No.'

'Then why would you ever believe that you would be able to create any? If it was that easy, the Ascendants would have created hundreds of worlds where humans had Gifts, and salve would be everywhere. You could study for your entire life, and never manage to recreate Tempest. Only gods can do it – not because they're better than us, but because only they have enough time on their hands.'

'Stop nagging me,' said Cael.

'I will, as soon as you stop being so stupid. Never, in other words.'

Cael glared at her. 'Horses can fly.'

'Ow.'

'Cows have ten legs.'

'Stop it.'

'Dogs can talk.'

Arrosa jumped to her feet, her fists clenched.

Cael laughed. 'What are you going to do – punch me?'

'I will if you don't stop lying,' she said. 'It hurts.'

Cael opened his mouth, and Arrosa swung her right fist. Cael tried to duck, and the blow struck the side of his head.

'You fucking little bitch,' he cried. 'You'll pay for that.'

Cole barged his way between them. 'I can't stand another minute of this!' he shouted. 'We have no food, our clothes are in rags, we're trapped on this useless world, and all you two do is squabble every day like children.' He raised his hands, and pushed Arrosa and Cael back from each other. 'We can't carry on like this; moving from place to place every few days whenever we run out of food. We are slowly starving to death; do you realise that? We can't hunt; we can't fish, and I'm fucking sick of eating fruit. More than that, though – I'm sick of you two. The only conceivable way that we're going to get out of this is if we work together, and yet you can't stand the sight of each other.'

Cole lowered his arms, then he turned and walked towards the waterfall.

'Where are you going?' said Arrosa.

'To the town I saw,' said Cole. 'I'm going to ask for help.'

'But...'

'You can stay here if you want,' said Cole. 'I don't give a shit any more.'

He walked through the curtain of water, and disappeared from view.

Cael got to his feet, and rubbed the side of his head. 'I don't think I've ever seen Cole that angry before.'

'We should probably go after him,' said Arrosa.

'Are you going to apologise for punching me?'

'You brought it on yourself,' she said.

He shook his head as he gazed down at her. 'You always have to be right, don't you?'

'It's not my fault that you are usually wrong. And besides, what did you expect? You lied to me three times; do you have any idea how that feels?'

Cael readied a response, his gaze fixed on her eyes, then his vision changed. He saw the interior of a dark cave, not the same cave where he had been standing with Arrosa at that moment. He was looking down at a figure who lay groaning in agony on the damp floor of the cave; then he realised it was Arrosa, and that he was crouching by her side. She was injured, or sick; perhaps she was dying, and a sense of helplessness close to despair was surging through him.

When he next knew where he was, he was on his knees in the same cave as before, with the waterfall in front of him. Arrosa was staring at him, a look of concern on her face.

'Are you all right?' she said.

'I... I saw something.'

'What did you see?' she said. 'Your eyes glazed over for a few seconds, then you fell to your knees. Are you ill?'

He shook his head. 'It was just a stupid prophecy.'

'Oh. Was I in it?'

He nodded.

Her eyes widened. 'Where were we? Please tell me we were back on the Star Continent. Were we? Do we make it home?'

'I don't know. It might have been World Three.'

He got to his feet, swayed, then stumbled over to the corner of the cave and picked up the blade he had used to activate the Sextant.

'Did I look older?' she said.

He shrugged.

'What was I wearing?'

'I can't remember. It was just a brief flash. I know you're desperate for a clue that shows us getting off this world, but there was nothing to prove it either way.'

'Did you see Cole?'

He shook his head. 'Only you.'

'We'd better catch up with him. He'll be thinking that we aren't going to walk with him to the town.'

'We shouldn't go to the town. It's a stupid idea.'

'Maybe.'

'There's no maybe about it.'

'Then we have six miles to change his mind.'

'We should each go over our abilities,' Arrosa said, as she, Cole and Cael trudged along by the banks of a stream. 'We should know what each of us is capable of doing, and what we can't do; in case the townsfolk turn out to be unfriendly.'

'Or,' said Cael, 'we should forget the whole idea. None of us look the same as the people we've seen here. And Cole and I are much taller than them. We're going to stand out as strangers, from the moment they lay eyes on us.'

'I can throw fire,' said Cole, 'and I can read thoughts. I can vision for hundreds of miles, at a push. In theory, I might be able to control lightning, but I've never tried it.'

'Does no one listen to anything I say?' said Cael.

'How do you know that you don't have battle-vision, Cole?' said Arrosa. 'Have you ever tried to... summon it?'

Cole nodded. 'I used to try it out when I was about fourteen. It's not there. My father didn't have it, either; and my mother had no mage powers.'

'I can detect lies,' said Arrosa. 'I guess you all know that. I can also detect others with Gifts, but that's not exactly very useful on World Three. And, I can turn people into glass, but only if I'm touching them. Dragons, too. All animals, probably. I once turned a rat into glass.'

Cole glanced at her. 'Why?'

'It was annoying me,' she said. 'What about you, Cael?'

'So you've remembered that I'm here?' he said. 'I thought for a minute that I was using my ability to turn myself invisible. I have vision but, like Cole, it doesn't include battle-vision; and aye, I've tried. I can dream vision, which means I can use my vision while I sleep, and I can also persuade people to do or say things. For example, I could persuade Cole to punch you in the face, Arrosa. The next time you try to hit me, I might do just that. I used to get prophecies now and again, but they're very rare nowadays; and almost all of them were completely useless, anyway. And I can talk to the Sextant. I think that's everything.'

'How should we combine these abilities to defend ourselves?' said Arrosa. 'I think Cole's fire and Cael's invisibility and persuasion are the most useful if we're attacked. Can you make people fall asleep?'

'We can both do that,' said Cole.

'Then why didn't you say so? This is confusing. Right; if the townsfolk try anything, you two can send them all to sleep. Then we'll steal their food and run away.'

'How noble,' said Cael.

'Would you rather starve?'

'I'd rather we turned around and found a new place to forage,' he said. 'Going to the town is a bad idea.'

'They might have a blacksmith's forge,' said Cole. 'Arrosa told us she could repair your sword.'

'The townsfolk will have woken up long before Arrosa is able to do that.'

'We might not have to send them to sleep.'

Cael rolled his eyes. 'Have you forgotten what we saw in the village? The decapitated bodies? Who do you think did that? This town is the only settlement for miles around.'

Ahead of them, the forest began to peter out, and they slowed their pace. Cael crept forwards, moving from tree to tree, his eyes scanning the area. He came to a halt by the side of a wide track that crossed in front of him. He looked to either side, and saw three men approaching, armed with axes and spears. Cael raised a hand to warn Arrosa and Cole, and they fell into silence. Cael crouched down in the undergrowth, the others next to him, and they watched as the three men walked along the track. They were barefoot, and shod in rough animal skins; and the blades of their axes were fashioned from stone rather than metal. Cael gripped the hilt of his black-edged sword as the three men passed their position, keeping himself ready. The three men kept walking, oblivious to the presence of Cael and the others hiding in the undergrowth and, within a minute, they had disappeared along the track.

Cael turned, and saw that Cole's eyes were glazed over. He waited until they cleared, then nudged his cousin.

'Were you inside their heads?' he whispered.

Cole shook his head. 'No. I was making sure they walked into the village. It's just round the corner, but there is a large gate, with more armed men standing close by.'

Cael glanced up at the sky. 'There's no smoke... no; wait – I see some, but that doesn't mean there's a forge.'

'There's no forge,' said Cole, 'or, if there is, it's hidden away somewhere. I looked from one end of the town to the other. I don't think they have the technology to build a forge.'

'Why did you create stupid humans, Cael?' said Arrosa.

'They're not stupid,' said Cael. 'Every society in history has gone through this stage, even the damn Gunstians. It takes time for...'

Arrosa laughed.

'I think she's taking the piss, Cael,' said Cole. 'Are you ready to walk into the town?'

'Will we get past the gate?' said Arrosa.

'Not if Cael's carrying that sword,' said Cole.

Cael frowned. 'I'm not leaving it here.' He took off his outer shirt, and wrapped it round the black blade. 'They probably don't have metal swords here,' he said. 'They won't know what I'm holding.'

'*Metal swords*?' said Arrosa. 'Is there any other kind?'

'Shut up.'

They got to their feet, then they eased through the undergrowth and onto the rough track. The forest started again on the other side of the track, but several of the trees had been cut down.

'Here's the plan,' said Cael, as they made their way along the track; 'we'll see if they will let us in; if not, I will use my powers of persuasion on them to turn a blind eye or I'll make us all invisible. If anyone threatens us, Cole and I will send them to sleep; and if anyone lies to us, Arrosa will scratch her fat arse.'

'We've barely eaten anything in days,' said Cole. 'I don't think that insult works any more.'

'You mean it worked before?' said Arrosa.

Cole raised his palms. 'That's not what I meant!'

Cael laughed. 'How about, *Arrosa scratches her ear*? Is that any better?'

'Much,' said Arrosa. The track bent to the left, and they halted as the town came into sight. A long, high wooden fence was blocking any view of the buildings, but a few wisps of smoke were rising into the blue sky. In the middle of the fence was the gate that Cole had mentioned. It was lying open, but four armed men were standing next to it.

'They've seen us,' said Arrosa.

'Act like we belong here,' said Cael, as he started striding towards the gate. 'Walk, don't run, and let me do the talking.'

'Aye, aye, Captain,' said Arrosa.

The four men at the gate stared at the three approaching figures, then one of them shouted something, but the words were unintelligible to Cael. The four men levelled their spears. They shouted something again.

'Do you understand what they're saying?' said Cole.

'No,' said Cael. 'But... I told the Sextant to embed the Holdings language into the human population of this world.'

'Use your persuasion on them,' said Arrosa.

Cael released his powers and sent them towards one of the men. He entered his mind through his eyes, but was confronted with a consciousness he couldn't comprehend.

Lower your spear, Cael said in the man's head. *We are not a threat. Tell the others to let us enter the town.*

There was no response from the man, except for a look of confusion on his face.

'It's not working,' said Cael.

Cole raised his right hand. 'Sleep.'

Nothing happened.

One of the men turned, and began shouting through the gate. A few moments later, more men appeared, also armed, and they flooded out of the town, and began to advance on Cael and the others.

'Stay calm,' said Cole. 'They're just curious.'

The large group of men surrounded the three strangers on the track, their spears aimed inwards. A loud cacophony of unintelligible words rose up from the gate, as more people came out to see what was happening. As Cael had predicted, he and Cole were by far the tallest there; but it was Arrosa the men were staring at.

'We're hungry,' she said. 'Do you have any food?'

One of the men reached out and pushed her in the shoulder.

'Hey!' she cried. 'Hands off.'

Another man lunged at her, and Cael punched him in the face. The force of the blow sent the man back a few feet, then the crowd rushed at them. Arrosa touched the arm of one man, and he screamed in agony, his spear falling to the ground. The scream cut off abruptly, as his flesh began to transform, and within seconds, a glass sculpture of him was standing in the middle of the track. At this, the other armed men ran back a few yards, their voices shouting and crying out in fear and anger.

'There's a lit fire just beyond the gate,' said Cael. 'Do you see it, Cole?'

'What?'

'Do you see the fire?'

'Yes. I see it.

'Use it!'

The men in front of them gathered themselves into a thick line, and lowered their spears. One of them shouted, and they charged at the three strangers. Cael pulled the shirt off the black-bladed sword, and its dark metal shone in the sunlight. He parried a spear that was aimed at his waist, then swept his arm out. The tip of the black sword ripped across a bare chest, and the man fell to the ground. More spears came at them, jabbing out, and Cael fended them off. One of the men swung a stone-bladed axe at Cael's head. Cael lifted the sword to block it, and the black blade snapped in two from the impact.

'Run!' cried Arrosa.

Flames rushed down from the sky like a snake striking at its prey. They smashed into the back of the gathered men, incinerating several. The rest broke in panic, fleeing in every direction.

'Go,' said Cole, his hand raised as he controlled the flames. 'I'll cover our escape. Head back to the waterfall.'

'We'll stay together,' said Cael.

'And what will you fight with – a broken sword?'

Arrosa grabbed Cael's arm and began pulling him back down the road. Three men ran out at them, and Cole moved his hand, directing the flames into their bodies. The three men screamed as the fire coursed through them. Cael and Arrosa reached the undergrowth at the side of the road, then Cael turned, the hilt of the broken sword still gripped in his hand.

'Cole; come on!' he shouted.

The fires began to die down, so Cole lifted a hand and guided some of the flames onto the tall wooden fence protecting the town. Its beams exploded as the flames took hold. With more fuel at his disposal, Cole erected a fiery wall between him and the town, a great barrier of flames from which the townsfolk fled in panic. Cole lowered his hand. He was about to turn, when a man rushed out from the forest, a large stone held in both hands. He raised his arms, and brought the stone down onto Cole's head. Blood streamed from the side of Cole's face, then he fell onto the track.

Cael started to run towards his cousin, but Arrosa was pulling his arm back.

'He's dead, Cael,' she cried. 'We have to run, or we'll be next.'

Cael stared at Cole. The man with the stone prodded Cole's bloody head with a foot, as the wall of flames weakened and died out. The townsfolk rushed forwards, gathering round Cole's motionless body, and blocking him from sight.

'Please, Cael,' whispered Arrosa. 'Run, before they see us.'

Cael turned, then he and Arrosa fled through the forest.

CHAPTER 18
ATTAINING ADULTHOOD

Colsbury Castle, the Holdings – 30th Day, Last Third Summer 544

'Because it would not only violate the laws of the City,' said Shella; 'it would also break our imperial obligations. We have a treaty with Emily and Daniel – a treaty that I helped to write – which clearly states that the Empire will respect the City's legal jurisdiction.'

'Then what other options do I have?' said Kelsey.

'You can lodge an appeal with the City courts,' said Shella.

'I've done that already.'

'I don't know what else to say, Kelsey. If you want to remain within the law, then there's nothing you can do but wait until the City's legal system issues its verdict.'

'But he abducted my children.'

'I agree, but my opinion is worthless. The only opinion that counts is that of the highest court in Ooste, which is why you'll have to await their decision.'

'But...'

Karalyn frowned from across the table. 'As much as I sympathise with your situation, sister,' she said, 'we are here for my daughter's birthday breakfast, not to discuss your on-going legal case against Van.'

'I agree,' said Thorn. 'Kyra is eighteen today; let us focus on that.'

Kyra glanced up from her untouched plate of food. Part of her was slightly amused that her mother and the Empress had agreed with each other for once, while another part had been content to remain in the shadows while Kelsey and Shella talked.

'It's Cael's birthday, too,' she said.

'Of course,' said the Empress, 'and we all miss him deeply.'

'This is the first birthday I've ever spent without him. When he first disappeared with Arrosa and Cole, I thought they'd be back within a few days. But when Elbannon told me about the flaws in Cael's sword, I started to think that they might be trapped on Cael's world. What if they never come back?'

'I have faith in Professor Elbannon,' said the Empress, 'but he requires time to work on the task he has been set. All we can do in the meantime is hope that Cael and the others are safe and well.'

'Cael will know much about the world they are on,' said Karalyn. 'It is his creation; he will understand it better than anyone. He, Cole and Arrosa are resourceful, and they each have powers and Gifts that will help them survive.'

'Don't pretend you care, Mother,' said Kyra.

Anger flickered over Karalyn's face, then she nodded and fell silent.

'We all care about the missing children,' said Cardova. 'It has been a painful summer without them, and we are doing all we can to bring them back. Our options, however, are limited. We are lucky to have Elbannon, but he is only one man and, as Her Majesty stated, he needs time to develop the means by which we can track down the Sextant.'

'Have you had a chance to think about your future?' said the Empress. 'If you wish, this year can be your last at the university, or, you can decide to stay on for a further year.'

Kyra glanced down again. 'I don't know. Do I have to decide now?'

'You have until the end of autumn to make up your mind,' said Kelsey. 'If you do decide to stay on for a fourth year, then you'll have to pick the subject you want to specialise in, and then we'll find you a tutor.'

'I think Professor Gallea would be a good choice,' said Cardova.

'But you don't have to do a fourth year if you don't want to,' said Karalyn. 'You could get a job, or you could go travelling.'

'If you want a job,' said Shella, 'I can find a place for you in the chancellery.'

'But that would mean living in Colsbury all year round,' said Kelsey.

Kyra stared at her plate of food as the others discussed her future. If she hadn't threatened to tell the Empress about Cael's use of the Sextant, then her brother would be sitting next to her. Arrosa and Cole would be there, too, and she would most likely be bickering with Cael. She shifted awkwardly in her seat, and felt the edge of her Quadrant digging into her leg. She was tempted to use it. With a single touch of her finger, she would be able to escape her own birthday breakfast.

The adults at the table fell silent as a staff officer from the Imperial Army walked out on to the upper balcony.

'Apologies for interrupting, Your Majesty,' he said; 'I have a message for Major General Cardova.'

Cardova got up from his chair and led the officer over to the side of the balcony, where they talked in hushed tones. Kyra watched as Cardova nodded a few times, his expression grim as he listened to what the staff officer was saying.

'Thank you for letting me know,' Cardova said.

The staff officer saluted, and left the balcony.

'What was that about?' said Kyra, as Cardova re-took his seat.

'Operational matters,' said Cardova. 'Let's get back to our discussion about your future.'

Kelsey's blocking abilities had no effect on Kyra's dream powers, so she drove her way into Cardova's mind, bypassing the protective layers that her mother had placed there to thwart ordinary vision mages; then she replayed the entire conversation that had taken place between him and the staff officer.

'I have told you not to do that,' said Karalyn. 'You must allow people to keep their secrets, Kyra.'

Kyra ignored her mother's words, and stared at Cardova. 'Eighty thousand?' she said.

Cardova narrowed his eyes.

'Our army has killed eighty thousand people in Rahain?' Kyra went on. 'And what was that about massacres being carried out by the Sanang? Are the Sanang so bad that even the marines are complaining about their behaviour?'

'War is never simple or painless,' said Cardova.

'It's been painless for our side,' said Kyra. 'The staff officer told you that we'd experienced a few dozen casualties in the entire operation. A few dozen against eighty thousand? Are we trying to slaughter everyone in Rahain? We're as bad as the Ascendants.'

The table fell into silence.

'Why are we doing this?' Kyra went on. 'Why can't we leave the people of Rahain alone? Twenty years has passed since Rahain last invaded the Plateau – you cannot seriously tell me that they are a threat to the Empire. So why are we sending dragons and ill-disciplined and barbaric Sanang forces against them?'

'Watch your language,' said Kelsey. 'There is no need to insult the Sanang.'

Kyra glanced at the Empress, and her features flushed.

'I am sure Kyra did not mean it that way,' said Thorn.

'I still think an apology is in order,' said Kelsey.

Kyra clenched her fists. 'You are slaughtering the Rahain, and you want me to apologise for a few words? What you are doing is a war crime. But why am I surprised? War crimes are my family's speciality. My mother, Corthie, Sable, and now you. I refuse to be part of this. You make me ashamed to be a Holdfast.'

She touched her Quadrant.

My room. Go.

The air shimmered, and she found herself sitting on her bed. Her mother would know where she had gone, but would anyone come to talk to her? She got to her feet, and locked her door. That wouldn't stop her mother, or Kelsey, if she had her Quadrant handy; but it would signal her intentions. She went back to the bed, and put her head in her hands. Her mind raced with images of Sanang soldiers butchering unarmed Rahain civilians in the dark underground cities where they lived in extreme poverty. It was a war of conquest and extermination, not a war of liberation; no matter what anyone tried to tell her. How could the Empress have allowed it to happen? Had she known what would occur when she had unleashed her Sanang divisions upon the Rahain? Did she care?

Kyra pulled a blanket over her and lay down. Could it be possible? Might the Empress not be the kind, benevolent, wise ruler Kyra had always believed her to be? The thought made her feel sick. For years, she had looked up to Thorn; had she been deluding herself? Was she just as bad as the others in her family who had been responsible for horrific crimes? If that was true, then what was left for Kyra?

Kyra was half-dozing when the air shimmered in the corner of her bedroom. Kyra braced herself for a lecture, then she realised that it was Sable who had appeared in her room.

'Happy birthday,' Sable said; 'though I hear it hasn't been as happy as you'd probably been hoping for.'

'What do you want, Aunty?'

'To talk. Do you want me to leave?'

'I don't care.'

Sable looked down at her. 'Stand up.'

'Why?'

'Because, if you don't, you're going to fall on your arse.'

Kyra glared at her, then she put her feet on the floor and stood. Sable put her hand into a pocket, the air shimmered again, and they appeared under a deep blue sky. Three dragons flew overhead, then Kyra glanced around. She and Sable were standing in the middle of a courtyard, with old stone buildings on three sides. Through the gap on the other side, she could see the ocean crashing against the shore.

'Where are we?' she said.

'We are on Haurn,' said Sable.

'Dragon Eyre?'

'That's right. This is where I lived for two years, after I was injured by some greenhides. It's called Nan Po Tana. It was from here that I planned the rampage that you would probably categorise as a war crime. I killed dozens of gods, hundreds of dragons, and thousands of Banner soldiers. And yet, it remains one of my favourite places on any world.'

'Why did you bring me here?'

'To get you away from Colsbury for a while. So we could eat, drink and relax in the sunshine. I might even go swimming. Lara has the children, or the tiddlers, as she calls them. I thought you might like a break.'

A squad of imperial soldiers emerged from a building, picked up a selection of tools, and headed off to the right.

'What are they doing here?' said Kyra.

'Building defences,' said Sable, 'in case Yearning falls to the Unk Tannic. It's unlikely, but one should be prepared. If we lose Yearning, Haurn will be next.'

Sable led Kyra over to one of the buildings, and they entered through the front door.

'This was my home,' said Sable. 'I lived on the ground floor, because I had trouble getting up and down stairs.' She gestured at a table, which had been laid out with plates and bowls filled with food. 'Olives, cheese, bacon, bread, and some of the local wine.'

Kyra folded her arms across her chest. 'How do you sleep at night, Aunty?'

'I sleep well, thank you.'

'Do you know what the Empire is doing in Rahain?'

'Vaguely.'

'And that doesn't bother you?'

'The Rahain have been living with violence and squalor for decades. They murder each other, enslave each other, and some of them do it in the name of their god. If you want that to end, there is a price to pay.'

'So the end justifies the means?'

'In this case, yes.'

'I can't accept that.'

'No one is asking you to accept it. You're eighteen, Kyra; old enough to make up your own mind. If you don't agree with what the Empire is doing, you have two choices – work within it in order to change it, or walk away. Calling me and your mother war criminals is also your right. I've been called worse over the years. It's a little ironic, though, because when you talk like that you remind me of your mother.'

'My mother killed a hundred thousand Rahain while they slept.'

'I know. And she has regretted it ever since. She did it to save your life, Kyra. If Colsbury had fallen to Agatha, you and your brother, along with every other Holdfast, would have been killed. Why do you think she visits the grave of your father every day?'

'Because she loved him?'

'It was his death that sparked her actions. Rage and grief are powerful emotions. Your mother hates violence. On the rare occasions when she uses it, it is when all other options have been exhausted. You may find this offensive, but you are more similar to her than you imagine.'

'I am nothing like my mother!'

'Then why does she agree with everything you said in front of Kelsey and the Empress? I didn't agree with it, but Karalyn does. I tend to believe that violence has its place; that violence sometimes works. Your mother thinks that notion is abhorrent; as do you, I suspect.'

'Why is my family like this? Why are we so murderous?'

'Because life isn't fair or easy. If you don't defend yourself, others will take all that you have. If you don't get rid of evil, it will swallow you whole. If you don't fight back, you will be walked over. If you believe that bad people will leave you alone because you refuse to resist them, all you are doing is inviting them to steal from you. In order to live in peace, you must be willing to fight to protect what you love. There is a place for generosity and mercy, but it comes after you have defeated your enemies, not before.'

'But then all we end up with is a cycle of violence.'

'Let me know if human nature suddenly changes; on that day, I might start agreeing with you. Now, I don't know about you, but I'm hungry, and I want to sit out under the branches of my favourite olive tree.' She smiled. 'Would you care to join me?'

Kyra eyed the wine. 'Can I get drunk?'

'Of course, as long as you pace yourself. We have all day.'

The next morning, Kyra awoke refreshed and well. She glanced around at her bedroom in Colsbury, then remembered that Sable had brought her back from Dragon Eyre at some point in the middle of the night. Sable had then slipped her a tiny portion of Salve, before leaving her collapsed on her bed.

Kyra had drunk far too much wine, and had even smoked a few of her aunt's weedsticks; and it felt strange not to be paying any price. She got out of bed, and went to the bathroom to wash. Her hair smelled of smoke, and her tongue tasted awful, so she brushed her teeth and started to run the hot water for a bath. Fragments of the previous evening came back to her as she waited for the bath to fill. She and Sable had argued, but her aunt had remained calm, refusing to react to Kyra's provocations. Or perhaps she had been unable to answer her niece's questions. After a few glasses of wine, and a long swim in the ocean, however, Kyra had started to relax, and the rest of the evening had been less acrimonious. She wiped the mirror as steam filled the room, and gazed at her reflection. Was she naïve to think that violence solved nothing?

A knock came from her bedroom door, and Kyra's shoulders sagged.

'Who is it?' she shouted.

'Your mother.'

'I'm having a bath.'

'I can hear the water running,' Karalyn said. 'This will only take a few minutes. Kelsey has already started ferrying the Imperial Court back to Plateau City, and I wanted to speak to you before you left.'

Kyra wrapped her bathrobe around her, and walked to the door. She opened it, but did not move aside to allow her mother to enter.

'Aye?'

'I'm sorry about your birthday,' her mother said.

'Don't be. I had a great time with Aunty Sable on Dragon Eyre.'

'Good. I'm glad that the breakfast didn't completely ruin your day.'

'What do you want?'

'I'm here to tell you that I will be coming to Plateau City in a few days from now.'

'So?'

'I will be living in the university for a while.'

Kyra frowned. 'Why? So you can keep an eye on me?'

'No. I will be there to help Elbannon. Lucius has agreed to look after Caitlyn and Carden while I am gone. Getting Cael, Arrosa and Cole back is my priority.'

Kyra took a step back, unable to think of anything to say.

'Therefore,' her mother went on, 'we shall likely be bumping into one another, and I wanted to let you know.'

'You're going to help look for Cael?'

'Aye. Why does that surprise you? He is my son.'

'But you haven't paid any attention to him in years.'

'I've had two small children to look after, while you and your brother spend most of each year not living in Colsbury. I know that you believe I have been neglecting you, but what else was I supposed to do? You and Cael are old enough to look after yourselves, but this... What Cael has done might well be irrevocable, but I helped Elbannon create a Quadrant, so maybe I can be of use to him. I fully expect that you will continue to assist him. You can also hear the voice of Tempest, aye? Between you, me and Elbannon, we might be able to create something that will track Tempest.'

'I… I don't know what to say.'

'Do you really believe that from the moment Carden was born, I no longer loved you and your brother? Kyra, you and Cael mean everything to me. Carden and Caitlyn haven't replaced you. I have two children from Lennox, and now I have two from Lucius; and I love you all equally. That will never change, and I don't understand why you think it would.'

Kyra stared at her mother.

'Your bath is probably full,' Karalyn said. 'I will come round and see you when I arrive in Plateau City, and I'll try not to embarrass you in front of your friends. Oh, and by the way, well done for standing up to Kelsey and the Empress yesterday. You made me proud.'

Kyra said nothing as her mother walked away. She closed the door, and walked back to the bathroom, hardly able to believe what her mother had said to her. It was guilt, she decided. Her mother was feeling guilty about having given all of her attention to her new children, and now she wanted to swoop in, so that she would be able to take the credit for rescuing Cael. She turned off the water, pulled off her bathrobe, and stepped into the bath. Aye, that was it. Her mother was selfish and self-obsessed. Perhaps Cardova had shamed her into taking action. As for feeling proud of her daughter, that was clearly an attempt to drive a wedge between Kyra and the Empress. Her mother was jealous of the fact that Kyra had loved Thorn more than her, and she was trying to stir up trouble.

She sank back into the hot water, going through every possibility that would explain why her mother had said what she had said – every possibility bar one. There was no way she had been telling the truth.

Two hours later, Kyra appeared in the forecourt between the Summer Palace and the Great Keep. Naxor was there, talking to a handful of courtiers, while a huge heap of luggage sat on the flagstones next to them.

'Ah, Miss Holdfast,' he said, as Kyra approached them; 'the disturber of breakfasts. I have been hearing tales about you, young lady.'

'Where's Aunty Kelsey?'

'She is in the midst of transporting the Empress to the Ministry of the Plateau,' said Naxor.

'I've missed the Empress?'

'You have. Was that not intentional? After your remarks concerning the Sanang yesterday, I had wondered if you perhaps wished to avoid Her Majesty this morning. After all, did you not refer to her as a barbarian?'

'No. I was talking about the Sanang in the Imperial Army.'

'Oh, is that what you're claiming? I like that – it would be wise to stick to that version of the truth.'

'It's not a *version* of the truth.'

Naxor smiled. 'If you say so. You might want to ready an apology, nonetheless. Otherwise, my advice to you would be to stay away from Her Majesty's presence, at least until she has had enough time to regain her composure. The Empress has many difficult decisions ahead of her, and she does not require a naïve idealist to be whispering defeatism and doubt into her ear.'

'You don't care that our soldiers have massacred eighty thousand Rahain?'

'Are you drunk? Why would I care about a few casualties? Should our army have marched into Rahain to hand out flowers? Or maybe we should have given them a stern reprimand, eh? That would have shown them we meant business.'

Kyra's anger simmered to the surface, but before she could respond, Kelsey appeared a few yards to their left, a Quadrant grasped in her right hand.

Naxor nodded to her. 'Your pacifist niece has arrived.'

Kelsey raised an eyebrow at Naxor, then she turned to Kyra. 'Are you ready?'

'For what?' she said.

'To go back to Plateau City,' said Kelsey. 'Why else would we be standing out here like numpties? The summer is over.'

'Happy Autumn's Day to you, Herald,' said Naxor.

'Aye, whatever,' said Kelsey.

'I'm ready,' said Kyra.

Kelsey glanced at the courtiers, then at the heap of luggage.

'Can I get taken straight to the university?' said Kyra.

'No,' said Kelsey. 'I have to take everything else to the Ministry of the Plateau. To take you straight to the university, I would need to work out the calculations first.'

'I have my own Quadrant,' said Kyra. 'I can take myself to the university.'

'Then do that,' said Kelsey. 'I'll be in touch.'

She swept her fingers over the Quadrant, and the forecourt emptied, leaving only Kyra standing on the flagstones. She glanced up at the façade of the palace. Kelsey had been right – summer was over. She placed a hand into her pocket.

University Quad. Go.

The air shimmered, and she appeared in the middle of the large quad. Several carriages were lined up by the entrance, bringing students back from their summer break. It was warmer, too, far warmer than it had been in Colsbury; and almost as warm as Haurn had been. She glanced up at the high spires surrounding the quad. Was this her real home now? If it was, then she resented the fact that she would have to share it with her mother. She spent much of her time at university downplaying that she was a member of the most powerful family on the Star Continent; how would she be able to do that if the famed Karalyn Holdfast was also present?

She crossed the Quad, and entered the wing that held the student accommodation. She ascended a flight of stairs, took her key from a pocket of her coat, and opened the door to the small apartment she shared with Dazi. No one was inside, but luggage was sitting on the bed in Dazi's room. Next to it was a hand-written timetable for Dazi's Autumn Term, along with a leaflet inviting her to an Autumn's Day party being hosted by Professor Achan. It was open to all students who had Achan as their tutor, so Kyra decided that she would go along. She locked the apartment and walked through the quiet university corridors until she reached Achan's rooms. She knocked, and the door opened. From inside, she could hear voices, so she entered the professor's quarters.

Dazi, Achan and half a dozen others were seated around a low table, drinking wine and talking.

Kyra smiled. 'Happy Autumn's Day,' she said.

Dazi got to her feet, and they embraced. 'Welcome back,' she said. 'Did you have a good summer in Colsbury?'

'It was... It could have been better,' she said.

'Take a seat, Miss Holdfast,' said Achan. 'Help yourself to a glass of wine, and tell us all what it is like to spend your entire summer with the high and mighty.'

A couple of students moved along to create some space, and Kyra sat.

'It's busy,' she said. 'People coming and going all the time. Parties, dinners, galas.' She thought about telling them what had happened to her brother, but decided against it. She didn't want people to feel sorry for her, but she would tell Dazi when they were alone.

'Did you get to see the Empress?' said a student.

Kyra smiled. 'I saw her every day. And the Herald, too. I mean, I was living with them all in the Summer Palace, just as I do every year. After a while, the novelty wears off. What were you all talking about before I came in?'

'Rahain,' said Achan.

Kyra's expression darkened. 'Oh.'

'Do you know anything about what's been going on there?' said Achan. 'Oops. Sorry. I shouldn't really ask you that question, not when it was your family who took the decision to invade.'

'What have you all heard?' said Kyra.

'Not very much,' said Achan. 'The official news coming out of the Ministry of the Plateau has been vague and insipid. That's why we've been speculating. What I'd like to know is the reasoning behind it all. What possible use could a country like Rahain be to the Empire? The Ministry stated that the purpose of the invasion was to help the unfortunate people of Rahain, but no one does that by invading! You don't help people by killing them and occupying their land. Does Rahain have reserves of natural resources to exploit? Or, is it just about power? Has the existence of a free Rahain irked the Empire so much that it has decided to crush its independence? That, my friends, is my own opinion. You all need to make up your own minds on the subject, based upon the evidence.'

'I think they have some coal and iron mines,' said one student; 'but Northern Kell has plenty of all that, so why would the Empire want to spend a huge amount of money invading Rahain, when they could get their resources from Kell?'

'Has the Ministry released any figures regarding casualties?' said Kyra.

'They have,' said Achan. 'Just yesterday, they stated that forty-nine Sanang soldiers, fifty-two Imperial Marines, and fourteen Holdings infantry had been killed in the invasion. What a waste. However, as far as wars go, that total does seem to be a little on the small side, and I suspect that they are perhaps massaging the figures.'

'They're not,' said Kyra. 'That's the correct figure. What about the number of Rahain who have been killed?'

'No figures have been forthcoming from the government on that account,' said Achan.

Kyra nodded, then she realised that everyone was looking at her.

'Do you know?' said Dazi.

'Aye. I do.'

'You don't need to say anything else, Kyra,' said Achan. 'We understand that you may have been entrusted with secrets that you are not allowed to divulge. I know – we'll change the subject, and talk about something else.'

'That's not the reason I don't want to tell you,' she said.

'No? What is the reason?'

Kyra glanced down. 'You won't believe me if I tell you how many have died.'

The room fell into silence.

'The invasion force has a dragon,' Kyra went on; 'did you know that?'

'No,' said Achan. 'A dragon? That... well, that seems a little disproportionate to the situation.'

'And have you heard about the Sanang divisions?'

'We know that they've been deployed to the front line.'

'Between the dragon, and the Sanang,' Kyra said, 'the casualties have been... high.'

Achan leaned forward, his eyes narrowing. 'How high?'

'Eighty thousand.'

'No,' said Achan. 'I can't...' He shook his head, and his eyes welled up. 'That can't be right, Kyra.'

'I wish it were wrong,' she said, 'but it's the truth. Eighty thousand Rahain have been slaughtered by the dragon, and by rampaging Sanang forces. Even the marines... the marines are complaining. They don't want to fight alongside such... such savages.'

Achan put a hand to his head. 'This is evil,' he whispered. 'Pure evil.'

'When I criticised the policy,' Kyra said, 'the Imperial Chamberlain called me a naïve idealist, and a pacifist.'

'Wear those insults with honour,' said Achan, as tears ran down his cheeks. 'It takes great courage to speak up to those who wield unlimited power, especially if they are members of your family.'

'I am ashamed at what my family is doing,' she said.

'You have no reason to feel shame, Kyra. You spoke up when others remained silent. And now, it is the duty of everyone with a conscience to also speak up about this. The Star Continent needs to know the truth about what our government is doing in Rahain.'

'Might that be dangerous, sir?' said Dazi.

'Not if we remain united,' said Achan. 'We will start by spreading the truth, and then we will call for a university walk-out, to demand a ceasefire. The Empress cannot arrest us all. We shall strike a blow against imperialism, and then we shall watch as the whole rotten edifice comes crumbling to the ground. But, before we can do any of that, we need to know if Miss Holdfast is with us. Well, Kyra, will you join us if we make a stand against this evil, corrupt government? Will you help us fight for the freedom of the Rahain people?'

Kyra looked up. 'Aye,' she said. 'I will.'

CHAPTER 19
FIRST DAY BACK

Plateau City, The Plateau – 1st Day, First Third Autumn 544

Cardova lit a cigarette, and put his feet up against the balcony railings. 'Has the townhouse belonged to the Holdfasts for a while?' he said.

'About forty years,' said Kelsey. 'Not long after the New Town was built by Emperor Guilliam. The Holdfasts were among the first residents.'

'You have a spectacular view over the Inner Sea. I had no idea, from looking at the front of the house, that it was actually built into the side of the sea wall.'

Kelsey said nothing, her nerves fraying.

'This would be my house,' Cardova went on, 'if Karalyn decided that she wanted to be Holder Fast.'

'Is that likely?'

Cardova laughed. 'No. Not in the slightest. You know Karalyn; she wants a quiet life.'

'When will she be arriving in Plateau City?'

'As soon as I've finished up here,' he said.

'Thanks for coming down from Colsbury for this. I'm so nervous, I might throw up later.'

'I'm your friend, Kelsey; and, it's nice to get out of Colsbury now and again.'

'We'll be back in Rahain in a few days.'

'Yes, but that's work.' He flicked some ash over the balcony railing. 'Have you spoken to Kyra?'

'We only got here yesterday, Lucius. I thought I'd let her settle back in before I talked to her about what happened over breakfast.'

'You're not going to be too hard on her, are you?'

'Nope. She's eighteen. Aren't all eighteen-year-olds idealists at heart? She doesn't understand our long-term aims for Rahain.'

'She had a point about the Sanang, though.'

'Aye, I know. If it were up to me, I'd court-martial the whole fucking lot of them. But, it's not up to me, is it? And the Empress doesn't want to offend the Matriarch.'

'It's not right that the Matriarch is being allowed to dump all of her unwanted criminals into the Imperial Army.'

'Once again, Lucius, I agree. But, I also agree that keeping them in Sanang might destabilise the whole country. I'm old enough to remember the Sons of Sanang; a more bloodthirsty, vicious bunch would be hard to imagine. What is it about some Sanang men? Perhaps we need to find them a decent off-world war to fight in. We could throw them against the Unk Tannic, or maybe against the Dragon Dominion. Anywhere but the Star Continent.'

Cardova smiled. 'If we had the Sextant, we could send them all to one of the Doomed Worlds.'

'Aye, it's tempting. But, we cannot repeat any of this to the Empress, or to Kyra, for that matter. How long are you prepared to look after Carden and Caitlyn on your own?'

'For as long as it takes,' he said. 'Karalyn is going to be coming back to Colsbury every few days for a visit, so I won't be completely on my own. I should still be able to get some work done.'

'You don't mind putting your job on hold to take care of children?'

'No.'

'Pyre's tits; you shame me, Lucius. This is exactly what went wrong with me and Van. I can't let go.'

'It's different for you,' he said. 'You're the Herald.'

'And you're the Imperial Constable.'

'Yes, but I sit at the top of a vast military hierarchy of officers. It's like a machine – a machine that can keep running on its own without me. A bit like one of Professor Gallea's steam engines. Feed it with coal, and it carries on. Without you, the Empire would grind to a halt. Do you think Naxor or Shella would be able to pick up your workload?'

'Shella would have been able to do it in her prime; she still might be able to manage.'

'But she would refuse to leave Colsbury. The Empress needs her Herald to be by her side, every day of the year.'

'My mother was Herald for years, and she wasn't by Bridget's side.'

'And look how that turned out.'

'Fair point.' She glanced at his cigarette. 'I'm almost inclined to start smoking again.'

Cardova laughed. 'The Empress would not approve.'

'Damn right she wouldn't. For a Sanang, she can be remarkably... temperate. She wasn't always like that, though. I can remember when she used to drink and smoke, back when she was with my brother. Mind you, being with Keir would drive anyone to alcohol.'

Cardova grimaced.

'He was my brother,' said Kelsey, 'and I'm allowed to say things like that. It doesn't mean that I didn't love the stupid bastard. If he'd survived the Ascendants, he would probably be running the Hold Fast estate with Celine, and Cole would have had a chance to get to know his father.'

The air shimmered in the large chamber behind them, and Kelsey got to her feet as Naxor appeared, along with Van, Calpurnia, and little Caelius. Kelsey ran into the room, crouched down, and embraced her children. She had told herself that she would not allow Van to see her cry, but the tears came unbidden, and she wept as she held her son and daughter close to her.

'Good morning, Van,' said Cardova.

'And to you, Lucius.'

'Do we need to discuss any arrangements?' Cardova went on.

'There's no need,' said Van. 'I appreciate you being here, but things have changed.'

'How so?'

'I am no longer the commander of the Banner of the Lostwell Exiles.'

Kelsey glanced up. 'What?'

Van glanced down at her. 'I have been relieved of my position, and given a new one,' he said. 'I'm not sure if it's a promotion or not, but I am now the official ambassador from the City to the Empire.'

'Ambassador?' said Cardova.

'Yes,' said Van. 'The king and queen felt that, as I know the Star Continent well, and due to my family commitments here, that I should take up the role with immediate effect.'

'It is a sign,' said Naxor.

'Of what?' said Cardova.

'That the City is ready to capitulate to the Empire's requests,' said the demigod. 'Am I right, Ambassador Van Logos? Are you here to negotiate the City's entry into the Empire?'

'What makes you think I would say anything to you before I speak to the Empress, Naxor?' said Van. 'I can tell you that Plateau City is to become my permanent home, at least until I retire, or get replaced. I'll need a place to stay.'

'You can stay here,' said Kelsey.

'In the Holdfast townhouse?' said Van. 'I don't think that would be appropriate. I have been given funds by the government of the City to purchase a property in the New Town of Plateau City; one suitable for an ambassador.'

'I will make enquiries upon your behalf,' said Naxor. 'Will your new accommodation require rooms for the two children?'

'Yes.' He turned to Kelsey. 'That's something we need to discuss; alone, preferably.'

'I can take Lucius Cardova back to Colsbury,' said Naxor.

'Thanks,' said Kelsey. 'I'll see you in a few days, Lucius.'

Cardova glanced from Van to Kelsey, then he nodded. Naxor slid his fingers over his Quadrant, and they both vanished.

'Go out on to the balcony, children,' said Van. 'Your mother and I need to talk.'

Kelsey waited until Calpurnia and Caelius had walked out of the room, then she slapped Van across the face.

'You bastard,' she hissed. 'How dare you take the children from me? Have you any idea of the torture you've put me through? Eight times I went to Ooste, to beg for a glimpse of them, but you wouldn't even do that for me.'

'I did what I had to do,' he said. 'I know you hate me for it. My lawyers in the City have drafted divorce papers. Shall I send them to your office in the Ministry of the Plateau?'

'Fuck you.'

'I'll take that as a yes. As ambassador, I have negotiated a schedule in which I'll be working two days out of every six. I'll need you to take the children for those two days. I will look after them when I'm not working. Do we have a deal?'

'After what you did to me, you think I'm in the mood to be reasonable?'

'Evidently not, but I know you can be reasonable; for the children's sake, not mine. Do we have a deal? I intend to start work tomorrow, so you will have them both then, and the day after. I can drop them off in the morning, and pick them up at sunset on the following day.'

Kelsey paced the floor, her rage barely under control. 'So, I only get them for one night out of every six?'

'Do you think you can handle more than that?'

'I want them every night, and I want you to fuck off back to the City.'

'That won't be happening. I didn't want to be appointed as ambassador, but I will do my duty; and my duty involves me living in Plateau City. I will agree to three nights each, then we switch, but only if you can guarantee that you will be there for them. I don't want you leaving them with nannies and childminders.'

'You know damn well that I can't agree to that without resigning my role as Herald. The Empress needs me to be available.'

'Are you saying you can't even manage one night in six?'

'As ambassador, you will be required to attend evening meetings.'

'And I will ensure that they are always scheduled for the night when you have the children.'

Kelsey stopped pacing. She put a hand to her face, and wiped away the tears she had shed. 'Stay here tonight, and go to work in the morning,' she said. 'Leave the children with me.'

'And then what? I can't stay in the Holdfast townhouse more than one night. It would compromise my position as ambassador. You know that.'

'We'll discuss it tonight, after I get back from work. I can't think of an answer right now, and I'm going to be late.'

Van narrowed his eyes. 'You're leaving already? We only just got here.'

'There's a meeting of the Imperial Court, the first meeting since getting back from Colsbury.'

'When will you be back?'

'At some point this evening.'

'Then I guess you'd better go.'

Kelsey took a coat from a peg, then she walked on to the balcony, where Calpurnia and little Caelius were sitting.

'I have to go to work now,' Kelsey said, 'but I'm very happy that you're both back here; and I'll see you when I get home.'

'I missed you, mummy,' said Calpurnia.

'I missed you, too,' said Kelsey.

She activated her Quadrant before she could start crying again, and appeared in the square courtyard in the centre of the Ministry of the Plateau. She took a moment to gather her thoughts, then she strode into the building. The corridors were bustling with staff who had returned from Colsbury the day before. Offices that hadn't been used for three thirds were being opened and cleaned, as the relocated government got back to work. Kelsey made her way upstairs to the chambers where the Empress lived, passing soldiers who saluted her, and courtiers who bowed and curtsied. She knocked on the door of a small dining room, and entered. Inside, the entire Imperial Court had gathered, except for Cardova and Shella.

'Sorry I'm a little late, Your Majesty,' Kelsey said.

'Please be seated, my Herald,' said Thorn.

Kelsey slung her coat over her chair, then she took her place by the Empress's right-hand side. Brogan and Caelius were further down the table on her right, while Naxor and Bedig were sitting opposite.

Thorn glanced at Naxor. 'Would you chair, Chamberlain?'

'Certainly, Your Majesty,' said Naxor. 'Might I begin by saying that it is good to be back in Plateau City? – and I would like to offer my thanks to Lord Bedig and Quartermaster Caelius for governing the Plateau in the absence of Her Majesty. Our first item today is Rahain. With Tahrana City firmly in the grip of imperial forces, the question before us consists of deciding our next steps. Should we consolidate, or should we press on towards the Rahain Capital before the snows of winter appear? Herald, what is your view on this matter?'

'Our initial plan was to consolidate,' said Kelsey. 'A slow, piece-meal approach, where we captured each city one-by-one, and remained there until peace and stability had been restored. Unfortunately, circumstances have conspired to make this approach undesirable.'

'Why, ma'am?' said Bedig. 'It still seems to me to be the best strategy.'

'It overlooks the behaviour of the Sanang divisions,' said Kelsey. 'Thirty thousand Sanang soldiers have been evacuated from Tahrana City, and they are currently encamped on the road leading south towards the capital. Originally, we had intended to use them as an occupying force, but, quite frankly, they are unsuitable for peacekeeping duties. We risk tarnishing the reputation of the Empire by allowing them to run wild in the streets of Tahrana City, so we can either withdraw them back to the Plateau, or deploy them against the Rahain Capital.'

'You have adopted a most curious tone, Herald,' said Naxor. 'As far as I can see, the Sanang divisions have proved to be the most efficient and effective force under the command of the Empire. Are you insinuating that they are untrustworthy? I think the Matriarch of that nation might well be angered by such a stance.'

'I am insinuating no such thing, Naxor,' said Kelsey. 'I am not criticising the offensive capabilities of the Sanang. Clearly, they are a formidable fighting force, but we need to deploy them in situations that match their talents. Policing civilians is not one of their strengths. Death rates have plummeted since the Sanang were pulled out of Tahrana City, and yet the city remains at peace. Do we want tens of thousands of unnecessary deaths on our hands? If the massacres carried out by the Sanang came to public attention, the Empire's good name would be badly damaged. Here is my suggestion – we use them to assault the Rahain cities, then pull them out once each city has been pacified. I also recommend that Lord Sigum and Commander Lahnos be withdrawn. This is not meant as a slight to their loyalty and skills; but, it is clear that the Rahain have abandoned the countryside to take shelter within their underground cities. The dragon is no longer required. I suggest that Sigum and Lahnos be redeployed to the Rakanese frontier.'

'Dragons from the Eastern Rim have already been assembling there,' said Bedig. 'Would adding Lord Sigum make much difference?'

'Lahnos and Sigum have been stationed there before,' said Kelsey. 'They know the area better than the volunteers Blackrose has rustled up for us. Furthermore, and let's be honest, events have shown that the Sanang on their own are more than a match for anything the Rahain can throw against us. The dragon is not needed, and his presence would only add to an already high casualty list.'

'Did you expect this war to be bloodless?' said Naxor.

'No,' said Kelsey. 'Do you consider eighty thousand Rahain dead to be proportionate to the amount of resistance we have faced? What are we doing in Rahain? Why did we invade? Was it to bring peace and prosperity to a region that has been suffering for decades, or is this a war of conquest and annihilation? Of course I was expecting casualties, but some of the complaints that have been coming out of Tahrana City have disturbed my faith in what we are doing.'

'Perhaps we should pull the Sanang divisions out of Rahain altogether,' said Brogan.

'And where would we send them?' said Kelsey. 'I do not wish to see thirty thousand Sanang soldiers sitting idle in border garrisons, not now that they have had a taste of war.'

'Once again,' said Naxor, 'you are skirting close to stating that you dislike the Sanang because they are Sanang. Is there something about this people that you find abhorrent, Herald?'

'Don't be a twat, Naxor; you know as well as I do that the Matriarch did not give us her best. She dumped thousands of murderers, rapists, thieves and brigands into those three divisions, and passed them over to us. Can you imagine if the Kellach Brigdomin had done the same? Or the Holdings? The Imperial Army and the Imperial Marines are professional forces, as are those from the Banner of the Sapphire Throne. The Sanang divisions are not. Their removal from Sanang society might well have benefitted the Matriarch, but they have not improved the morale, discipline or cohesion of the imperial armed forces. We cannot disband them; we cannot send them home; we cannot allow them to fester in remote border garrisons; and we cannot allow them to police the streets of occupied Rahain cities. What then, is left to us? We throw them into battle. We have them lead the assault on the Rahain Capital.'

'In the hope that they are wiped out?' said Naxor. 'Is that your ultimate aim for these brave warriors – that we use them as fodder, to be cut down in order to protect the more favoured peoples of this world?'

'Fifty Sanang were killed in the capture of Tahrana City,' said Kelsey. 'I hardly think that amounts to them being wiped out.'

'But...'

'I have heard enough,' said the Empress. 'I have given my word to the Matriarch of Sanang that her divisions shall be fairly treated;

disbanding them or sending them home in disgrace is not an option. While my Herald is correct that some of their actions have been less than reputable, my Chamberlain is also correct that they have distinguished themselves in the initial assault upon Tahrana City. Therefore, I decree that the attack upon the Rahain Capital should proceed as quickly as possible, in order to avoid the harsh Rahain winter, and that the Sanang divisions shall be in the van of that assault, supported by the marines and the regular army. I also authorise the redeployment of Lord Sigum and Commander Lahnos to the Rakanese frontier. What is the next item on the agenda, Chamberlain?'

'It is a trivial matter, Your Majesty,' said Naxor.

'It is not trivial,' said Brogan. 'It greatly affects imperial tax receipts, and it has been stuck in the courts for nearly seven years, awaiting a decision. If you would please give it a few moments thought, Your Majesty, the situation could be easily resolved.'

'What is this matter, Treasurer?' said the Empress. 'I will give it a fair hearing.'

'Thank you, Your Majesty,' said Brogan. 'It concerns the imperial monopoly bestowed upon the Severton Distillery Company by Empress Bridget. Under that agreement, only goods produced by that company are officially allowed to be purchased by any imperial buyer, and only they are liable for taxation. This has allowed several new distilleries in Lach to open up without any imperial oversight, and their products are untaxed. Severton is demanding that we use military force to close these distilleries, while the Lach are demanding that they be recognised as legitimate producers.'

'What course do you recommend, Brogan?' said the Empress.

'I think my mother was correct to assign monopoly status in the first place,' she said, 'but times have changed, and the law should be altered to reflect that. I recommend granting official status to the Lach distilleries. The tax receipts arising from the decision would greatly benefit the treasury.'

Naxor shook his head. 'Aila will be most displeased at having her whisky taxed, and Severton will be furious. One can always trust the treasury to provide solutions that please no one.'

'That may be true,' said the Empress, 'but I am inclined to agree with Lady Brogan. Abolish the monopoly and recognise these new distilleries. It might do Severton some good to have a little competition. Let us now break for lunch. Herald, would you please remain here?'

The others in the Imperial Court rose to their feet, bowed, and filed out of the chamber.

Thorn turned to Kelsey. 'Naxor told me that Van and your children are back in Plateau City.'

'Aye, Your Majesty. They arrived just before this meeting started. That's why I was late.'

'Have you come to an agreement with the new ambassador?'

'His solution requires me to have two free days and one free evening out of every six, Your Majesty.'

'Would you be able to work on those days?'

'No, Your Majesty. I would be needed to care for Calpurnia and Caelius.'

'I cannot afford to lose one third of my Herald's workload. Could you not find a suitable nanny?'

'Van... doesn't wish me to employ nannies, Your Majesty. He wants me to be there in person. I think this is something I need to do.'

Thorn frowned. 'It seems that having children is incompatible with the duties of Herald.'

'Do you wish me to offer my resignation?'

'Absolutely not. You are invaluable to me, and the Empire needs you.'

'Van will begin his role as ambassador tomorrow, Your Majesty, and he is expecting me to absent myself from work for that day and the next. Might I try this new schedule? It has been many years since I had a day off.'

'Looking after two children hardly amounts to a day off, Kelsey,' Thorn said. She shook her head. 'Very well; I shall allow you leave for the next two days, as a trial period. However, you should be aware that others will move forward in an attempt to take your place while you are not here. An Empress needs her Herald. I am not Bridget, and you are not Daphne; and I will not tolerate a situation whereby my Herald is not present.'

'Thank you, Your Majesty. Might I be excused from the rest of today's meeting? I had planned to visit Athumia tomorrow, but that will have to be moved to today.'

Irritation flickered over the Empress's face. 'What choice do I have? So be it. Go.'

Kelsey picked up her coat as she got to her feet. She withdrew her Quadrant from a pocket, bowed to the Empress, then slid her fingers over the copper surface. The air shimmered, and she appeared in a bleak volcanic landscape. The sky overhead was blocked by thick clouds of ash, while, on the ground, the Tempest mine was laid out, with rows of squat stone buildings, patrolled by soldiers from the Banner of the Sapphire Throne. Kelsey pushed the Quadrant back into her pocket, and walked along the ash-filled road towards the headquarters of the garrison commander.

Three hours later, the air shimmered again, and Kelsey appeared by the rear of the Dragon Palace on Zamata. She brushed the accumulated ash from her outer coat, and walked towards a palace entrance. The soldiers stationed by the doors recognised her, and, within a few minutes, Kelsey was standing in front of President Bauchlie and his ministers in the grand circular audience chamber.

'Greetings, Herald of the Sapphire Empire,' said Bauchlie, as he rose to shake her hand. 'Would you like a tour of the new island defences that you have generously paid for? The expansion of the Chain Castles is almost complete, and Handshore Naval Base is bustling with construction work. The two dragon carriers are being thoroughly refitted, at your request. Of course, we have no dragons to sail on them, but it's your money.'

'Thank you, but no,' said Kelsey. 'As for dragons, would you be interested in hosting two or three to defend Zamata? Dragon Eyre dragons, naturally, not those of the Dominion variety. It is important that Zamata remains impregnable.'

'It is important to us,' said Bauchlie, 'but I fail to see how it is important to you.'

'A strong, free Zamata prevents either the Gunstians or the Dominion from gaining the upper hand upon this world,' said Kelsey. 'The defensive alliance we signed with your government shows that the Empire is pledged to maintain your independence.'

'Without asking us for anything in return?' said Bauchlie. 'A most one-sided document. However, I have learned not to spurn acts of generosity, especially those which come with no strings attached.'

'I have another list of spending proposals to show you,' she said. 'The Empire believes that a small squadron of, say, eight frigates, would be a powerful addition to your naval armoury.'

Bauchlie smiled. 'They would indeed. Who would pay the sailors required to crew these vessels?'

'We would,' said Kelsey. 'The rates would be high enough to entice sailors from Irlan to join the Zamatan navy.' She withdrew a few papers from her coat. 'Would you care to read the details?'

'I would be delighted to do so,' said Bauchlie. 'Let us retire to a smaller meeting room, and we can hold a frank discussion. Are you hungry?'

'I am, aye.'

'Then we shall see you well fed, Herald. After all you have done for us, it is the least we could do.'

The sun had set by the time Kelsey reached her last stop of the day. She appeared outside the gates of the mountaintop monastery of Zamata Gataza, where Lord Bailey was waiting for her.

'Lady Holdfast,' said the god. 'Welcome back to my humble abode.'

'There's nothing humble about it, Bailey. How have you been?'

I am well,' he said. 'There is little for me to do here, except read, relax, and gaze out at the view. You just missed today's sunset – a pity. Will you be staying long enough to enjoy the sunrise?'

'Not this time,' she said. 'I need to ask your advice about something.'

'Then come inside. I have dinner prepared for you.'

Kelsey smiled, and decided it would be impolite to mention the fact that Bauchlie had already laid on a banquet for her. They entered the ancient monastery, and climbed the steps to one of the upper floors, where the old prelate had previously lived before Bailey had taken the building into his possession. They stepped on to a rickety wooden balcony, as the stars came out. They sat, and Bailey filled two glasses with wine.

'This is from Chesson,' he said. 'A fine little vintage.'

'Thank you,' she said. 'Tell me – is Tempest traceable?'

Bailey raised an eyebrow. 'Why would you ask that?'

'Because we've lost the Sextant.'

Bailey's face changed colour, and he almost spat his wine out.

'One of the younger Holdfasts took it to a new world he has created,' said Kelsey; 'it's not in the hands of our enemies.'

'Well, that's something, I suppose. I presume this little rascal has yet to return with it?'

'Aye. Is there any way to find it? We have Elbannon working on the problem, but I thought I'd ask you, considering your experience in these matters.'

'I will need to think deeply about it,' he said. 'Nothing springs to mind, but I may find something if I reflect upon some of my older memories. I think my sister devised a technique to locate deposits of Tempest ore on another world, long ago. Leave the problem with me for now, and I shall be in contact if I remember anything.'

'I'd appreciate that. On a related question, do you know why the Sextant would refuse to relocate the Palace of the Almighty?'

Bailey stared at her. 'By that, do you mean that the palace remains upon the Star Continent?'

'Aye. It's in a place called the Holdings; just sitting there like an enormous lump of granite.'

'It is an enormous lump of granite. This news alarms me, Kelsey; I advised Karalyn years ago to ensure that she destroyed that infernal building.'

'We tried. The Sextant refused to cooperate. It said something vague about being unable to carry out our request to shift the palace to a safe location. It is also extremely difficult to damage. We had teams of workers trying to break it apart, but they barely scratched it.'

'Do not break it apart, I beg you,' Bailey said. 'There are things in there that should never be allowed to see the light of day.' He gazed into the distance for a few moments. 'Edmond was able to transport the palace from Implacatus to the Star Continent – correct?'

'Aye.'

'I wonder... perhaps Edmond was able to move it because he was the architect who built it. He must have known every detail of the interior. It was designed to prevent Quadrants from being able to penetrate the interior, so maybe one has to fully comprehend the structure of the palace before one can move it? It's only a theory.'

'It sounds reasonable.'

'So, the Palace of the Almighty is still on the Star Continent? I had assumed it had gone. I know the interior quite well, having been imprisoned there for... let's just say quite a long time. If the Sextant is found, then I might be able to move it. In the meantime, might I ask a favour?'

'Of course.'

'My sister is still inside the Palace of the Almighty,' he said. 'Tortured for millennia by Edmond, is it not time that Theodora should be allowed to rest? Will you grant me permission to enter the palace to find her? I would place her body onto a funeral pyre, and lament my grief to the heavens.'

'Your sister is dead, Bailey. She isn't suffering.'

'Her reanimated flesh is a mockery of all she stood for. Theodora, the First and Greatest Ascendant, reduced to a shuffling, decayed, wrinkled old corpse. She will be wandering the halls of the palace, Kelsey, not alive, but not yet fully dead. Allow me to put an end to this misery, this travesty of justice and humanity.'

'But you just said that the palace should remain sealed up. You told me that there are... things inside that might be dangerous.'

'Yes. All of that is true. Be assured – I would be very careful.'

'No, Bailey. I'm sorry, but I cannot allow that. If your sister was alive, then of course I would be willing to help, but no.'

Bailey smiled. 'Of course. I had to ask. More wine?'

CHAPTER 20
FOR THE BEST

Tahrana City, Rahain – 4th Day, First Third Autumn 544

Lahnos and Efizel strode down the clean, well-lit tunnel. It was wide enough to fit four carriages side by side, and the wall lamps had been repaired by teams of workers brought in from the Holdings. Along with the soldiers from that country, the Holdings workers were seemingly ubiquitous in Tahrana City. They were loathed by the majority of the Rahain civilians, but were still seen as a great improvement over the withdrawn Sanang.

Lahnos and Efizel ducked their heads to enter a square-cut cavern, where a mixture of soldiers, officials and representatives of the local Rahain population had gathered. A few people turned to glance at Lahnos and his Bullan sergeant major, but most were watching a heated argument in the centre of the room.

'We still have no clean water,' said an old Rahain man, using the language of the Holdings. 'You promised us clean water. Where is it?'

'You must be patient,' said a Holdings officer. 'The reservoir that used to serve this city has been neglected for decades, and it will take time to repair the dam that controls the flow of water.'

'Without clean water, I cannot guarantee the stability of the population. They have suffered enough, and now they are suffering anew. Many of them think I am a traitor for even speaking to you.'

The Holdings officer frowned. 'Would you rather we hadn't come? Would you prefer the gangs to still be in charge?'

'Nobody wants to go back to those days,' said the old Rahain, 'but you have to prove to the people that you are not just another foreign overlord. We remember the old times, when Guilliam invaded. That was the beginning of our troubles, and here you are again – Holdings, Kellach, and... and the Sanang. What happened in Rainsby last time should have been a lesson to you, but it seems you have forgotten your history.'

'What's he talking about?' Lahnos whispered to another officer.

The Rahain turned and saw him. 'I was referring to the mass slaughter of the Rahain inhabitants of the town of Rainsby, Commander Laimos. It took place the last time the peoples of this world united to invade us. Guilliam unleashed the Sanang upon the town – he gave them a free hand for three days to loot, murder, and terrorise the civilians. And now we have a blasted Sanang as the Empress! Is it any wonder they rampaged through Tahrana City?'

'Do not disrespect the Empress,' cried a Holdings officer.

'She is your Empress, not mine,' said the Rahain. His tongue flickered out for a moment, and many of the Holdings officials grimaced. 'When will the water supply be restored?'

'It may take another ten to fifteen days,' said an officer. 'We have four hundred workers up at the reservoir; we are not stinting in our efforts.'

'Fifteen days? And what about the heating? The winter will be upon us sooner than you think. Can you assure me that the caverns will be warm when the snows begin?'

'The heating system hasn't worked for twenty years,' said an official. 'We cannot simply turn it back on and expect it to function. It needs a complete overhaul. The pipes, the boilers, the valves. We have requested experts from Plateau City to come down here to assist us.'

'And what would the people of Plateau City know of such things?'

The official shook his head. 'You have no idea, do you? Did you know that there is an entire university faculty entitled The Department of Recovered Rahain Technology? While you fell into the abyss, we were doing our utmost to preserve the inventions and discoveries that once made these cities the envy of the world. Most houses in Plateau City now have some version of the same heating system that used to operate here. Tell me – what happened to your experts?'

The Rahain waved his hand. 'They are long dead. Very few of the older generation have survived the last few years.'

'You survived,' said Lahnos.

'I am one of the few, Commander. I was once a member of the Rahain aristocracy; free, and wealthy. Now, I am as poor as anyone else in the city. I remember when Laodoc was Chancellor, and when Ghorley was High Protector. They were both flawed men, but it is Guilliam I blame for our downfall.'

'Forget the past,' said Lahnos. 'How do we make life better for the future?'

'Leave,' said the old man. 'You have removed the gangs that used to rule these caverns. Your job is done; now go, and leave the Rahain to govern Tahrana City.'

'The Rahain are not ready to rule themselves,' said a Holdings officer. 'If our army and staff withdrew, you would be back in the abyss within thirds, maybe days. You had better get used to us being here. There will be no retreat from Rahain this time.'

'What is that supposed to mean?' said the old Rahain man. 'Are you going to attempt to annex us into your damn Empire?'

'That will be for the Empress to decide,' said a senior officer.

'Ah, so we have no say in the matter? I see. Once again, foreign imperialists treat Rahain as their personal possession.'

'We left you alone for twenty years,' said the senior officer. 'In that time, you did nothing to save yourselves. Instead, you sank deeper into the mire with every passing year. We are here to civilise this land, old man, and there's nothing you can to do stop us. We will fix the heating, and the fresh water supply, and the sewer system, and the roads and the farms, and we will make this city inhabitable. A decade from now, Rahain will be back to its former glory, and it is the Empire that will deserve the credit. When you are fit to govern yourselves, you will be permitted to form your own, localised administration but, until then, we are in control. Decide now if you want to work with us to better yourselves, or piss off out of this chamber, and leave the reconstruction of Tahrana City to the professionals. '

The half dozen Rahain in the cavern fell into silence.

'Shall we, uh, discuss food supplies?' said a Holdings official. 'We have an estimate of the imports we shall need to get us through until the next harvest is available.'

The old Rahain man's tongue flickered again. 'We shall be happy to discuss the food supply. Thank you.'

The senior officer watched as the Rahain sat down with a group of officials, then he turned to Lahnos.

'Was it advisable to tell the representatives of the Rahain to piss off?' said Lahnos.

'Probably not, Commander,' said the officer, 'but I was starting to lose my patience with them.' He gestured to an aide, who handed him a sheaf of documents. 'Which regiment were you looking for, Commander?'

'The Eleventh Mixed Regulars,' said Lahnos. 'They were based along the Great Tunnel.'

The officer leafed through the pages, then stopped. 'They arrived in Tahrana City three days ago, Commander. Do you wish to speak to the colonel in charge?'

'No. Where have they been posted?'

'The south-western district.'

'Thank you. Good luck with the negotiations.'

The senior officer smiled. 'With any luck, Commander, the Rahain will soon realise that we are here to help them. Between me and you, the Sanang have a lot to answer for. If they had behaved with an ounce of decency, the Rahain wouldn't be acting as though we were monsters.'

Lahnos said nothing, then he and Efizel retreated from the cavern.

'Why did you not agree with the officer, sir?' said Efizel. 'His comments on the Sanang mirrored your own.'

'Yes, but Sigum and I were also responsible for many of the deaths, on the road down from the Grey Mountains. We're not exactly innocent.'

'You and Lord Sigum cleared the gang encampments along the road, sir. You did not massacre civilians once the city had been taken.'

'Do you think they'll use us to attack the Rahain Capital?'

'I think that to do so would be a tactical error on the part of the Empire, sir. The Rahain are all well aware by now that a dragon rules the skies, and they have fled underground. I think you and Lord Sigum would have little to do.'

'I can live with that.'

They came to a large junction, where several tunnels branched away.

'This is where I leave you,' said Lahnos. 'I'm going into the south-western district.'

'Are you sure this is a wise idea, sir?'

'It's not even slightly wise, but I have to try.'

'Should you take an armed escort along with you, sir? That district can still be unruly at times.'

Lahnos laughed. 'I think I'll be all right. I'll see you later.'

He turned, and took a tunnel that led off to the left. He passed teams of Holdings workers, busily repairing old heating pipes, while a few soldiers stood guard to protect them. With his horns, Lahnos was one of the most easily-recognisable figures in the city, evoking respect and terror in equal measure from the imperial army and the Rahain civilians. A few Rahain eyed him from a dark cavern, and they visibly relaxed after he had passed by. Lahnos didn't care. He had never felt so fearless, so invulnerable. His Gifts and his self-healing had altered his perception of himself over the previous few years. In that time, he had been injured often, but he had always healed, and he rarely felt any pain.

He walked for four miles, passing through some of the worst-ravaged areas of Tahrana City. Some of the tunnels looked close to collapse, and there were sections where the lighting had yet to be repaired. For all the neglect and squalor, there were dozens of crews out working, cleaning the accumulated grime from the walls, shoring up damaged tunnels, and fixing the lamps.

He came to a roadblock, and halted.

'Are you from the Eleventh Mixed?' he said to the soldiers on duty.

'Yes, sir,' said a Holdings man.

'I'm looking for Lieutenant Dolwyn,' said Lahnos. 'Sixth Company.'

'You want to go down to the left of here, sir,' said the soldier, 'until you reach a cavern. The Eleventh Mixed has set up its headquarters there, and the officers will be gathering at this time of the day.'

Lahnos nodded his thanks, then he followed the soldier's directions. He emerged into a large cavern, where workers were suspended from the ceiling, as they fixed the lamps that hung down from chains. He saw a group of officers walk out of a building and start to disperse, and walked towards them. In their midst were several Kellach, along with officers from the Holdings, and he caught sight of Dolwyn, who was talking to another Kellach woman.

'Hello,' said Lahnos.

Dolwyn glanced over, and came to a halt.

'How have you been?' Lahnos said.

'Fine, sir. I'm due to lead a patrol out into the neighbouring streets. I don't want to be late.'

'I want to talk to you.'

'Is that an order, sir? My squad are waiting for me.'

'I've missed you.'

Dolwyn took a slow breath.

'I was hoping that we might be able to spend some time together,' Lahnos went on.

Dolwyn frowned. 'Why, sir?'

'I think I made a mistake.'

'I haven't seen ye since the First Third of Summer, sir. It took me a while to get over ye, and I don't want to go through that again. You were right; your arguments convinced me. We don't belong together. May I go now?'

Lahnos raised his palms and stepped aside. 'I'm not stopping you, Lieutenant. I had to try.'

Dolwyn gave him a strange, sad smile, and then she re-joined the group of officers and they disappeared into a tunnel. Lahnos remained where he was for a few moments. Part of him had been shocked by her response, and that made him feel embarrassed – had he expected her to run into his arms and pretend that nothing had happened? His embarrassment started to turn into disappointment. He noticed that a few of the nearby officers and soldiers were glancing in his direction, but he didn't care. He turned, and began the long walk back.

A visitor was waiting for him when he returned to the central cavern where he and the Bullan were stationed. Lahnos walked out on to his balcony where she was sitting with Efizel, and saluted.

'Ma'am,' he said.

'Commander,' said Kelsey, remaining seated. 'Where have you been? I don't have the time to be waiting here all day for you.'

'I was off duty, ma'am. I went for a walk.'

'Sit.'

Lahnos took a spare seat on the balcony next to Kelsey. She looked annoyed, and tired.

'I have news for you,' she said.

'Good or bad, ma'am?'

'That depends upon your point of view.' She yawned.

'Would you like a cup of coffee, ma'am?' he said.

'I will be happy to make it for you, Madam Herald,' said Efizel.

Kelsey frowned. 'Is it that obvious that I'm knackered? Aye, alright; I'll take some coffee. Thanks, sergeant major.'

'No problem, ma'am,' said Efizel, standing. 'Would you like some, sir?'

'Yes, please,' said Lahnos.

Efizel bowed his head, then he strode from the balcony.

'He's loyal, that one,' said Kelsey. 'He wouldn't even tell me what you were doing when I asked him.'

'I was chasing an old girlfriend,' said Lahnos. 'I'd heard that her regiment had been deployed to the city.'

'Was it that Kellach woman you brought to Colsbury for Summer's Day?'

'Yes.'

'Did you find her?'

'I did.'

'And?'

'She said no.'

'Tough luck, Lahnos. Maybe it's for the best, though.'

'Have you seen your children?'

Kelsey paused for a moment, then she nodded. 'I've just spent two full days and a night with them.'

'I'm happy for you. Is the situation resolved?'

'This is none of your business, Lahnos.'

'I know, but I'm available if you want someone to talk to about it; someone unbiased, who will be honest with you.'

'You know my sister well,' she said.

'Not as well as you'd think. I spent two years living with her and her family in Colsbury, but Karalyn is a difficult woman to get to know. I probably talked to Lucius and her children more than I talked to her. She was easier to understand when she was Lyla, and she couldn't remember anything.'

'I'm going to overlook the fact that you just referred to your commanding officer by his first name.'

'I thought we were talking informally.'

'Aye, I noticed you dropped the *ma'am* as soon as your Bullan sergeant major left the balcony.' She gazed out into the interior of the vast cavern. 'I can't win, no matter what I decide to do. I love my children, and I love my job.'

'Why can't you have both?'

'I don't have time for both.'

'But you must have servants and staff who could help you. What about your husband?'

'We've separated.'

'Sorry to hear that, but there must be some arrangement you can make.'

'You would think so, but neither my estranged husband nor my employer is willing to compromise.'

'I don't have any children, so I'll readily admit that I haven't experienced what you're going through; but they're still young, aren't they?'

'Calpurnia will be eight next third; and Caelius will be five at the beginning of winter.'

'Regret is a powerful emotion,' he said. 'It's useless, but powerful. You might want to take steps to ensure that you don't end up riddled with it. Your children won't be young forever, but the job of Herald will always be there.'

'This is bullshit,' she said. 'If I was the father, no one would be batting an eyelid.'

'Back on Zamata,' he said, 'I confess that I used to think that women should stay at home to look after the house and the children. It was the traditional way, and I didn't question it; not until I arrived here and saw how things could be done differently. I've seen plenty of capable Kellach and Holdings women in the army and marines. The only branch of the armed forces that doesn't take women are the Sanang divisions, and... well... the less said about them, the better. In other words, what I'm about to say has nothing to do with the politics of it – I'm just suggesting that you, personally, might end up regretting your decisions if you choose work over your children. It might be bullshit, but feelings are feelings.'

'I'm going to feel regret no matter what I do. I'll either let down the Empress, or let down my children.'

'Ten years from now, which of the two would you rather look in the eye, and know that you had done your best for?'

Kelsey fell silent as Efizel walked back on to the balcony with two mugs. He bowed his head, then passed one to Lahnos, and the other to Kelsey.

'Thank you,' said the Herald.

'It was my pleasure, ma'am.'

'Take a seat, sergeant major,' she went on. 'This news also affects you.'

Efizel sat, as Lahnos sipped the hot, sweetened coffee.

'The Imperial Court has recently come to a few conclusions regarding the future of the campaign in Rahain,' she said. 'The main decision was that the assault on the Rahain Capital will now go ahead before the onset of winter. We have momentum on our side, not to mention the three Sanang divisions, who are eager to continue the campaign.'

'We had guessed that this might be the case, ma'am,' said Lahnos. 'Do we have a date for the assault?'

'We do, but you will not be taking part.'

Lahnos frowned. 'Ma'am?'

'You and Sigum did a great job of clearing the road between the Grey Mountains and Tahrana City, Commander,' she said, 'and this is no reflection upon your abilities; but the Rahain have fled from the countryside, to take shelter within their underground cities. Now that the element of surprise has been lost, your effectiveness in the air has correspondingly reduced. You would be of more use elsewhere.'

Lahnos glanced at Efizel. 'You were right, sergeant major.'

Efizel tilted his head, but said nothing.

'Pack up your things,' said Kelsey, 'and let Lord Sigum know the news. I'll come back for you at the same time tomorrow, and I'll meet you all outside, where we met before.'

'Where are we being deployed, ma'am?' said Lahnos.

'I cannot tell you that right now,' she said, 'as I don't want a whisper of this to get out. You will be fully briefed upon arrival at your new destination tomorrow.'

'Understood, ma'am.'

'Do you have any other questions, Commander?'

'No, ma'am. To be honest, we'll be glad to get out of Tahrana City. I barely get to see Sigum, and I hate living in a glorified cave. I assume that the Bullan will be coming with me?'

'Of course. They are Lord Sigum's support team; we wouldn't separate you.'

'Thank you, ma'am.'

Kelsey drained her mug of coffee and got to her feet. Lahnos and Efizel also stood.

'I will see you all tomorrow,' she said, as she took her Quadrant out of a shoulder bag.

The air shimmered, and the Herald of the Empire vanished.

Lahnos and Efizel re-took their seats.

'I will give the news to the other Bullan, sir,' said Efizel.

'Thanks. Will we have time to pack up everything?'

'We will work through the night, if need be, sir. Might I ask how it went with Lieutenant Dolwyn?'

'It went badly.'

'I see, sir.'

'She's not interested in restarting anything. I blew it.'

'It might be for the best, sir.'

'That's what the Herald said.'

'With us being redeployed tomorrow, sir, if she had been willing to rekindle your relationship, you would now be having to say goodbye to her.'

'I know. That was the first time a woman has ever turned me down.'

'Really, sir?'

'Really. It's not as though I've asked that many women, but still, my brain doesn't know how to deal with it. I want to go back there and try again, even though it would be pointless.'

'You have plenty of time to find someone else, sir.'

'Plenty of time? Efizel, I have all of damn eternity to find others. Five hundred years from now, I'll still look twenty-one, which I hate, by the way. I'm nearly thirty, and I look like a boy. I'm never going to find the perfect woman, because she will grow old and die, and I'll still be looking like a fucking boy.'

'There is one option that you do not seem to have considered, sir.'

'Yes? What's that, then?'

'You could find someone who shares your immortality, sir.'

Lahnos laughed. 'A literal goddess? You're setting the bar a little high, are you not?'

'It would make sense, sir. Any children produced by such a union would almost certainly possess self-healing abilities.'

'Wouldn't the Holdfasts hunt us down?'

'The Holdfasts are producing immortal children at a steady rate, sir. Their views on gods will no doubt change as the present mortal generations grow old and die, while their immortal offspring come into their maturity. Things may look very different twenty years from now.'

'You might be right. All the same, it's Dolwyn that I want. What about you and the other Bullan? Five hundred years from now, I want your great-great-great-great grandson to be by my side. You'd better see to that soon.'

Efizel laughed. 'I don't know if the Klediomira Haga are capable of having children with any of the peoples of this world, sir.'

'Well, I would rule out the Rahain,' said Lahnos. 'And probably the Rakanese. The Kellach and the Holdings can have children together, obviously. Witness the Herald – she was from such a union. If you found the right Holdings woman, you might have a part-Bullan son who has battle-vision. That would be something to behold.'

'It would, indeed, sir.'

Lahnos got to his feet. 'I'm going up to the surface to find Sigum.'

The next fifteen minutes were spent climbing the long staircases that cut through the mountain to the slopes outside. Lahnos passed a small squad of marines who were guarding the entrance to the stairs, and stepped out into the cool mountain air. Three of the Bullan were attending to Sigum under some over-hanging cliffs, and Lahnos smiled as he approached.

'Greetings, rider,' said the large silvery-green dragon. 'I was hoping to see you this day. Shall we fly together?'

'I'd like that,' said Lahnos, 'but first, I have some news.'

The three Bullan stopped what they were doing and gathered round.

'Tonight will be our last night in Tahrana City,' Lahnos said. 'We're being redeployed. We are to assemble here tomorrow at noon, and the Herald of the Empire will transport us to our new location. Before you ask – I don't know where we're going, but it will be somewhere interesting; otherwise, the Herald wouldn't have kept it a secret. Pack up everything, and have it ready to be transported.'

'Does this mean,' said the dragon, 'that we shall not be taking part in any assault upon the Rahain Capital?'

'That's right. Shall we go for that flight now?'

'Let us do so.'

The dragon stepped out from under the cliffs, and Lahnos pulled himself up into the harness. He strapped himself in, and Sigum ascended into the clear, cold air.

'I will miss these mountains,' said Sigum, as he rose ever higher, 'but I shall not miss waging this unequal war. It was all too easy. There is little honour to be found here. Wherever we are sent, I hope it comes with a more honourable challenge.'

'As far as the Empire is concerned,' said Lahnos, 'we are weapons.'

'Mighty weapons.'

Lahnos smiled as the chill air whipped against his face. 'The best.'

CHAPTER 21
ON THE RUN

World Three – (4th Day, First Third Autumn 544)

Cael moved his vision over the vast expanse of thick forest. He delved down into a long valley, crossed the river, and allowed his sight to scan the opposite bank.

Where were they?

For five days, he and Arrosa had been chased by hunters from the town where Cole had been killed, with only Cael's vision powers keeping them at bay. No matter how tired and hungry he felt, he knew that if he didn't find the group that was pursuing them, they would be ambushed as soon as night fell, and both he and Arrosa would die.

He pushed his vision along the bottom of the valley, checking both sides. He caught a glimpse of movement, close to where he and Arrosa had spent the previous night. Cael peered in closer, and saw over a dozen armed men from the town, rooting about in the patch where Cael had slept. They examined the surrounding area, noted a few marks made by the two fugitives, and set off again, following the bank in the direction of Cael and Arrosa's new hiding place.

He brought his vision back to his body, and opened his eyes to a blinding headache.

'Did you see them?' said Arrosa.

He turned to her. She was sitting on the ground with her knees drawn up, and she looked exhausted.

'I saw them,' he said. 'They've found last night's camp, and are running down this side of the river. They'll be here in about two hours.'

Arrosa's shoulders sagged, and she bowed her head.

'We're going to have to cross the river,' he said. 'If we don't, they'll find us. They notice everything, even a broken blade of grass. If we cross the river, we might be able to lose them for a while.'

'I'm so tired, and I miss Cole.'

'We can't give up.'

'We're trapped here forever, aren't we? The Tempest sword is broken, and half of it is still lying on the road by the town. We'll never see home again.'

'I didn't mean to break the sword.'

'I know.'

'It shouldn't have broken like that.'

'You shouldn't have been using it as a weapon. I told you it was fragile, but you didn't listen. You should have guarded it with your life.'

'That doesn't make any sense. To use the Sextant, you need me as well as the sword. Without me, you wouldn't be able to operate it.'

'Without you, we wouldn't be here in the first place. Without you, Cole would still... Sorry. I didn't mean that. Cole's death was not your fault.'

'Are you sure about that? This is my creation, and I brought us here. If I hadn't been so angry, so frustrated with everything that was going on in my life, Cole would be at home on the Hold Fast estate, and we... You know, I don't know what date it is any more. Is it still summer, do you think?'

'I don't know.'

'Either way, it doesn't matter. This is all my fault, Arrosa. I brought us to the one place where we couldn't be found, not even by my mother. When I first planned this world, I had such high hopes for it. I know you think it was unrealistic of me, but I had imagined a beautiful world, with salve, and Tempest, and humans with the same powers as you'd find on the Star Continent. Instead, all we have are the heat, the flies, and the endless forest. I hate this world now. My own sub-created humans killed Cole, and they will kill us, too, if they catch us.'

'I thought you said we shouldn't give up.'

'We shouldn't. There has to be a way to survive here for long enough to work out how to get home. We need to get the broken half of the sword back, but first, we need to cross the river to put some distance between us and our pursuers.'

He got to his feet, and extended his hand. Arrosa took it, and he pulled her up. They left the small clearing where they had been resting, and Cael glanced down at the tracks they had made.

'What if we walk back up the same way we came for ten minutes, and then cross the river there? Do you think that might confuse them?'

'I don't know. Maybe.'

'Let's try it. Try to place your feet in the same positions as they were when we walked here.'

Arrosa gave him a look. 'I can't see where I placed my feet.'

'Try anyway.'

They set off, following the track that they had walked along earlier that day. The river was on their left, and Cael waited until it drew closer to the track. He stopped, and looked at the rocky bank separating him and Arrosa from the fast-flowing water.

'If we clamber over those rocks,' he said, 'we might not leave any tracks behind. Then, we'll dive into the river, and swim across.'

'Swim?' she said. 'Can't we wade across? The current looks strong.'

'It might carry us a hundred yards downstream,' said Cael. 'You can swim, can't you? I saw you swimming back when we were staying in the cave.'

'That wasn't swimming; that was paddling about.'

Cael narrowed his eyes. 'Can you swim, Arrosa?'

'A little bit.'

'Let's get moving, then,' he said.

He jumped up onto a large boulder, and scrambled down to the edge of the river. Arrosa joined him, and they stared down at the swift current, which was flowing from right to left. On the opposite bank was a forest that looked identical to the one they were already in.

'It's only twenty yards,' he said. 'Are you ready?'

'I don't think I can do it.'

He took her hand, and jumped into the river, pulling Arrosa in after him. He kicked out with his feet as the current started to bear them away to the left, and felt Arrosa struggling. Her head dipped under the water, and Cael gripped her shoulders and pulled her back up.

'Stop writhing about,' he cried. 'You'll take us both down. Relax, and trust me.'

With one arm round her, Cael kicked out again, and they began to cross the river, while still being carried downstream. He felt exhaustion sap his strength, but kept going, as Arrosa clung on to his arm. When they were three quarters of the way across, Cael felt the ground beneath his feet, and they waded the last few yards. They crept into the forest on the far bank, and collapsed next to a stand of trees, panting, and soaked through.

'You need to learn how to swim better,' Cael said, while lying on his back.

'You need to learn not to break Tempest swords,' she said.

'Fair point. How far do you think the river carried us?'

'I have no idea. I had my eyes closed for most of the time.'

Two men burst into the small clearing. One swung his axe down at Cael, and Arrosa reached over and placed her palm against his bare leg. The man screamed and dropped the axe, as he turned into glass. Cael picked up the axe as the other man stared at his companion, then he jumped to his feet and brought it down two-handed onto the man's head, splitting his skull open. The second man fell to the ground, while the other was frozen in his tortured pose, another glass statue to add to the one Arrosa had created in front of the town.

Shouts rang out from the forest, from both sides of the river. Cael stared at the man he had killed, then he took hold of Arrosa's hand again, and they took off through the forest at a run. A spear flew past his head.

'How are they all around us?' Arrosa cried.

'The river must have swung back on itself,' said Cael.

'But you said we had two hours.'

'Then there must be another band out hunting for us.'

They reached a tree that had fallen over, its trunk covered in ivy and moss. It was too high to climb over, so they squeezed under it. On the other side was a steep incline, and they tumbled down the slope, landing in a soft marshy pool of stagnant water. Insects buzzed around them as they sat in the thick mud, and Cael checked the hilt of the Tempest sword was still attached to his belt.

He pulled himself upright. 'We have to keep moving.'

Arrosa crushed an insect that had landed on her arm. 'They're going to smell us before they see us.'

They ran onwards, struggling up the other side of the steep valley, then they realised that the river was in front of them again. Behind them, more shouts and cries rose up from the forest.

'We'll have to go back in the water,' said Cael. 'We have no choice. Let it take us much further downstream this time.' He glanced at Arrosa. 'Are you ready?'

She took his hand. 'Don't let go.'

'I won't,' he said, then they dived into the river.

Wet, exhausted and miserable, Cael and Arrosa climbed the rocky slope towards the caves they had seen. The sun was low in the sky to their right, but they had survived another day. They staggered into the first cave they came across, and sat down, out of breath.

'I'm so hungry,' Arrosa gasped. 'This is a nightmare. We're going to die here, aren't we?'

Cael said nothing.

'Why did I have to dare you to use the Sextant?' she said. 'This is my fault, too. I thought it would be fun. Now, Cole's dead, and we... we're running out of time.'

'I think the river might have carried us about twenty miles downstream,' he said. 'We should be safe for tonight.'

'What about the morning? Those bastards know the forest better than we do. They'll find us.'

The temperature dipped in the shadows of the cave as the sun fell below the horizon. Arrosa, her clothes soaked through, began to shiver from the cold.

'You should try to sleep,' Cael said. 'I'll use my vision powers to take a look at our surroundings.'

'Sleep?' said Arrosa. 'How am I supposed to sleep? My clothes are soaking, it's cold, and I'm too frightened.'

'You must have been in worse situations over the years.'

'None like this.'

'Talk to me. Tell me about a time you managed to escape a difficult situation.'

She glanced at him.

'It will take our minds off things,' he said.

'I was stuck in the snow once,' she said.

'Aye? Where?'

'On Elidus.'

'Is that one of the Doomed Worlds?'

'Yes. I was with your mother, when she was still in Lyla's body. Elbannon and Gallea were there, too, and so was Belle. Do you remember Belle?'

'Was that Elbannon's dog?'

'Yes. I liked that dog. You know, Cael, I don't think I ever forgave you for the fact that I wasn't allowed a dog. When your mother and I arrived in Colsbury, I asked if we could get a dog, but you threw such a tantrum that Lyla... I mean Karalyn, was forced to agree to placate you.'

'I don't remember that.'

'Well, it happened. You owe me a dog, Cael. When we get back, I demand that you get me one.'

'If we get back, it will be the first thing I do.'

'Good. Anyway, we were stuck in a frozen wilderness, with blizzards and ice. We had a forge with us, and...'

'Why was there a forge in the middle of ice and snow?'

'Gallea brought it along by accident. We burned whatever we could find in the forge, but we were running out of wood. It was so cold. I thought we were all going to die. All we had was this thin tarpaulin sheet between us and the blizzard.'

'What happened?'

'Bailey appeared. He saved us. He had felt something when Elbannon's Quadrant had brought us there.'

'Why didn't you use the Quadrant to escape?'

'Because it only had one jewel, and it had exploded. I don't think Bailey is going to save us this time.'

'I should have placed some Serpent Eye jewels on World Three.'

'Do you think that would have worked?'

'Probably not. All right; it's my turn. I have also been stranded on a strange world. I was with my sister and my mother, and Aunty Aila. We were trapped in a volcanic wasteland, and we had to rummage through a rubbish midden for food. I remember sending rats to sleep, so that they wouldn't bite us.'

'How could you do that, if you can't get into the minds of the humans who live here? I'm going to guess that rats don't understand our language.'

'I'm not sure,' he said. 'Maybe I was imparting a feeling, rather than a spoken command. Anyway, after a few days, a dragon found us, and...'

'Let me guess – the dragon's name was King Gahad.'

'Aye.'

'I think I know this story. Your mother killed King Gahad, and plunged Athumia into a massive war.'

'Something like that. I don't understand it, though – why would my mother return to Athumia, when she had me and Kyra? She communicated with Lahnos, but she didn't think to do the same with me or my sister?'

'She felt guilty. She had also killed Lahnos's father when she murdered Gahad.'

'Gahad was intending to imprison us.'

'Maybe, but she still killed Lahnos's father. She helped Zamata rise up against the Dominion, and she even caused the deaths of a few dragons. That's why the dragons wanted revenge on her, so they forced her into Lyla's body.'

'Did my mother... kill Lyla?'

'From what I heard, the dragons killed Lyla first, then they put your mother into her body. But they couldn't have completely killed her, because your mother could still remember pieces of the old Lyla's life. That really confused her for a while but, over time, the Lyla memories faded away.'

'And now she is in Albany's body?'

Arrosa nodded.

'With ordinary gods, if you cut off their heads, they die. My mother might... never die. Ever. In a few thousand years from now, she won't remember anything about us; but Caitlyn and Carden will still be there.'

'Do you wish you were immortal?'

'No. I can't even imagine how awful that would be. To live on and on forever, watching kingdoms rise and fall, wars, suffering, all endlessly repeated. Seeing every mortal you love wither away and die, until you shut yourself off from all sympathy towards them, in order to stay sane. Life... is precious because it doesn't last forever.' He glanced at Arrosa. 'Some people think I'm jealous because Caitlyn and Carden have self-healing powers. I'm not. I feel sorry for them.'

'Then why are you so jealous?'

'I'm not jealous. I'm...'

'Angry?'

'Aye. Angry. Angry that I had to live without a father, and angry that my mother kept vanishing for years at a time. Then, when she finally does come back, she brings you along with her – as though you were going to replace me and Kyra. It was too much for my ten-year-old brain to take. The reason I don't remember preventing you from getting a dog is that I had so many tantrums that they've all blurred into one. I wasn't easy to be around back then.'

'Do you think you have been much better recently? I wanted to be your friend, Cael; I wanted a big brother.'

'I don't want to be your brother.'

'See? Why do you say such cruel things to me? I didn't choose to have my family massacred when I was eight. All I wanted was a family, and yet you refused to accept me. Even Kyra, who I never got along with, was polite to me; but you? You have been mean to me for years. That's why I fight with you all the time; if you stopped being horrible, then so would I.'

'You don't understand. I don't want to be your brother, because... because that would mean...'

'That would mean what?'

'It doesn't matter. Forget it.'

'I'm not going to forget it,' she said. 'I can't believe this. After all we've been through, and after Cole's death, you still hate me. Why? If you told me, then maybe I would understand. You said it doesn't matter; well, it fucking matters to me.'

'I can't tell you,' he said. 'If I did, then... everything would change. I don't understand it myself. I would rather be your enemy than have you laugh in my face.'

'Why would I laugh?'

Cael closed his eyes in frustration. He had already said far too much, about feelings that he barely comprehended.

'We could die tomorrow,' Arrosa said. 'Tell me.'

'No.'

She punched him on the arm. 'Tell me, you bastard! Tell me why you hate me.'

'I don't hate you!' he cried. 'I love you.'

Arrosa's mouth opened as she stared at him.

Cael got to his feet and walked out of the cave. He paused by the entrance and raised a hand to his face.

'What the fuck have I done?' he whispered to himself.

He turned, and saw Arrosa standing next to him. She was still staring at him, but at least she wasn't laughing.

'You *love* me?' she said.

'I don't know. Maybe. Aye. I look at you, and... I don't want you to be my sister, because then nothing could ever happen between us. Kill me now, Arrosa. I couldn't be more humiliated if I tried.'

'You don't need to feel humiliated,' she said. 'How long have you known?'

'Not as long as you'd like. I really have been an arsehole to you for years.'

'I'm not saying no.'

He gazed down at her.

'I'm not saying yes, either,' she said. 'I need time to think about what this means. I can't suddenly change my mind about you. You've been so horrible to me that I might never be able to look past all that. Will you do one thing for me, though?'

'What?'

'Never lie to me again.'

Cael watched Arrosa sleep. Her clothes had dried out, and she was curled up in the corner of the cave, her breathing soft and quiet. He felt relieved at having finally been honest with her, but he knew that she would probably never return his feelings. Why would she? He had treated her so badly for so long, that he didn't deserve her forgiveness, far less her love. He tried to remember the first time that he had looked at her differently, but his memories were confused.

Did he really love her? While Cole's death had yet to sink in, he knew that, if it had been Arrosa who had been killed, he would have been too distraught to carry on. He frowned. He didn't like what that said about him as a person. His cousin was dead, a cousin he had grown up close to; and yet, as painful as that was, it paled next to his feelings for Arrosa. Whatever else happened, he would protect her, even if it meant his own death. Was that love? He would kill every sub-created human on World Three to save her; he would burn every forest down, and destroy every town and village, if it meant that she was safe.

He tore his eyes away from her, and gazed out of the cave's entrance at the stars. If he loved her, he would do whatever it took to get them home; and, to do that, he needed to locate the broken piece of his Tempest sword. He closed his eyes for a moment, preparing himself for another use of his powers. Despite the hunger and exhaustion, he would push himself to his limits again. What else could he do? He refused to accept defeat.

He opened his eyes and unleashed his vision powers. He reckoned he was more than thirty miles from the town, but the river was reflecting the starlight, and he was able to follow it upstream. The distance glided by beneath him. On either side of the faint ribbon of glistening water, there was nothing but the great forests that covered the land like a thick blanket. Darker shadows on the horizon marked where the mountains rose to the north, and the vast ocean was somewhere in the other direction, hemming them in from both sides.

After an hour or so, he caught a glimpse of tiny lights, and moved his vision closer to the town where Cole had died. He skirted around the tall perimeter fence until he reached the town gate, and then he saw the place where he, Cole and Arrosa had been attacked. There was no sign of any bodies, and the fire damage was too indistinct to be recognisable in the light. He focussed on the road that led up to the gate, scanning every inch of it. He went back and forward over the place where his sword had snapped, but there was no sign of it. Had it sunk beneath the mud? But there had been no rain since that day; so where had it gone?

He glanced up at the town. Perhaps the local inhabitants had found it, and taken it as a souvenir, or a relic. Its black metal would have been unfamiliar to them, as unfamiliar as the appearance of three strangers that day. Strangers who could turn people into glass; strangers with the power to control fire; strangers who carried black-bladed weapons. Their arrival had probably been the most momentous event of their lives; and with two of the strangers still loose in the forest, the townsfolk were probably as scared of Cael and Arrosa as they were of them.

Cael lifted his vision over the town, and gazed down. There were no obvious streets, and the layout seemed haphazard and chaotic. Circular timber huts with thatched roofs sat in little clusters, while groups of armed men were standing close to the few fires that had been lit. Cael's attention fell upon the only building in the town that had more than one storey. It was a rectangular wooden structure, near the centre of the town, and more armed men were standing by its front door, as though they were guarding it.

Cael's vision entered the building. On the ground floor was a large hall, which was full of people shouting at each other. Cael was unable to hear what was being said, but, as their language was incomprehensible to him, that didn't matter. A small number of old men and women were being berated by the large crowd, as though they were being blamed for something. The elders were seated along one side of a low table at the end of the hall, and they were arguing back with their accusers. Cael scanned the hall, and smiled. Sitting on the table in front of an old man was the broken Tempest blade, on show as if it were a crucial piece of evidence.

Tempers among the crowd rose further as a side door was opened, allowing more people to enter from the floor above. Several of the townsfolk looked close to hysteria, so violent was their anger at whoever was being led through the doorway.

Cael froze. A man was bound in thick ropes, and had a hood over his head. His hands were tied behind his back, and he was being pushed along by the tips of several spears. Even with the hood on, Cael knew who it was. He watched as the figure was pushed down onto his knees in front of the crowd. Several armed men formed a cordon to keep the crowd from reaching the bound prisoner, as a few of the elders got to their feet and began talking to the people in the hall. The crowd calmed a little, then the bound man was led off again, being pushed and shoved back through the door.

Cael severed his vision connection, and gazed out of the cave entrance. He jumped to his feet and ran over to Arrosa. He put a hand on her shoulder, and shook her awake.

'What is it?' she said. 'Do we need to run again? Have they found us?'

'They haven't found us,' he said.

'Then let me sleep. We can talk in the morning.'

He smiled down at her.

'What?' she said. 'Why are you looking at me like that?'

'Cole's alive,' he said. 'I found him.'

CHAPTER 22
THE NEW ACOLYTE

Plateau City, The Plateau – 4th Day, First Third Autumn 544

'Not like that, you stupid girl!' Elbannon cried. 'Do I have to do everything for you?'

Karalyn rolled her eyes, and Kyra laughed.

'What are you chortling about?' snapped the old professor.

'I have never heard anyone speak to my mother like that before,' Kyra said.

'I know something that will wipe that smile off your face,' said Elbannon. 'Consider this, Kyra Holdfast – in a few short years from now, you will look older than your own mother. And a few short years after that, people will start to think that you are her mother, rather than her daughter! Won't that be amusing? Well, they probably won't think that, because you look nothing alike, but you get my point.'

'Have you finished?' said Karalyn. She glanced at Kyra. 'This is what he was like on Athumia.'

'He's like this every day in class,' said Kyra.

'Do you know what's wrong with this university?' said Elbannon. 'The bloody students. At least in Tell Hoard I was allowed peace in which to work. Now I have nothing but gawkish teenagers harassing me all day with their manifest ignorance.' He plucked the slender hammer from Karalyn's hands, and proceeded to tap the small metal device that he had been fashioning. 'Like this,' he said. 'We're trying to bend the metal, not batter it into submission.'

'I sometimes forget how strong I am in this body,' said Karalyn.

'I preferred it when you were Lyla,' Elbannon said.

'What does this device do?' said Karalyn.

'Well, let's see,' said Elbannon. 'It has a small Zamatan Coil at its centre, and it is powered by a single Serpent Eye. The device is coated in copper, naturally, to dampen down the Tempest.'

'Aye,' said Karalyn, 'but what does it do?'

'Nothing,' he said. 'Absolutely nothing. It is but a casing, an outer shell, lacking the vital ingredient.'

'What ingredient?' said Kyra.

'The ability to actually track Tempest,' said Elbannon. 'I built this little device so that you people would think I had been making some sort of progress. The truth is, however, that I am no further forward in accomplishing the task you set me in summer. If there is a substance that can track Tempest, I have yet to find it.'

'Have you tried every alloy from your old book?' said Karalyn.

Elbannon stared at her as though she was stupid. '*Every* alloy, young lady? How long do you think I have been working on this project, eh? I would need twenty years to test *every* alloy. I have had three months. And the books provide no clues, as none of the prefects of the Tempest Cogitarium were looking for any such traceability. I have considered magnetism, and I have discovered how to fashion a decent compass that would aid any sailor lost at sea. Is that of use to you?'

'It might be of use to the navy,' said Karalyn, 'but it's of no use to us. So, you have done nothing that will help us find the Sextant?'

'Nothing? How dare you? I have built a prototype!' He picked up the small device. 'See? It fits snugly into the palm of one's hand. Do you see the jewel? And the little dial with the arrow? That took days to build. It is hinged along one side to allow easy access to the interior; thus.' He pressed a catch, and the lid of the device sprang open. Karalyn and Kyra peered into the innards of the new device. 'There is the small Zamatan

Coil; see?' he went on. 'And I have included a space for the missing component, so that when we finally make a breakthrough, it can be slotted into position. How dare you say I have done nothing?'

'It's like a tiny Quadrant,' said Kyra.

Elbannon smiled. 'I call it *Tammy*, after Tamid, the Eighth Ascendant. It could actually be used as a Quadrant in its present state, although, as your mother could testify, it would only transport someone along a horizontal plane.' He pointed at the gap in the interior of the device. 'I have also prepared some Tempest wires, to funnel the power from the jewel into our missing component, and there are other wires that lead to the dial. In theory, if we can find a material that can detect the presence of Tempest, all we need to do is fit it into the available space.'

'How do we go about finding that material?' said Kyra.

Elbannon placed the device onto his workbench and leaned over to pick up a large journal.

'I have been recording my unsuccessful experiments in here,' he said. 'I have tried mixing small amounts of Tempest with various metals, but it is like trying to find a single grain of wheat amid a granary. As your mother knows all too well, there are thousands of possible alloys to choose from. More pertinently, there might not be any alloy that works. We simply don't know if Tempest gives off any signal that can be tracked.'

'It must,' said Karalyn. 'I am able to detect the presence of the Sextant if it is upon any world that I have sensed before.'

'Only if the Sextant is active,' said Kyra. 'You can't do it if the Tempest sword has been taken out.'

'Aye, that's true. It needs to be active.'

'I shall concede,' said Elbannon, 'that an active Sextant may indeed give off some sort of signal, but that in no way implies that any Tempest alloy would be able to detect said signal. It is as likely that a piece of cheese would be able to do the job.' He scratched his head. 'Have we asked Bailey? That degenerate god might have an insight into his sister's mind.'

'We've asked him,' said Karalyn. 'He's thinking about it.'

'Well he might. As for now, if you are truly here to assist me, Lyla...' He smiled. 'Whoops. I meant Albany; no, wait, it's Karalyn. Silly me. If you are truly here to offer assistance, there's an apron and some gloves hanging by the door. You can fire up the forge and make a start on some basic zinc alloys. Kyra, you can begin by...'

'I have a class with Professor Nadia,' Kyra said.

'Skip it,' said Elbannon.

'I can't. I can help you during the mornings before classes start, and in the evenings, when classes are over, but I have exams at the end of this term.'

Elbannon rolled his eyes. 'Then go; you wouldn't have been much use anyway, in all honesty.'

'I will see you later,' said Karalyn.

Kyra nodded. 'I guess so.'

She picked up her bag, slung it over her shoulder, and walked out of Elbannon's laboratory. There was a sign posted up on the outside of the door, stating *Professor Elbannon's classes are cancelled until further notice. Any students entering without permission will be beaten around the head with an iron poker. You have been warned.*

Kyra made her way along the busy corridor, dodging the groups of milling students who were talking about their autumn schedules. A few first years were wandering around, looking lost, while others were staring at the notice on Elbannon's door. Kyra climbed a flight of stairs, and hurried to Professor Nadia's classroom. The door was lying open, and she walked in. Dazi waved to her from a desk, and Kyra sat down next to her.

'Where were you at breakfast?' Dazi said.

'I was talking to Professor Elbannon.'

'Oh yeah? Why have his classes been cancelled?'

'I think he's working on something important.'

Professor Nadia walked into the room, and the dozen students quietened. She closed the door and strode over to her long desk.

'Good morning and welcome to third year,' Nadia said. 'This term, we shall be doing something a little different. The Imperial Army, as some of you will no doubt be aware, has recently entered a place in Rahain called Tahrana City. There, they have found that the city's old heating system has been neglected for several decades; and they have requested assistance from the university in helping to make the system operational again. To that end, I have procured the old designs for the heating system.' She smiled. 'As some of you might remember, I was once responsible for the maintenance of the heating system in the Rahain Capital, so this happens to be my particular area of knowledge. We are going to split into groups, and each group will examine one specific aspect of the heating system, and then we shall look at formulating a list of recommendations for the army to follow. Winters in Rahain are far harsher than on the Plateau, and our work will contribute to the comfort of my fellow Rahain who dwell in that city. Now...'

Kyra raised her hand.

'Yes, Kyra?' said the old professor.

'Is it moral to help an invading army, ma'am?'

The Rahain woman blinked. 'I don't think I understand the question. Our work will be of great help to the citizens living in Tahrana City. There is much reconstruction work to be carried out there, and we are in a privileged position to lend our expertise.'

'But if we help the Imperial Army, ma'am,' Kyra went on, 'wouldn't we become complicit in their crimes?'

'I don't know to which crimes you are referring,' said Nadia. 'I deem it perfectly moral to help repair an old, broken heating system. Would you rather the Rahain freeze this winter?'

'I would rather the Empire put an end to its illegal invasion of another country, ma'am.'

Nadia narrowed her yellow eyes. 'I see. Tell me, Miss Holdfast – why do you think the Department of Recovered Rahain Technology was founded by Empress Bridget?'

'It was founded so all that knowledge wouldn't be lost.'

'Indeed. And for whose benefit was this done?'

Kyra frowned. 'For ours, ma'am?'

'Correct; but it was not done only for our benefit. It was also done so that, one day, if the Empire ever returned to Rahain, we would be in a position to help restore their cities to their former glory.'

'But you are a Rahain, ma'am,' Kyra went on. 'Are you saying that you are in favour of the invasion of your country by a foreign army?'

Nadia laughed. 'My dear girl,' she said, 'I have been advocating an imperial invasion of Rahain for many years, and I am delighted that it has finally come to pass. Anything which can put an end to the decades of chaos and suffering in my homeland is welcome in my eyes.'

'But thousands of Rahain have already been killed.'

'And each individual death is a tragedy. However, to restore order, the armed gangs that ruled Tahrana City had to be eliminated. If one is guarding a henhouse, one does not leave the wolf in charge. It may seem easy for you to lecture me on morality, Miss Holdfast, but I have personal experience of living under the oppressive regime that has held Rahain in its iron grip for all these recent years.'

'But the Sanang have...'

'I earnestly hope that the Sanang slaughter every single gang member, Miss Holdfast, and you can quote me on that. I would now ask you to please leave my classroom, so that I can teach those who are willing to help my suffering countrymen and women; rather than have to humour those who merely wish to carp from the sidelines.'

The chamber fell into utter silence as Kyra got to her feet. Dazi stared up at her with her wide Rakanese eyes, as Kyra slung her bag back over her shoulder.

'And close the door on the way out,' said Nadia.

Kyra left the classroom, and shut the door. She felt a little deflated, but proud that she had stood up for her beliefs. She considered walking downstairs to Elbannon's laboratory, but that would mean having to spend time with her mother, so, instead, she ascended another flight of stairs and walked to the rooms of Professor Achan.

The Hammer professor was sitting at his desk marking students' assignments, and he smiled up at Kyra when she knocked upon his open door.

'Come in, Kyra,' he said. 'Take a seat. How can I help you?'

Kyra sat down opposite Achan. 'Professor Nadia just threw me out of her class for questioning the invasion of Rahain.'

'Ah. I see.'

'But Professor Nadia is from Rahain, sir. I don't understand why she is in favour of the Empire attacking her homeland.'

'Professor Nadia has lived in the Plateau for many, many years, Kyra,' said Achan. 'It would be natural to assume that she has absorbed some of the imperialist notions that dominate the political landscape here. You know, I recall meeting many Hammers in the City who were in favour of their own enslavement. They would actually claim that the tribe of the Rosers were better suited to ruling, and that the Hammers owed them their loyalty. It is a bizarre experience, to see those who are oppressed, champion their oppressors. Bizarre, but, unfortunately, all too common. I tend to see it as a coping mechanism. If one has to live under oppression, one might be tempted to rationalise it away, to pretend that the system must be there for a good reason; otherwise, their lives would be too difficult to bear.'

Kyra nodded.

'When I was arrested by the Blades for sedition,' Achan went on, 'there were very few Hammers who were willing to speak up for me. Some thought I deserved to be sent to the penal colony of Tarstation, when all I was demanding was equal rights; their equal rights.'

He paused as he opened a drawer in his desk. He removed a thick sheaf of papers and set them down in front of Kyra.

He smiled. 'What do you think?'

Kyra gazed down.

'I had them printed last night,' Achan went on. 'One thousand copies altogether. Several students are going to help me post them up all over the city tonight. The language is a little sensationalist, but it will help to get our message across to the citizenry.'

Kyra picked up one of the printed leaflets. *80,000 Dead Rahain Civil-*

ians, it stated at the top of the page, in bold letters. Below that was a condemnation of the Imperial Army, and the government of the Empire, who were being blamed for committing a series of atrocities against the innocent population of Rahain. Details of a planned protest were included at the bottom, with the date and location.

'Is it right to refer to them all as *civilians*?' she said.

'Rahain has no army,' said Achan, 'so, therefore, everyone living there is, by definition, a civilian. In the grand scheme of things, I deem this to be a harmless exaggeration. Will you consider coming along to the protest? I anticipate a gathering of several hundred, perhaps more.'

'I will do more than come along, sir,' she said. 'I will help post up these leaflets tonight.'

'I knew I could rely on you, Kyra,' he said. 'As I have always suspected, not every member of your family favours the repressive imperialism advocated by the Empress and her bloodthirsty Herald. I, uh, have heard that your distinguished mother is staying in the university at the moment. Do you at all think that she might...?'

'No, and I wouldn't even waste my time asking her. My mother probably disapproves of the invasion, but she will not budge from her position of non-interference in the affairs of the Empire. It has been the guiding principle of her entire life.'

'Then I shall be happy to respect her wishes.'

'What would you do, sir, if you were in charge of the Empire for a day?'

'I would dismantle it,' he said. 'Each province would be free to govern itself, in its own way. The Imperial Army would be abolished, along with the marines, and the mercenary Banner forces, who are the very symbol of imperialist aggression. I would institute democracy for the Plateau, which would become an independent republic with a proper, written constitution that safeguards the rights of every citizen. Most importantly, I would set up state-funded schools, so that every child, no matter their background, would be given a free education. Taxes would be raised for the wealthy, to pay for this.' He smiled. 'I could go on all day in this manner, for I am just getting started.

However, I have dozens of assignments that I need to mark. It was very nice to see you, Kyra, and I look forward to seeing you again this evening, when we shall nail up our leaflets all over this city. We are meeting in the Quad one hour before midnight, so wrap up warm.'

Kyra got to her feet. 'Thank you for talking to me, sir.'

'No problem at all. My door is always open to you.'

Later that afternoon, when Kyra had attended her last class for the day, she made her way down to Elbannon's laboratory. She walked through the entrance, and saw her mother and Elbannon peering down at a few samples laid out on a workbench to the left of the forge.

'Useless, useless, and yes, useless,' said Elbannon. 'Do we need bother trying any more zinc alloys? These results seem fairly conclusive to me.'

'We have wasted the entire day,' said Karalyn. 'Another day in which my son, Arrosa and Cole remain stranded.'

Elbannon stared at her, then he started to laugh.

'Did something I say amuse you?' said Karalyn.

Kyra frowned and walked forward. 'He didn't know who had taken the Sextant, Mother. It was supposed to be a secret. Did nobody tell you before you opened your big mouth?'

Karalyn eyed her daughter. 'I think Kelsey might have mentioned something regarding this, but I fail to see the point in keeping it a secret.'

Elbannon slapped his thigh. 'Your son is the mysterious Sextant-thief, eh? What a mischievous scamp. And that little brat Arrosa is with him? For that reason alone, I am tempted to abandon this entire project. Let them fester!'

'I hope you are making a joke,' said Karalyn. 'I did not come all the way to Plateau City for the Sextant; I am here to bring my son home. If you present me with any difficulties, I will use the death powers I inherited from Albany to rot your insides.'

Elbannon shook his head, his smile gone. 'I actually believe you. Bloody Holdfasts. You're as bad as that Sable woman.'

'I can be worse, if angered.'

Elbannon glanced at Kyra. 'And what do you want to be when you grow up, girl – a mass murderer like the others in your family, eh? Imagine threatening an old man. For shame.'

'I am opposed to all forms of violence,' said Kyra.

Elbannon shook his head again. 'That's almost as bad as being whole-heartedly in favour of violence. You enjoy handing over your sweets to the playground bully, do you?'

'But you just said...'

'Ignore him,' said Karalyn. 'Half of what comes out of Elbannon's mouth is nonsense. His greatest pleasure in life is seeing the reaction he gets when he provokes people.'

'What utter claptrap,' said Elbannon. 'My greatest pleasure in life is revelling in my own genius; though provoking others does come a close second, I'll admit.'

'How about you use some of that genius to work out which alloy we should try next?' said Karalyn.

Elbannon rubbed his chin. 'Let's see. Iron is out, as I have conducted many experiments in the past with iron, mostly for the benefit of the Empire's armaments programme. Lead is definitely out. It does strange things to Tempest, but nothing that would benefit us in any way. Zinc seems useless, and as for copper, I would rather cut my own throat than endure another round of creating copper alloys. Quicksilver would be interesting, but we don't have any to hand. Tin? Carbon? Nickel? Take your pick.'

'Carbon isn't a metal,' said Kyra.

Elbannon sighed. 'I'm glad to see that your daughter's university education hasn't been completely wasted, Karalyn. Well done, Kyra. Carbon is indeed not a metal. It can, however, be added to metals to create alloys. Have you ever heard of steel?'

Kyra's face flushed.

'Don't tease her, Elbannon,' said Karalyn. 'Why don't we schedule some experiments with tin for tomorrow?'

Elbannon nodded. 'I suppose I have nothing better to do.'

The air shimmered in the corner of the laboratory, and Bailey appeared, a Quadrant in his left hand.

Elbannon groaned. 'Look who it is – the man who brought Arden and Albany to Athumia.'

Bailey bowed. 'The man who saved you from the icefields of Elidus, I would have thought, Prefect Elbannon.'

'It's *Professor* Elbannon. I haven't been a prefect for eight years.'

'How are you, Bailey?' said Karalyn. 'Do you have anything for us? Have you remembered any details from your memory that might help?'

Bailey smiled. 'I might have.'

He walked over and took a seat next to the workbench. 'I see you have been busy.' He picked up Elbannon's new device.

'Put that down,' said Elbannon.

'Does it work?' said the god.

'No,' said Karalyn. 'Open it. Press the little catch on the side.'

Bailey put his thumb against the catch, and the lid sprang open.

'Ah,' he said. 'The jewel is connected to a tiny Zamatan Coil.'

'Do you see the empty space?' said Karalyn. 'If we can create something that is able to locate Tempest, it will fit there.'

Elbannon snatched the device from Bailey's hand. '*Tammy* is mine, I say! I made it.'

'Named after Tamid, I assume?' said Bailey. 'I never liked Tamid. He was always very rude to me. Who was it that killed him?'

'My brother,' said Karalyn.

'Ah yes, the mighty Corthie Holdfast. Anyway, on to business. I have spent the last few days reviewing my enormous library of memories, in order to help you regain the missing Sextant. When the Ascendants first moved to Implacatus, my sister brought a large supply of Tempest ore with her, in case she ever decided to build another Sextant. She didn't, as it turns out, and the reserves of Tempest were instead used by Nathaniel to create the Quadrants. At that point, both Theodora and

Nathaniel, who happened to be allies during that period, became concerned that the Tempest stocks would be exhausted.'

'Why didn't they just make some more?' said Elbannon.

'None of the surviving Ascendants knew how to *make* Tempest,' said Bailey.

'Then where did it come from?'

'Haven't I already covered this? Theodora brought it with her when she moved to Implacatus.'

Elbannon clenched his fists. 'You stupid god! I meant how was it created in the first place? They surely didn't just stumble across it one day.'

'Ah. I see. Tempest was created by other Ascendants, long before my sister built the Sextant. Back in those days, there were Ascendants with powers that no longer exist. One of those powers was the ability to transmute metal. It's a bit like stone powers today, only these Ascendants would alter the composition of metal, and, thus, Tempest was born. None of those Ascendants survived long enough to reach Implacatus, hence, there are no gods living today with that particular power.'

Elbannon sighed. 'Five minutes with Bailey can sometimes feel like a lifetime of study.'

'May I continue?' said the god. 'As I was saying, Theodora and Nathaniel were worried. They came up with the idea that they could use the Sextant to create a world with deposits of Tempest; after all, the Sextant was full of the stuff, and they assumed, correctly, that the device would be able to create more on a new world. Therefore, my sister started to plan the creation of Athumia. Nathaniel had parted company with Edmond and Theodora by this stage, so my sister carried on her work unaided. A further worry came to her mind – what if she created Tempest deposits, but could not find them? Would she have to dig up the entire world to discover any? She asked the Sextant to help her find a way to detect these underground reserves and, as far as I know, she was successful.'

Karalyn frowned. 'As far as you know?'

'Yes. I wasn't with my sister very often by then; I was too busy enjoying my reign as Emperor-God of the world she had created for me. She mentioned her plans to me once or twice, and from that I gathered that she had found a way to locate raw Tempest ore.'

'Nathaniel certainly knew how to find the Tempest deposits upon Athumia,' said Elbannon. 'It was the first place he visited, and he took back samples with him when he left Gahad in charge.'

'He probably asked the Sextant to find it for him,' said Karalyn.

'In that case, we are back at the beginning,' said Elbannon. 'We need the Sextant to find the Tempest located inside the Sextant.'

'Do not despair,' said Bailey, 'for there was one further detail I recalled. My sister did not wish to have to take the Sextant with her when she travelled to Athumia, which, in the end, she never did. Instead, she created something portable, just as you are trying to do.' He reached a hand into a pocket. 'I don't know how she did it, but I know it involved this.'

He withdrew his hand, and dropped a coin onto the workbench.

Elbannon peered at it. 'Ordinary silver? But silver mixed with Tempest creates a pale alloy that does not react with anything else. It is inert.'

'I am only telling you what I remember,' said Bailey. 'My sister likened the effect to that of magnetism, though, of course, silver is not magnetic. It was an analogy. Somehow, the silver was essential. That's all I know. Say, are there any good restaurants in Plateau City? One can tire a little of the fare upon Zamata.'

'I will take you out for dinner this evening,' said Karalyn; 'as a thank you for bringing us this information.'

'Don't spend all your money on him,' said Elbannon. 'We'll need a heap of silver for tomorrow's experiments.'

'I'm sure I can afford it,' said Karalyn. 'Would you like to come, Kyra?'

'I have plans for tonight, Mother.'

'Very well. I will see you both tomorrow morning. Let's go, Bailey. I know a few good places.'

Kyra frowned as her mother walked out of the laboratory with the god.

'Are you leaving right away, girl?' said Elbannon.

'No.'

'Do you happen to have any silver?'

'I have some, aye.'

'Then fetch it, get yourself back here, find an apron, and we'll get started.'

'What, now?' said Kyra.

'Yes. Now. You want your brother back, don't you? Also, I want to prove to your mother that I don't require her assistance. Let us surprise her in the morning when she sees the progress you and I have made together.'

Kyra smiled.

'I see that got your attention, girl. A little rivalry with your mother won't do you any harm.'

'I'll go to my room for the silver.'

'Excellent,' said Elbannon. 'And bring a flask of coffee, and some of those cream cakes from the canteen. Oh, and remember to call me sir.'

Kyra narrowed her eyes. 'Aye, sir.'

Elbannon laughed. 'That's the spirit, girl. Don't forget the cream cakes.'

CHAPTER 23
THE TRUE POWER

Tahrana City, Rahain – 5th Day, First Third Autumn 544

The air shimmered, and Kelsey appeared on the side of the mountain. Standing to her left, under the overhang of a cliff, stood Sigum, Lahnos, the seven Bullan, and their equipment and luggage.

'You are late, Herald,' said the silvery-green dragon.

'I know. Sorry,' she said. 'We're supposed to be going to the Rakanese frontier, but there's been a complication. I'll explain when we arrive at our new destination. Is everything ready to go?'

Lahnos nodded. 'We're ready, ma'am.'

Kelsey activated her Quadrant, and they appeared in the forecourt on Colsbury, between the Summer Palace and the Great Keep.

Lahnos raised an eyebrow.

Cardova approached from an entrance to the palace, and Lahnos and the Bullan came to attention and saluted.

'You can relax,' said Cardova. 'Consider the next couple of days as leave.'

'Thank you, sir,' said Lahnos. 'Is there a problem at the Rakanese frontier?'

'There are several problems,' said Kelsey, 'but only one of them concerns you. Queen Blackrose has sent eight volunteers from Dragon Eyre to the frontier, but they are objecting to the presence of Lord Sigum.'

Sigum's eyes shone a cold blue. 'Am I to be insulted by this, Herald?' he said.

'I would rather you be patient, Lord Sigum,' said Kelsey. 'I will fix this, but it might take a day or so. In the meantime, you can stay here and enjoy a short break. We have set aside rooms for Commander Lahnos and the Bullan on the ground floor of the palace, and Frostback and Halfclaw will be here soon.'

'Why are they objecting, ma'am?' said Lahnos.

'It's the same nonsense that caused Blackrose to take exception to Lord Sigum on Summer's Day,' said Kelsey. 'The dragons from the Eastern Rim are saying that they will refuse to cooperate with a dragon from Athumia. And, Commander, it didn't help that you called their queen stupid to her face.'

'Perhaps I should object to working with them,' said Sigum. 'Tell them I cannot cooperate with gullible fools who spread false rumours about dragons they have never met.'

Kelsey frowned. 'Do you really want me to say that to them?'

Sigum lowered his head a fraction. 'No. I spoke in anger. For the sake of harmony, I shall accept your advice, and remain patient. This wounds me. It stings my pride to be thought of as a liar and a breaker of oaths, when I have done neither. I was isolated upon Athumia because I refused to betray my vows; and now it seems I am isolated within the Empire, by those who would name me liar without proof.'

'It is unfair,' said Cardova. 'Those of us who know you, Lord Sigum, are assured of your honesty and honour, and we shall work hard to correct the wrong impression of you that exists among the dragons of the Eastern Rim.'

'It was Sable who accidentally caused this,' said Kelsey. 'I have spoken to her, and she will now endeavour to clear up this misunderstanding.'

'How?' said Lahnos.

'Sable has agreed to speak to the eight dragons currently by the Rakanese frontier,' said Kelsey. 'She will vouch for Lord Sigum's honour in person.'

'Will they accept that?'

'The dragons of the Eastern Rim would crawl over broken glass if Sable asked them to,' said Kelsey. 'They will accept it.'

Shella and Olo'osso walked over from the direction of the small harbour.

'It's good to see you all again,' said Shella. 'I heard about your little difficulties with the dragons of Ulna, and I want you to know that you're very welcome here. Colsbury gets very quiet at the start of autumn each year and, usually, I'm glad to get the place to ourselves again; but in your case I'll make an exception. And, let's be fair, the weather is far better here than it is in Rahain.'

'Do any of you horned lads know how to sail?' said Olo'osso. 'We have an excellent clear day ahead of us; perfect for sailing.'

'I know how to sail,' said Lahnos. 'Well, I did. My skills, poor as they were, have probably withered through lack of practice.'

'We'll soon put that right, Lahnos,' said the old pirate. 'My little yacht is at your service.'

'I might take you up on that,' said Lahnos.

'We've ordered in enough food for everyone,' said Shella. 'More than enough.'

'Treat this as a well-deserved holiday,' said Kelsey. 'You all did a fine job for the Empire in Rahain, so make yourselves at home in Colsbury until I hear back from Sable. She'll be arriving by the Rakanese frontier at some point tomorrow, so you have at least a day, probably two.'

'Thank you Herald,' said Sigum. 'I might stretch my wings in the warm winds over the lake, and await the arrival of Frostback and Halfclaw from the air.'

'I'm sure they would like to fly with you,' said Kelsey.

'I will see you soon, my rider,' said the silvery-green dragon. 'Pray do not drown in the lake.'

Cardova gestured to a soldier, as Sigum rose into the sky. 'Show Commander Lahnos and the Bullan to their quarters.'

The soldier saluted. 'Yes, sir.'

Kelsey stood back a little and watched as the soldier led their guests towards the palace.

'They seemed to accept it with good grace,' said Cardova.

'Thank Pyre for that,' Kelsey muttered. 'Those damn self-righteous Eastern Rim dragons. I'm not surprised Sigum was feeling insulted. After all he's done for us, to be treated like that by our allies is unacceptable.'

'Are you off to Dragon Eyre now?'

'Aye, but it has nothing to do with Sigum's troubles,' she said. 'I need to check on how the defences at Yearning are progressing.'

'Have you told Blackrose about the two dragon carriers that are being refurbished on Athumia?'

'Not yet. I don't think a Quadrant will be able to transport either of them to Dragon Eyre. We'll need the Sextant for that, and I figured there was no point mentioning anything while it remains lost.'

'Will President Bauchlie object to us taking the two ships?'

'Bauchlie is more than happy to see us shower money over his little island. I signed the contract for the eight frigates yesterday. They're being built in a place called Irlan.'

'Is that on Zamata?'

'No. Zamata doesn't have any ship-building facilities. Irlan is a region to the south of Zamata. It used to be occupied by the Dominion, but it's regained its independence. The crews will also be Irlanian.'

'Can we trust them?'

'I held out the promise of future orders,' she said. 'Their shipyards are the equal of anything on Dragon Eyre. If they do a good job, we could order an entire fleet. Anyway, I'd better go. Thanks for agreeing to host Lahnos, Sigum and their Bullan.'

'It's no problem. I'll catch up with you later.'

Kelsey glanced down at her Quadrant, then she slid her fingers over its surface. The air shimmered, and she appeared on a long quayside under the warm sunshine of Dragon Eyre. Several marine officers were standing in the shade of a harbour building, waiting for her, and she walked forward.

'Welcome to Yearning, ma'am,' said one. 'I am Major Tylon Greenhold, commander of the Yearning garrison.'

Kelsey extended her hand, and the major shook it.

'How are our defences shaping up?' she said.

'We have reached the stage where we should be able to repel any attack from the Western Rim, ma'am,' he said, 'whether by sea or air. Would you care to see the new artillery batteries?'

'I'd like that, aye,' she said.

The major led her to the long wall that surrounded the small island's harbour district. They ascended a flight of stairs up to the battlements, and the major gestured to the locations of several towers.

'Each tower has a battery of six forty-eighters,' he said, 'capable of launching explosive projectiles either into the sky, or at any approaching enemy vessel. We have removed the old ballistae from the towers and placed them into storage. Would you care to witness a small demonstration, ma'am?'

Kelsey nodded.

The major signalled to an aide, who put a whistle to his mouth. Three short blasts were emitted, and a green flag was raised from one of the towers. Moments later, all six of the forty-eighter machines on that roof released their payloads, and dozens of small explosive devices were shot up into the sky. Four seconds later, all of them exploded in a crackle of noise, smoke and light.

'Each projectile is packed with shrapnel, ma'am,' the major said, 'and each volley contains two hundred and eighty-eight such projectiles. The forty-eighters are capable of loosing a barrage every ten seconds, and if all five towers are in action at the same time, we are talking in the region of around eight and a half thousand projectiles a minute; enough to fill the sky with shrapnel. It should be sufficient to take down any hostile dragon.'

Kelsey smiled. 'That sounds more than sufficient. How much ammunition do you have on hand?'

'We have some sixty thousand projectiles stored within the harbour district, ma'am.' He pointed at a squat stone building that stood alone in an empty part of the quayside. 'They are being kept in there. Civilian workers from the imperial staff are about to begin constructing blast walls on all four sides of the storage facility, to dampen down the effects of any accidents.'

'How many marines are posted here?'

'One hundred and eighty, ma'am,' he said, 'along with a dozen expert advisors from the Banner of the Sapphire Throne, three hundred imperial staff, and four hundred and fifty natives from the Eastern Rim.'

'Food supplies? Fresh water?'

'All of it is being shipped in from Haurn, ma'am. We receive deliveries every ten days from the camp that has been established there.'

'Sable's old home?'

'I believe so, ma'am. Nan Po Tana is its name. They in turn receive their supplies directly from Throscala. If Yearning were to fall to the enemy, a secondary line of defence has been created along the western tip of Haurn.'

'Has there been any Unk Tannic activity?'

'A few dragons have been spotted in the vicinity, but none have entered the range of the forty-eighters. They are keeping their distance, so far, ma'am. Might I make a suggestion?'

'Of course.'

'It might be misleading to refer to the enemy as Unk Tannic, ma'am; it might give the impression to the decision-makers of the Empire that our foe consists of a handful of wild-eyed religious fanatics in black robes. The truth is that the dragons forcibly transported by Sable Holdfast to the Home Islands have taken control of the Unk Tannic terrorist groups. It is the dragons of Wyst whom we face, and they are greatly aggrieved by their fate. With thousands of their kin stranded on Rigga, the hundreds who have settled on Gyle and Na Sun Ka have vowed vengeance upon Queen Blackrose and the Holdfasts. They are determined to force their passage through the Eastern Rim, so that they can return to their old homes on Wyst.'

'And all that's stopping them are a hundred and eighty marines and thirty forty-eighters?'

'Yes, ma'am.'

'What else do you need?'

'A fleet of warships would be useful, ma'am.'

'What about a ship that can carry up to five dragons at once? A ship capable of crossing oceans? Would that be handy?'

The marine major frowned. 'There are no ships on Dragon Eyre with those specifications, ma'am.'

'I know. But there are ships like that on Athumia and, right now, the Empire is funding their refurbishment. If I could organise their transport to Dragon Eyre, what would you recommend I did with them?'

The major gazed out to sea for a moment. 'In my opinion, ma'am, ships like that would be best suited to patrol the gap between Wyst and Alef. As everyone on Dragon Eyre knows, no dragon can fly between those two island groups, as the distance is too great. If we were to position them there, dragons from the Eastern Rim would be able to lend support to Alef and Olkis, thereby relieving the pressure on Yearning. The Wystian dragons and their Unk Tannic allies would be confounded by this move, for they do not expect any attack from that direction.'

'That would also allow oil supplies from Alef to reach Ulna safely.'

'That is correct, ma'am.'

'I will take your suggestion under consideration, Major; thank you.'

A junior officer approached, and bowed his head. 'Lunch is served, ma'am, sir.'

The major smiled. 'Shall we adjourn to the wardroom, Herald?'

'Lead on, Major,' she said. 'After that, I want to speak to the marines, to let them know how much the Empire appreciates their efforts.'

'I am sure they will be happy to hear that, ma'am.'

. . .

It was late afternoon when Kelsey returned to her office in the Ministry in Plateau City. The hot sun of Dragon Eyre, along with the copious amounts of food the marines had served her was making her drowsy, and she filled a mug with fresh coffee from a pot on a warm stove. She sat down at her desk, and loosened her belt. Everywhere she went, people expected to feed her, and she had learned never to refuse their hospitality. All the same, if it carried on for much longer, she would need a new wardrobe.

Naxor strode into her office and slapped a sheet of paper down onto her desk.

'Have you seen this?' he said.

'So far today,' she said, 'I have been to the Rakanese frontier, Tahrana City, Colsbury, and Yearning on Dragon Eyre. Can I not have five minutes to drink my coffee?'

Naxor prodded the paper with a finger. 'Read it.'

Kelsey sighed, then she picked up the sheet of paper. Its four corners were torn, as though it had been ripped down from a wall, but it was the headline at the top that caught her eye.

80,000 Dead Rahain Civilians.

'Shit,' she muttered.

'There are hundreds of these leaflets, posted up all over the New Town, and some have been seen as far afield as the Kellach Quarter and the old peasant district. Hundreds, Kelsey. This is a public relations disaster of the highest magnitude.'

'People are allowed to express their opinions, Naxor,' she said, 'even if those opinions amount to utter bullshit.'

'But it's not merely *opinion*, is it? From where did the author of this diatribe pluck the figure of eighty thousand? That was a state secret, known only to a select few. There has been a breach of security, plain and simple. Someone within either the palace or the military has leaked this to our enemies.'

'There must be at least a hundred people who had this information,' she said; 'from clerks in the Ministry of the Plateau, to junior officers serving with the Imperial Army in Rahain. The bigger problem is that the figure is true. If it were an outright fabrication, we could release evidence to disprove it. I recommend saying and doing nothing. It will blow over.'

'What about the protest that is being planned two days from now?' said Naxor. 'Did you read the details at the bottom of the leaflet? Perhaps we should consider passing an emergency decree, banning such demonstrations in wartime.'

'That would only make it worse. Let them protest. The army will be able to peacefully contain a couple of hundred students and pacifists.'

Naxor smiled. 'I note your use of *students*, Kelsey. How prescient of you, seeing that I can prove these leaflets were printed upon the university press.'

'What proof do you have of that?'

'My dear Kelsey, there are five operational printing presses within Plateau City – two in the Ministry of the Plateau, one in the Holdings Embassy, one in the offices of the daily newspaper, and, yes, one in the university. Several years ago, I meddled with each. I swapped out certain types, and adjusted others, so that, at a glance, I would always be able to tell from which machine any printed material had originated.'

'You did all that? You sneaky little bastard.'

'Quite. However, my endeavours seem to have finally paid off.' He pointed down at the leaflet. 'Do you see here? Do you observe how the punctuation is slightly misaligned? Only the printing press in the university bears that characteristic. Therefore, these seditious leaflets were printed there.'

Kelsey peered down at the leaflet.

'It was Achan,' Naxor went on. 'It is quite obvious. I recognise his Hammer rhetoric and hyperbole.'

Kelsey said nothing.

'Do you realise what this means?' said Naxor. 'If someone is leaking government secrets to Achan, then who knows what the next leaflet shall be about? Does Achan already know about our plans for the Rakanese frontier, for example; or has he learned the date for the assault upon the Rahain Capital? What about our secrets regarding the Tempest mine, or our defence installations on Yearning? It is imperative that we find the source of the leak and plug it up, for good.'

'Have you spoken to the Empress about this?'

'Yes. Her Majesty is greatly irritated by the prospect of a traitor in our midst. She asked me to work with you towards a resolution.'

'I will go to the university,' she said.

'And let them know that we are aware of their perfidy? Shouldn't we raid the place with two hundred soldiers?'

'I will go alone. I want you to brief Lord Bedig and the city garrison about the planned demonstration. Order them to let it proceed, but to keep an eye out for any troublemakers.'

Naxor eyed her for a moment. 'Would I be wrong to imagine that you are not facing this crisis with as much gravity as one might expect, Herald?'

'I hardly think that a few disgruntled students and their radical professor are likely to bring down the Empire any time soon, Naxor. Let's deal with it calmly, and proportionately. I will go straight to the source, and make some enquiries.'

'I beg you not to reveal to them how we know the university press was responsible.'

'I won't mention that aspect.'

She drained her coffee and got to her feet.

'I think this is a mistake,' said Naxor. 'I suggest we find a sympathetic student we can trust to infiltrate Achan's little band of malcontents. He or she could then feed us information about Achan's plans.'

'Are you aware that Kyra is most likely a member of this little band?'

'Of course.'

'But I noticed that you have neglected to mention her.'

'Are you asking me if I think your niece is the one divulging our secrets?'

'Aye.'

'Then, unfortunately, I would have to say that she is one of my chief suspects. We know that Kyra heard about the figure of eighty thousand, and we know that she was very upset about it. I also heard from my sources in the university that she was thrown out of a class by Professor Nadia yesterday. Can you guess why?'

'Why don't you tell me?'

'She was criticising the invasion of Rahain.'

Kelsey frowned. 'In front of Nadia?'

'Precisely. You can imagine how Nadia reacted.'

Kelsey took out her Quadrant. 'Speak to Bedig and the garrison, Naxor. I will deal with Kyra.'

She slid her fingers over the copper surface, and appeared by the corner of the university quad. A few students noticed her arrival, and Kelsey perceived a slight difference in the way they were looking at her. A few half-torn leaflets were still posted up by the walls of the canteen, and ripped fragments of text were fluttering around the quad in the autumn breeze. Kelsey set off for Elbannon's laboratory. The day's classes were coming to an end, and she guessed that it was the most likely place for Kyra to be.

She entered the buildings on the northern flank of the Quad, and ignored a few stares from passing students. She came to Elbannon's door, shook her head at the threatening notice pinned outside, and walked in. By a workbench next to the forge, Elbannon, Karalyn and Kyra were examining a few trays filled with samples of metal.

'Hello,' said Kelsey.

They turned.

'The answer is no,' said Elbannon.

'Which question are you answering?' said Kelsey, as she walked forward.

'We have not succeeded in our task,' Elbannon went on, 'and you coming here will not speed up our progress. We require time and peace, not constant interruptions by the Herald of the Empire.'

'This is the first time I've been here,' she said, 'and I wasn't going to ask you about progress. I'm here to speak to Kyra.'

Kyra turned back to the workbench. 'I'm busy.'

'It will only take a moment.'

'No. Sorry, Aunty. I'm too busy.'

Karalyn raised an eyebrow. 'You're not that busy. You can spare a few minutes.'

Kyra glared at her mother, then she got off her chair and walked over to where Kelsey was standing. She folded her arms across her chest.

'What do you want?'

'A chat,' said Kelsey; 'in private.'

'Anything you wish to say can be said in front of Elbannon and my mother.'

'Very well. This will be a one-sided chat. I want you to listen very carefully to what I have to say, Kyra. Please don't interrupt me until I have finished.'

Kyra rolled her eyes.

'It has come to my attention,' Kelsey went on, 'that someone in the university has been breaching the oath of confidentiality sworn by all members of the military and imperial staff. You yourself have sworn this oath, Kyra. This breach is in regard to the illegal dissemination of secrets to those who may harbour ill designs against the Empire. I am not accusing you of anything. I am merely pointing out that I would like this behaviour to end, immediately. If it ends, no further action will be taken by the imperial authorities. If, however, I learn that more secrets have been leaked, then I will be unable to prevent a full, criminal investigation from taking place. No member of the Holdfast family is above the law, and the penalties for breaching the Imperial Secrets Act can be quite harsh. I would not want this to happen; therefore, I am appealing to you for your cooperation in this matter. Do I have it?'

Kyra stared at her.

'I said, do I have it, Kyra?'

'No. You can't stop me from attending the protest in a few days' time, Aunty. I thought the Empire allowed freedom of speech?'

'I don't care about the protest; attend it if you like. You are free to demonstrate your anger against the government, but no one bound by the Imperial Secrets Act is free to divulge state secrets. There is a difference.'

'Are you denying that eighty thousand Rahain have been slaughtered in this so-called war?'

'I am neither denying nor confirming anything, Kyra.'

Kyra shook her head. 'You are such a disappointment to me, Aunty.'

Kelsey took a breath to steady her rising anger. 'Am I?' she said. 'And what emotion should I feel when someone close to me has betrayed my trust? You were placed into a very privileged position recently, Kyra, a position that allowed you to hear all manner of secrets.'

'Why should there be any secrets?' said Kyra. 'Why are you keeping the truth from the people you are supposed to serve?'

'Because, in certain cases, the truth would lead to casualties. If we advertised our operational plans to our enemies, then our enemies would be prepared and ready. Do you wish to endanger the lives of the men and women who protect our freedoms?'

'You are twisting everything!' Kyra cried. 'It's the government who is placing us in danger, by recklessly invading its neighbour! Eighty thousand men, women and children, Aunty! The Empire has become wicked, but you are too close to the Empress to see it. Your hands are covered in blood, and you lecture me on preventing casualties? You are a hypocrite.'

Kelsey felt her temper boil over. 'You have no fucking idea what you're talking about!' she cried. 'I work day and night to protect the people of this Empire and, right now, I am trying to protect you from prosecution, you ungrateful little...'

'That's enough,' said Karalyn, striding over. 'Get out, Kelsey. I will not stand here and watch you shout at my daughter. For the record, I don't think she's done anything wrong. All she did was tell the truth; it's not her fault that the truth is so unpalatable. If your soldiers hadn't been slaughtering their way through Rahain like wild dogs, then Kyra would have had no reason to act as she did.'

Kelsey glared at her sister. 'She has broken the law.'

Karalyn extended a protective arm in front of her daughter. 'Then arrest her; I dare you.'

Kelsey took a step back. 'Kyra,' she said, 'I am revoking your court privileges, with immediate effect. You are no longer permitted to sit in at any meetings of the senior military or civilian leaders of the Empire. If you wish to appeal to the Empress on this matter, arrange an appointment with Her Majesty. And tell Achan that if he publishes any more secrets, I will send soldiers here to arrest him.' She glanced at her sister. 'There is such a thing as the rule of law, Karalyn, and, god or no god, you are not exempt.'

'Take your threats and get out,' said Karalyn.

Kelsey activated her Quadrant, and appeared on the street outside the Holdfast townhouse, less than a quarter of a mile from the university. The sun was setting, and a few workers were out, lighting the streetlamps. Kelsey walked up the steps to the front door of the townhouse, and let herself in. The house was shrouded in shadows and silence. With no servants living within the building, and with Van looking after the children from his new apartment next to the Holdings Embassy, Kelsey was getting used to returning to an empty house.

She hung up her coat and walked into the ground floor kitchen. When alone in the townhouse, she tended to visit only a small handful of rooms – the kitchen, her study, the bathroom, and her bedroom, leaving the rest of the large house undisturbed. She unwrapped a loaf that still smelled fresh, and cut off a couple of slices. In three days' time, Van would be arriving at the front door to drop off Calpurnia and Caelius, and the house would once again become a hive of noise and activity, but, until then, Kelsey had nothing but the silence.

Kelsey sat down, and chewed a mouthful of bread. She wondered what the population of the Empire would think if they could see her, alone, sitting in the half-darkness of her kitchen, with nothing but her own thoughts for company. Wasn't she supposed to be the second most powerful woman upon any of the known worlds?

She almost laughed at the thought. Thorn might be Empress, and Kelsey might be Herald, but they all knew who the real power was, the unspoken power that stood behind them all – a power that was slow to anger, but devastating if provoked. A power that was often overlooked, but one whose existence it was always wise to remember.

Her sister, Karalyn.

CHAPTER 24
A BAD FIT

Colsbury Castle, the Holdings – 7th Day, First Third Autumn 544

Lahnos lay back on the deck of the small yacht, as the sunshine touched his skin. It wasn't as warm as a Zamatan summer, but he was glad to be out of the chill winds that swept the Rahain mountains. Shella and Olo'osso were laughing together by the wheel at the stern, but Lahnos was able to ignore them both as the craft bobbed up and down on the swell of the lake.

'This is nice,' said a voice. 'I might have to get myself one of these yachts.'

Lahnos opened his eyes, and saw Sable smiling down at him.

'Does this mean our break in Colsbury is over?' he said.

'I'm afraid so. I'm here to take you all to the Rakanese border.'

Lahnos leaned up on one elbow. 'You spoke to the dragons, I assume?'

'I did.'

Shella staggered over the deck towards them. 'Hey, horned boy, who let that ugly stowaway on board?'

'Good morning, Shella,' said Sable. 'I would never have taken you for a sailor.'

Shella laughed. 'It's more that I'm being taken *by* a sailor.'

'I'm glad to see that your level of humour has remained in the gutter, Shella,' said Sable. 'And where is this sailor? Oh, wait – I see him. I hope you're behaving yourself with the Imperial Chancellor, Olo'osso.'

'Why would I want to do a thing like that, eh?' said the old pirate. He put his arm round Shella's waist and began to nibble her ear.

'Gods above,' said Sable. 'Sometimes, Lahnos, I wish I could wipe my own memories.'

'They're both drunk,' said Lahnos. 'They've been drinking gin since dawn.'

'And what of it?' said Shella. 'Are only young folk allowed to have fun?'

'The young don't know how to enjoy themselves any more,' said Olo'osso. 'Our horned friend, for instance – he's refused to take even the tiniest sip of gin since he got here. And he's only a lad.'

'I knew I could be called back to duty at any moment,' said Lahnos. 'I needed to remain sober.'

Sable eyed him. 'You have self-healing powers. You can sober yourself up in seconds if you become inebriated.'

'Can I do that?' said Lahnos.

Olo'osso swayed on the deck. 'Learning how to sail whilst inebriated was one of the best things I ever did.'

'More pertinently,' said Sable; 'can Shella swim?'

'I'm bloody Rakanese,' Shella said; 'of course I can swim.' She glanced around. 'Where are your children?'

'I didn't bring them,' said Sable. 'They're at home with Lara.'

'You come out of retirement, have you?'

'No. I am undoing an earlier mistake.'

Shella cackled. 'Which one? There are hundreds to choose from.'

Olo'osso joined in the laughter. 'You're not wrong, sweet woman of mine. Your wisdom is matched only by your outstanding taste in men.'

Sable and Lahnos glanced at each other as Shella and Olo'osso began to kiss.

'Shall we?' said Sable.

'Please,' said Lahnos.

She put a hand into a pocket, the air shimmered, and Lahnos found himself lying on the grass of the gardens behind the two keeps on the isle of Colsbury. Sable extended a hand, and helped him up.

'If they're not careful,' Lahnos said, 'they're going to drown in that lake.'

'It would be a fitting end, I feel,' said Sable.

'Thanks for speaking to the dragons on our behalf.'

'Well, it was my fault.'

'It wasn't your fault,' he said. 'You told Blackrose that Sigum was honourable eight years ago. You can't be held responsible for her forgetting that detail. How did it go?'

'Fine. I told the eight dragons that I had complete trust in Sigum's honesty and integrity, and that if they refused to work alongside him, I would take it as a personal insult. That seemed to do the trick. Watch out for Gallantmorn; he's the oldest of the eight, and he has taken command of the others. He's a member of Blackrose's court, and I think he's trying to impress the queen.'

'Who is officially in command?'

'You will be under the authority of the Imperial Army; the same as all the other dragons at the frontier. Technically, none of you will be superior to any other. However, Gallantmorn seems to think that he's in charge.'

Lahnos nodded. 'I'll soon set him straight.'

'I'm sure you will, Lahnos. He's dark orange, almost black in places, but his underside is paler.'

'Thanks for letting me know.'

'You go and get dressed and packed. I've already told Sigum and the Bullan to get ready. I'll meet you in the forecourt in twenty minutes.'

When Lahnos emerged from the Summer Palace twenty minutes later, Sable and Cardova were talking and smoking together in the forecourt, while Sigum and the Bullan had gathered by their luggage. Sable saw him, stubbed out her cigarette, and walked over.

'I'll be taking you to an imperial camp just behind the wall that marks the Rakanese border,' she said to the assembled group. 'The eight dragons from the Eastern Rim are expecting you. If they give you any shit, let me know, and I'll be back here in a shot to have words with them. But, they have given their word that they will treat you with respect, so I'm not anticipating any problems. Their riders have also been told to behave themselves. The officer in charge of the camp is called General Brigon – he's from Kellach Brigdomin, in case you hadn't realised that from his name. He's army, and he knows what he's talking about. He will brief you on the operation.'

Lahnos smiled. 'This is very different from when Kelsey takes us places,' he said. 'She doesn't usually tell us anything.'

'Yeah, but Kelsey travels back and forward a dozen times every day,' said Sable. 'Give her a break; she has her own problems to deal with right now.'

'I wasn't meaning that I didn't like her,' said Lahnos. 'I have a lot of respect for Kelsey Holdfast.'

'I'm glad to hear it. Are you all ready?'

No one spoke out in dissent, so Sable put a hand into her pocket. The air shimmered, and they appeared in the middle of a large grassy field. Ahead of them, the border wall was visible, rising above the rows of tents and campfires, while, to their left, eight dragons were standing in a long row, their eyes on Sigum.

'I'll leave you to it,' said Sable. 'Good luck.'

She placed her hand back into her pocket and disappeared.

'May I offer you my greetings, Sigum of Athumia?' said a large dark orange dragon.

'You have my thanks,' said Sigum, tilting his head slightly. 'May I know your name?'

'I am Gallantmorn of Throscala,' the orange dragon said. 'We have heard many things about the dragons of Athumia.'

'And I have heard much about the dragons of the Eastern Rim.'

Gallantmorn glanced down at Lahnos and the Bullan. 'What are these... people?'

'Seven of them belong to the noble warrior tribe of the Bullan, brave Gallantmorn,' said Sigum. 'The other is my rider.'

The orange dragon stared down at Lahnos. 'You are Commander Laimos?'

'I am.'

'The one who can deliver pain with a mere gesture?'

'Yes.'

'Why do you have horns?'

'My grandfather was a Bullan soldier.'

Gallantmorn said nothing as he stared at Lahnos for a few more moments; then he turned. 'Riders of the Eastern Rim,' he said, 'introduce yourselves to our... guests.'

Five young men and three young women stepped out from the shadows between the dragons. Lahnos walked forward to meet them, then he shook the hands that were presented to him.

'Were you in the invasion of Rahain?' said one.

'I was, yes,' said Lahnos. 'Up until a couple of days ago, we were in Tahrana City.'

'Is there going to be an invasion of Rakana? Is that why we're here?'

Lahnos smiled. 'I was hoping that you'd be able to tell us why we're here.'

'The Imperial Army has told us nothing so far,' he said. 'They've been waiting for you to arrive.'

Lahnos looked around. 'Where are they? I was expecting to see a few officers.'

'They're keeping back for now,' said a female rider. 'They wanted the dragons to meet Sigum without anyone thinking they were interfering.'

Lahnos glanced over his shoulder. Sigum was talking to the eight dragons, but their cautious, almost tense postures belied the politeness of their discourse.

'I hope none of your dragons treats my dragon with any disrespect,' Lahnos said to the riders.

'Sable has already told us that it's all been a big misunderstanding,' said one.

'Is it true, though?' said another. 'Do most Athumian dragons lie?'

'I don't know about most,' said Lahnos, 'but I've met a few who do. Some of them were complete bastards, in fact. And, perhaps you should know that many of the dragons of Athumia didn't care much for Sigum, because he was often the only honourable one among them. It used to get him into trouble from time to time.'

'Do the... Bullan speak?' said another.

Lahnos gestured to Efizel and the others. 'Come over here and say hello.'

The Bullan approached, their features composed and expressionless.

'What are your names?' said a rider.

'We do not give our names to strangers,' said Efizel.

'Don't take it personally,' said Lahnos. 'I've been with them for years, and I know only two of their names. All you need to know about the Bullan is that they're loyal, courageous, and extremely good fighters.'

One of the riders nudged his colleague. 'Here come the officers.'

Lahnos glanced over to his right, and saw several army officers striding over the field, accompanied by a few Rakanese civilians.

'They must have judged that we're not about to start killing each other,' said Lahnos.

The dragons also broke off their conversation to gaze down at the approaching officers and civilians. In the lead was a tall, well-built Kellach man with red hair, who was wearing general's insignia upon his lapels.

'I'm glad to see you all getting acquainted,' the Kellach man said. 'My name is General Brigon, and I am the overall commander of the imperial forces posted by the Rakanese border. To my left is Colonel Hazen, who will be acting as liaison officer to the dragons, their riders, and support staff. Before I hand you over into his authority, I wanted to brief you on the nature of the forthcoming operation.'

'Are we to be led by a colonel?' said Gallantmorn.

'Aye, that's right,' said Brigon. 'Colonel Hazen reports directly to me, so if you have any questions or concerns, he will see that I hear them. What I am now about to tell you is confidential – not a word of this must be repeated to anyone without the highest military clearance.' He swept out a powerful arm, and gestured at the border wall. 'For fifty years, that wall has divided the Plateau from Rakana. It was originally built by the Holdings, in order to prevent the Rakanese population from migrating into the Plateau. Nowadays, the situation has changed, and the wall is primarily used by the Rakanese military authorities to prevent any of their citizens escaping from Rakana. Beyond the wall lie dozens of large refugee camps, filled with starving and destitute Rakanese civilians. The Empire would be happy to help them, but the Rakanese army does everything in its power to stop them crossing the border. For the sake of stability, the Empire has allowed this situation to remain in place for many years, but, if the orders are received, that state of affairs will soon be coming to an end.'

'Did you say, *if* our orders are received, General?' said Sigum.

'That's right. We are still awaiting final confirmation from the Empress herself. There is a small chance that nothing will happen, but, from what I am hearing, it is likely that we will soon get approval to put our operation into action. Once approval has been received, we will proceed without any further delay. The premise of the operation is simple – we are going to tear down the border wall in over two dozen separate locations all the way along the frontier; opening up breaches large enough for the Rakanese refugees to be able to flee into the Plateau. On my right is the Honourable Radahannarati, a member of the government of Amatskouri. She is in charge of the civil side of the operation. Rada, would you like to say a few words?'

'Thank you, General,' said the Rakanese woman, who looked tiny next to the huge Kellach officer. 'We in Amatskouri have been preparing for this day for many years. However, at this present time, the crisis in Rakana has developed into a catastrophe. Due to corruption, incompetence and mismanagement, the Republic of Rakana is enduring a terrible famine, and the number of refugees trapped behind the border has grown alarmingly. Usually, at any given time, we would expect around ten thousand Rakanese civilians to be gathered on the other side of the wall, but, according to our latest reports, that number has increased to over a quarter of a million. To provide relief, Amatskouri has purchased enough food, medical supplies, tents, fuel, fresh water and clothing for every refugee that enters the Plateau. All along the wall, you will see our emergency encampments. Each one has been positioned close to where the breaches will take place. If you see panicking and fleeing refugees, please guide them to the nearest encampment.'

She glanced up at the general.

'Thank you, Rada,' he said. 'Now we shall turn to the role of the dragons. You will be spread out along the frontier, each with your own sector to monitor. You will remain on the ground until told otherwise. You must not, I repeat not, ascend into the air while the wall is being breached. If you do so, you may be injured. Red flags will be raised during this time; once they have been lowered, that will be your signal to take to the skies. The refugees are being penned into their camps by an estimated forty thousand Rakanese soldiers. You will prevent those soldiers from hindering the escape of the civilians.' He gestured to a Rakanese man in an unfamiliar uniform. 'Todi here volunteered to wear the uniform of the Rakanese army today, for your benefit. Take a close look. Anyone in that uniform who tries to stop a refugee from fleeing into the Plateau must be considered a legitimate target. Thank you, Todi. The dragons are to remain within a mile of the border wall in either direction. Do not be tempted to press on further into Rakana – your job is to shepherd the refugees safely into the Plateau, where Rada's teams will look after them. Any questions?'

'I have one,' said Gallantmorn. 'What will the army of the Empire be doing during this time?'

'Units of the Imperial Army will first be deployed to ensure that each breach is passable. They will remove any lingering obstructions, and then they will occupy each breach. We are under orders not to allow military personnel to enter the territory of Rakana. To do so will be perceived as an act of war. This is not an invasion. This is a humanitarian intervention. Our purpose is to alleviate the suffering of a quarter of a million starving Rakanese, not to start a conflict.'

'How will the wall be breached, sir?' said Lahnos.

General Brigon smiled. 'Good question, Commander. At present, I am unable to provide you with these details. Rest assured, if and when the time comes, you will have an excellent view of the methods we plan to adopt.'

'I have one more question, sir,' said Lahnos. 'If we, and by we, I really mean the dragons – if we incinerate several battalions of Rakanese soldiers, because they are trying to stop the refugees from escaping, won't that also be perceived as an act of war?'

'We have our orders, Commander,' Brigon said, 'but I think it safe to say that this question falls under the category of what I would call political risk. How it shall be interpreted by the Rakanese government is another matter. I would say, however, that it would be extremely inadvisable for any dragon to *land* on Rakanese territory. In other words, you are free to burn the bastards from the air, but do not violate their territorial integrity.'

'Now I begin to see why we were invited here,' said Gallantmorn. 'We shall do from the air what your soldiers cannot do from the ground.'

'You're not wrong,' said the general. 'If there are no more questions, I will leave you in the capable hands of Colonel Hazen. My command tent is one mile north of this position, but I am confident that the colonel will be able to see to your needs. Carry on, Colonel.'

'Thank you, General,' said the Holdings man.

General Brigon led the Rakanese civilians and the other officers away. Hazen waited until he had gone, then he turned to the dragons and riders. 'It is my pleasure to be appointed your commanding officer for this operation. I have a cavalry background, and I am more used to riding a horse than I am looking up at such magnificent dragons.'

'Enough with the flattery,' said Gallantmorn. 'Let me make one thing clear to you – you are not our commanding officer. We answer to our beloved Queen Blackrose, ruler of the Eastern Rim, and to no one else. You would be wise to remember that.'

Hazen's eyes widened a little. 'Do you speak for every dragon here, Lord Gallantmorn?'

'He does not speak for me, Colonel,' said Sigum. 'Lahnos and I work for the Empress of the Star Continent, and we are content to fall within the chain of command. However, Lahnos was commanding officer of the invasion of Rahain, and it seems somewhat like a... demotion to now be taking orders from a colonel.'

'It is a temporary secondment, Lord Sigum, not a demotion, and I am grateful for your support.'

Gallantmorn laughed. 'Imagine taking orders from a human,' he said to the others from the Eastern Rim. 'I would die of shame.'

'You're happy to take orders from Sable Holdfast,' said Lahnos.

'That is true,' said Gallantmorn. 'Tell me, horned rider – does this little man seem in any way comparable to the great liberator of Dragon Eyre? How many Ascendants has Colonel Hazen killed? How many gods has he slain with his bare hands? Sable is unique, is she not? The love and admiration we bear her was earned through blood, death and grim victory – her credentials speak for themselves. What has this little man done?'

Colonel Hazen cleared his throat. 'I commanded a regiment of imperial cavalry at the Battle of the Vineyards.'

Gallantmorn eyed him. 'Did you fight on the side of the usurper Bryce?'

'Uh, yes, I did, and...'

The dragons from the Eastern Rim laughed.

'This is most disrespectful,' said Efizel. 'An army cannot function without discipline and a clear command structure. If it comes to a battle, the dragons must be prepared to obey orders.'

'Must we?' said Gallantmorn. 'I think not; besides, there will be no battle. Did you not hear the general? We are to be shepherds, gently herding a flock of miserable Rakanese to safety. Did you know that their blood is amphibian? Though, looking at the horns and tails possessed by the Bullan, one might suspect that they contain more than a little bovine heritage.'

A smaller, green dragon tilted her head. 'We were asked to be respectful, Lord Gallantmorn.'

'We were asked to show respect to Lord Sigum of Athumia and his rider, and we have done so,' said Gallantmorn. 'No one told us that we also had to respect starving amphibians, cattle that stand on two legs, or even that frightened little colonel. We are not subjects of this Empire; we are free dragons of the Eastern Rim.'

The Bullan bristled with anger, and Sigum raised a forelimb to restrain them.

'Let us not fall out on our first day together,' the silvery-green dragon said. 'We will, each of us, prove our worth when the time comes. You should be aware that these Bullan are dear to my heart, and I will defend them against insults and aggression. Perhaps you did not know this, brave Gallantmorn; but you know it now. Let us listen to Colonel Hazen. It may be that he will lead us to where we might eat, and then we can feast together as comrades.'

Gallantmorn stared at Sigum for a long moment, then, finally, he tilted his head a fraction. 'As you wish, Sigum of Athumia.'

'Thank you,' said Colonel Hazen. 'Food, yes. Come this way.'

Less than an hour later, Lahnos was sitting in a large tent with the eight riders from Dragon Eyre, while Sigum, Gallantmorn and the others were eating from a row of long troughs outside in the sunshine. The Bullan had also been invited to eat, but they had refused, choosing instead to inspect the area where they would be staying. Lahnos had been inclined to go with them, but Sigum had persuaded him to eat with the riders.

'We were told we would be helping humans,' one of the riders said, as the others ate. 'The Rakanese may look human, but they aren't. I was told that they are descended from frogs. Why are we risking our lives to save frogs?'

'We are allied to the Empire,' said another. 'They're helping us in Yearning, so we're helping them.'

'Yes, but frogs? I was hoping for something a little more... heroic.'

One of them glanced at Lahnos. 'How long have you been Lord Sigum's rider?'

'About eight years.'

The others nodded with approval.

'You must have been young when you started,' said one. 'That's the same as on Dragon Eyre. We were all chosen to be riders at around the age of ten. Do they have schools for dragon riders on Athumia?'

'No. They have something called the Dragon Corps, which is like a branch of the army. The Dragon Corps look after all the dragons of the Dominion, but none of them are riders. I'm the only rider from Athumia. The other dragons refuse to carry humans. They think it's degrading.'

'Degrading?' said one. 'Why?'

'The dragons are treated like gods, and gods are too high and mighty to carry people around on their backs.'

'They sound like the Unk Tannic,' said another. 'They act as though all dragons are gods. Where do the dragons of Athumia come from?'

'Dragon Eyre,' said Lahnos.

The others frowned, and a few shook their heads.

'A great god transported them to Athumia over a thousand years ago,' Lahnos went on. 'They are from a place called Na Sun Ka, or something like that.'

'Are you descended from Na Sun Ka?'

'No. I'm a native of Athumia.'

'Is that why you have horns?'

'Gallantmorn has already asked me this question. I have horns because my mother's father was Bullan. Like the Rakanese, I am not completely human. Remember this the next time you ask yourself if the Rakanese are not worth saving – as far as I'm concerned, if you can speak, and think, and reason, then you have the same rights as anyone else. I've spent years being called a demon, or a sub-human, and I don't appreciate that kind of language. Is that understood?'

One of the female riders glanced at him. 'I'm sorry we said those things.'

'Don't apologise to him,' said another rider. 'He's not one of us.'

'Didn't the settlers from Implacatus call us sub-created?' she said. 'They called us that because they thought we were inferior.'

'At least we're human.'

Lahnos got to his feet. 'I'll not eat where I am unwelcome.'

He strode from the tent.

'Wait,' said a voice.

He turned, and saw the young woman rider who had spoken up.

'What?' he said.

'I apologise on behalf of the others,' she said. 'Gallantmorn's rider can be... proud at times. Like his dragon. We're not all like that. My name is Ora'lya.'

Lahnos eyed her. 'Let me guess, your dragon is the green female?'

She raised an eyebrow. 'Her name is Quicklime. How did you know?'

'Because she was the only one who spoke up in front of Gallantmorn,' he said. 'Do all riders from the Eastern Rim mirror the personalities of their dragons?'

'Maybe we do,' she said. 'We are moulded by our dragons from a young age; and we are taught to see everything from their point of view, so that we are better equipped to serve them.'

'There's the difference,' he said. 'Sigum is my friend. I don't serve him; nor does he serve me. We are equals.'

Ora'lya laughed nervously. 'You had better not let Gallantmorn hear you say things like that.'

'I'm not afraid of that oaf. You know, Athumian dragons are not as different from the ones from Dragon Eyre as you might believe – they are just as rude and arrogant.'

She narrowed her eyes at him. 'Not all of them are as rude and arrogant as Gallantmorn. Quicklime is brave and kind-hearted. If you insult her again, I will take exception.'

Lahnos felt his anger dissipate. 'Then I, too, apologise. I meant no offence to you or your dragon, Ora... Ora – sorry, what was it?'

'Ora'lya.'

'Ora'lya,' he repeated. 'Thank you for setting me straight.' He glanced over his shoulder. 'The dragons have finished eating,' he said. 'If you'll excuse me, I want to see how Sigum is doing.'

He walked away from the tent. Sigum was standing apart from the other dragons, and he watched as Lahnos approached.

'How did the meal go?' said Lahnos.

'It was awkward,' said Sigum. 'Gallantmorn dominates the others, which is a pity, as some of them might well prove to be more reasonable, if they were given a chance to speak.'

'It was much the same with the riders,' said Lahnos. 'One of them was all right – a woman called Ora'lya. She's Quicklime's rider.'

Sigum gazed up at the blue sky. 'No matter where we go, my rider,' he said, 'it seems as though we shall always be the outsiders. It is a hard thing to accept.'

'We're exiles,' said Lahnos. 'You, me, and the Bullan.'

'It grieves me that not one of us has a mate.'

'We have each other,' said Lahnos. 'I guess that will have to be enough.'

'Indeed. Look up, rider; the sky is pure and clear. Shall we fly?'

Lahnos smiled. 'I'm always ready to fly.'

CHAPTER 25
TINDERBOX

World Three – (7th Day, First Third Autumn 544)

Cael pushed his vision into the room where Cole was being held. He was lying on a wooden floor with his wrists bound behind his back. His ankles had also been tied together, and a thick hood covered his head, secured by a cord wound round his neck. Cael gazed down at his cousin in the dim light coming through the gaps in the wooden beams. Apart from a faint rise and fall of his chest, Cole appeared to be dead. Cael wished he could enter his cousin's mind, to assure him that he and Arrosa would do whatever it took to free him, but the hood was too thick to penetrate.

A door was opened, and one of the townspeople entered. He was holding a long spear, and he prodded Cole with its sharp, stone tip. Cole groaned, and flinched away. The man laughed, and prodded him again, a little harder.

Enraged, Cael drove his powers into the man's thoughts.

Free him, he said in his mind.

The man looked around, as though he was aware of the voice in his head. His confused and alarmed expression showed that he had not understood the words Cael had said, and he stared at Cole, as if he had suspected the voice had come from him.

Free him, you stupid bastard! Cael shouted.

The man dropped the spear and placed his hands against his ears. Cael tried to read his thoughts, but was faced with a language that was incomprehensible to him. In his frustration, he lashed out, and accidentally wiped the man's mind, severing the connections between his memories and his consciousness. The man fell to the floor, and began convulsing. Cael withdrew from his mind, and stared down at what he had done.

Foam appeared on the man's lips, then he screamed. Within seconds, four other townsfolk ran into the room. Their eyes widened at the sight of their prostrate comrade. One crouched down and tried to restrain him, while the others began shouting at Cole. More townsfolk entered the room, including one of the elders, and they began arguing about what to do. The convulsing man was dragged out of the room, then several of the others began beating Cole, kicking him, and using the butts of their spears to strike his body.

Cael gazed down at the scene, feeling powerless as he watched his cousin being punished for something he had done. A desire for revenge surged through him, and he pushed his way into the mind of the elder. Though he could not understand what was going through the old man's mind, he knew he had power over him. He remembered what his mother had done to Belinda, and scoured the old man's mind clean, obliterating his identity, memories and personality.

The old man's eyes rolled up into his head, and he fell forwards onto the floorboards. The others cried out, stepping back from Cole in a panic, and Cael carried on, entering their minds one by one and doing the same thing, until more than a dozen bodies were piled up on the floor between Cole and the door. A tremendous headache pounded behind Cael's temples, and he broke off the connection. He fell onto his knees in the cave, and threw up that morning's meagre breakfast over the cold, stone floor.

Arrosa glanced up at him from where she lay curled up in a corner. Cael gripped the sides of his head as the pain began to subside.

'What's wrong?' said Arrosa.

He gazed at her. She looked ill and tired; and thin, too thin.

'I think I might know how to beat them,' Cael gasped, 'but it fucking hurts.'

'Did you see Cole?'

'Aye. He's still alive, but I don't know for how much longer. We'll have to rescue him today.'

'I don't know if I can move,' she said. 'My stomach... I have terrible cramps.'

'I can't leave you here,' he said. 'The hunters will have found our trail by now. Going down the river might have thrown them off our scent, but they will know by now that we doubled back towards the town.' He chewed his lip. 'How bad is it?'

'I haven't felt this sick in years,' she said. 'I think it was something I ate. Something that your Kellach body probably thought was fine.'

'We should have brought salve with us.'

'Only salve?' she said. 'We should have brought a proper Tempest sword, and a Quadrant, and about a hundred other things. Is there any water?'

Cael walked to the cave entrance, where a small rivulet ran down the smooth rock. He cupped his hands together to collect some of the water, and went back to Arrosa. He crouched down, and she drank from his hands.

'What did you discover?' she said. 'How can you beat them?'

'I can scour their minds.'

'What does that mean?'

'It doesn't kill them, but it renders them helpless. I can destroy their memories and thoughts. It's as if I can return them to being like newborns.'

'Like what happened to Lyla?'

'Maybe; I'm not sure. I was fine when I did it to one of them, but after about a dozen or so, it got too painful.'

She narrowed her eyes. 'You did that to a dozen of them?'

'Aye. The bad news is that they might blame Cole. We need a way to make them think that it was us, that we are on the offensive. They're scared of us.'

Arrosa smiled weakly. 'I doubt they'd be scared of me.'

'Are you joking? You are the witch who can turn people into glass. They'll be terrified of you. They're scared of Cole, too, because they saw him control fire. It's me that they'll be underestimating.' He paused. 'You know, the forest is dry. It hasn't rained in days, and the sun is baking hot.'

'It's a strange time to be giving me a weather report.'

'If I can start a forest fire, then they might think that I have the same power as Cole. Then, when they panic... *if* they panic, we can sneak into the town and free Cole. And we can pick up the Tempest blade while we're there.'

'How am I supposed to walk, Cael? I don't want to sound dramatic, but I am in agony.'

'I'll carry you,' he said. 'You can climb onto my back. Stay here for now. I'll see what I can do about getting a fire started.'

'Do you know how to start a fire?'

'Uncle Corthie showed me when we were in Kell. The ground was frozen, and we needed to warm it.'

'See?' she said. 'You did learn something from being sent all over the Star Continent.'

Cael walked to the cave entrance. His headache had cleared, so he sent out his vision to make sure that no hunters from the town were close. Satisfied that their cave had not been found, he made his way down the slope. There was a light breeze coming from the south, and the town was located to the north-east of the cave. He began to gather armfuls of dry bracken and fern fronds, and heaped them by the base of a withered old tree. When the pile was high enough, he crouched down next to it and unwrapped the sword hilt that he carried everywhere.

He spent the next thirty minutes trying to create a spark that would ignite the dry leaves and twigs. The sparks came easily, from grinding what was left of the contaminated Tempest blade against the side of a rock; the difficult part was trying to get the foliage to catch light. He thought about Arrosa as he worked. Neither of them had spoken about the admission he had made three days before, but there had been a definite change in Arrosa's demeanour towards him. He had also changed. Gone were most of the petty barbs and insults, and he hadn't once lied to her in order to cause her discomfort. They had also been working together better, although that had come to an end with the onset of her illness. Cael suspected it was due to a batch of mushrooms they had eaten. He hadn't experienced any ill effects, but his Kellach constitution protected him from most cases of food poisoning. If the mushrooms had been toxic, then Arrosa might not improve without medical attention; but where upon World Three was he going to be able to find that? He tried to push his darker thoughts out of his mind. There was nothing he could do to help Arrosa except to ensure that she was comfortable, and that she drank plenty of water; if he lost himself to worry, he would become useless to her and to Cole. They were both depending upon him, and he knew it.

A spark landed onto a fern frond, and a small flame appeared. Cael watched it for a moment, then he began to feed the tiny fire, holding other pieces of fern above it, and then using them as brands to light other areas of the heap. The bracken crackled, and grey smoke arose into the forest. Cael would have to move as soon as the first tendrils of smoke lifted above the uppermost branches, as every hunter in the vicinity would see it. He continued to tend his small fire, coaxing it towards the dry trunk of the withered old tree. More smoke came from the thick layer of bark around the trunk, and insects began to flee, emerging from the rotten heart of the tree. After a slow start, the fire seemed to take on a life of its own, and the heat forced Cael to back away. He gathered more dry undergrowth, and heaped it onto the flames. A cry echoed out from the distance, followed moments later by another. Cael dumped one more large armful of brown fern fronds on the fire, then watched as the breeze lifted the flames ever higher. The branches of the withered old tree ignited, and the flames rose higher still. The neighbouring trees began to smoke, and still Cael waited, his right hand grasping the broken hilt of his sword. As soon as flames leapt across the gap to envelop another tree, Cael began to move. He turned away from the flames, and ran straight into a hunter. Without thinking, Cael drove the hilt of his sword into the man's stomach. He twisted the blade, and pulled it out, bringing blood and intestines spilling out in its wake. The man fell to the ground, and Cael picked up his spear. He lodged the sword hilt into his belt, and ran back up the slope. He raced to the cave, ready to kill anyone who had found Arrosa, but she was alone, lying where he had left her.

'Did you manage to start a fire?' she said.

'Aye. We have to leave. Now.'

He ran over to her and tried to help her stand. She gripped her stomach and groaned, then nearly collapsed, but he kept her upright, and pulled her close to him. He held the spear out in his right hand, and they staggered over to the entrance.

Arrosa stared, her mouth opening. Ahead of them, the fire was raging and spreading down the side of the valley. A dozen more trees had ignited in the time it had taken for Cael to collect Arrosa, and a thick wall of smoke was billowing up into the blue sky.

'Let it burn,' Cael said, as they watched the flames for a moment. 'Let it all burn.'

'It's going to burn us if we don't escape,' Arrosa said. 'It's coming this way.'

Cael knelt on the ground. 'Get onto my back, and hold on.'

He felt her weight against his back, then her arms went round his neck, and she clasped her fingers together. Cael tensed his legs and got to his feet.

'I was going to make a joke about how heavy you are,' he said, 'but I can barely feel you. You'd better not fucking die on me, Arrosa.'

'I'll try not to.'

A wave of smoke gusted into their faces from the approaching flames. Cael coughed, then he turned to their right, and began to climb higher up the slope.

Arrosa glanced over her shoulder. 'How did you set fire to the whole forest?'

'All that came from one little spark,' he said.

A scream of agony came from the valley below them, then it was drowned out by the roar of the flames, as the wind carried them further to the north. Cael coughed again as he reached the brow of the hill, then he began to descend to the other side, where the air was a little clearer. He knew where the town was in relation to their position, and he set off along a track at a half run, keeping the spear held out in his right hand. He wanted to use his vision to check the way ahead, but he had to concentrate on every step. The track led them back into the path the smoke was taking, and Cael could see nothing more than a few feet in front of him, as though a thick fog had descended. His eyes began to sting, but he kept going, moving as quickly as he was able. They came to a junction in the path, and Cael chose the route that went to the left, as the other led to the gate at the front of the town. They reached a small gully where the smoke lessened and Cael set Arrosa down, and crouched next to her.

'Why have we stopped?' she said.

'The town is only a couple of hundred yards away,' he said.

'What? You mean that cave we were in was right next to the town?'

'Aye.'

'Why didn't you tell me?'

'You were too ill to notice much when we got to the cave,' he said. 'The next part is going to be trickier. We're going to have to climb over the fence at the back of the town, and then sneak into the building where Cole is being held. I will deal with anyone who sees us, but I don't know how many minds I can scour before the pain gets too much.'

'I will only slow you down,' she said. 'I can hide in the undergrowth until you come back with Cole.'

Cael glanced up at the smoke. 'No. If the fire doesn't get you, the hunters will.'

'You don't understand. Cael. My insides feel as though they are being ripped apart.'

'I'm not leaving you here,' he said. 'We'll get Cole, and then we'll find somewhere you can rest until you get better. After that, we'll work out how to fix the sword and go home.'

She stared at him. 'When did you become such an optimist?'

'I'm not giving up. We're going to get out of this, Arrosa. We just need to deal with one thing at a time, and right now, that one thing is Cole. Climb onto my back again.'

Arrosa grimaced, then she clambered onto his back and held her hands together under his throat. Cael got back to his feet. He patted the broken hilt by his waist, and headed back into the thickening smoke. Trees less than fifty yards to their left were aflame, and the roar of the fire almost drowned out Cael's thoughts as he ran along the track. After a few minutes, he saw a ditch running along the track to his right, and beyond, the wooden fence that surrounded the town. Cael ran down the slope to the bottom of the ditch, and gazed at the upright wooden beams.

'The ditch might be wide enough to save the town from the fire,' he said.

Arrosa said nothing, her mouth clenched shut in pain. Cael dropped the spear he had been carrying, and looked for a way to climb the fence. He found nothing, so he picked up the spear again, and drove it into the ground, pushing it down with all his strength. It snapped, leaving a foot's length poking out of the ground. He placed a boot up onto the broken spear, and reached out as he stepped up. His height enabled his fingers to reach the top of the fence, then he hauled himself up, straining his muscles to their limit, as Arrosa clung onto his back. He managed to get an elbow over the top of the fence, then another, as his feet dangled clear; then he raised his left leg and got it up and over. Arrosa slid off his back, falling to the ground on the inner side of the fence, and Cael drew his other leg up, and dropped down next to her. They had landed between the fence and the rear of a circular wooden hut, amid the competing sounds of the approaching fire and the cries of panic and fear coming from those in the town. Cael checked on Arrosa, then he crawled to the side of the hut until he had a better view of the town. Many of the townsfolk were standing in the middle of the settlement, arguing about what to do. With them were two of the town elders, and Cael sent out his powers. He entered the head of an old woman, and stripped it bare, scouring her mind; then he withdrew as the woman fell to the ground, and did the same thing to the old man. He felt his head throb and ache as the townsfolk stared at the two fallen elders. Someone screamed, and several people ran for the town gates, while others gathered their children and fled back to their huts.

Cael crawled over to Arrosa.

'One more time,' he said. 'I've cleared our path.'

Arrosa gazed at him, then she tried to climb onto his back as he crouched next to her. He heard her sobbing from the pain, but tried not to think about it. He pulled her arms over his head, and held her wrists together as he stood.

'We're going to make it,' he whispered to her. 'Nothing on this fucking world is going to beat us, Arrosa. Do you understand? Nothing.'

He set off, circling the hut until he saw the large, two-storey building in the centre of the town. The two fallen elders were groaning and weeping on the ground, and the others had fled from them, leaving the area close to the larger building empty. Cael braced himself, then he sprinted towards the building with his head down. He barrelled through an entrance, and an armed man turned to face him, his spear extended. Cael drove his powers into the man's mind, and he fell screaming. Cael entered the main hall, where he scoured the minds of two more armed townsfolk, then he raced up the stairs. The dozen bodies of those he had scoured earlier were lying in rows in a room on the upper floor, being tended by a few anxious-looking townsfolk. They gazed up at Cael and Arrosa, and a few reached for their weapons. Cael pointed at one of them, and wiped his mind clean. The others dropped their spears and cowered against the wall of the room. Cael pointed to the stairs, and the townsfolk fled in a panic, pushing each other to get away from Cael and Arrosa.

Cael swayed for a few moments, feeling the pain in his head increase. He nearly fell to his knees as it peaked, and he saw flashes of light as he opened his eyes. He moved his legs again, staggering towards the room where he had seen Cole. He placed a hand against the door, and pulled it open. Inside, Cole was lying in the same place as before, the hood still in place, along with the tight cords that bound his ankles and wrists. Cael stumbled into the room, then he closed the door and set Arrosa down on the floor. She curled up into a ball, her features anguished, as she gripped both hands round her stomach. Cael crouched down next to Cole. He removed the broken hilt from his belt, and cut through the cords by his cousin's ankles, then he moved the blade up to his wrists, and sliced through the ropes there. He then cut the cord that was securing the hood round Cole's neck. He placed the hilt on the floor, and pulled the hood from Cole's head.

Cael grimaced. Cole's face was bruised and swollen, with cuts by his eyes, nose and mouth. By the back of his head, his hair was matted in dried blood.

'Cole,' Cael whispered. 'Can you hear me?'

His cousin did not respond. Cael felt for a pulse by his neck, and found it. He listened to Cole's breathing, then shook his shoulder.

'Cole,' he said, in a louder voice. 'Can you walk? I can't carry both of you. Say something. Can you hear me?'

Cole opened his eyes. 'Cael?' he gasped.

'We're here,' said Cael. 'Arrosa and I are here. We thought you were dead, or we'd have come sooner. Can you stand?'

Cole shook his head. 'My leg's... broken.'

Cael glanced down at Cole's legs, but neither seemed obviously broken to his eyes.

'My left leg,' Cole gasped. 'Below the knee. They did it... to stop me running away.'

'All right,' said Cael. 'We can work this out. Arrosa – are you able to walk, even just for a little bit, so we can get back to the fence? I can carry you over one at a time.'

Arrosa said nothing.

'Arrosa?'

She groaned. 'Leave me here,' she said. 'I can't move.'

Cael felt frustration ripple through him. He got to his feet, unsure what to do. What could he do? After having struggled to reach Cole, he refused to leave either him or Arrosa behind when they fled the town. Despite having had no cigarettes since shortly after his arrival on World Three, he felt a desperate craving for one, as though that would solve his problems. He glanced down at Arrosa and Cole. He noticed a large crack in the wooden beams of one wall, and peered through the gap. The flames had reached the town. Four or five thatched roofs were ablaze, and entire portions of the wooden fence surrounding the settlement were in flames. The townsfolk had abandoned any attempt to extinguish the flames, and were running for the main gate, carrying small children as they fled into the forest.

Cael turned back to Cole and Arrosa. 'I will carry you out of here one at a time,' he said. 'The town is almost deserted, and I don't think anyone will try to stop us.' He paused. 'Are either of you listening to me?'

'I'm listening,' gasped Cole. 'What's wrong with Arrosa?'

'I think some mushrooms might have poisoned her.'

'You idiot,' Cole gasped. 'Why were you letting her eat mushrooms?'

'Let's get out of here, and then you can give me a telling off,' Cael said. 'I'll take Arrosa first, and come back for you; all right?'

Cole nodded. 'The sword blade... I saw it downstairs.'

'I'll find it,' said Cael. He crouched down by Arrosa and took her hand. 'I'll carry you in my arms this time,' he said, 'so you won't have to hold on.'

Arrosa nodded, but said nothing.

Cael got back to his feet. He pushed at the door, and it opened. He knelt by Arrosa, and picked her up in both arms, as she clutched her stomach.

'When we get back to the Star Continent,' he said, as he gazed down at her, 'every time I look at a mushroom, I will think of you.'

Arrosa attempted a smile. 'How romantic.'

He stepped out of the small room into the upper hallway of the two-storey building. Something moved to his right, but before Cael could turn to see what it was, the butt end of a spear connected with the side of his head. The pain sent him to his knees, as he clung on to Arrosa, then the spear-end lashed out again, and everything went dark.

CHAPTER 26
BUILDING FOR THE FUTURE

Plateau City, The Plateau – 7th Day, First Third Autumn 544

'Therefore,' Professor Achan said to the class, 'we have to consider *why* the authorities governing the City decided to suppress the discoveries made under the rule of Prince Aurelian. While Professor Gallea will focus upon the practicalities of the Aurelian papers in her classes, I intend to concentrate upon the political aspects. What was it about steam power and weaving machines that God-King Malik and God-Queen Amalia were so afraid of? To that end, I would like you all to write me five hundred words on the reasons for the prohibition against technological advancement placed into force by the ruling gods of the City. For tomorrow, if you please.' He smiled. 'No. Wait a moment. I have heard that many of you might be rather busy this evening; so I shall give you all one more day to complete this assignment. To those of you who are attending this evening's demonstration, I would like to offer a word of warning – do not provoke the armed authorities into making a violent response. Be firm, but polite. Resolute, but peaceful. Angry, but restrained. All right; you are free to go.'

The students got up from their desks and filed towards the door.

'Are you going tonight?' Dazi said, as she and Kyra walked out of the classroom.

'I'm not sure,' Kyra said.

'I thought you were keen.'

Kyra shrugged as they walked along the university corridor.

'Has something happened?' Dazi said. 'I know – has the Empress forbidden you to go?'

'No. The truth, Dazi, is that I haven't seen the Empress since my birthday. My Aunty Kelsey, she...'

'Yes?'

'I'm not sure if I'm allowed to tell you. Fine; I'll tell you, but you mustn't tell anyone else. Aunty Kelsey revoked all of my court privileges. She found out that it was me who told Achan about the eighty thousand deaths in Rahain.'

'What does that mean? What privileges did you have?'

'I was allowed to come and go as I pleased in the Ministry of the Plateau, and I was allowed to attend any meetings, even the secret ones. I could just walk into the Empress's presence without needing an appointment. You know – things like that. Now, I'm not even allowed to enter the building without written permission.'

'Wow. You must have really pissed them off. I mean, they're your family.'

'It could have been a lot worse,' said Kyra. 'I could have gone to jail.'

'For telling the truth?'

'Don't worry; it was never going to happen. Do you know why? I still can't believe it, but my mother actually stood up for me. She was sitting quietly while Aunty Kelsey was berating me, and then, before I even knew what was happening, my mother threw Aunty Kelsey out of the room. Can you imagine? The Herald of the Empire, being ordered about by my mother.'

'I can believe that. Your mother can be... intimidating.'

'You've never met her.'

'No, but I've heard the stories. Didn't she murder a hundred thousand Rahain soldiers while they slept? And didn't she kill all the gods who invaded the Star Continent? And, the biggest one of them all, didn't she change her body? She died, so she went and picked a brand new body to live in? That's not normal, Kyra. That's about as far from normal as it's possible to get. I'd bet you that even the Empress is secretly frightened of her.'

'But what am I to do, Dazi? I've spent the last ten years being much closer to the Empress than to my own mother. In that time, I've said a lot of rude things about my mother, to her face, as well as behind her back. And, every opportunity I got, I defended the Empress. I can't go back on all that now, but if I want my privileges reinstated, I'm supposed to make a grovelling apology.'

'The two most powerful women on the Star Continent, and both are competing over your love, Kyra? There are worse situations to be in.'

'I know, but if I make a mistake now, I might end up with neither.'

They descended a flight of stairs.

'Are you coming to get a coffee?' said Dazi.

'I can't. I'm due to be helping my mother and Professor Elbannon.'

'Again? You help them every morning and every evening, Kyra.'

'I know, but it's important.'

'What is?'

Kyra smiled. 'You know I can't tell you. Elbannon would fail me.'

'So, if it's an imperial secret, you don't mind telling people, but you won't risk annoying Elbannon?'

'That's about right.' She halted by a side corridor. 'I might see you later at the demonstration. I can't promise it, though.'

'Professor Achan will be looking for you tonight,' said Dazi. 'You're his most famous student, and if you're not there, he'll be disappointed.'

'I'll think about it.'

Dazi nodded, then she descended another flight of stairs. Kyra turned, and walked to Elbannon's laboratory. She opened the door and strode in, to see Elbannon and her mother in the midst of an argument.

'That fool Bailey was clearly mistaken,' Elbannon was saying. 'Silver? It's ridiculous. The coin he gave us wasn't even made of pure silver; it was an alloy.'

'Bailey's memories are all we have to go on,' said Karalyn. 'If you refuse to keep working with silver, I will do it myself.'

Elbannon laughed mockingly. 'Oh will you, indeed? Good luck with that. You'll have to make your own *Tammy* first, because I won't let you use mine.'

Kyra walked over to the workbench. She placed her bag on a chair, and peered down at the contents of a small dish.

'Is that a Zamatan Coil?' she said. 'It's the tiniest one I've ever seen.'

'It isn't merely *tiny*,' said Elbannon; 'it's made of pure silver. Of course, as I predicted, it's utterly useless. And that type of intricate metalwork is called filigree. I'd like to see your mother try to replicate it; that would be amusing.'

Karalyn eyed her daughter. 'Elbannon has given up, already.'

'I have not given up!' he shouted. 'I am simply stating that Bailey must have been mistaken. I am not abandoning the project.'

'But we haven't gone through every possible silver alloy,' said Karalyn.

'What have you tried?' said Kyra.

'We have experimented with placing a simple, small ingot of pure silver into the gap within the Compass,' Karalyn said.

'*Tammy*,' Elbannon muttered. 'At least get the name right.'

'And we have tried ingots of the most common silver alloys in the same gap,' Karalyn went on. 'None of them worked. Now, we've just tried Elbannon's filigree silver Zamatan Coil, and...'

'Guess what?' said Elbannon. 'That didn't work, either.'

'No, it didn't,' said Karalyn. 'I then suggested that Elbannon make a few coils from different alloys, and that's when he decided to throw a tantrum.'

'It's a waste of time,' said Elbannon.

'Have you tried to make a Tempest-silver alloy?' said Kyra.

'That was the first alloy we tried,' said Elbannon. 'We then tried hardened silver, which contains a little copper; that's what most silver coins consist of.'

'But we haven't tried a hardened silver coil,' said Karalyn.

'Make it your damn self,' said Elbannon. 'It would be pointless, anyway. It would tarnish.'

'Why do you think the silver should be in the shape of a Zamatan Coil?' said Kyra.

'Because we couldn't bloody think of anything else,' said Elbannon.

'Can I ask you something on an unrelated topic? Why did the gods of the City try to destroy all of the discoveries made by Prince Aurelian?'

Elbannon pulled a face. 'Isn't it blindingly obvious, girl?' he said. 'To stop the stupid mortals under their rule from being able to build contraptions that could kill them. If mere mortals had been allowed to develop science and technology on their own, the gods would have been finished. Anyway, that's Professor Gallea's area of expertise, not mine. I couldn't care less about her idiotic steam engines.'

'It was for one of Professor Achan's assignments.'

'Then you shouldn't be asking me, girl. The point of the exercise is to think for yourself, not to ask another professor.' He stretched his arms. 'I'm calling it a day. Perhaps inspiration will come to me in a dream.'

He took hold of his walking stick and got to his feet. He frowned at Karalyn, then he walked out of the laboratory.

'Don't forget to lock up,' he called out, before he slammed the door.

'Are you going to make a coil of hardened silver?' Kyra said to her mother.

'Of course not,' she said. 'Those skills are beyond me. Have you spoken to Professor Nadia yet?'

Kyra shook her head.

'You should,' said her mother. 'If you don't, you will fail that class.'

'But if I attend her class, I will have to do work that helps the imperial military's occupation of Rahain.'

'There's no harm in repairing old heating systems, Kyra. That will benefit many people who would otherwise freeze in those caverns this winter. Sometimes, it is acceptable to compromise.'

Kyra smiled and shook her head. 'Since when have you ever compromised, Mother?'

'I am a bad example,' Karalyn said. 'I'm as stubborn as my own mother, and I can see it in you. Promise me you'll think about it.'

'All right.'

She gazed down into the innards of the Compass. 'How did you solve the problem of making Quadrants?'

'By luck,' Karalyn said. 'King Gahad had told the Tempest Cogitarium to create a copper-coloured alloy, so the prefects spent hundreds of years trying to do exactly that. Gahad, however, was wrong. It wasn't an alloy – it was pure copper.'

'Why don't Quadrants turn green?'

'It's something to do with the jewels. It stops a patina from forming.'

'How?'

'I have no idea, Kyra. The man who could answer that left the room a few minutes ago.'

'Could the same process stop the silver from tarnishing?'

'Maybe. I don't think pure silver tarnishes, but I might be wrong.'

'Sorry for asking such stupid questions.'

Her mother smiled. 'Your questions are never stupid, Kyra, and I love being able to spend time with you. I've missed this.'

'You've missed it for eighteen years, Mother.'

Karalyn glanced away.

'Sorry,' said Kyra, 'but when have we ever talked like this? We've probably spent more time together in the last few days than we have in the last ten years. And it's not for my benefit, is it? You're here because you want to find Cael.'

'I would do the same if it were you who had gone missing.'

'Aye. I know. I do believe you when you say you love me, but your love feels theoretical, rather than practical. What I mean is, you were never there for me when I needed you.'

'I'm here now.'

'And worse, you look the same age as me. I know it shouldn't matter, but you don't look like my mother. You look like a stranger.'

'I can't do much about that.'

'But, this is still an improvement,' Kyra said. 'I like talking to you every day. It's not too late, is it? It's not too late for us to be friends?'

'Is *friends* the right word?' said Karalyn. 'You are my daughter. That's more than just being friends. I gave birth to you; well, my old body did. I remember that day vividly. It was one of my first memories when I woke up as Lyla. I would rather be a good mother than a friend.'

The door opened. Kelsey stepped into the room, then halted.

She raised her palms. 'I'm not here to argue with anyone,' she said. 'I'm here to pass on a message. Can I come in?'

'Aye,' said Karalyn.

Kelsey strode over to the workbench. 'Any progress on the Compass?'

'Not really,' said Karalyn. 'Elbannon and I have been trying out Bailey's advice, but with no success so far. Do you have any suggestions?'

'Who, me?' said Kelsey. She smiled. 'I should be flattered that you think I understand the first thing about any of this. Thank you for, you know, not... shouting at me.'

'We're sisters, Kelsey. We argue; we fight; but that will never change. Unless, of course, you're going to try to arrest my daughter again?'

'The Empress wants no further action to be taken about that,' said Kelsey. 'It's done; it's over. The message is from the Empress, and it's for Kyra.'

'For me?' Kyra said.

'Aye. You have been invited to the Empress's quarters this evening.'

'Invited, or summoned?' said Kyra.

'Invited.'

'So, I don't have to go?'

'No. It's up to you. If I were you, though, I'd go.'

'Will I have to apologise?'

Kelsey shook her head. 'The Empress wants a chance to explain her actions to you in person.'

'On the same night as the demonstration? That can't be a coincidence.'

'It's not a coincidence. The Empress hopes to dissuade you from going; but, she won't try to stop you.'

Kyra glanced at her mother.

Karalyn raised an eyebrow. 'Are you asking for my advice?'

'Aye,' said Kyra.

'There's no harm in going,' said Karalyn. 'Perhaps you owe it to Thorn to listen to what she has to say. If you don't like it, you can leave.'

Kyra nodded. 'All right. I will go with you, Aunty.'

Kelsey took out her Quadrant.

'Do you have the children tomorrow?' said Karalyn.

'Aye,' said Kelsey. 'Van will be dropping them off in the morning.'

'Do you need any help?'

Kelsey blinked. 'Uh, aye. Thanks. Maybe tomorrow evening, if you're free?'

'I'll come round to the townhouse after I've finished up here.'

'I'd appreciate that.'

Kelsey slid her fingers over the Quadrant. The air shimmered, and then she and Kyra appeared in the inner courtyard in the centre of the Ministry of the Plateau.

'Is your mother feeling all right?' said Kelsey. 'I walked into the laboratory thinking she might throw me out again; instead, she offers to help me with Calpurnia and Caelius.'

Kyra shrugged.

'Is that how it's going to be, Kyra?' said Kelsey. 'Are you just going to ignore me?'

'I am here because my mother thought it would be a good idea.'

'Aye, right. You've suddenly decided, after eighteen years, that you're going to listen to your mother?'

Kyra glanced away. 'You have blood on your hands.'

'Aye. I guess I do.'

They walked into the building, and Kelsey escorted Kyra up to the floor where the Empress's private quarters lay. They walked to the front door, and Kelsey gestured towards it.

'Go in,' she said. 'It's you Her Majesty wants to speak to, not me.'

'And what will you be doing, Aunty? Waging more wars upon our innocent neighbours?'

'That's very funny, Kyra. If you get kicked out of all your classes, you could have a career as an entertainer. Do you know how to juggle?'

Kyra glared at her, then she opened the door. Naxor was standing close to the entrance of the small audience chamber, and he smiled out at Kyra and Kelsey.

'Would you please step inside for a moment, Herald?' he said. 'The Empress has a couple of announcements for you.'

Kelsey nodded, and she accompanied Kyra into the chamber. The Empress was sitting at the head of a table, a mountain of paperwork piled up next to a large coffee pot in front of her. Kyra and Kelsey both bowed their heads, as Naxor closed the door.

'Thank you for coming, Kyra,' the Empress said. 'Please take a seat while I talk to my Herald for a moment.'

Kyra pulled out a chair and sat down.

'Herald,' said the Empress, 'I require two messages to be sent out; could you see that both reach their recipients this evening?'

'Aye, Your Majesty,' said Kelsey.

'Inform General Brigon that the operation at the Rakanese frontier is to proceed,' the Empress said; 'and then please let the commanders in Tahrana City know that the assault on the Rahain Capital has been approved.'

Kelsey took out her Quadrant. 'I will deal with both messages right away, Your Majesty.'

She swept her fingers over the Quadrant, and vanished.

The Empress turned to Naxor. 'Please leave us, Chamberlain.'

Naxor bowed low, then he strode from the chamber and closed the door.

'I didn't originally intend for you to hear either of those messages, Kyra,' the Empress said, 'and I trust that you will not inform others of what has just transpired.'

'You are attacking the Rahain Capital?' said Kyra. 'After everything that happened in Tahrana City? How many more have to die, Your Majesty?'

'There will be casualties,' said the Empress; 'of that, I have no doubt. The responsibility of governing an empire can weigh heavily, and some of the decisions that must be taken for the good of that empire may seem cruel or arbitrary to you; but I make no apology for trying to alleviate the suffering of some three million Rahain who have been living in the utmost squalor for decades. My mother, if you recall, was a prisoner in Rahain for many years. She often spoke to me about the conditions she suffered under the oppressive and violent rule of the gangs. As often happens in these situations, it is the women and children who suffer the most, and I only wish the Empire had been ready to conduct such an operation sooner. Will the armed thugs who hold the civilian population in their lawless grip be ruthlessly exterminated? Yes, Kyra, they will die brutal deaths. But look at the reward – Tahrana City is now at peace, thanks to our army and marines. Lighting, heating, sewerage, fresh water supplies – all are now being repaired, because of our intervention. The same thing will happen to the Rahain Capital. There will be a violent storm, followed by peace and reconstruction. Without that storm, the cities of Rahain would continue to struggle on in degradation and poverty. Such are the decisions faced by any who rule over such a vast empire.'

'But, Your Majesty, there must be a better way.'

The Empress regarded her. 'One would hope so, but bitter experience has taught me that nothing will prise power from the hands of the unworthy other than the application of force. One cannot negotiate with the armed gangs of Rahain; therefore, if one wishes to help the people of that land, one must first eradicate those gangs.'

'But not every Rahain killed was in a gang. There must have been innocent casualties.'

'Yes. I wish it were not so, Kyra. I wish all peoples of the Star Continent were free and at peace. One must weigh up the terrible and unforeseen consequences of the short term, and see if they balance the good that will come from the liberation of Rahain in the long term. I believe that many more people will benefit from my decisions in Rahain than will suffer, and thus I am guided to act. Does that mean I am unfeeling towards those innocents who die in our invasion? You know me, Kyra; you know me well. Am I unfeeling?'

'No, Your Majesty.'

'Do you believe that I have been misled by my advisors?'

Kyra frowned.

'The truth is, Kyra,' the Empress went on, 'that I receive differing advice, and I must reach my own conclusions. My Lord Chamberlain, for example, counsels a more aggressive approach, while my beloved Herald is a voice for caution and restraint. Does that surprise you? I know that you have said harsh words to Kelsey, but did you realise that my Herald has consistently spoken up for the rights of the innocent? If you wish to be angry with anyone, aim that anger at me. The strategy for the liberation of Rahain is my responsibility.'

'How can you call it *liberation*, Your Majesty?' said Kyra. 'Your Sanang divisions have carried out the most dreadful atrocities.'

'My Sanang warriors are the perfect assault troops,' said the Empress, 'but I will admit to making a mistake with the initial occupation of Tahrana City. Do you hear me, Kyra? I made a mistake. I misjudged the suitability of the Sanang divisions when it came to peacekeeping duties. Major General Cardova warned me in advance what might happen, but I disregarded his advice. I will not be repeating that mistake in the Rahain Capital, nor in any of the other cities of Rahain that my armed forces shall liberate. Divisions of Holdings soldiers are ready to take over from the Sanang as soon as the Rahain Capital has been subdued.'

'That mistake cost thousands of lives, Your Majesty.'

'Do you think I am unaware of this?'

Kyra said nothing.

'The Imperial Court would prefer that I did not reveal any more secrets to you,' the Empress went on, 'since you have previously flouted the oath you took; but I want to prove that I still trust you, Kyra. Am I right to do so? If so, then let me confide further in you. The order I gave to Kelsey regarding the Rakanese frontier – do you have any inkling of what that meant?'

'No, Your Majesty. I earnestly hope that it won't be another invasion.'

'It is not an invasion. When the orders are received, my armed forces will tear two dozen breaches in the frontier wall that divides Rakana from the Plateau. This will allow a quarter of a million starving, destitute refugees to flood into the lands of the Empire. A quarter of a million, Kyra; that is the same number as those who dwell within Plateau City. The cost to the treasury of feeding and housing these Rakanese refugees will be exorbitant; yet, it is the right thing to do. Some will probably die in the crossing of the border, as the army of Rakana is determined to prevent any of its citizens from leaving. Should that cost outweigh the good that will come? Tell me.'

'I don't know, Your Majesty.'

'One generation from now,' the Empress went on, 'those refugees and their descendants will be productive members of the Empire, but they will first be a burden that must be borne. Similarly, the liberated cities of Rahain will cost the treasury dear, but they too, in time, will contribute to the Empire. I am working towards a future that I may not be alive to see; nevertheless, it is a future worth building.'

Kyra said nothing.

'Speak to me,' said the Empress. 'I have opened up to you; tell me your thoughts.'

'It seems to me,' said Kyra, 'that you are saying the end justifies the means. But, Your Majesty, I cannot support this policy if the *means* involves the slaughter of innocent people. Violence is wrong. Sending our soldiers out to kill unarmed civilians is wrong. All my life, I have looked up to you. I thought that you would rule with compassion and kindness. It is inexplicable to me that you have now decided to use overwhelming force to beat our neighbours into submission. I used to think my mother was naïve, but now? It pains me to say this, but I believe that she is right in this matter, and that you are wrong.'

'Have my words had such little effect on you?'

'Your words have only served to confirm my worst suspicions.'

'Then you plan to attend this evening's demonstration?'

'Will you allow me to attend?'

The Empress smiled, but Kyra could see the pain in her eyes. 'I would never forbid anyone from expressing their honest opinion, Kyra. Of course you are free to attend; but beware those who would use your name to advance causes that, if enacted, would bring great harm to the Empire. Beware those who shout simplistic slogans in the face of complicated problems; and those who condemn policies without offering any solutions. Life is not simple, and the Empire would not survive without difficult compromises. Be as demanding of your new comrades as you have been of my policies; question them as you have questioned me.'

Kyra lowered her gaze. 'Am I no longer your chosen successor, Your Majesty?'

'It is far too early to make such a sweeping remark. You are eighteen, Kyra, and you have shown that you need time and space to come to your own conclusions. I do not expect any successor to agree with me on every issue, but the Empire must come first. I will make my decision based upon that, in due course.'

'Am I free to leave?'

'You are.'

Kyra got to her feet. She tilted her head slightly, then she walked out of the audience chamber.

Thirty minutes later, Kyra was hurrying along a main road that cut through the New Town. A few extra soldiers were on duty, standing by the larger junctions that led to the university. As Kyra approached, she began to hear the noise of a crowd, their voices raised in unison. The streets around the university were crammed with hundreds of people. Most were gazing up at a small group that included Professor Achan, who was standing on a raised platform by the entrance to the quad. A large banner had been hung up behind them, which read: *Demand Peace – End the War*.

One of the men on the platform was delivering an impassioned speech, but Kyra could barely hear what he was saying over the noise of the crowd. She pushed her way through to the front, and Achan grinned widely when he saw her. He stepped down from the platform and waited for Kyra to reach him.

'I'm so glad you could make it, Kyra,' he said. 'I knew you wouldn't let down the cause of peace.'

'I have just been with the Empress,' she said.

'I see. Was she attempting to dissuade you from attending this evening's protest?'

'Aye.'

'Then I presume she failed, for you are here.'

'I told her that I did not agree with her. I told her that violence was wrong.'

'Your courage never fails to astound me.' He took her arm. 'Come up with me onto the platform, so that the crowd can see that a Holdfast stands with them.'

Kyra frowned, but allowed Achan to help her up onto the platform. Achan leaned forward, and whispered something into the ear of the man who was speaking. The man paused, and turned. He saw Kyra, and stood aside. Achan gently pushed Kyra forward, until they were standing at the front of the platform, in full view of the crowd.

'Hush for a moment,' Achan said, raising his arm. 'Please, everyone, hush. Do you see who I have standing by my side? The daughter of Karalyn Holdfast! A scion of the mightiest family on the Star Continent! This very night, Kyra Holdfast has confronted the Empress in her lair, in order to tell Her Majesty that she is wrong! If someone like Kyra can stand up to the imperialist war machine, then what is stopping the rest of us? Take heart from her courage, and stand united as we condemn the atrocities carried out in our name!'

Achan took hold of Kyra's left hand. He raised it into the air, and the crowd roared.

CHAPTER 27
THE TWO-THIRDS HERALD

Plateau City, The Plateau – 8th Day, First Third Autumn 544

Kelsey glanced at the large clock in the corner of her study. It had been made in the craft workshops of Amatskouri, and had cost her a small fortune, but she had come to rely upon it when organising her schedule.

Her time was almost up. She had arisen one hour before dawn that morning, in order to do as much work as possible before Van arrived to hand over the children. She had completed the detailed orders and reports on the situation on the Rakanese frontier, and she had read and commented on the army's account of the previous evening's demonstration. Over two thousand people had attended the protest, and they had all seen Kyra up on the platform. Despite their differences of opinion, Kelsey could not help but admire her niece's act of defiance. After everything the Empress had said to her, she had decided to stand with those who had denounced Her Majesty's government as cruel, warmongering imperialist oppressors, who were ravaging Rahain for profit and power. In doing so, the disaffected of Plateau City had found their new champion, and it was a Holdfast.

The doorbell rang, and Kelsey glanced at the clock again. She laid down her pencil, got to her feet, and walked to the front door of the townhouse. She took a breath, smoothed out her expression, and mentally prepared herself for two days of staying at home with the children.

She opened the door.

'Good morning,' said Van. He gestured to Calpurnia and Caelius. 'In you go, children. Say hello to your mother.'

The two children entered the house, and Kelsey embraced them both.

'You are looking very smart in your new ambassador's robes,' said Kelsey.

'Thank you,' said Van.

'You are also fifteen minutes early,' she said.

'You and that damn clock,' said Van. 'Not everyone runs their lives according to such precision, Kelsey. You have to allow a little leeway.'

'Are you off to the Ministry?'

'Yes. The king and queen of the City are arriving for an audience with the Empress today, and so I shall be there to support them.'

Kelsey stared at him. 'Emily and Daniel will be here, today? Why did no one tell me?'

'The decision was only taken this morning,' said Van. 'Remember the time difference. Dawn arrived in the City while it was still night here.'

'But I need to be there,' she said.

'As do I, and I am the ambassador. You cannot renege on your promises, Kelsey.'

Kelsey glanced at the children. 'Go into the living room,' she said. 'There are cakes on the table.'

Calpurnia and Caelius hurried away.

'Cake for breakfast?' said Van.

'I didn't want them to hear what I have to say to you,' she said, 'and that was the first thing I thought of.'

'I don't have time to stand here while you issue a reprimand,' said Van. 'It's just bad luck that the king and queen will be here while you are looking after the children. It's not a conspiracy to keep you away.'

'Why are they here? Have they reached a decision about joining the Empire?'

Van smiled at her. 'You know that I am not at liberty to discuss such matters with you. Any announcement, if there is an announcement, must first be made to the Empress. That's the correct protocol, and I am not going to deviate from it.'

Kelsey narrowed her eyes.

'I heard that Kyra was at last night's protest,' Van went on. 'It's nice to see that someone in your family possesses a conscience.'

'Says the former mercenary who used to work for the Ascendants.'

'It's my experience which qualifies me to speak on these issues. The Empress wishes to expand the area under her control; this isn't a secret. She wants Rahain and the City absorbed into the Empire, no matter the cost. That is my considered opinion.'

'Go fuck yourself, Van. That's my considered opinion.'

'I see you remain as charming as always, Kelsey. I will be here at sunset tomorrow to collect the children. Oh, and before I forget...' He slipped a hand into his robes and removed a large envelope.

'What's that?' said Kelsey.

'Our divorce papers,' he said, holding out the envelope. 'I have already signed. All you need to do is add your signature to the bottom of each page and our marriage will be over.'

'Is this what you want?'

He nodded. 'Yes, Kelsey. It's for the best. We have tried, but, we have failed.'

'Is there another woman?'

'No. I have never been unfaithful to you, and I have no plans to jump into another relationship, at least not any time soon. You will be a free woman again. I honestly wish you all the best, and...'

She took the envelope and slammed the door in his face. She turned, and saw Calpurnia looking up at her.

'What does *go fuck yourself* mean, mummy?' she said.

'It means *I hope you have a nice day,*' said Kelsey, 'but it's a secret language that only your daddy and I know, so don't repeat it to anyone else.'

'Do you and daddy hate each other now?'

'I don't hate your father, sweetie. We won't be living in the same house any more, but you must remember that we both love you and your brother. Where is Caelius, by the way?'

'He's eating all the cakes.'

Kelsey took Calpurnia's hand and they walked into the living room. Caelius was standing on a chair, scooping up the cakes with his hand. Kelsey lifted the plate out of his reach, and Caelius began to cry.

'I think you've had enough cake for now,' said Kelsey. 'Why don't you have an apple?'

'I don't want an apple,' said the boy.

'We've already had breakfast,' said Calpurnia. 'Daddy gave us eggs and toast.'

Kelsey placed the plate on a high shelf. 'What's your new house like?'

'It's not as big as this one,' said Calpurnia, 'and the maid keeps moving my things. I couldn't find my shoes this morning.'

'You have a maid?'

'She comes round every day to clean daddy's house.'

'Is she pretty?'

'She's an old lady, mummy.'

'She smells,' said Caelius. 'I don't like her.'

'What are we doing today, mummy?'

'You have lessons this morning and this afternoon,' she said to her daughter. 'Your arithmetic tutor will be here in an hour, and your languages tutor will be coming after lunch.'

The girl's face fell. 'Why can't I go to a normal school?'

'You're a Holdfast, and your mother is the Herald of the Empire. It's too dangerous.'

'Why?'

'Because there are bad people who might try to hurt you. I would have to surround you with armed guards.'

'Can we go to Colsbury?' said Caelius.

'Not today,' said Kelsey.

'Can we go to Dragon Eyre?'

'We'll be staying here for today. Your Aunty Karalyn will be coming round to visit this evening.'

'She's scary,' said Caelius.

'I am sure she will be on her best behaviour. Do you want to go to your room to read for a while?'

'Will you read to me, mummy?' said Caelius.

Kelsey smiled. 'Of course I will.'

'I am not a childminder, ma'am,' said the arithmetic tutor. 'A parent is always supposed to be present in the house while I am conducting my lessons.'

'I won't be gone for long,' said Kelsey, 'and I'll be taking Caelius with me.'

The middle-aged woman frowned. 'This is most improper, ma'am. It is in breach of my terms of employment.'

'What if I were to supply you with a little bonus, to say thank you for all the good work you've done?' said Kelsey. 'I think you deserve a bonus. Say, twenty sovereigns?'

'Are you trying to bribe me, ma'am?'

'Obviously,' said Kelsey. 'One hour, and I'll be back. You won't even be halfway through your lesson by then.'

'What if there is an emergency?'

'Leave the house if there's a fire; take shelter under the table if there's an earthquake; hide in the basement if the city is invaded by gods; and lock the front door if wild dogs are roaming the streets. Does that cover everything?'

The woman narrowed her eyes.

'You'll find the twenty sovereigns in the desk drawer,' said Kelsey. 'Do we have a deal?'

The tutor remained frozen for a moment, then she gave an almost imperceptible nod.

'Thank you,' said Kelsey. She turned to the door. 'You can come in, Calpurnia.'

The girl walked into the living room.

'Have a good lesson, sweetie,' said Kelsey. 'I'll see you soon.'

Kelsey left the room, and found Caelius sitting in the kitchen, trying to get into a locked cupboard.

'We're going on a little trip, Caelius,' she said.

'Are we going to Colsbury?'

'No, Caelius, we are going to the palace.'

'The new palace?'

'The new palace won't be finished for another couple of years. We're going to the Ministry of the Plateau, but that doesn't sound quite as exciting. Now, I'm going to need you to behave. All right? No shouting, running, screaming, jumping or anything like that. If you are good, you can have some more cake when we get back. Stand next to me.'

She took out her Quadrant, and slid her fingers over the copper surface. The air shimmered, then they appeared in the inner courtyard at the centre of the Ministry. She placed the Quadrant into a deep pocket, and took Caelius's hand.

'Remember to behave,' she said. 'Sit quietly, or there will be no cake.'

They walked into the building, and two soldiers saluted as they passed. Kelsey led Caelius up the stairs and along a corridor, until they reached the main audience chamber. The doors were open, and the Empress was sitting upon her throne, flanked by Naxor, Brogan, Caelius Logos and Bedig. Ambassador Van Logos was standing a few yards away, and he narrowed his eyes at the sight of his estranged wife.

'Good morning, Herald,' said the Empress. 'I wasn't expecting you here today.'

'Is it all right if Caelius and I sit quietly to observe proceedings, Your Majesty?' Kelsey said.

Naxor frowned. 'Are you working, or aren't you?'

'I'm not working, Naxor,' she said, 'but I would rather not miss what might be about to happen.'

The elder Caelius strode forward and ruffled his grandson's hair.

'Lovely to see you, little Caelius,' he said, then he leaned in closer to Kelsey. 'Sorry to hear about your troubles with my wayward son,' he whispered. 'He's a fool, and I've told him so. If you ever need any help, let me know.'

'Thank you, Caelius,' she said.

'You may remain here, Herald,' said the Empress, 'but I would ask that this does not become a common occurrence. If you are here, you should be available to work; otherwise, your presence might cause confusion and uncertainty. I do not like these half measures.'

'I understand, Your Majesty.'

Kelsey walked over to a row of seats by the back wall. She seated Caelius on one, and sat down next to him.

'Should we appoint an interim Herald for these occasions, Your Majesty?' said Naxor. 'Someone who can pick up the Herald's work while she is unavailable?'

'I do not want an interim Herald,' said the Empress. 'I want a full-time Herald.'

'Alas, Your Majesty, it seems that the present Herald is unable to fulfil such a simple demand, as she can only work four days out of every six. She is a two-thirds Herald; a little way short of full.'

'We can deal with this later,' said the Empress. 'Ambassador Van Logos, do you wish to address this throne?'

Van walked out in front of the Empress and bowed. 'Thank you, Your Imperial Majesty. Would it please you to have the king and queen of the City deliver a short address?'

'It would.'

'Then I shall escort Their Majesty's into your presence.'

He bowed again, and strode towards the door.

'Daddy!' cried little Caelius.

Van gave his son a wink, then he left the hall.

'Be quiet, son,' Kelsey hissed in his ear. 'Quiet, or no cake.'

Naxor glanced at Brogan. 'Do you have the financial accounts of the City to hand?'

'Yes, my lord,' she said.

'And the annexation agreement? Is it ready to be signed?'

'It is, my lord. I have also organised ink and quills for the signing ceremony.'

'We do not know if any of that will be required,' said the Empress.

'But, Your Majesty,' said Naxor, 'we would look foolish if the king and queen have come here in order to join the Empire, and we are not prepared.'

'If that does happen, I do not wish to give the impression that we had assumed it would be so.'

'Therefore, Your Majesty,' said Naxor, 'we shall do our utmost to appear surprised and delighted, and we will take a little longer than necessary to retrieve the agreement and the ink.'

Van walked back into the hall. 'I am honoured to present to the Imperial Court King Daniel and Queen Emily of House Aurelian, sovereign rulers of the City.'

Emily and Daniel strode into the hall, wearing their royal regalia.

'Greetings, Your Majesties,' said Naxor. 'We are pleased to see you both in such fine health. Do you wish to address Her Imperial Majesty Empress Thorn, Holder of the World?'

'We do, Lord Naxor,' said Daniel.

'Then you may proceed,' said Naxor.

Emily and Daniel took a few steps further forward. They glanced at each other for a brief moment, and as soon as Kelsey saw the pain in their eyes, she knew exactly what they were about to do.

'It is our considered opinion, Your Imperial Majesty,' said Emily, 'that we do so desire for the City to be admitted into the Empire of the Sapphire Throne, under the conditions laid out in the agreement authored by the Imperial Chancellor Princess Shellakanawara.'

The Empress smiled.

A tear slid down Emily's cheek, but she held her head up. 'Does it please Your Imperial Majesty to admit the City into this Empire?'

'It does,' said the Empress. 'Chamberlain, please prepare the necessary documents.'

The demigod bowed low. 'With tremendous pleasure, Your Majesty.'

Naxor strode out through a back door of the hall, taking Brogan with him.

'I wish to say a few words before our signatures are appended to any document,' said the Empress. 'The Empire and the City have been friends for many years, and this will not change. As a token of the affection I feel for the Empire's newest province, I hereby double the usual subsidy for the coming year.'

Daniel's eyes widened. 'Double, Your Majesty?'

'Indeed. As rulers of the Province of the City of Salve, you are free to allocate the funds and resources in any way you see fit, with one exception. All military concerns will now be separately funded by the Empire, and an imperial appointee will assume command of the Great Wall and its associated infrastructure.'

'Why is the lady crying?' said little Caelius in a loud voice.

'Hush,' said Kelsey. 'Sorry about that, everyone.'

Emily glanced over at Kelsey and the boy, then she wiped the tears from her face. 'I could not help but weep, young Caelius,' she said, 'to hear my realm referred to as a province for the first time.'

The Empress narrowed her eyes slightly.

Naxor strode back into the room with Brogan. They walked over to a large table on the right-hand side of the hall, and laid out documents, ink pots and quills. Naxor made a fuss of making sure everything looked neat and perfect, then he turned to the Empress.

'The agreement is ready to be signed, Your Majesty.'

The Empress rose from the throne, and descended the two steps to the floor of the hall. She waited until her court was flanking her, then they walked over to one side of the table. Van stepped forward, and accompanied Emily and Daniel to the other side. Naxor pulled out a chair for the Empress, and she sat. As soon as she was seated, the others did the same.

The Empress eyed Naxor. 'Thank you for getting these documents prepared so quickly, Chamberlain.'

'It was no trouble at all, Your Majesty.' He dipped a fresh quill into a pot of ink, and handed it to the Empress. He pointed at the last page of the agreement. 'Sign there, Your Majesty.'

The Empress studied the document for a few moments, then she wrote her name at the bottom in large swirling letters. She handed the quill to Naxor, who signed his name under that of the Empress. Kelsey watched as, one by one, the other members of the Imperial court added their names, then Naxor handed the documents to Van, who laid them out in front of Emily and Daniel.

'A little ink, my darling Emily,' said Daniel, 'and it will be done.'

Emily took the quill, and for the briefest of moments, Kelsey thought she was going to refuse to sign. The moment passed, and Emily wrote her name, then Daniel and Van did the same. Brogan sprinkled sand onto the lower half of the document, then she tipped the excess onto a silver tray.

'Store that in the treasury vaults,' said Naxor.

Brogan nodded. 'I shall, my lord.'

The Empress stood, and the others did the same. She made her way back to the throne, and sat down. The court re-assumed their positions next to her, while Emily, Daniel and Van walked into the middle of the room, then turned to face the Empress.

'Her Imperial Majesty now wishes to hear your oaths of loyalty,' said Naxor.

Emily and Daniel glanced at each other again, then they lowered themselves to their knees.

'We swear,' they said together, 'to faithfully serve the Empire of the Sapphire Throne, and we do pledge our undying loyalty to Her Imperial Majesty the Empress, and to all who reign after her.'

'You may rise,' said Naxor.

'You have our eternal gratitude for what you have done this day,' said the Empress. 'May all who witnessed this occasion remember it with the same joy that now burns brightly within my heart. At one stroke, the Empire gains another two million citizens, and I am proud and honoured to be their ultimate sovereign authority. May the City flourish under our rule, and may every province be bestowed with peace and prosperity. I will now allow you a few moments to change out of your formal royal regalia, then we hope you will join us for an informal reception, to celebrate these momentous events.'

Van bowed. 'Their Majesties would be pleased and honoured to attend such a reception, Your Imperial Majesty.'

The Empress smiled. 'Everyone is dismissed for ten minutes. We shall reconvene in the smaller reception room, where food and drinks will be served.'

Emily and Daniel bowed low, then Van accompanied them out of the hall.

Naxor clenched his fists in delight. 'We got them! Well done, Your Majesty; beautifully played. The glory of your Empire will shine through the ages.'

The Empress eyed her chamberlain, a hint of a smile on her lips. 'The congratulations should be shared among all members of the Imperial Court. Go, and prepare the small audience chamber. I wish to speak to Kelsey alone for a moment.'

The members of the court bowed and left the room, and Kelsey got to her feet.

'Stay where you are,' said the Empress, as she stepped down from the throne. 'I shall come to you.'

'That went well, Your Majesty,' said Kelsey, as the Empress walked over to her.

'I think it did. It was painful for them both, but they have done the right thing for the Empire, and for the City. We are stronger together. Will you stay for the reception?'

'I should probably be heading home, Your Majesty. Calpurnia's tutor wasn't too pleased when I told her I was coming here.'

The Empress eyed Kelsey for a long moment. 'I made a great sacrifice,' she said, 'when I chose never to have children. At first, I made my pledge to prove that I would not repeat the mistake made by my predecessor Empress Bridget, when she tried to have her son placed onto the throne. In time, however, I have come to understand that there were other reasons, which were equally valid. For instance, without children, I have nothing to concentrate on but my role as Empress. I have no conflict of interest to worry about, and nothing to distract me from what needs to be done. I can give everything to the Empire, Kelsey. Can you say the same?'

'I have given everything for the past ten years, Your Majesty.'

'I know. You have been a remarkable Herald, and I do not wish to lose you. Nevertheless, I require a Herald that is always available. As Naxor said, I do not want a two-thirds Herald.'

'But I am still able to work for four days out of every six, Your Majesty.'

'What if there is a sudden crisis, and I cannot find you?'

'I will remain in the Holdfast townhouse.'

'Hire a damn nanny, Kelsey. There is no need for you to personally care for the children. Between nannies and tutors, you should be able to resolve this. What about placing them into a boarding school?'

'I can't do that, Your Majesty. Van and I have brokered an agreement, and...'

'Damn him! He cannot dictate what you do with your life. I need you, Kelsey.'

'So do my children.'

'I cannot accept this current situation. You are either completely with me, or...'

'Or what? You'll replace me? With whom – Naxor? Brogan?'

'No one is irreplaceable; not even you or me. If you cannot do the job, then you know the honourable course of action.'

'All I'm asking for is a little flexibility. Is it so hard to accommodate my requests? I have sweated blood in this role. I have been utterly loyal, even when you've made mistakes. Can you not show me the slightest bit of understanding?'

'It's quite simple, Kelsey. Make arrangements that will ensure that you are always available to me; or step away. You are distracted. You have lost your focus. The Empire deserves better.'

Kelsey lowered her gaze.

'Let me know what you intend to do as quickly as possible,' said the Empress, 'and never bring your children to court again.'

Kelsey remained where she was as the Empress strode to the back of the hall and left through a concealed door. The two strongest relationships in her life were slipping out of her reach, and she felt powerless to prevent it. Her husband was demanding a divorce, and the Empress was demanding the impossible. She looked down at her son, who was sitting still in his chair for once.

'Was I good, mummy?' he said. 'Can I get some cake now?'

Thirty minutes later, Kelsey was sitting in her kitchen, while Caelius was filling his face with cake. She knew she should stop him, but the cake had kept him quiet for as long as it had taken her to write her letter of resignation. She wiped her eyes with a dish cloth. Some of her tears had fallen onto the single sheet of paper that bore her words, and the ink had smudged a little. For six thirds short of ten years, she had been Herald of the Empire; and, as Daniel had said, a little ink, and it was over.

She signed her name at the bottom, and folded the sheet in half. She reached into a pocket, and withdrew the envelope that Van had given her. She took out its contents, and readied the quill again. Her eyes went over the legal wording of the divorce agreement, but Kelsey's mind was too distracted to take much of it in. She dipped the quill into an ink pot, and scribbled her name at the bottom of every sheet. She crammed the documents back into the envelope without waiting for the ink to dry, and got to her feet.

'I'll be back in two minutes,' she said to Caelius, but he was too busy paying attention to the cake to notice.

Kelsey activated the Quadrant, and appeared in the large audience chamber. She walked through a back door, and entered the smaller hall where the reception was taking place. Courtiers, officers and officials were mingling with the king and queen of the City, while the Empress was talking to Van and the members of her court. Kelsey walked through the hall, then she bowed her head in front of the Empress.

She handed over her letter to the Empress, then she gave the envelope to Van. Before either could respond, Kelsey triggered the Quadrant again. She appeared in the university quad, and headed for the northern wing. Calpurnia was still with her tutor, and Caelius wouldn't miss her for another couple of minutes. A few students eyed her with suspicion, and she wanted to scream at them, to tell them all that the Empire was now none of her concern, that she had given it all up to satisfy the Empress's demands.

She came to Elbannon's laboratory, and opened the door. Inside, Karalyn and Elbannon were bickering about something, but, to Kelsey's relief, Kyra wasn't there. Karalyn glanced over, then her eyes narrowed.

'Are you all right?' she said.

Kelsey ran over to her sister, and burst into tears. Karalyn embraced her.

'Are the children all right?' said Karalyn. 'Kelsey, what's happened?'

'I've just signed away my marriage and my job,' Kelsey sobbed.

'Where are Calpurnia and Caelius?'

'In the townhouse.'

Karalyn glanced at Elbannon. 'You'll have to work on your own for the rest of the day. My sister needs me.'

The air shimmered, and they appeared in the front hall of the townhouse. Karalyn led Kelsey through to the kitchen, where Caelius was drinking water straight from the tap. Karalyn sat Kelsey down, then crouched by her.

'I'm here, Kelsey,' she said. 'Tell me everything.'

CHAPTER 28
THE PRETEXT

Plateau/Rakana Frontier – 8th Day, First Third Autumn 544

Lahnos opened his eyes as the morning bugles blared out over the military encampment. He had been sleeping out in the open, between Sigum's flank and a long silvery-green forelimb, and he pulled the blanket free where it had tangled round his legs. The Bullan were also outside, having sat up for much of the night around their small campfire. The dragon moved a little, and Lahnos got to his feet. The Bullan had already started work for the day, and some were warming water over the restarted fire. Over to the left, the other dragons had been resting in a different part of the field from Sigum. Their riders were emerging from a large tent, a tent that Lahnos had refused to enter.

'We're lucky it didn't rain last night,' Lahnos said, as he approached the campfire.

'It did rain, sir,' said Efizel. 'Lord Sigum extended a wing for us, to keep us dry.'

'I didn't notice,' said Lahnos. He sat down by the fire, and rubbed his face. 'I need a bath.'

'Certainly, sir,' said the Bullan sergeant major. 'We shall heat enough water and find a tub for you.'

'No, don't. We need the water for breakfast; don't waste it all on me. I'll manage with a quick wash.'

'Very well, sir. Coffee?'

'Definitely.'

Efizel lifted a pot from the metal grid that had been placed over the fire, and poured some into a small coffee pot.

'It will just be a minute, sir.'

Lahnos glanced over at the other riders. They had their own campfire, and a few were attempting to re-light it.

'I should try to mend some bridges today,' he said. 'We could be here for a long time, and the contingent from Dragon Eyre are supposed to be our allies.'

The silvery-green dragon moved his long neck, so that his head was a few yards from the campfire and the Bullan.

'I will also try to remain civil,' he said, 'even if Gallantmorn and the others attempt to provoke me.'

Efizel filled three mugs from the coffee pot. He handed the first to Lahnos, then gave one to the corporal, and another to the next Bullan in line.

'Thanks,' said Lahnos.

'We have nothing to sweeten it, sir,' said Efizel.

'I'll manage. It's a miracle that we have coffee out here; I'm not going to complain about a lack of sugar.'

One of the Bullan pointed. 'Sir,' he said; 'officers.'

Lahnos sipped some of the scalding-hot coffee, then he got to his feet. A large group was entering the dragon field from the right.

'I recognise General Brigon,' said Sigum. 'I wonder what this means.'

The group came to a halt in front of the eight dragons from the Eastern Rim, then one of the officers gestured over in the direction of Sigum, Lahnos and the Bullan. A junior officer was dispatched, and she hurried over to the campfire where Lahnos was standing.

'Commander Laimos, sir,' she said. 'General Brigon invites you, Lord Sigum and the Bullan over to hear today's orders.'

'Why should we have to move?' said one of the Bullan.

'It makes sense,' said Lahnos. 'There are eight of them and only one of us.' He glanced at the lieutenant. 'We'll be along in a moment.'

The officer saluted, then she hurried back towards the general and the other dragons.

'You heard the commander,' said Efizel. 'Let's find out what we shall be doing today.'

Lord Sigum stood, and stretched out his long wings, casting a large shadow over their corner of the field. The Bullan also got to their feet, and Lahnos led them and the dragon over to where General Brigon was waiting for them. Colonel Hazen was also there, but he was remaining in the background, and would not look up at Gallantmorn or any of the other Eastern Rim dragons.

'Good morning,' said Brigon, his voice carrying over the field. 'Last night, just before midnight, we had a visitor from Plateau City – the Herald of the Empire.' He paused for a moment, as he regarded the nine dragons. 'The operation has been approved. Her Imperial Majesty has ordered us to carry out the plan to allow the Rakanese refugees trapped on the far side of the border wall to reach the Plateau. Throughout the night, as you all slept, my soldiers have been meticulously preparing for the operation. In little under an hour, the plan will be put into motion, and the wall shall be breached.' He gestured at a red flag flying from a tall post near the centre of the camp. 'All along the frontier, these red flags have been raised. It is imperative that all dragons remain on the ground until those flags have been taken down. If any dragons disobey this instruction, the Empire shall not be held responsible for any injuries or deaths that may occur. As soon as the flags have been lowered, each dragon shall ascend into the air, and fly to their designated section of the frontier. Once there, they will assist the fleeing refuges, and eliminate any member of the Rakanese armed forces who tries to hinder their escape.' He paused again, allowing his words to sink in. 'The Empire thanks you all in advance for the work you shall do this day. I have no doubt that the service you will provide shall be instrumental in making this operation a complete success. I do not know at this stage how long it will take for every refugee to cross the frontier. It may take several days, or it might all be done by sunset. Regardless of its duration, you will be on duty until all of our objectives have been met. Are there any questions?'

'Will there be any other flags flown, General?' said Sigum. 'A recall flag, for instance, to signal us to return to this side of the frontier?'

'No.' said Brigon. 'Once you are in the air, you will be acting independently, as you will have a far better overview of what is happening compared to those of us on the ground. Remember not to land on the Rakanese side of the border, and use your judgement to direct your actions. I would like to wish you all good luck. Carry on.'

The general turned, and led the other officers from the field.

An hour later, many of the dragons were growing impatient. Nothing seemed to be happening over by the border wall, but formations of imperial soldiers were gathering in large numbers, preparing to rush forward as soon as the breaches appeared. The delay allowed Lahnos and the Bullan to wash and tidy up their camp, then they waited in silence, their eyes on the wall.

A whistle blasted out three times, and the imperial soldiers lifted their shields, as though to protect themselves from something. A moment later, a series of deafening explosions began to rip through the wall, sending tons of rubble flying up into the air like a hailstorm. A hundred yards in front of Lahnos, a huge breach appeared amid the cloud of dust and rubble, and the ground shook under his feet. Pillars of smoke rose along the line of the wall, stretching out to the north and the south of their position, as the other breaches were ripped through the structure. A few fragments of rock landed close to where Sigum was standing, and they lay smoking on the grass in front of him.

'It is time to prepare for the operation, I think, sir,' said Efizel.

Lahnos nodded, then he hurried to the silvery-green dragon's flank, and began climbing up onto the harness. He fastened the leather belt round his waist, and gazed over at the red flag.

'Get ready,' he said.

'I am ready, my rider,' said Sigum. 'I am not daunted by a few explosive devices.'

'I wonder how many tons of explosives were needed for what we just witnessed. Twenty-three breaches? I'm glad we're not fighting against the Empire.'

The red flag was pulled down, and Sigum launched himself into the air. He was the first dragon airborne, as the riders from the Eastern Rim were still running towards their dragons.

'Our sector of the wall is a mile to the south,' Sigum said, as he banked. 'We shall be there in a moment or two.'

Sigum put on a burst of speed, and soared away to the right. Lahnos glanced down. Companies of imperial soldiers were charging towards the breach closest to them and, as Sigum ascended further, Lahnos could see the same thing happening behind the other breaches. The wall had been smashed apart at regular intervals, with each breach around ten yards in width. Rubble was strewn around each, and several bodies were lying on the Rakanese side. Refugees were stumbling around in a daze as they stared at the destroyed sections of the frontier wall, while the soldiers on that side were rushing about, unsure what they were facing. Sigum banked again over the broken line of the wall, and flew to the south. They reached the sector they were responsible for, and Sigum dived down, scaring away a group of Rakanese soldiers who were tentatively approaching one of the breaches. Imperial soldiers arrived on the spot, and began clearing the gap. A few of them clambered up onto the rubble, and waved their arms in the air, calling on the Rakanese civilians to flee over to the Plateau. At first, the refugees stared at them, none moving, then a few ran forwards. Rakanese soldiers tried to stop them from reaching the breach, and Sigum dived down again. He picked up two soldiers in his forelimbs, and threw them through the air, and the others panicked and fled. The first refugees arrived at the breach, where the waiting imperial soldiers helped them climb over the rubble. At the sight of this, the huge mass of refugees still in the camps surged forward. Rakanese soldiers loosed their crossbows at them, and Sigum soared down. He opened his jaws and emitted a thin but powerful blast of fire, incinerating the soldiers standing between the refugees and the breach. The soldiers screamed as the flames ripped through them, then the refugees charged across the ground.

'It's working,' said Lahnos. 'I think they've got the right idea now.'

'Yes, but it will take a long time for everyone to fit through the breaches, my rider.'

'Can you see the other dragons?'

Sigum pulled his attention away from the breach below them, and scanned the skies. While he did so, Lahnos stared out along the line of the wall to the north. Next to each breach, refugees were gathering in their tens of thousands, while, on the other side, thin streams of them were issuing through into the Plateau, where they were being met with food and blankets carried by the Amatskourians.

'The dragons of the Eastern Rim have not obeyed their orders,' said Sigum. 'We are the only ones at our correct posts, my rider. The others are clustered together, and are fighting as a group.'

'What is wrong with those arseholes?' said Lahnos.

'They are proud, Lahnos,' said Sigum. 'They are showing General Brigon that they care not for his orders. Rakanese civilians will pay the price for their arrogance.'

Sigum soared down again, heading for the other breach within their sector of the wall. He sent a wide barrage of flames down onto a Rakanese army blockade that was standing by the entrance of one of the refugee camps, and the soldiers were killed in seconds, rendered to ash by the heat of the dragon fire. The refugees gazed up at the dragon in terror, then some of them ran towards the breach, joining the others who had already gathered there.

'The other dragons are coming our way,' said Lahnos.

'I see them. They must be sweeping down the entire length of the frontier wall.'

Lahnos watched as the eight Eastern Rim dragons got closer. Several were spraying fire down onto the crowds of Rakanese, killing many soldiers, but burning dozens of civilians who happened to be close to them.

'Greetings, Lord Sigum,' said Gallantmorn, as he reached the silvery-green dragon. 'This is a fine day for sport.'

'You should fly to the locations to which you were assigned by the general, brave Gallantmorn,' said Sigum; 'that is my humbly-given advice.'

'We shall do as we please,' said Gallantmorn. 'Brigon was correct in one respect – we have a far better view of the wall from up here. It makes sense to concentrate our fire.'

'I disagree,' said Sigum. 'Who is monitoring the many breaches to our north and south?'

'Have you always taken your orders from humans?'

'I agreed to obey orders when Lahnos and I joined Her Imperial Majesty's armed forces.'

'You may be honest, as Sable herself has sworn you are,' said Gallantmorn, 'but that does not mean you are not a fool, Lord Sigum of Athumia. Even a fool may tell no lies.'

'You have proved that by your own words and deeds, brave Gallantmorn.'

'You dare mock me?'

'I dare. Do you wish to challenge me?'

'I do not fight the elderly. How old are you, Athumian? You seem to have lost any vigour you might have possessed in your youth.'

'I have seen four hundred and sixty-two winters thaw into spring. Challenge me, or cease your impertinence and be gone from my sector.'

Gallantmorn laughed. 'Come, my Eastern Rim dragons; let us leave this withered old fool to his dotage. He is wasting our time; time that could be better spent roasting more amphibians.'

The eight dragons gathered round Gallantmorn as he soared off to the south.

'Just so I know for the future,' said Lahnos, 'if you ever get into a fight with another dragon, do I use my Gift of Pain on them or not?'

'You will not,' said Sigum. 'If I am ever attacked by more than one, feel free to do so, but I reserve the right to destroy my enemies unaided. Gallantmorn is fortunate that he fled my challenge. My teeth would have ripped out his throat in mere minutes.'

He soared down again, and chased away a group of soldiers who were trying to re-group. His claws raked through the back of one, slicing him in two, and the others scattered in terror.

'Run to the breach!' Sigum called out to the refugees. 'I will protect you from the air. Run to the breach!'

A terrible, howling scream echoed out from the south. Sigum ascended, and Lahnos saw a blue dragon plummeting from the sky, its head completely gone. Gallantmorn and the other six from the Eastern Rim were flying in all directions, circling in a panic as they tried to work out what had caused their companion's death. The headless blue dragon crashed into the middle of a refugee camp, crushing dozens and ploughing through the soft ground.

The head of a red dragon exploded in a great burst of blood and flesh, showering Gallantmorn and the others with fragments of scales and tissue. Gallantmorn cried out in alarm, then he began spraying flames down onto the Rakanese indiscriminately. The refugee camp where the blue dragon had fallen went up in flames, its high fences preventing the refugees from escaping the raging fires. The other dragons copied Gallantmorn's example, and six streams of fire raged down on the Rakanese side of the wall.

Sigum shot off towards them, putting on a burst of speed that made Lahnos close his eyes due to the searing wind. Lahnos opened them just as Sigum collided with Gallantmorn, sending the younger dragon spinning backwards through the air. A white dragon extended his claws in Sigum's direction, and he reacted by gripping the white dragon by the throat, and squeezing.

'I am assuming command of the air,' Sigum called out, his voice booming out. 'Either challenge my right to do so, or obey my orders. Fly to your assigned sectors and do as you were commanded to do. I will deal with the Gifted one who is killing our numbers. Obey me, or die.'

Gallantmorn cried out in rage, and soared at Sigum. The silvery-green dragon released his grip on the throat of the white dragon, then he deftly moved to the side, and allowed his claws to rake down Gallantmorn's right flank as he charged past in a fury.

The head of the white dragon exploded in a crescendo of noise and blood. His headless body lingered in the sky for a moment, then he fell, smashing into an unbroken section of wall.

'Do as I command,' roared Sigum, 'or you will all die this day.'

'I will obey,' said Quicklime. 'Gallantmorn, you have led three dragons to their deaths this day.'

Gallantmorn glanced down at the wound inflicted upon his flank by Sigum's claws.

'I will also obey, Lord Sigum,' said a dark red dragon. 'Come, Quicklime; let us hasten to our positions.'

The dragons began to scatter to the north and the south, leaving only Sigum and Gallantmorn above the burning refugee camp.

'I will not forget this insult,' said Gallantmorn.

'I care not for your hurt feelings, brave Gallantmorn,' said Sigum. 'Be gone.'

The dark orange dragon turned, and sped away.

'Lahnos,' said Sigum; 'use your Gift to subdue the entire area before I lose my own head.'

Lahnos extended his right hand, aimed it at the huge crowd, and unleashed the Gift of Pain. Dozens, then hundreds of Rakanese cried out in agony, falling like cut wheat onto the ground around the burning refugee camp.

'There is no way of knowing if the Gifted one is down there,' said Sigum. 'And what manner of Gift can cause a dragon's head to disintegrate?'

'It's Rakanese flow powers,' said Lahnos, as he kept up his barrage of Pain. 'Shella can do it. The important question is this – why didn't the imperial army know that there was a flow mage in the vicinity?'

He dropped his Gift, and stared down at the writhing masses of people. By the left of the burning camp, Rakanese soldiers were trying to drag away a woman in dark robes, pulling her unconscious body away from the wall.

'Set me down,' said Lahnos. He pointed. 'There. Set me down, Sigum.'

'Are you also willing to disobey orders, my rider?'

'I will be happy to tell General Brigon exactly why I did so. We can't let her get away, Sigum; it has to be her – she's the only one the soldiers are trying to protect.'

Sigum tilted his head, then he soared down, passing through the smoke billowing up from the incinerated camp. Lahnos unbuckled the strap, and leapt to the ground. He rolled as he landed, and his powers healed the bruises and strains in an instant. He sprinted towards the soldiers, racing past groaning bodies still recovering from his Gift. A few of the soldiers saw him, and one loosed his crossbow. The bolt ripped through Lahnos's right shoulder, but he hardly felt it. He raised his right hand, and sent Pain into the fleeing group. He ran over to them, and pulled the soldiers away from the unconscious woman. He rolled her onto her front, pulled off his belt, and used it to bind her wrists together. He waved at Sigum to descend, then he lifted the woman, slung her over his shoulder and ran to where the dragon was landing in a cleared area.

'Flee to the breaches!' the dragon called out to the refugees. 'Flee to safety!'

Soldiers over to the right began loosing their bows at the dragon, and he sent a flood of flames in their direction, killing them all. Lahnos reached Sigum's flank, and climbed up to the harness. He secured their unconscious prisoner to the straps of the harness, and the dragon lifted back into the air. He ascended high into the sky, and Lahnos gazed down. The bodies of the three dead dragons were visible where they had fallen, but little had changed along the other stretches of the wall. Refugees were flooding through the breaches in their thousands, while most of the Rakanese soldiers had given up trying to stop them. To the north, Gallantmorn was burning entire encampments of the Rakanese military, and the roads leading to Arakhanah City were clogged with escaping soldiers.

The woman on the harness next to Lahnos opened her eyes, then she cried out in fright as she realised that she was a hundred feet above the ground.

'Three dragons,' said Lahnos. 'Not bad.'

The woman stared at him, her eyes widening.

'Yes, I have horns,' he said. 'You are now my prisoner. I know that you can't use your mage powers without your hands, and you should know that I could kill you with a single touch.'

'You have started a war,' she said, her accent heavy. 'Do you think I am the only Rakanese patriot with flow powers?'

'What I think is none of your business. Sigum, let's hand our prisoner over to the army.'

The silvery-green dragon swooped down to the Plateau side of the wall, and landed close to the cluster of large command tents. Lahnos unfastened the straps holding him and the prisoner to the harness, then he picked her up and climbed down to the ground. Her fingers brushed the skin on his arm, and he felt a sharp pain through his body, as the mage tried to stop his heart. Lahnos dropped her onto the grass.

'You should be dead,' she said.

'I'm not that easy to kill,' he said. 'That hurt, though; I'll be honest.'

Several officers and soldiers ran over.

'She's a flow mage,' Lahnos said. 'It was this one who killed the three dragons.'

'Careful, everyone,' said an officer. 'We'll need gloves for her, and a hood. No one must touch her with their bare hands. Sergeant, the colonel has a set of metal gauntlets brought along for this purpose; fetch them.

'Yes, sir,' said the sergeant.

'You knew there might be flow mages?' said Lahnos.

General Brigon approached. 'We were aware that there was a small risk that some might be present,' he said. 'Thank you for your actions in the air, Lord Sigum, and thank you, Commander Laimos for apprehending this mage. You did, however, land on the Rakanese side of the frontier, and I shall have to report this to the imperial authorities.'

'I felt I had no choice under the circumstances, sir.'

'I know. Had I been in your position, I would have done the same thing. There will be no court martial, and no disciplinary action shall be taken; but I must report it all the same.'

The air shimmered, and Naxor appeared, a Quadrant in his right hand.

The officers bowed their heads.

'I have been watching this morning's events from a distance,' said the demigod, 'and I deduced that the time was right for an intervention.' He glanced down at the Rakanese mage. 'First of all – kill her. She ended the lives of three of Queen Blackrose's dragons, and I would not like to have to explain to the ruler of the Eastern Rim why we allowed her to live.'

Brigon gestured to a captain. 'See to it.'

The captain bowed, then he walked forward, drawing his sword.

'Should she not be questioned first?' said Lahnos.

'I have already read her mind,' said Naxor. 'She has nothing useful to give us.'

The captain glanced at the general, who gave him a brief nod. The captain crouched by the prisoner, then he cut her throat with the blade of his sword. Lahnos watched her blood stain the grass, then he turned away.

'Where are you going, Commander?' said Naxor.

'Back to Lord Sigum,' he said. 'Our job isn't done.'

'I saw you land on the far side of the wall,' Naxor went on. 'Technically, you have committed an act of war.'

Lahnos laughed. 'Are you going to arrest me?'

'Of course not – you and Lord Sigum were the only ones in the sky who actually obeyed the orders you were given.' He smiled. 'I have new orders for you. Take to the air, gather the other dragons, and drive the Rakanese military all the way back to Arakhanah City. If we are at war, gentlemen, let us at least act in the proper manner. Destroy the

Rakanese army in its entirety, Commander Laimos; chase them to the outskirts of their city, and burn their defences and military installations. Is that clear?'

'I thought this was a humanitarian operation.'

'It was, Commander,' said Naxor; 'it is now a war. Take no more prisoners, and show our enemy no quarter. Lord Sigum, you are now in charge of the five surviving dragons from the Eastern Rim. Does anyone have any questions before you set off?'

'What shall the ground troops be doing, my lord?' said the general.

'I want our army to secure both sides of the wall,' said Naxor, 'as well as the roads leading to Arakhanah City. However, do not advance into Rakanese territory until the dragons have first completed their tasks.'

'I have a question,' said Lahnos. 'Where's Kelsey?'

Naxor eyed Lahnos and the officers. 'It is with the greatest regret that I have to announce the immediate resignation of the Herald of the Empire.'

The officers gasped.

'The Herald has resigned from her post, my lord?' said General Brigon.

'She has. She remains Lady Holdfast, or Holder Fast, whichever you prefer, but she no longer has any role in the government of the Empire. Her Imperial Majesty has asked me to take over all operations on the Rakanese frontier. I shall be setting up my headquarters here, so that I can monitor the progress of the war, which I hope shall be swift and overwhelming.'

'Why did she resign?' said Lahnos.

Naxor smiled. 'To spend more time with her children.'

'Are you the new Herald?'

'Her Majesty has not yet decided who should take over the role of Herald. The Empress shall make her choice in due course. Now go; there is a war to be won, Commander.'

Lahnos walked back to Sigum, and climbed up onto the harness. The silvery-green dragon ascended into the air. He flew out over the wall, then he swept to the north, where Gallantmorn was burning another military encampment.

'We have new orders, brave Gallantmorn,' said Sigum.

The dark orange dragon eyed him. 'If you are here to ask me to retreat in shame, I shall disobey.'

'There will be no retreat,' said Sigum. 'I have been placed in command of the invasion of Rakana. We are to seek out and destroy the entire Rakanese army on the roads leading to their city. Will you obey that order, Gallantmorn?'

The dark orange dragon laughed. 'I most certainly will, Lord Sigum.'

'Then gather your kin, and we shall begin the offensive.'

Gallantmorn tilted his head slightly, then he soared away to where the other dragons from the Eastern Rim were patrolling over the wall.

'Are you ready for another war, my rider?' said Sigum.

'It will be the road to Tahrana City all over again,' said Lahnos. 'Only this time, there will be six dragons, not one.'

'I fear the carnage will be immense,' said Sigum. 'By sunset this day, tens of thousands of Rakanese will lie dead on the ground.'

'Is this my fault?'

'No, Lahnos. I suspect the noble Lord Naxor was searching for any excuse that would permit him to expand the terms of this conflict.'

Gallantmorn returned, bringing the other four dragons with him. They circled round Sigum, waiting for him to speak.

'We shall form ourselves into a wide arc,' said Sigum, 'and I shall lead. Let not a remnant of the Rakanese army survive this day of blood and fire. No retreat; no prisoners; no mercy! Follow me, and we shall kill them all!'

The other dragons, including Gallantmorn, roared out their approval of Sigum's words.

'Lead us into battle, Lord of Athumia!' cried Quicklime.

The dragons formed into a curving line, with Sigum in the centre. Lahnos gazed down at the columns of retreating Rakanese soldiers, who were filling every available road leading away from the wall.

'To war!' cried Sigum.

He soared down towards the soldiers, and the other dragons followed him. The soldiers saw them coming, and tried to run, turning the retreat into a chaotic stampede. As one, the dragons opened their jaws. Six great bursts of flame came down onto the fleeing army, and the armed might of Rakana was reduced to ash.

CHAPTER 29
SPILLAGE

Plateau City, The Plateau – 8th Day, First Third Autumn 544

'She's still a warmonger,' said Kyra.

'She is your aunt,' said Karalyn. 'Family is important.'

'You sound more and more like Granny Daphne, Mother,' said Kyra. 'She was always talking about how important the family was. The Holdfasts were everything to her.'

Karalyn frowned. 'I am not my mother.'

'Then why do you talk like her?'

'If my mother was still alive,' Karalyn said, 'then you would see what a real warmonger looks like. Kelsey is not the same.' She glanced down at the tray of silver ingots. 'She asked if I minded if she lived in Colsbury whenever she has the children.'

'What did you say?'

'I told her it was fine. She thinks that, now she's resigned, Van will reconsider how many days they each get with Calpurnia and Caelius. She's hoping that they might reverse the current arrangement, so she can have them for four days, while he has them for two.'

'Are they really divorced? I mean, is that it?'

'They have both signed the papers. Legally, their marriage is over.

I'm glad my mother wasn't around to see that. It would be the second time she would have to watch one of her children getting divorced.'

Elbannon glared at them. 'Stop all this idle gossip, and pay attention to the molten silver.'

'Don't get agitated,' said Karalyn. 'We're watching it.'

Elbannon squeezed in between them at the forge, then he leaned over and picked up a cylinder with a long pair of tongs. Inside the cylinder, molten silver was bubbling away. As he moved it back from the heat of the forge, he knocked into Kyra, and a large drop of silver spilled out, landing close to Kyra's bare hands.

'Pyre's arse, Elbannon!' Karalyn shouted. 'You could have seriously burned my daughter.'

'Well, you shouldn't be in the damn way!' Elbannon shouted back. 'It's not my fault if you're both stupid.'

'You asked me to watch the silver,' she said; 'that's why we were standing here. And put that damn cylinder down before you drop any more.'

'You can't tell me what to do,' he said. 'This is my laboratory. Any more complaints, and I shall refuse to cooperate. Do you think you'll manage to find your idiot son without my help, eh?'

Kyra glanced down at the spillage as her mother continued to argue with Elbannon. The Compass had been lying close by with its lid open, and some of the silver had splashed into the interior. Kyra peered down at it, then she pulled the small device towards her. A penny-sized nodule of cooling silver had landed on the Zamatan Coil, and had run down its side, where it was overlaying some of the tiny Tempest wires.

'Uh, maybe you should take a look at this,' she said. 'I don't think this can be good.'

Karalyn glanced over, and her eyes narrowed. 'Shit.'

'What is it?' said Elbannon.

Kyra pushed the Compass over so that he could see into it.

His eyes widened. 'You have killed my *Tammy*!' he cried. 'All that work – wasted! You incompetent, clumsy, foolish oafs!'

'It was you who spilled the silver, Elbannon,' said Karalyn. 'You should be directing those insults at yourself.'

Elbannon set the tongs and the cylinder down, then he tore off his gloves and threw them onto the floor.

'That's it,' he said. 'I have reached my limit. I quit.'

'You will not quit,' said Karalyn, 'not while my son, my nephew and Arrosa are trapped upon another world.'

'You can't stop me.'

'You're wrong, Elbannon. I can stop you. All it would take is for me to enter your mind, and you would do whatever I suggested.' She glanced at Kyra. 'Lunchtime must be over by now. Go to your class, and I'll deal with Elbannon, and clean up the mess he's made.'

Kyra looked at the old professor, who had taken a few nervous steps away, his eyes tinged with fear. She picked up her bag from the back of a chair, and strode out of the laboratory. Another day was passing, and they were no closer to finding Cael. The disappointment was crushing, and she was starting to lose hope that her brother would ever be found. Compared to that, the exhilaration she had felt during the previous evening's demonstration seemed petty. The crowd of protesters had roared out her name, but what was it all worth without her twin?

She walked along the university corridor, then she remembered that the class she was due to attend was that run by Professor Nadia. She almost came to a halt, then she decided that it was time to confront the old Rahain woman. She ascended a flight of stairs and walked into the classroom just as the lesson was about to start.

Professor Nadia cleared her throat. 'And just where do you think you are going, Miss Holdfast?'

'To my seat, Professor,' she said.

'No. Not until I hear you promise to keep your obnoxious political opinions to yourself.'

'Don't you believe in freedom of speech, Professor?'

'It is one of my most dearly-held beliefs, Miss Holdfast; however, there is a time and a place for everything, and my classroom is not the appropriate location for political diatribes. If you wish to exercise your freedom of speech, do so in the canteen or, perhaps, in the classroom of Professor Achan. You will not do it here. Do I have your agreement?'

Kyra gazed at the faces of the students who were watching the exchange. Several of them had been at the demonstration, and a few of them had even suggested that morning that the Herald had lost her job as a direct result of Kyra's attendance alongside the other speakers at the protest.

'I will respect the rules of your classroom, Professor,' she said.

'Very well,' said Nadia. 'Please return to your seat.'

Kyra walked over, and took the empty chair next to Dazi.

'We shall continue with our examination of the faults that have been found by the imperial engineers,' said Nadia. 'The heating system of Tahrana City was first designed and installed over six centuries ago, and it has gone through countless modifications, repairs and improvements since then. Remarkably, however, a few extremely old components are still in use, and it is to these components that we will be paying particular attention. Take out your textbook on fluid dynamics and turn to page two hundred and eleven. Read the page in silence, and then we shall examine how that knowledge can assist with the repairs.'

The first hour of Professor Nadia's class passed quickly, and Kyra begrudgingly admitted to herself that she found it fascinating to study how the theoretical equations held within the book would help repair the ancient heating system of Tahrana City. They were examining a large schematic of the furnaces that heated the enormous boilers under the city, when the door to the classroom burst open, and her mother walked in.

'Another Holdfast,' said Nadia. 'How delightful.'

'I need my daughter to be excused,' said Karalyn.

'Might I ask why?' said Nadia.

'It's a family matter.'

'Of course it is. The Holdfasts always come first, don't they?'

Karalyn frowned. 'Don't take that attitude with me, Nadia. Kyra, pick up your things; we're going.'

Kyra glanced around at her classmates, embarrassed that her mother was there, but also quite pleased by what she had said to Nadia.

'Your daughter will fail this subject if she keeps missing classes,' said Nadia.

'Some things are more important,' said Karalyn; 'and this is one of them.'

Kyra stood, and slung her bag over her shoulder.

'I'll take notes for you,' said Dazi.

'Thanks.'

She followed her mother out of the classroom, and shut the door.

'Where are we going?' she said. 'Is everyone all right?'

'We are going back to the laboratory,' Karalyn said. 'I need you to confirm something for me.'

'So, there's no emergency? You had me worried for a moment, Mother.'

They descended a flight of stairs and walked to the laboratory. Karalyn opened the door, and they strode inside. Elbannon was hard at work over the hot forge, feeding ingots of pure silver into more heated cylinders. Karalyn led Kyra over to a workbench, where the Compass had been set down.

'It hasn't been cleaned,' said Kyra. 'There is still silver inside it.'

'You have touched pure Tempest before, haven't you?' said Karalyn.

'Aye. Once. I heard it scream. Is it the same with you? Can you hear it?'

'I can hear it. Do you see where the silver spillage is coating the edge of the Zamatan Coil? Place your finger on it and tell me what happens.'

Kyra narrowed her eyes, then she extended a finger, and touched the small splash of cooled silver. At once, her vision clouded, and she heard a small, whispered cry. Her vision wouldn't clear, and it was like looking into a dense fog. She took her finger off, and her vision went back to normal. Her mother peered at her.

'Well?' she said.

'That was... odd,' said Kyra. 'I couldn't see you for a moment. All I saw was... fog.'

Karalyn smiled and turned to Elbannon. 'She sees it, too.'

Elbannon kept his gaze on the forge. 'That doesn't mean it will work.' He withdrew a cylinder of molten silver from the forge, and poured a small amount into a cast, covering a tiny ingot of Tempest. The silver coated the ingot completely, then it began to cool.

'We're going to insert that into the space in the Compass,' said Karalyn.

'Remove the damaged Coil from *Tammy* first,' said Elbannon.

Karalyn took a pair of thin-nosed pliers and leaned over the Compass. She lifted the silver-splashed Zamatan Coil from the inside of the device, and set it to the side. She then picked up a clean coil of the same size, and inserted it into the space where the damaged Coil had been.

'It's ready,' she said.

Elbannon picked up the cooling ingot of silver-coated Tempest, and placed it into the empty space within the Compass. He put down the tongs, closed the lid of the device, and handed it to Karalyn.

Kyra watched as her mother handled the device.

'Damn it,' said Karalyn. 'Nothing.'

Elbannon growled and clenched his fists. 'I knew it would be useless!' he cried. 'And yet you insisted we waste our time pandering to your delusional feelings. *I heard it whisper* – you said. Pah. What utter nonsense.'

'We are on the right track; I know it,' said Karalyn.

'I heard it, too,' said Kyra.

'Did you?' said Elbannon. 'That only proves that you're as crazy as your mother.'

Karalyn sat down, with the device in her hand. She opened the lid and stared inside.

'I really thought this would work.'

'Should I go back to my class?' said Kyra.

Karalyn nodded.

Kyra gazed at her mother. Far from looking defeated, Karalyn's eyes were burning with defiance and determination. Kyra turned, her bag still over her shoulder, and went back to Professor Nadia's lesson.

'But who would be a suitable replacement?' said Achan to the small group. 'We all know that Kelsey Holdfast was a ruthless imperialist warmonger, but will the new Herald be any better? I know much about the disgraceful Lord Naxor. It became well known in the City that he could not be trusted; and yet the Empress has decided to give him considerable authority. Whether that was through her naivety, or her cunning, I wouldn't like to say. Major General Cardova has a better reputation than the duplicitous Lord Naxor, but he is a military man who obeys whatever orders he is given. Therefore, even after the resignation of Kelsey Holdfast, the prospects for peace continue to look remote.'

He paced up and down the room.

'The only thing that will change the balance of power,' he went on, 'is the complete removal of the imperialist political apparatus. Swapping one ruthless Herald for another is nothing but a cosmetic change; a change that will allow the Empress to do two things – firstly, she will be able to blame every past mistake upon her old Herald; and, secondly, it will allow her to pursue exactly the same policies as before. This so-called humanitarian intervention on the Rakanese frontier makes me anxious. Imperialists do not decide to feed and house a quarter of a million starving refugees out of the goodness of their hearts; if, indeed, the refugees are actually starving – for all we know, that could be just a pretext to begin a new conflict. This will be the test, then – if it turns out that I am wrong, and the Empire does nothing to violate Rakanese sovereignty, then I will hold my hands up and admit my mistake. If, on the other hand, this *intervention* leads to a new war, a war that causes untold suffering among the Rakanese, then we will see the Empire in its true colours.'

Kyra raised her hand.

'Yes, Miss Holdfast?'

'I have been led to believe, sir, that my Aunt Kelsey was a restraining influence upon the Empress. That is what I have been told.'

'A restraining influence?' said Achan. 'Gods above – if she was a restraining influence, then I dread to think what the Empire has in store for us next. Is your source reliable?'

'I think so, aye, sir.'

'And what is your opinion of Lord Naxor?'

'I... well, he has been loyal to the Empress, as far as I know; but... he, well, he acts in his own interests. It just so happens that his interests coincide with those of the Empire.'

'A succinct summation of my own feelings, Miss Holdfast,' said Achan. 'Lord Naxor will serve the Empire, as long as the Empire continues to serve him.'

'What can we do to oppose them, sir?' said another student.

'Good question,' said Achan. 'We should continue to send out our message of peace, by using the printing press in the university to create a newssheet to rival the official propaganda published by the imperial authorities. We shall need money, an editorial board, and a team of young journalists. We should continue to consolidate our strength, without bringing the wrath of the authorities down upon us. That means we shall have to be discreet. A few martyrs for the cause might be helpful, but we cannot resist the imperialist war machine if we are all in jail. Lastly, we should be patient. It takes time to bring down an Empire; time to gather our resources; time to persuade the masses of the citizens that we are correct in our beliefs; and time to build up our numbers.'

'And then what?' said Kyra. 'What is our aim, sir?'

'Ultimately?' said Achan. He smiled. 'Revolution. Only by eradicating all traces of the imperialist political structures can we truly be free. Revolution. Outside of the little group, that is not a word that we should ever use, for it inspires fear in the hearts of those too cowardly to act; and anger in the hearts of those who benefit from the present regime. But make no mistake, revolution is the only way forward, and I have no doubt that, some day, a revolution will sweep away the old order, and prepare the allied worlds for a bright new dawn of brotherhood and peace.'

Kyra, said a voice in her head.

She frowned. *What is it, Mother? I'm in the middle of a lesson.*

Come down to the laboratory. Now.

But...

Now, Kyra.

The voice disappeared from Kyra's mind, and she frowned.

'You look troubled, Miss Holdfast,' said Achan. 'Have my words disturbed you?'

'It's not that, sir. My mother has just been inside my head. She wants me to meet her.'

'Then you should,' said Achan. 'Your mother is a mighty woman, and I would not wish to keep her waiting. She is also, in my humble opinion, one of our greatest hopes. If Karalyn Holdfast were to oppose the Empire, then it would crumble into dust within minutes. Her policy of non-intervention may be a noble one, but imagine how powerful we would be if she decided to act on our behalf.'

'I wouldn't count on that happening, sir.'

'Maybe so, but if anyone can persuade her, it is you.'

Kyra got to her feet. 'I shall return as soon as I see what she wants, sir.'

'Take as long as you need.'

Kyra walked out of the classroom and closed the door. She made her way downstairs towards Elbannon's laboratory, feeling annoyed with her mother for the brusque manner in which she had been summoned. She opened the laboratory door and strode inside.

Her mother was wearing travelling clothes, and she had a bag over her shoulder.

Kyra eyed her. 'Thinking of going somewhere, Mother?'

'Aye,' said Karalyn. 'We've done it. Are you ready to find your brother?'

Kyra's mouth fell open.

Elbannon laughed. 'Look at her face,' he said. 'She doubted my genius.'

'It wasn't your genius that brought us success,' said Karalyn. 'It was an accident. If you hadn't spilled the silver, we would be no further forward.'

'Yes, but who spilled the silver, eh? That's right; it was me.'

'What are you both talking about?' said Kyra. 'The last time I was here, the experiment failed.'

Karalyn held out the Compass and opened the lid. 'What do you see?'

Kyra peered inside. 'Is that a silver Zamatan Coil?' she said. 'But we've already tried that.'

'It's a Tempest Coil,' said Elbannon, 'coated in an extremely thin layer of pure silver.'

'But there is nothing in the gap.'

'Nothing is required,' said Karalyn. 'All we needed to do was coat the Zamatan Coil, and it worked.'

'It was my idea,' said Elbannon.

'When our vision clouded,' said Karalyn, 'it wasn't just because the silver was touching Tempest, it was because it was touching a Tempest Coil.'

'Try it,' said Elbannon. 'There is a lump of pure Tempest hidden somewhere within the laboratory. See if *Tammy* can help you find it.'

'Why is it hidden?' said Kyra.

'So that you can bloody test it, girl!' said Elbannon.

Karalyn held out the Compass, and Kyra took it.

'What do I do?' she said.

'Place your thumb on the circle,' said her mother. 'That's where the Tempest wires are in contact with the outer casing.'

Kyra glanced down at the small device, and saw that a penny-sized circle had been engraved into the copper surface. She pressed her thumb down against it. For the briefest of moments, she saw the jewel begin to glow, then her vision clouded. She could still see the vague outlines of her mother and Elbannon, and then she saw the hazy outline of the forge. She glanced around the room, and saw a sharp, bright orange light coming from a drawer in a wall cabinet. She took her thumb off the device, walked over to the cabinet, opened the drawer, and saw the lump of Tempest lying there.

Elbannon clapped his hands together. 'I want a mansion for this.'

'It works,' said Kyra.

'A mansion on the beach,' Elbannon went on, 'with a dozen pretty girls to serve me fine wines all day.'

Kyra glanced at her mother. 'What now?'

'Now I am going to attempt to locate your brother,' she said. 'I will have to look far afield, beyond this world, until I can pick up the Tempest inside the Sextant. I will try to locate the Tempest mine on Athumia first, as a trial; then I will expand the search.'

'Can I try?' said Kyra.

Her mother narrowed her eyes.

'Please?' said Kyra. 'Let me try.'

'All right,' said her mother. 'Take a seat, relax, and you can try.'

Kyra dropped her bag to the floor, and sat down. She took a long slow breath, then placed her thumb against the engraved circle. Her vision clouded again. She waited a moment for her senses to adjust, then she lifted her vision out of the laboratory, sending it through an open window. She glanced down at the vague outline of the quad, and sensed a few faint traces of Tempest coming from several locations within the university, including the room where her mother slept each night. The Weathervane – it had to be. Kyra turned her attention to the rest of Plateau City. She saw more traces of Tempest coming from the Imperial Armoury, where new weapons and armour were being designed and forged, then she focussed.

Show me Athumia.

Her vision switched to a large landmass, where the ocean was crashing against the shore.

Show me eastern Inopei.

Her vision changed again, and she saw a dark landscape of mountains under a heavy cloud of smoke and ash. She couldn't make out any details of what she was seeing, so she began to search around. She detected a faint glow, and raced her vision towards it. The glow became brighter, clustered around the base of several volcanoes, then it became too bright for her eyes, and she had to pull away.

'I found the Tempest mine on Athumia,' she said, taking her thumb off the Compass.

Karalyn smiled. 'Well done.'

'I could talk to the device, just like I can talk to Quadrants,' she said. 'I told it to show me Athumia, and it did.'

'That trick will only work for you two,' said Elbannon.

'And Sable, most likely,' said Karalyn.

'Fine, her too,' said the old professor. 'Everyone else will have to search manually.'

'How?' said Kyra.

Elbannon shrugged. 'I only have you two freaks to work with. Your sensitivity to Tempest has allowed me to make this breakthrough; but I would need a normal person to try it out before I could answer that question. Perhaps Kelsey might be willing to try? I hear that she has some time on her hands.'

'Later,' said Karalyn. 'All right, Kyra; expand your search to all other worlds.'

Kyra nodded, then she placed her thumb back on to the engraved circle. To her surprise, her vision took her straight back to the Tempest mine on Athumia, where she had last been looking. She pulled away from the vicinity of the mine.

Search all other worlds for Tempest.

Her vision deteriorated into a blur, as images whipped past too quickly for her to make out. She caught two quick flashes of Tempest in the City, and then another on Dragon Eyre, and she realised that she had just seen the locations of the Axe of Rand and the two Fated Blades. She moved on, and everything turned too dark to see, as the Compass hunted through the other worlds in existence.

Time passed, but Kyra had no means to know how much, then

finally, her vision slowed again, and a faint glow appeared. She drew in closer, and saw a tangled mass of Tempest pipes, coils and wires, all tightly clustered together. It was difficult to make out the environment surrounding it, but Kyra judged that it might have been a forest, with cliffs and stone ledges.

She took her thumb off the device and handed the Compass to her mother.

'I think I've found it,' she said.

'Where?' said her mother.

'Put your thumb on it,' Kyra said. 'It should remember where I was last looking.'

'It does that? All right.'

Karalyn placed her thumb onto the Compass, and her eyes glazed over. She smiled, and lifted her thumb away.

'On your feet,' she said to her daughter.

'Are we going now?'

'Of course. What we saw is definitely the Sextant. I'd recognise it anywhere. And now that I've seen the world it's on, I will be able to travel there.'

Kyra stood up. 'Do we need to bring anything? Won't you need the Weathervane? I sensed it in your room.'

Karalyn nodded, then she vanished. A few moments later, she re-appeared, with a sword strapped to her waist.

'You had better come back,' said Elbannon. 'I don't wish to go through the effort of having to make another *Tammy*.'

'The Empress will probably ask you to make ten,' said Karalyn. She glanced at her daughter. 'Ready?'

Kyra nodded.

The air crackled and spat, and Kyra found herself standing on a long rocky ledge, next to the edge of a dark forest. In front of her and her mother was the Sextant, sitting close to the entrance of a cave.

'Cael!' her mother shouted. 'Cole! Arrosa!'

A few birds rose up from the nearby trees, but there was no other response to Karalyn's words.

'Is this Cael's world?' said Kyra. 'Did he make all this?'

'Aye,' said Karalyn. 'This is his creation.'

'Then... where is he?'

'We can search for him with the Sextant.'

They walked up to the huge device.

'It's inactive,' said Kyra.

Karalyn eyed her, then she placed a hand on the hilt of her sword, and drew the Weathervane from its scabbard. She walked round to the side of the Sextant, and inserted the Weathervane into the correct slot. It began to hum, and lifted a little off the stone ledge.

'I will search this world from top to bottom,' Karalyn said. 'If your brother is here, I will find him.'

CHAPTER 30
HELD TO ACCOUNT

World Three – (8th Day, First Third Autumn 544)

Cael awoke on a filthy wooden floor, his hands bound behind his back. One side of his head was throbbing, and the pain increased as soon as he opened his eyes. He saw nothing but darkness, then he realised that a hood had been placed over his head. He closed his eyes again, and drew on his dream vision, which did not require his eyes. His vision lifted up from his body, and he glanced down at himself. He was in a small room, the same room within the two-storey building where Cole had been imprisoned. He glanced to his left, and saw Cole and Arrosa lying on the floor next to his own body. Cole's hands had been re-bound, and cords were binding Arrosa's wrists together. Like him, they also had hoods covering their heads.

Cael turned his attention to what was going on outside. He squeezed his vision through the gaps in the wooden beams and gazed down at the town. Half of it had been destroyed in the forest fire, and several dozen circular huts had been reduced to rings of ash and rubble. A large section of the outer fence had also gone, along with whole tracts of the nearby forest. In the distance, smoke was still rising from where the fires continued to rage, sweeping through the tinder-dry forest.

A few townsfolk were rummaging through the ruins. Charred skeletons had been laid out in a line, and many of those gathered there were weeping. Cael watched their tears, knowing that he was responsible for every death caused by the fire. His own sub-created humans – dead because of him. He tried to feel pity for them, but couldn't. How could he feel any sympathy towards those who displayed nothing but hostility toward him, Cole and Arrosa? Had he done something wrong when he had created them? Had he made a mistake that had turned his created humans into savages? Or, more unpalatably, did all humans have the potential to behave like savages? Cael knew the answer to his question the moment he had posed it – he had made no mistake.

He gazed back into the room where his body was lying next to Arrosa and Cole. He couldn't access their minds, but he could see that they were both breathing. Arrosa was curled up into a tight ball, and Cael's anger rose at the sight of her. His rage drew him back outside, and he selected someone at random, a man who was standing by the burnt-out ruins of a hut. Cael drove his powers into his mind, and scoured the man's memories, wiping his thoughts clean. The man cried out and fell to the ground, convulsing. The other townsfolk cried out in panic, and several ran over to crouch by the man, while others started pointing up towards the room in the two-storey building where Cael was lying.

The man's body was lifted by two others, and Cael followed them, as they carried the man to a large hut. They took him inside, and Cael went in after them. Laid out on the floor was every person whose mind Cael had destroyed. They were in rows, being nursed by a handful of the other townsfolk. Some were babbling nonsense, while others were staring into space, or had foam on their lips. The new arrival was laid down next to the others. A woman crouched down by his side and took his hand, as she wept and cried out laments. Another woman placed a hand on her shoulder to comfort her, and Cael retreated from the display of grief.

His vision went back outside, and he watched as a few elders spoke to a growing crowd of armed men and women. One of them gestured towards the building holding those whose minds had been destroyed, and then he pointed at the two-storey building. The crowd raised their weapons, and began marching in the direction of the large building. They entered through the main doors, and rushed up the stairs. Cael followed them. As soon as a man placed his hand onto the door leading to the room where Cael, Arrosa and Cole were lying, Cael drove into his mind and destroyed it. The man fell to the floor, but the others were still coming. Cael went into the next man's mind, and wiped it clean, and he, too, fell to the floor, as the pain in Cael's head increased. Three more times he did it, and three more townsfolk fell, their bodies being dragged away. The door was kicked open. Cael struck down the man who had done it, then the pain became unbearable, and his vision connection was severed. Back in his body, he felt his shoulders being gripped, then his ankles. He was lifted up, and carried out of the room, then he heard Cole and Arrosa being brought out behind him. Cael threw up inside the hood, and nearly gagged, choking and coughing. He sensed his body being carried downstairs, then he was taken outside and dropped onto the ground. Moments later, he heard the sound of two others being set down next to him.

Cael managed to send his dream vision out again, despite the agony in his head. In a daze, he stared at the sight of his body lying on the ground. Arrosa was on his left, and Cole on his right, but neither were moving. The townsfolk brandished their weapons, and one knelt down by Arrosa, a long knife in his hands. With a last effort, Cael entered the man's mind, and destroyed it. Almost blinded by pain, Cael cried out. Someone kicked him in the ribs, then Cael saw the body of the man who had knelt by Arrosa be carried away. Another picked up the knife. He crouched by Arrosa, but Cael was too weak to stop him. He raised the knife to Arrosa's throat, and she seemed to awaken. She struggled against the ropes binding her wrists together, and another man leaned over. He took hold of her hands to stop her moving and, the moment he had done so, he was transformed into glass. Screams broke out, and the glass statue of the leaning man was knocked over in the panic. It shattered against the ground, splintering into a thousand pieces that rained down onto Cael and Cole. Cael felt slivers of glass cut his hands, and more dig into his legs. Cole rolled over, a sharp fragment of glass clutched in his bound hands. The townsfolk backed away, and three strung their bows.

One of them was handed an arrow. He nocked it to his newly-strung short bow, aimed at Arrosa, and loosed. The arrow struck her in the stomach, and Arrosa screamed. Another arrow was nocked, and aimed at Cael, but, before the arrow could be loosed, the man was incinerated in a violent burst of flame that hit him from above. His entire body was enveloped in flames as the other townsfolk stared, then more balls of fire came down on the town, striking the people from above. Cael tore his gaze from Arrosa and saw Cole, his hood off, his bloody hands freed, and his arms raised. Cole got up onto one knee, a look of deranged anger and hatred in his eyes as he pulled in the fires burning in the forest, and rained them down upon the town. He struck a group of women who were fleeing towards the gate, incinerating them in seconds, then he brought a huge wave of fire rolling over the fence, devouring everything in its path, including the hut where those stricken by Cael's powers were lying. He swept his arm to the left, and the wave of fire passed over the two-storey building, consuming it, then he guided it over the rest of the town, leaving only a small circle untouched in the centre.

'Die, you bastards!' Cole screamed, as the last of the townsfolk were enveloped in the conflagration.

Cael felt the intense heat all around him, but the flames remained outside the circle where he and Arrosa lay, and from where Cole had obliterated the town.

Sobbing, Cole lowered his arms, and the fires died down. He turned to Cael and, using a shard of green glass, he cut through the bonds by Cael's wrists. Cael pulled off his hood, then he and Cole knelt by Arrosa. Cole cut through her bonds, and Cael lifted the hood from her head.

'Arrosa, can you hear me?' said Cael.

She opened her eyes, as blood appeared on her lips.

'You're going to be all right,' said Cael, as he took her hand.

'Not this time,' she gasped.

Cael broke down, as tears fell onto his cheeks. 'No,' he said. 'Stay with me.'

'I love you, too,' she whispered, then her eyes closed.

A strong hand pushed Cael to the side, and he went sprawling to the dirt. He looked up, and saw his mother leaning over Arrosa. She ripped out the arrow from Arrosa's stomach, and placed a hand onto her forehead. Arrosa convulsed, then she choked up blood and opened her eyes.

'Mother?' said Cael.

Arrosa sat up and gazed around in confusion. 'Thank you, Karalyn. What happened to the town?'

'I killed them all,' said Cole.

Karalyn turned to the two cousins. She raised her hand, and Cael felt his body being healed. Next to him, Cole cried out as his broken leg aligned itself, and the cuts on his hands closed up. Kyra appeared, stepping gingerly through the remaining flames, then she ran at Cael and threw her arms round his shoulders. Then she pulled away, and slapped him across the face.

'You fucking idiot,' she said. 'Don't ever do that to me again.'

Cole got to his feet and gazed around at the destruction he had caused. 'I did this,' he said. 'I could have scared them away, but I didn't. I killed them all; just as my father would have done.'

'I saw what happened,' said Karalyn. 'They were trying to kill you. Why?'

'Can we go home now?' said Arrosa. 'Please?'

Karalyn frowned as she looked at the three ragged teenagers. 'You're all very fortunate that Albany had healing powers,' she said. 'Do you have any idea how long we've been looking for you? You are forbidden from touching the Sextant again, Cael. I will place it somewhere out of your reach, until you are responsible enough to know how to use it properly. Why did you do it, son? Why did you come to a world you knew I would struggle to find?'

'I dared him to do it,' said Arrosa. 'I am as much to blame.'

Kyra narrowed her eyes. 'Are you standing up for Cael, Arrosa?'

'Things have... changed. Please don't adopt me, Karalyn.'

'Why not? I thought you wanted to be a Holdfast.'

'I do, but I don't want to be Cael's sister.'

Kyra nodded. 'That's the Arrosa I remember. You two still hate each other, don't you?'

Cael gazed at Arrosa, and she took his hand.

'No, Kyra,' she said. 'I love him.'

Karalyn smiled and shook her head. 'On your feet, you two. Cole, stand closer.'

Cael and Arrosa stood. Cael looked out over his creation at the smoke and ruins, then the air crackled loudly, and he found himself standing next to the others in the forecourt of Colsbury, between the Summer Palace and the Great Keep.

'Where is the Sextant?' said Cael.

'Somewhere safe,' said his mother. 'Go inside, all of you. You need a bath and a good meal before I take you to see the Empress.'

The sound of laughter came from their right, and Cael saw Shella and Olo'osso walking over from the direction of the little harbour.

'I see you found the missing delinquents, Karalyn,' Shella said. 'Nice rags, you three, and several matching blood stains; very fetching. Did you enjoy your holiday?'

'The weather was nice,' said Arrosa.

Cole started to cry.

'It's all right,' said Karalyn. 'You're safe. I doubt the Empress will punish you, Cole; it seems that you were the only reluctant member of this little party.'

'It's not that,' said Cole. 'For years, I have been frightened of turning into my father. I have tried to keep my temper, and I have tried to make people happy. Today... today I let my anger take over. I killed women and children. I burnt the flesh from their bones, and... and I wanted them to die. I wanted them all to die.'

'You are not your father, Cole,' said Karalyn. 'You are nothing like him. It is not surprising that you might have cracked under the pressure you were under.'

'They were going to kill us,' said Cael. 'I'm glad you killed them, cousin.'

'Spoken like a bloodthirsty little Holdfast,' said Olo'osso. 'Still, they are all back, safe and sound. You have to allow the young folk to get up to some mischief, eh?'

'They practically ruined summer,' said Shella. 'Everyone was worried about them, and no one could do anything about it.' She frowned. 'How did you find them, Karalyn?'

'It was Kyra who found Cael's world,' Karalyn said. 'I'll tell you all about it later, Shella; I will be moving back to Colsbury again, now that our little crisis is over.'

'Lucius will be delighted to hear that,' said Olo'osso.

'Where is he?'

'He's in the palace with the children,' said Shella. 'Your other children.'

Karalyn glanced at Cael, Cole and Arrosa. 'Inside. Baths. Now.'

They set off for the Summer Palace, leaving Karalyn talking to Shella and Olo'osso. Kyra ran after them and followed Cael into the building, passing the Holdings soldiers on duty by the doors.

'You and Arrosa?' she said to her brother. 'How is that possible?'

Cael shrugged, then he took Arrosa's hand as they climbed the stairs. 'It's true. I am in love with her.'

'Oh. But... Cole, how did it happen?'

'This is the first I'm hearing of it,' said Cole, his eyes red. 'I'm all for it, if it stops them arguing all the time.'

'This is harder to believe than you taking the Sextant in the first place.'

'I wouldn't have taken it,' Cael said, 'if you hadn't threatened to tell Aunty Kelsey about what I had been doing.'

'I wasn't really going to tell her, Cael. I was trying to frighten you; that's all. And now the Empress will probably want to punish you. Don't worry too much though; Mother won't let anything too bad happen to you.'

Cael narrowed his eyes.

'Mother and I have been getting along much better,' Kyra went on. 'We had to work together to find you, and... and maybe I have been too harsh on her. She stopped Aunty Kelsey trying to arrest me.'

'She tried to arrest you?'

They reached the floor where their rooms were located, and came to a halt.

'I'm glad you're back, brother,' Kyra said.

'Why did Aunty Kelsey try to arrest you?'

'I'll tell you all about it after you've had your bath. You stink. You all stink. Was it worth it?'

Cael hesitated. He glanced to his side, where Arrosa was standing, and she smiled at him.

He smiled back at her. 'Some parts were worth it.'

Three hours later, Karalyn led Cael, Cole and Arrosa into the presence of the Empress. Her Majesty was sitting on her throne in the main audience chamber. She smiled at first when she saw who had walked in, then her eyes narrowed, and a frown appeared on her face.

'I shall have to remember that I am quite angry with you all,' the Empress said; 'despite the fact that I am overjoyed to see you. Karalyn, how was it done? Do I owe Professor Elbannon a debt of gratitude?'

'Elbannon would like a mansion,' said Karalyn; 'well, that's what he told me. A mansion on the beach.'

'I am sure that can be arranged.'

The four arrivals halted in front of the throne.

'And the Sextant?' said the Empress.

'I have taken the liberty of hiding it somewhere my errant son will not be able to find it,' said Karalyn.

'And it is working properly? It wasn't damaged?'

'It's fine,' said Karalyn.

The Empress puffed out her cheeks in relief. 'That is good to hear. Well done, Karalyn.'

'Kyra deserves some thanks, too,' said Karalyn. 'I asked her to be here today, but she felt that she wouldn't be welcome.'

'Kyra will always be welcome in my company,' said the Empress, 'despite our recent disagreements. It is a pity that our opinions seem to have diverged, but I retain hope that she will come round to my point of view in time. Now, I suppose we shall have to consider suitable punishments for those who stole one of the Empire's most valuable assets.'

'Might I first allocate some blame in this matter?' said Karalyn. 'Not all three were equally responsible. Cole, for example, tried to dissuade my son from absconding, and he did not wish to be taken away. He is blameless in this.'

'Very well,' said the Empress. 'Cole, there will be no consequences for your part in this, and no punishments. Do you wish to go back to the Hold Fast estate?'

'Might I attend university this year, Your Majesty?' Cole said. 'I don't want to go back to the estate; not yet.'

'That shouldn't be a problem,' said the Empress. 'Is Arrosa also innocent?'

'I dared Cael to do it, Your Majesty,' said Arrosa. 'I thought it would be funny.'

'I see.'

'I would have done it anyway,' said Cael, 'even if she hadn't dared me, Your Majesty. Let all the blame fall onto my head. I am willing to take whatever punishment you decide.'

The Empress regarded him for a few moments. 'For that attitude, Cael,' she said, 'I will do as you ask. Arrosa, you will also escape punishment. You will attend university, along with Cole.'

'Thank you, Your Majesty,' said Arrosa.

'Then it is just Cael's punishment that we have to consider,' said the Empress. She glanced at the members of the Imperial Court, who were flanking the throne. 'What do you suggest?'

'The gallows, Your Majesty?' said Caelius Logos, then he smiled.

'My little joke. Prison, perhaps? It would send a powerful message that even members of the Imperial Family are not above the law; but it would also draw attention to the fact that we allowed the Sextant to be stolen in the first place.'

'I don't think prison is the answer,' said the Empress. 'What is his mother's opinion?'

Karalyn gazed at Cael. 'His father was a marine. A spell in the armed forces might do him some good.'

'I would not be averse to that,' said the Empress. 'What do you think, Cael? Shall we say a minimum service of three years, serving the Empire?'

Cael bowed his head. 'If that is your decree, Your Majesty, I accept.'

'Lord Marshal,' said the Empress, 'see that Cael is given a junior commission in the Imperial Marines. He can begin his training tomorrow.'

'As you wish, Your Majesty,' said Bedig.

'That seems a fitting solution,' said Caelius Logos. 'There's no harm in a soldier's life.'

'I won't be a soldier, sir,' said Cael. 'I will be a marine.'

Caelius laughed. 'You will indeed, lad.'

'Then we are settled,' said the Empress. 'Cole and Arrosa will attend university, and Cael will serve in the marines. It will be good to have a Holdfast in my armed forces again, but I will ensure you are treated the same as any other trainee, Cael. There will be no special favours due to your family name.'

'I wouldn't have it any other way, Your Majesty,' Cael said.

'Once again, Karalyn, thank you for retrieving our lost sheep, and thank you for bringing back the Sextant,' said the Empress. 'Will you be returning to Colsbury?'

'I shall,' said Karalyn. 'I will travel there tomorrow, after Cael has left to begin his new career.'

'Enjoy your time together,' said the Empress. 'You are dismissed.'

All four bowed their heads at the Empress, then they walked from the audience hall.

'The university?' said Karalyn.

The others nodded, then the air shimmered, and they found themselves in the middle of the quad.

'I need to speak to Elbannon,' said Karalyn. 'Shall we meet for dinner, two hours from now?'

'Aye, Mother,' said Cael; 'and... thanks. Thanks for coming to get us.'

Karalyn put a hand on his arm. 'You are my son,' she said, 'and I love you more than words can say. Never forget that.'

She vanished, leaving Cael, Arrosa and Cole alone again.

Cole glanced at the other two, then smiled weakly. 'I get the feeling you'd rather be by yourselves,' he said. 'I'll go to reception and register for classes; and see if there are any spare rooms to rent. Do you still have your old room, Arrosa?'

She patted a pocket. 'I picked up the key for it while we were in Colsbury,' she said. 'Are you coming to dinner?'

Cole nodded. 'I'll be there. I... I'm sorry I lost my mind in the town. I shouldn't have killed all those people. I...'

'You did what you had to do,' said Cael. 'If you hadn't done it, we'd all be dead.'

Cole nodded, then he turned and walked away.

'Do you think he'll be all right?' said Arrosa, as they walked in the opposite direction.

'He'll have you and Kyra to keep him company.'

'But not you.'

'No. Not me.'

'The sodding marines?' said Arrosa. 'But I thought...'

'I know,' said Cael.

They entered the building, and climbed the stairs to where Arrosa's room was located.

'When will I see you again?' she said.

'The marine base is just outside Plateau City,' said Cael. 'I'll visit as often as I can. At least you will be in the same place as Cole and my sister. And I get to follow what my father did. It seems... right.'

'Well, it's better than fucking prison, I suppose.'

He smiled. 'You actually seem quite upset about this.'

'Of course I'm upset,' she said. 'You and I, Cael, we've only just... started something, and you're leaving. Who will I argue with now? Who is going to annoy the crap out of me every day? These last few months...'

'Thirds.'

'Oh shut up. You know what I meant.' They stopped outside the door to Arrosa's room. 'We're here,' she said. 'I wonder if it's in the same condition as I left it. You know, sometimes they put other people in here during Spring Term, when I'm on the Hold Fast estate.'

She opened the door. 'It looks the same. Are you coming in?'

'Are you asking?'

'I thought I just did. A few months on World Three certainly didn't do anything to cure your stupidity.'

They walked into the small room, and Arrosa closed the door. She walked up to Cael.

'We're alone,' he said; 'we have a room, and we have two hours. Whatever shall we do?'

She leaned up and kissed him. 'Let's find out.'

AUTHOR'S NOTES

AUGUST 2024

Thank you for reading ***Creator of Worlds***, the first book of the Twins Trilogy. I wrote a large part of this book inside a tiny wooden hut halfway up the side of a hill in the Scottish Highlands. I had been hoping for fair weather, imagining long walks by the rivers and through the forests; but the rain was persistent and torrential, and I sometimes felt as though the winds were going to send the hut tumbling to the bottom of the hill. There was, indeed, nothing to do but write.

I hope you enjoyed it.

RECEIVE A FREE MAGELANDS DOMINION SHORT STORY

Building a relationship with my readers is very important to me.

Join my newsletter for information on new books and deals and you will also receive a Magelands Dominion short story that is currently EXCLUSIVE to my Readers' Group for FREE.

www.ChristopherMitchellBooks.com/dominion

ABOUT THE AUTHOR

Christopher Mitchell is the author of the Magelands epic fantasy series.

For more information:

www.christophermitchellbooks.com
info@christophermitchellbooks.com

Printed in Great Britain
by Amazon

46250468R00253